EMPIRE OF ALEXANDRIA

Book Five of The Alexandrian Saga

Thomas K. Carpenter

Empire of Alexandria

Book Five of The Alexandrian Saga

Hardcover Version
by Thomas K. Carpenter

Published by Black Moon Books

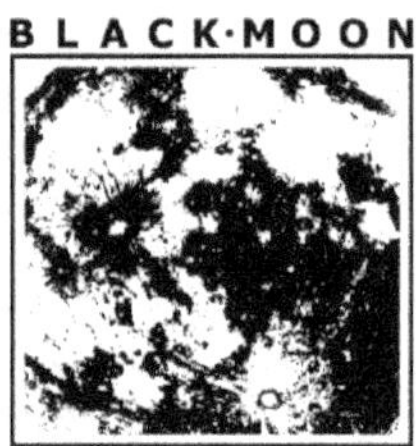

Cover design by
G&S Cover Designs

Chapter Headings design by Aleks49011

Discover other titles by this author on:
www.thomaskcarpenter.com

ISBN-13: 978-1-958498-15-6

ALEXANDRIAN SAGA
Fires of Alexandria
Heirs of Alexandria
Legacy of Alexandria
Warmachines of Alexandria
Empire of Alexandria
Voyage of Alexandria
Goddess of Alexandria

Other Books by Thomas K. Carpenter

The Dashkova Memoirs
Revolutionary Magic
A Cauldron of Secrets
Birds of Prophecy
The Franklin Deception
Nightfell Games
The Queen of Dreams
Dragons of Siberia
Shadows of an Empire

The Kingmaker Saga
The Stone Tree
The Crystal Bard
The Ghost Tower
The Champion's Prophecy
The Shadow Labyrinth
The Autumn Empire

The Hundred Halls Universe
SEASON ONE

THE HUNDRED HALLS
Trials of Magic
Web of Lies
Alchemy of Souls
Gathering of Shadows
City of Sorcery

THE RELUCTANT ASSASSIN
The Reluctant Assassin
The Sorcerous Spy
The Veiled Diplomat
Agent Unraveled
The Webs That Bind

GAMEMAKERS ONLINE
The Warped Forest
Gladiators of Warsong
Citadel of Broken Dreams
Enter the Daemonpits
Plane of Twilight

ANIMALIANS HALL
Wild Magic
Bane of the Hunter
Mark of the Phoenix
Arcane Mutations
Untamed Destiny

STONE SINGERS HALL
Song of Siren and Blood
House of Snake and Tome
Storm of Dragon and Stone
Sonata of Shadow and Thorn
Well of Demon and Bone

THE ORDER OF MERLIN
The Order of Merlin
Infernal Alliances
Tower of Horn and Blood

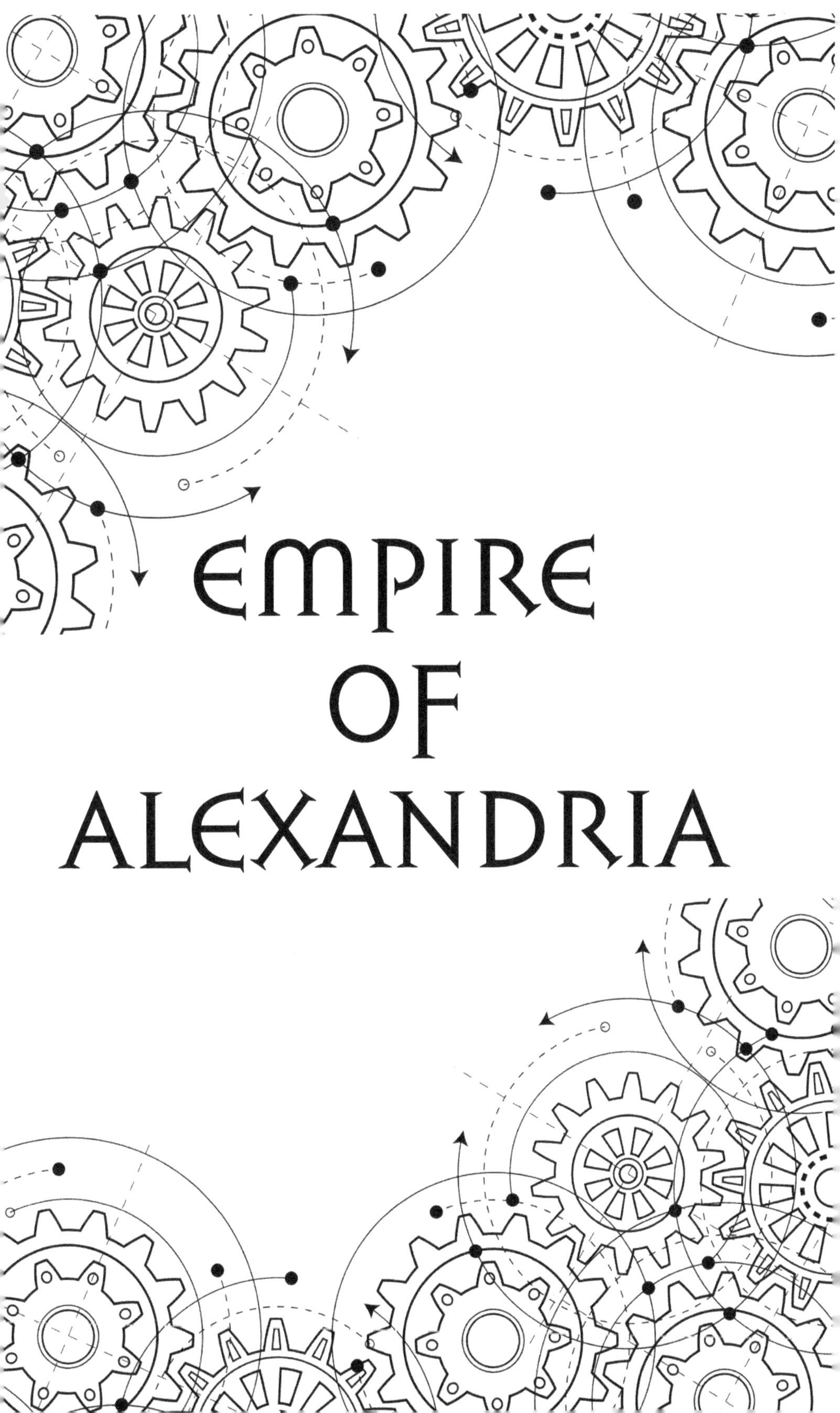

EMPIRE
OF
ALEXANDRIA

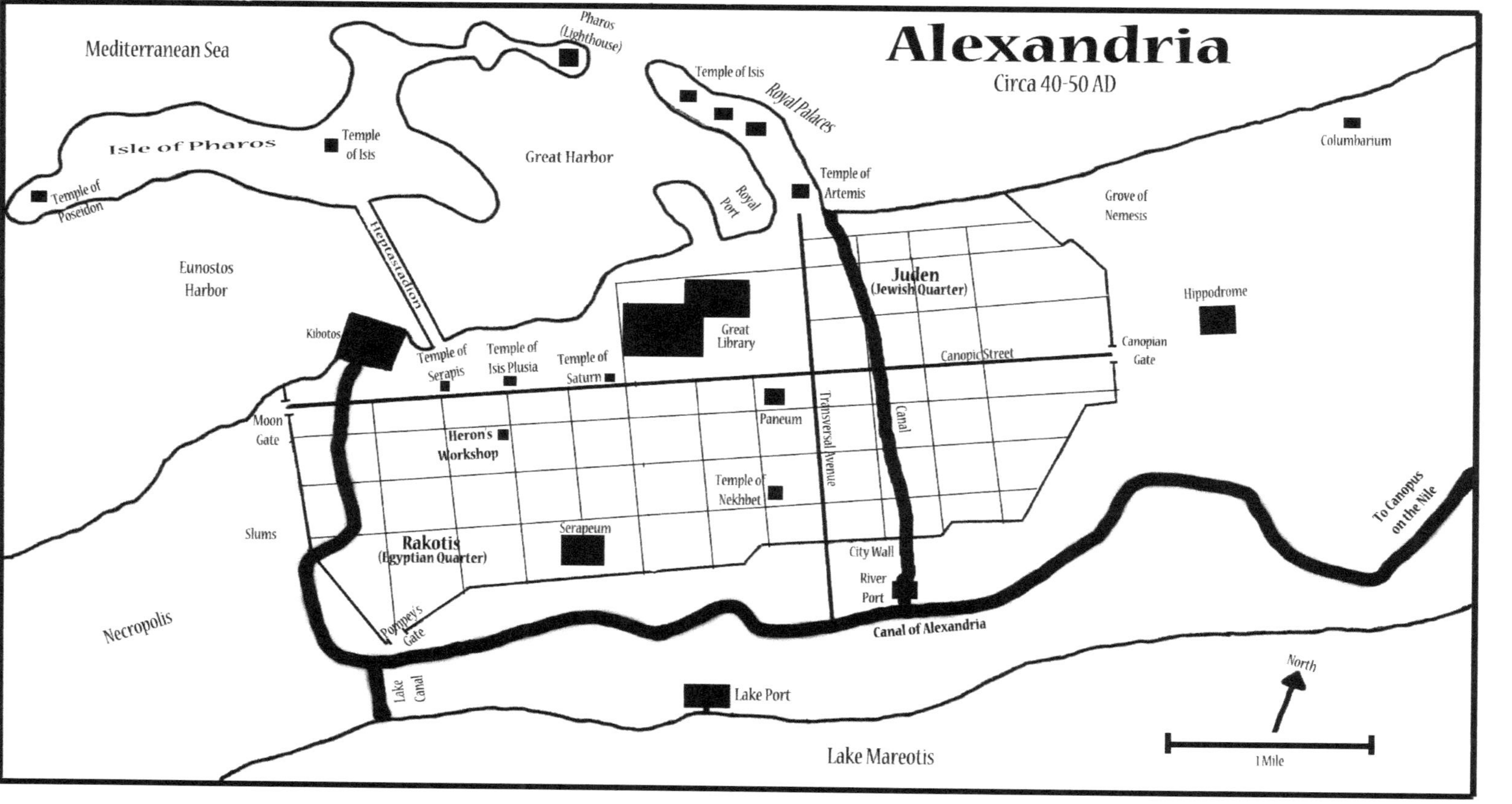

Alexandria
Circa 40-50 AD
Mediterranean Sea
Pharos (Lighthouse)
Temple of Isis
Royal Palaces
Columbarium
Isle of Pharos
Temple of Isis
Great Harbor
Temple of Poseidon
Royal Port
Temple of Artemis
Grove of Nemesis
Eunostos Harbor
Juden (Jewish Quarter)
Hippodrome
Heptastadion
Great Library
Canopic Street
Canopian Gate
Kibotos
Temple of Serapis
Temple of Isis Plusia
Temple of Saturn
Paneum
Transversal Avenue
Canal
Moon Gate
Heron's Workshop
Temple of Nekhbet
Slums
Rakotis (Egyptian Quarter)
Serapeum
City Wall
River Port
To Canopus on the Nile
Necropolis
Pompey's Gate
Canal of Alexandria
Lake Canal
North
Lake Port
Lake Mareotis
1 Mile

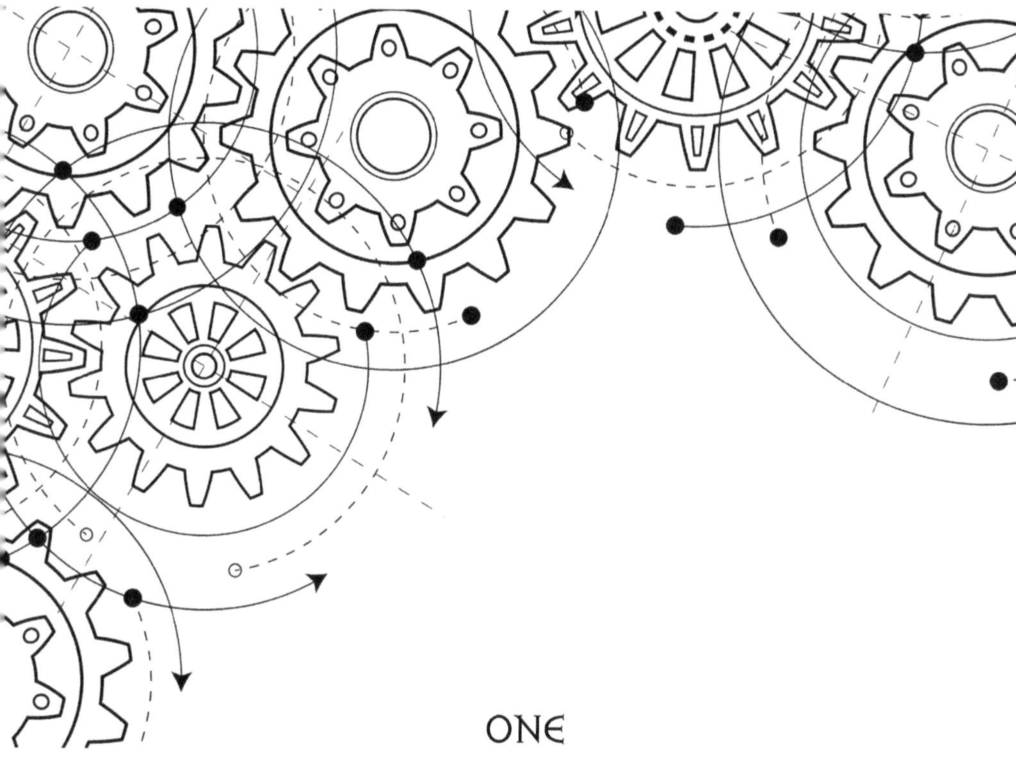

ONE

If you must break the law do it to seize power: in all other cases observe it.
-- Julius Caesar

Cold, driving rain pounded the clay tiles of the domus, rattling the brass lampworks set into the marble pillars. The inner courtyard, a wide space that in drier times had seen bright adornments and heard the laughing cadence of Roman Senators at work and had even welcomed Emperors to dine on sweet, sticky figs, was now deluged by the sudden storm.

A growing pool formed on the tiles, and Dominitus watched his servants fight through the knee-high water to unplug the drain. Never had he seen so much water at once. If he were a godly man, he might blame them, but he'd been in Rome far too long not to know that men and their ambitions were the real danger.

A searing white brilliance, as if day had come to night, burst over the house and with it a teeth shattering blast. Sitting in his favorite chair next to a smoky fireplace with a pile of warm blankets on his lap, Dominitus doubled over in pain, brought on by the vibration attacking his abscessed tooth at the back of his jaw.

When the spots had faded from his sight and the throbbing pain in his jaw had reduced enough to allow him to breathe again, Dominitus sat back against his chair and shoved his arthritic hands deeper into the blankets. It was only then he noticed a shape standing in the shadows.

"Is that you, Cultri?" he asked.

The shadow turned into a man, wearing the style of a merchant with a leather coin purse at his side and etched leather wrist guards, a fashion that had fallen to the common folk last autumn. He had an ordinary look, descended from conquered tribes, and a face that was easy to forget. Which in his profession, was a boon rather than a curse.

Dominitus cleared the phlegm from his throat in a series of coughing growls, which left him exhausted when he was finished. "You're a man of many talents, Cultri," said Dominitus. "How you reached my estate without getting a drop of rain on you is a mystery."

"A humble practitioner of the arts never reveals his secrets," said Cultri.

"Come sit," he said, patting the chair next to him, "this tired old man can hardly see across the room."

Cultri moved into the light but no further. "I cannot stay long. There is much to do since the Alexandrians took the Empire from us."

Dominitus chuckled. "Is that how you see it? Can a jackal take a lion, no matter how fierce it is, if it's crawled inside the lion's belly?"

Another crash of thunder interrupted them, this time far enough away that Dominitus could ignore the ache in his jaw. Cultri, true to his nature, did not react except to glance toward the courtyard.

"You don't see them as conquerors?" asked Cultri.

Dominitus shrugged. "An empire this size cannot be tamed by a few barbarians. A coup from the provinces, that's what this is. Once they try to rule and bed down with the Senate, they will find it a bed of vipers."

Cultri wandered to the edge of the room where the water had crept in, tapping his sandal into it, making a sucking, splash sound. "Then what line will you take? There are many courses of action that suggest themselves."

The smile was broken by a brief cough, but still Dominitus was pleased. If Cultri saw them, Dominitus would not have to guide his direction so tightly, letting the man take action where he saw fit. Especially in these chaotic times, when no one knew who still held power.

"Too much is unknown to act too rashly. I must see how Silius and his Wolves deal with the new emperor," said Dominitus.

"Isn't Tiberius a member of his faction? The legate that lost Antioch. A winter on the road with the new emperor gave him more influence than he deserves," said Cultri with disdain.

"And he seeks to discredit our former Consul Magnus," said Dominitus, "by siding with Silius and seeking reparations for family members lost in the war. A bold move, considering Tiberius shoulders some of the blame for Rome's loss."

Cultri pulled a knife from some hidden location, and began cleaning his fingernails with it. Dominitus had never known the man not to have a half-dozen blades on him, even if he appeared to be unarmed.

"Supporting their cause," said Cultri looking up from his work, "could lead to furthering ours."

Another rumble put a pause in the conversation, the storm was dying down, and Dominitus thought he caught a whiff of honey cakes. He'd sent a servant to the kitchens before the worst of the storm hit, though it was certainly possible the ovens had cooled for the night and the cakes were taking longer to make.

"A neck extended is a neck ready for chopping," replied Dominitus with a smile.

"What about Pallas? He was the one to kill Claudius when he tried to sneak out of the city with that gold, though I suspect Pallas supplied the gold to give reason to kill him."

"Pallas?" chuckled Dominitus. "It's not Pallas that rules that faction. He's a tired old man that's only recently rose to prominence. His wife, Aelia, she's the one that wields the power, and remember, Claudius was married to her once. She's held a vicious grudge since he set her aside for a younger wife. I'll remind myself of her long memory if I ever seek to cross her."

Cultri crossed his arms across his stomach, and when he did, the knife that had been in his fist disappeared as if it'd turned to smoke. "I'd forgotten about that."

"Don't underestimate Aelia and her group," said Dominitus, "what they lack in size and influence, they make up for in cunning. They're fiercely loyal to Magnus, yearn for the power Silius won't share with them, and own half the poisoners in Rome. Personally, I love my mealtimes a little too much to wait to see if my tasters fall over dead first."

"Then that leaves the Protectors, which I know you won't deal with," said Cultri.

"It's not that I won't deal with them, dear Cultri, it's that Messalina and his fellow Senators are zealots. Above everything else, they revere the power of the Senate as a force for good, and despise everything about the other two factions due to their aristocratic natures." Dominitus paused. "But that does not mean we cannot use them. A cat that spies a mouse in a mirror will launch itself into the glass with no regard for its face."

Cultri wrinkled his nose, and knotted his brow, and then his lips screwed up in thought. Dominitus watched and waited, he had patience enough to let him work through it.

"The Alexandrians, then? I've heard Emperor Wodanaz plans on leaving the inventor Heron in the city to rule in his stead while he chases down Magnus. Would you trust yourself to those fools?" asked Cultri.

"Fools? I'm not sure. This Heron intrigues me. He seems to be Aristotle, Archimedes, and Alexander all rolled into one. A man who convinces the Egyptians to start building a new pyramid when they haven't attempted one in centuries, and during a war, gives me pause. His name has turned up time and time again in the taking of Alexandria, and don't forget it's his inventions that made this conquest possible. The future of Rome balances on Heron's mechanical fist."

"Trusting to a machine?"

Dominitus felt the rumble in his stomach match the distant thunder and hoped the honey cakes would arrive soon. "His arm and leg may be a machine, but his mind is still flesh and blood like you and I."

"But will he have a mind for politics? It's a different game. A dangerous place, even for players. And Rome is the most dangerous of stages," said Cultri.

"Truth in every word," said Dominitus. "That is why I will watch and wait. And if this Heron proves to be adept at Rome's famous game, then and only then, will I offer my support, for besides the power that he so handsomely wields, there is another reason to support him, we share a common interest."

"And what common interest is that?" asked Cultri, intrigued.

"We both wish to free the Empire of slavery."

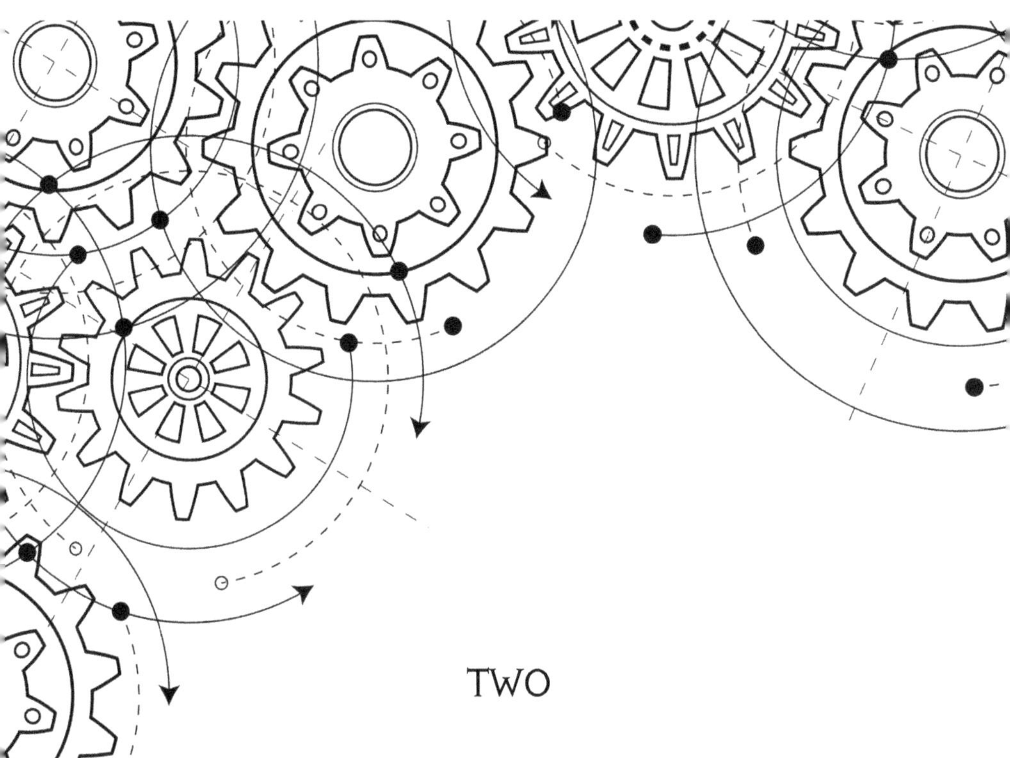

TWO

A great cloud of dust rose to the sky like a host of locust after a great feeding. The heat of summer filtered the air, casting mirages across the city behind and the marching army ahead.

The russet mare shifted beneath Heron, and she placed a hand against the dusty neck, careful to use her flesh hand. The beast had already reared up twice from the whirring and clicking of her mechanical arm, eyes white with fright, making her regret not taking a steam chariot.

Vestalis rode beside her, the flat stare of amusement lining his lips, as his white stallion pranced. The golden breastplate he wore reflected the sun beneath his crimson epaulets.

"I should have never let you talk me into riding a horse," said Heron. "They don't like me and I can't say I blame them. I make more noise than a bucket of rats."

"These Romans need to see you as one of them, and the steam chariots are too foreign to make an impression," replied Vestalis.

"These horse hooves will make an impression in my skull when it throws me and tries to stomp out the noise," said Heron.

"You're being difficult," said Vestalis. "The Parthian mounts carry a hundred stone of mail armor."

Heron smiled briefly. "The lecture's unnecessary, good Vestalis. I'm merely venting. I still can't seem to fathom why Agog left me in charge of Rome. I'm an inventor, not a politician."

Vestalis swung his mount around and they plodded towards Rome. Between the hills ahead, the dark smoke of industry rose, and behind that, the gleaming pillars of the Senate. This city dwarfed Alexandria, and reminded Heron of Old Babylon in size. From her vantage, she could only see part of the city, while in Alexandria, even from the Palace on the hill, the whole of the city could be seen. It didn't help that Rome stretched across seven hills.

A slight nudge spurred her mount to catch up to Vestalis, and she felt a surge of pride that she'd done so without thinking about her mechanical leg. Heron stared at the reins held limply by the brass fingers, wishing they could match the usefulness of the lower limb.

She looked to Vestalis, noting his trim soldier physique, and merciless gaze. He rode comfortably on his stallion, bouncing in time with his horse's gait, back straight and tall. Even this short ride strained her thighs as she clamped tight in case of another sudden startle.

"Now that Agog is gone, I can do what I want," said Heron.

The only response from Vestalis was a raised eyebrow in her direction. Even speaking as such made her feel like a petulant child.

"That you can," he said.

"I could give the Consulship to you," said Heron. "I'd stay in Rome and help, but it would allow me to focus on what I do best. I have so much to do with the Archimedes texts."

Vestalis nodded. "Ask me that a few years ago and I might have taken it. But now, I cannot. I need to solidify the Alexandrian-ness of the army. There are only a few Northman officers that didn't go with Agog, and the loyalties of the native Alexandrians are even more tenuous now that we're in Rome. My duty is to the army and making sure the technologies that you made, that helped us take Rome, do not help our enemies take it back."

"You make all too much sense," said Heron. "But I had to try."

"I wouldn't wish your position on my worst enemy," said Vestalis with a rare smirk.

"Ah, the truth at last," she laughed.

Despite the ache in her thighs, she settled into an easy ride beside Vestalis. The soreness in her legs had been earned honestly, and though she would limp a little deeper in the next few days, in the end her legs would be stronger for it. The aches and pains she would receive dealing with the Senate would be nothing of the sort. Even now her stomach twisted with the duplicitous smiles she would receive. Heron had kept herself from the ranks of the nobles in Alexandria, only visiting when it served the needs of her workshop. Here in Rome, everyone would find need of her and peck her to death like piece of bread at the mercy of a ravenous flock of crows.

"Good Vestalis," she said, pausing in case she had intruded in his thoughts. A breeze shifted, blowing hair away from her forehead and bringing with it a smell unlike Alexandria. Rome was rich with gardens and estates, opulent wealth displayed like a peacock to draw in potential mates. Though the scents of flowers and scrubbed clean estates were quite lovely on the nose, Heron preferred the gritty stench of the foundry, or the simple earthy breads that woke her each morning through the workshop window.

"Yes, Consul Heron?" he replied stone-faced.

"Do you have advice for me? I'm ill-suited to the game of politics, but since I have no choice, I had best get on with it."

"A wise course of action," he replied. "Those that complain about the rules of the game are usually the first to fall by the wayside."

"And your advice?"

Vestalis narrowed his gaze towards the Senate house, a monument of the city set across from Palatine hill. "Glory and achievement is the coin and currency of the city's elite. First, you must find out the score and what each side seeks, knowing that whatever they say is only a glamour to hide what they really want."

"Each side?" she asked as their mounts descended down a winding road that led toward the Forum. While they had been riding, citizens of Rome passed them, eyes widening with surprise at the identity of the two riders. Before Heron spoke again, she wondered at the safety of traveling without guards. "What sides are there? Or even, how many?"

"Three," said Vestalis briskly. "Though my knowledge of the city's politics are outdated, the three sides have not changed since I left. The old elite, the aristocratic families that have placed their sons into the Senate for generations, they are the oldest and most dangerous of the three factions. They are led by Senator Silius. The commoners call them the Wolves of Rome, because they claim lineage to Remus and Romulus."

"I've heard Tiberius speak of Silius with Agog," said Heron.

"Yes, that prig, he tried to make it sound like he was a close confidant of the man, but think nothing of his claim. Tiberius may have gained influence by turning to our side, but Silius will only use him as far as that."

Heron sighed. "And the other two?"

"Senator Pallas represents the new elite, those who came up through the Roman Legion by skill and achievement, rather than purchased influence," said Vestalis. "They venerate Magnus like a god, but killed Claudius as we approached Rome. Some deeper meaning hides there."

"These truths thrill me with anticipation," deadpanned Heron. "And the third?"

"The last are the smallest, but the most passionate. The Protectors of the Senate. They were natural enemies of Claudius and his imperial powers, so I find it odd that it was Pallas who killed him," said Vestalis.

"They hate the other two factions then?" asked Heron.

"They would feast on their entrails if given the opportunity," said Vestalis, "or at least augur the future with them."

"Did I mention I was thrilled?"

A wry smile flickered across his lips. "Their hatred for each other can be your advantage. Nothing upends plans like frothing untempered passion."

"I shall keep that in mind," said Heron.

Vestalis gave a brief nod. "You asked for advice and I have given you none. Only information that could be obtained by asking a fruit merchant outside the Coliseum. My real advice is to stay mysterious. Already the city is abuzz with your presence."

He nodded toward a child gaping slack jawed at her as they rode by, at least until his mother yanked on his arm and pulled him down the street, but Heron had caught her glance, as well. It was just briefer than her child's.

"And what will I do with this mysteriousness?" she asked.

Vestalis shrugged. "Use your strengths, whatever they are. Once you get the lay of the land, you'll figure it out."

Heron buried her pithy comments and turned her head toward the climbing archways of the Coliseum. Already, she felt like a gladiator battling for her life in front of tens of thousands.

Nearing the Domus Alexandria, the former palace of Claudius, taken and renamed by Agog before he left, Heron yanked on the reins until her mount settled into a restless prance.

"Care to join me for mealtime?" she asked Vestalis. "I could use more of your Roman insight."

"Apologies, *Michanikos*, I must visit the legions tonight. The loyalty of the legates will only be bought with time and coin," he said.

"Well, then, may your wooing bear fruit."

"I have a request before I go," he said, his brow hunched in seriousness.

She nodded.

"Archimedes' final gift," he said, glancing around to make sure no one was near. "It was a great weapon for defeating the Roman army, but it's useless for holding power."

"What do you need?" she asked.

"The Legion's practice of decimation, you've heard of it right?"

"Only in passing, explain for my illumination," she said.

"When a legion fails in its duty, through dereliction, mutiny, or cowardice, it cannot be thrown away like an old toy. So like a malignant growth, the rottenness of the legion must be cut away. When a legion fails, one man in ten is chosen and the other nine must beat him to his death. A legion has never had to decimate twice. The lesson learned is learned forever."

"Your request grows faint like day at dusk," said Heron.

"I need a way to use Archimedes' final gift to project power without destroying everything. If you appointed me the destroyer of the city, I could reduce it to rubble in a few weeks using those barrels. But keep it? I cannot do that without some way to keep the legions in line and not give them the tools to overthrow us."

Heron sighed. "Good Vestalis, you don't ask very much, do you?"

"Only what is necessary," he replied.

"I will think upon it, though I cannot promise anything," she said.

"The duty of the Empire calls."

"Consul Heron, *Michanikos*," said Vestalis as he turned his mount to steer away. "The Empire is a grand machine, fit with great gears that turn on the axis of the Earth. Take care not to get caught in its works."

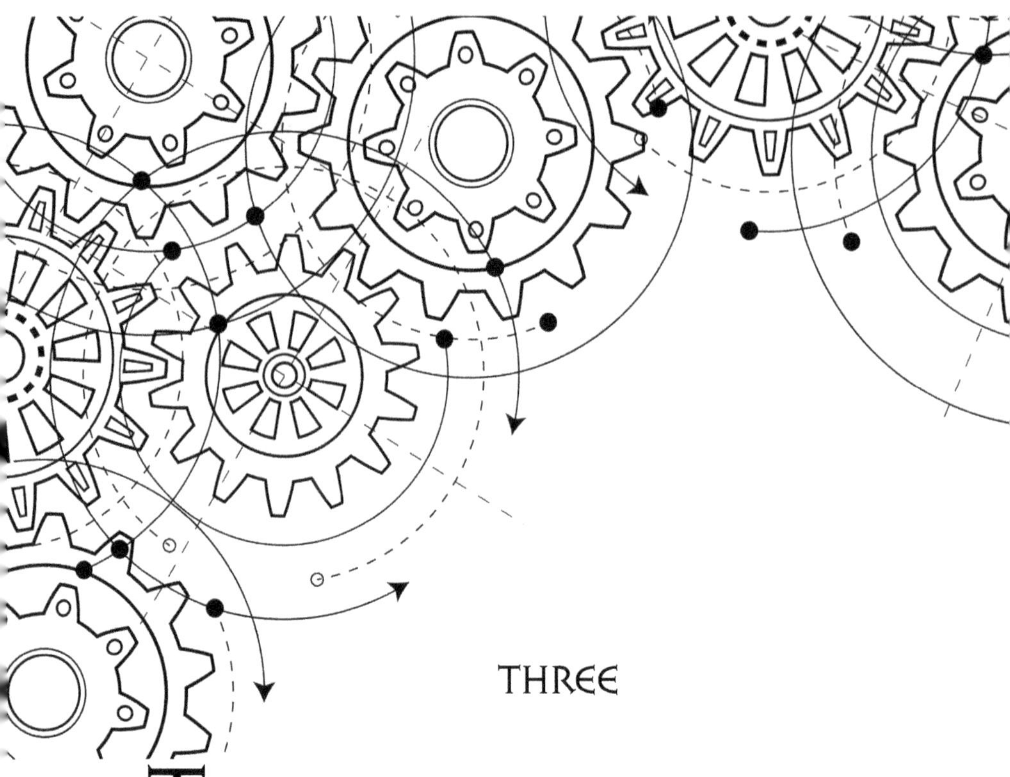

THREE

The cinereous undergarment hitched up around Sepharia's waist, so she tugged it back down discreetly with a stretch and a wiggle. She wasn't used to wearing the ochre stola, preferring the tunics she wore in the workshop, but this was Rome, and only common men wore tunics and prostitutes wore togas.

Like Alexandria, the streets bustled with a tangible energy, men and women bumping into each other as they passed the stone stacked buildings of the merchant district. Sepharia had no particular destination in mind, letting the crowd and her whimsy carry her forward.

But unlike Alexandria, the abundance of slaves surprised her. Not that Alexandrians did not have them, but it seemed there were five slaves to every citizen.

A man with an ample waist, soot-streaked arms, and an olive complexion bumped into Sepharia. His horrid breath assaulted her as he pushed past, forcing her to cringe against the stone wall and resulting in her catching an elbow on an errant piece of stonework.

Pain shot up her arm as she clamped her eyes closed. Sepharia shook it off and readied herself to rejoin the flow when she saw the bald man in robes staring at her. The direct eye contact was like a shock and before she could get a good look at him, a team of horses came between them.

She couldn't place the name or how she knew him, but she did, and a cold shiver ran through her. Sepharia kept watching the spot until the wagon passed, but he was gone. She searched the crowd frantically, feeling like an antelope nervously drinking from the Nile.

Someone grabbed her arm, and she let out a yelp. The man standing behind her wore a leather jerkin and iron bands around his thick arms. He had an exotic quality that she knew only came from east of the Parthian Empire. He nudged her in the arm, mumbled something in a guttural language she didn't recognize, and when she didn't move, he yanked her out of the way.

Disoriented and caught by the flow of the crowd, Sepharia was swept along. Glancing over her shoulder, she thought she caught a glimpse of a bald head, but she ran directly into the backside of a perfumed drenched merchant in a silken beige toga and had to swerve away from a soldier marching directly through her path.

When the street turned, Sepharia spied a curtained doorway and before the brief hole could close, she threw herself into it, fighting through the fabric like a spider web at dusk.

Inside and blinking away the sunlight, she had the impression of rows of furry beasts watching her. It wasn't until the last bright spots faded from her vision that she realized she was in a wig shop.

She made sure she wasn't going to run into anything before moving deeper into the store. Before she moved to explore, she peeked through the door curtain to make sure the bald man had not followed her.

The aroma of perfumed powders tickled her nose as she surveyed the rows of wooden heads covered with a wide variety of wigs. These shops weren't uncommon in Alexandria, but she'd never had reason or want to enter one, since they hadn't been the fashion while she was sequestered in the Palace.

Sepharia ran her fingers along a particularly grand waterfall of blonde hair, feeling the silky strands beneath her fingertips. It looked fit for a Queen, or at least a vain woman trying to emulate one. Or maybe, as she had read in the scrolls Heron had given her, a revered prostitute in the halls of Caligula.

The hair felt real enough, and after the brief bit of terror in the street, it felt soothing. So she kept touching the wigs, expecting the merchant to yell at her for dirtying his goods, but no rebuke came.

A short black manly wig of hair, very Roman, very soldier-like, caught her eye. It was right on the other side of a short wall. A disguise like that could be useful. Twice, she'd had to cut her hair for a disguise, once to escape the workshop and the other was during the hunt for the Archimedes text. She didn't know what Rome was going to be like, especially since her father was in charge of the city while Agog was away chasing down Magnus, but it wouldn't hurt to be prepared.

Sepharia grabbed the wig and yanked, but it didn't come off the wooden head. When she yanked again, getting her shoulder into it the second time, a cry of pain startled her.

The wig turned into a head of hair, very connected to a very Roman, very soldier-like man, who stood up and spun around red-faced, his hand going to his belt, though no weapon was hanging there.

"By the Empire, what is the meaning...?"

He was taller than most Romans, had a prominent nose, and eyes as green as a summer storm. Sepharia put a hand to her throat.

"Apologies, I thought you were a wig," she said.

"A wig," he responded in mock injury, "I've been called a lot of things, but never a wig. Are you in the custom of wearing men's wigs?"

She hesitated. His voice was as smooth as a dream, but with steel beneath it.

"Only when I want to see how the dumber sex lives," she said, and after the words fled her lips, she prepared herself to flee the shop, for this was Rome and she wasn't bantering with Plutarch in the workshop.

The silence was shattered when he laughed, a mirthful light in his eyes shining right through her.

"And what are you doing in a woman's wig shop?" she asked quickly.

He crossed his arms. "Are you in a habit of assaulting, insulting, and interrogating strangers?"

"Are you in a habit of disguising yourself as a wig?" She smiled.

"Could I at least have your name?" he asked.

"Sepharia."

"Sextus," he replied.

For the first time, Sepharia really noted the cut of his tunic, the gold-lined leather wrist bands, the fine sandals, and fat coin purse at his side. He had the earthy musk of a warrior, but the crispness of an aristocrat. Sepharia noted that Sextus only gave his *praenomen* name, failing to add the *agnomen* or *cognomen*, which would have identified his family.

"Sextus, are you in the habit of disguising yourself as a wig?"

"Yes, Sepharia," he said putting emphasis on her name and crinkling his eyes in a smile, "I hide amongst the wigs and trap unsuspecting wom-en."

"And what do you do with them once you've captured them?" she asked.

He grinned. "Usually, I sell them back to their fathers, or trade them on the spot for one of their slaves, but since you have none with you..."

He let the words trail off and she could only guess at his implica-tions.

"Nor do you."

Sextus shrugged and put a hand to his chin. His long limbs had a strength to them, like a fisherman, earned honestly, or at least she hoped.

"I sent them on other errands. I did not expect the wig merchant to be so long, but he had to finish fixing the wig my mother had left with him," he said.

"And who is your mother?"

"The woman who birthed me," he said impishly. "And who is your father?"

"The person who raised me," she replied.

He tilted his head slightly at her, appraisingly. "You're not from Rome."

"That took you long enough," she said.

Sextus chuckled. "I knew it right away since you have an odd accent and the way you spoke about your father seemed very non-Roman. I just thought if I said so, you'd tell me where you're from. Rome is the crossway of the world."

Alexandria is the crossway of the world, she thought, but decided against saying it. Partly because she didn't know who this young handsome man was connected to, and partly on a whim.

"I'm from all sorts of places," she told him. "I spent time in Syracuse, and on the seas of the Mediterranean, and I've even lived in the sky."

"Lived in the sky?" he repeated, "What a strange thing to claim, yet you seem absolutely convinced of what you just said." He paused and a mischievous look bloomed on his face. "You're one of the Alexandrians, aren't you?"

"And why would you say that?" she asked as plain-faced as possible.

"Well," he said, seeming to question himself, "it just seemed right. What with the *Michanikos* and his mechanical limbs, the steam chariots, and other fantastical things. Magic, even. It just seemed like something an Alexandrian would say."

He was boyish as he spoke, excitement in every word.

"Well, you're wrong. I'm not from there."

"Yes, you are," he said, grinning. "You're educated, but you don't have slaves attending you, so you must be new in the city. Is it true there are metal soldiers that walk the streets of Alexandria?"

"I wouldn't know," she said, crossing her arms.

He grinned like an idiot, even putting his hand on her arm familiarly. She shook it off.

"What about the steam chariot races?" Sextus asked, undaunted. "Will they bring them to the Circus Maximus? Surely they must, Rome would love those."

"I'm telling you, I don't know," she said, shrinking upon herself.

"And have you ever met the inventor Heron? Mother says...well, I'd love to meet him. There must be metal soldiers in Alexandria if he has metal limbs? If you can make an arm or a leg, then you can make a soldier. I can't say I'd like to face one."

When the wig merchant burst from the back room with a red-haired wig under his arm, he said, "Ave, Sextus—oh...another customer, my apologies."

Sepharia used the distraction to rush from the cramped wig shop, pushing through the crimson curtain, and getting immediately swept up in the crowded street. She thought she heard her name being called out from the shop.

A colorfully dressed Nubian woman attended by a pair of Thracian slaves, stepped on Sepharia's foot, but she didn't care. Sepharia let the crowd carry her as she stumbled along numbly. Then she shook off her malaise, remembering that it didn't matter, in a city the size of Rome, it was unlikely she would meet Sextus again. Whatever happened in the wig shop was a nice distraction, but it was better this way. She was the Consul's daughter, and until they returned to Alexandria, she had to be realistic about potential entanglements. Her dealings with Prince Vima and Ramses the Exile had taught her the price of her naiveté. She wasn't going to make the same mistake again.

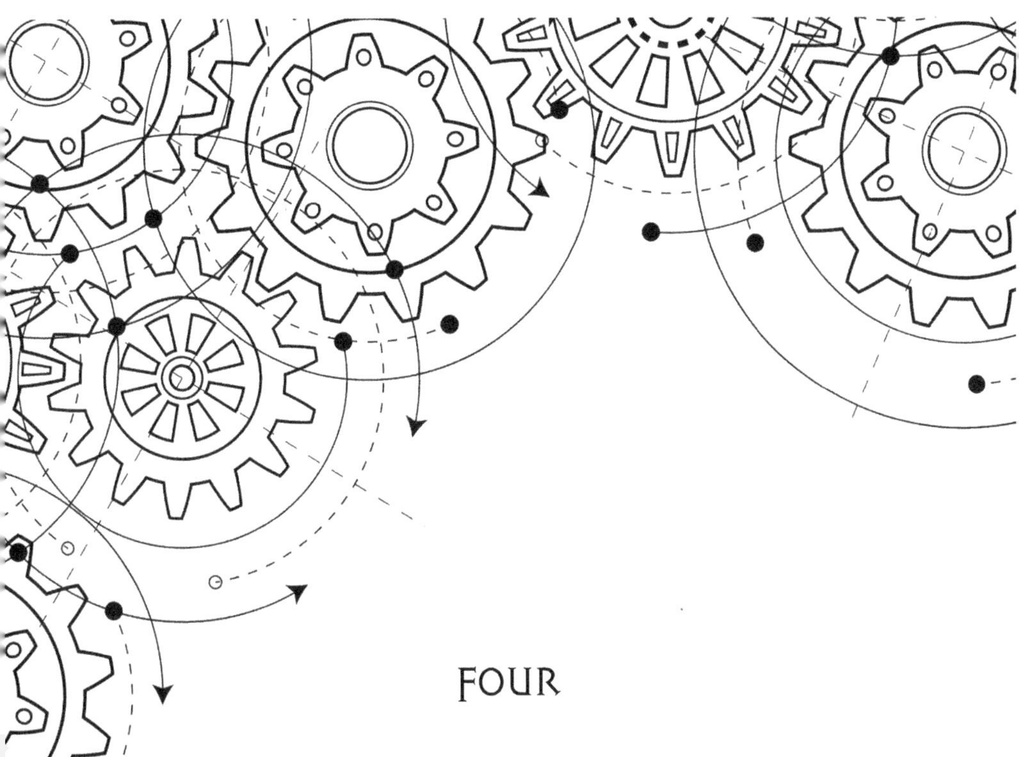

FOUR

Heron regretted taking Domus Alexandria for her place of residence in Rome while she was Consul. She stood at the back of the flowering courtyard, bees buzzing around the bushes, trying to remember which archway took her to Sepharia's room.

The domus was as large as her workshop, except her workshop was mostly empty space. If she needed to find someone, she could see them across the grounds, even through the scaffolding that usually filled the space like vast wooden spider webs.

A flurry of movement caught her eye across the courtyard. A servant, she gathered, by the plain white tunic.

"Ave!" she called.

The servant, if he'd heard her, disappeared into a passageway, leaving Heron to plod on alone. She circled the courtyard with the scrolls under her good arm, examining each archway in turn. The one carved with sea monsters, giant eel-like creatures that sprung from the waves with ship-sized fangs, led to the dining area.

A little further on, a pair of archways confounded her. One was adorned with expertly painted soldiers wielding gladii and scutums; the other had carvings of the great monuments of the Empire.

She'd been living in the domus for three months, but had never needed to find Sepharia personally. A word to a servant brought her daughter to wherever she was, but today was different. She wanted to find her personally, if only to ease the disappointment.

Heron closed her eyes, bringing the sounds of the city. A few streets over, a marketplace seethed with activity, shouts and merchant-calls flooding the air with commerce. Looking up, she could only see pale sky; the domus had two floors which blocked the view of Palatine hill.

"Father, are you having a walking dream?" asked Sepharia from down the monument hallway.

Sepharia greeted Heron with a kiss to the cheek. The aqua stola she wore shimmered like the sea, blue-green with whitecaps. A silvery lace had been sewn over sections, giving the impression of expensive netting.

"You've certainly taken to Rome," said Heron, holding Sepharia at an arm's length and regretting the need for the errand she would set her daughter upon.

Sepharia's gaze sparkled with a fierce intelligence. "We must each play our part."

"Hopefully not for long," said Heron, sighing. "Agog hasn't been gone a month and already I feel stifled by this city. Everyone wants something from me."

"Then you have the power they need," said Sepharia, "an advantageous position."

Heron started to reach out to Sepharia with her metal arm, but pulled it to her chest instead, cradling it with her other arm while keeping the scrolls tucked.

"I need you to be away from the city today," she said, "especially looking like that."

"Looking like what? I thought I would be here to help you with Senator Silius? Today is the first real test of your Consulship," said Sepharia.

Sepharia's cheeks were blushed with a light pink and her hair fell into flaxen curls. Despite the appearance of a soft exterior, Heron knew that the events of the last few years had changed her daughter. Her help would be appreciated in the meeting today, and Heron would have gladly welcomed it, except for the message that Vestalis had sent.

"I need you to take these scrolls to the docks. A ship waits to take them to Alexandria and to the workshop," said Heron.

"But Father, my place is here with you," said Sepharia. "I might be young, but I've had more experience with politics than you."

"That might be true," said Heron, "but still, I need this errand and it can only be you."

Sepharia crossed her arms, the pink in her cheeks turning crimson. Heron considered telling her about the message from Vestalis, but decided against it. She'd already been through enough with Vima.

"Would it help to know that it's Hoth the Black who waits at the docks for these scrolls?" she asked.

Sepharia, to her credit, did not react as she expected. Keeping her chin high and lips pursed together, Sepharia asked, "When did he arrive in Rome?"

"Last night."

"And why doesn't he come visit?" asked Sepharia. "Surely you could use his help."

"Hoth claims his days on land are finished and from the stories I've heard about his new iron ship, he'll have little need to leave it again."

Sepharia let out an exaggerated sigh. "Well, I suppose I can take these scrolls, if he cannot come to Rome."

Heron handed them over, wondering how bad things had gotten that she was sending Sepharia to Hoth for safe keeping.

"Take a steam chariot, and plenty of guards with you," said Heron, "I think it's less than safe for either of us to move about Rome alone. Vestalis gives me daily reports on the schemes brewing in the noble families."

Heron watched Sepharia leave with trepidation in her heart. She wasn't sure if she was making the right choice. It might be advantageous to have her daughter by her side during the meetings with Silius, but the decision had been made, so Heron put it out of her mind.

By the time early afternoon arrived, Heron was waiting in the map room. When Claudius had lived in the domus, he'd spent hours in the room, pouring over details of the Empire. When Heron had first visited the map, she'd been surprised at the difference between it and the one at the Palace in Alexandria. This one comically expanded the size of Rome and the lands around the city until it dwarfed other sections of the map, while the map in Alexandria was more geographically accurate.

Heron wondered how much this warped view of the landscape had led to the Roman Empire's underestimation of Alexandria, which appeared only as a tiny dot on the map along the south edge of the Sea. She hoped in turn they weren't overestimating the importance of Rome in keeping this new Alexandrian Empire, but there was little she could do now with Agog chasing Magnus across the north.

"Ave, Consul Heron," said a strong voice from the entryway, "may the Empire be eternal."

Heron turned carefully, so not to unbalance and make a fool of herself upon first meeting.

Despite leading what the populous called the Wolves of Rome, Senator Silius was often called the Lion of the Senate. His mane of gray hair and strong, wide face, held the countenance of the noble beast.

The sash of purple, which normally noted the position of a Senator, had been replaced with a wrap turning his whole toga purple, except for the sleeves and a portion below the knees, a strong statement that bordered on imperial. His tan jeweled hands were clasped in front.

"I trust you speak of the Alexandrian Empire," said Heron.

Senator Silius inclined his head. "As long as the rule of law and the office of the Senate still stands, then we speak of the same thing."

"We have no need of disturbing the Senate, it's workings provide a useful engine to the new Empire," she said.

"And what of this new Empire?" he scowled as he motioned toward her. "Will you turn us to machines?"

Heron lifted her mechanical arm, flexing the fingers before gripping them into a powerful fist. "My machines are here to serve us, just as the wheel, or catapult, or aqueduct serves us now."

"Romans are not Alexandrians," countered Silius. "We do not accept such strange devices in our midst easily. It would be a shame for the people to become spooked and rise up against your government."

Heron smiled. Vestalis had warned that Silius and his allies had been holding secret meetings with prominent members of the *plebs*. "Your concerns are appreciated, but not necessary. Just last week, I sent designs free of charge to the workshops of the city for some of the common machines that Alexandrians enjoy like self-trimming lamps, or wind-powered mills. Not all had the funds to make these machines, so we made lower interest loans available to facilitate their manufacture."

Senator Silius shrugged dismissively. "It matters not to me, I was only passing along a warning. Roman politics can be an infuriating endeavor, and I thought you might enjoy some inside information."

"Your generosity is appreciated," said Heron trying hard to force her lips into a pleasant smile. "How can I serve your needs?"

Silius coughed and waved her off. "Oh, no. My needs are few and easily taken care of. I come on behalf of those that cannot speak for themselves. This is the Republic, after all."

Heron repressed a frown. "And these needs?"

His shoulders slumped considerably, and he wandered to a chair to lean heavily upon it with both hands gripping the ornate backing.

"This war was a terrible, terrible thing," he said.

"Of course," said Heron. "War is always terrible."

"But this one, this one was worse than ever before," whispered Silius before clearing his throat. "When an army loses a fight, they usually have time to surrender once it's known they will not win."

Heron crossed her arms. "And your point?"

Silius stood and sighed with all the exaggeration of a theater performance. "Forgive my poor words here, I'm a man of peace better known as a champion of the people, not a eloquent speaker like Cicero."

Heron stifled her laughter, even she knew Silius was more dangerous than swimming in a pool of vipers, and had never been even remotely called a champion of the people. Vestalis had told her that once a street merchant had been crucified for his donkey's dung fouling the edge of Silius' toga.

"Your weapons, terrible, terrible weapons. Though I was not there, I heard the stories. Your sorcery cast fire and earth into the midst of the legions, destroying them as simply as snapping your fingers. They had no time to surrender, only die."

"Are you getting to a point here?" she asked.

He leaned heavily on the chair. "So many families lost firstborn sons in the war. And not just firstborns, seconds, and thirds, too. Almost six full legions were killed that day, nearly thirty thousand men. An unheard of death toll in our time, or any time."

Even Heron was not unmoved by the obscenely large number. Winning the war had come with a price, but it was a price she was willing to pay to put a stop to the Empire's slaving ways.

"As you said, war is terrible."

"Without their sons, many of these families will not survive," he pleaded. "I know it's unprecedented for the losing side to ask for reparations, but it would go a long way in securing peace for the Empire."

Heron blinked hard, twice. "You want us to pay the families for the soldiers killed?"

A smile bloomed on Silius' face. "Yes, it's a small thing, but I think you would gain loyalty for the new government. I've even offered deaneries from my own coffers to the families to ease their suffering."

Heron turned to the map to hide her disgust. If they gave coin to the families of the slain soldiers, it would only anger the Alexandrians who had fought and won. And even then, Silius would get all the credit for the payment, not the Consulship.

"While I sympathize with the fallen, the Empire is in a period of reorganization, and we're still fighting a war. At this time, we cannot afford such a payment, however noble the purpose might be."

"Surely this new Empire must be flush with coinage? Why it is the talk of the city that you freed your house slaves and made them freemen. Why, if you can afford to pay them, can't you afford to pay the families?"

"Apologies, but as I said before, we're still fighting a war. Please pass my condolences along to those families, but that's all we can offer at this moment."

"You want me to pass along condolences to thirty thousand families?" he asked.

"No, of course not," she said, sighing, feeling like a street vendor taking orders for roast bear. "Can I help you with anything else?"

"Nothing at this moment," he said bowing, but before he turned to leave, he raised his arms slightly, "though there is one thing, a small thing."

Heron raised an eyebrow. "A small thing?"

"Yes, a trifle, barely worth mentioning."

"Then don't mention it," she replied, stone-faced. This 'Lion of the Senate' was nothing as she expected.

Silius cleared his throat. "There's a minor rule in the Senate, one that's lingered from centuries past, but as rules are, they're easier to implement, but harder to eliminate."

"And you want my support on eliminating the rule?" she asked.

"Well, it's more than your support. Since the powers of the dictatorship are in effect, and you are acting Dictator while the Emperor pursues the traitor Magnus, you could change the rule with the flick of a quill."

"What is this rule?" she asked carefully.

"It's an old rule, one long since passed out of usefulness. I feel it is my duty to eliminate such waste in our laws, but others thwart me out of spite for my position. The law proscribes the paying of fines to the Empire in bronze, a practice necessary four hundred years ago before silver and gold were readily available. It puts a drag on the Empire, and costs it funds by its arbitrary nature."

Heron had been expecting all manner of laws, but not this one. It could be that he would get some minor benefit out of it, and he was just testing the waters with her, but she couldn't see what.

"It seems a law that I might consider eliminating," she said.

"I would most appreciate it," said Silius. "It would put me quite into your debt."

"I suppose."

Silius bowed again. "You'll find I can be a staunch ally. There's a group of Senators, whom I am a part of, that wishes to be helpful. With the right favors, this new Empire can enjoy our valuable support."

"And what are the right favors?"

The smile that rose to Silius' lips made Heron want to retch. Had she not been warned by Vestalis, this request would have shocked her. Now, it only made her ill.

"I seem to be in-between wives at the moment," he said, imploring her with open hands. "Your daughter is of age and is said to be quite attractive. A binding of our two families would make this new Empire quite strong."

Heron took a deep breath and said the words she had been practicing all morning. "Apologies, Senator Silius. It is my deepest regret that I cannot offer my daughter's hand to you. She is promised to Admiral Hoth and is boarding his vessel to return to Alexandria as we speak."

"Oh, I had not heard," he said, looking around feverishly. "Well, then, I must be going. The duty of a Senator calls."

"Of course."

Before he left, Silius raised a hand in farewell. "And I shall not forget that favor. Small things can have great effects. I am much appreciative."

When the Senator was gone, Heron slumped into a chair, and whispered to herself, "Oh, why again did I agree to this?"

FIVE

The waiting was intolerable.

The tight blue-green fabric shifted with each bump, drawing the silky stola across her taut nipples. Sepharia held her arm over her chest as the steam chariot thundered through the streets, drawing stares and open-mouthed gapes.

Sepharia barely noticed them, faces mutely passing, the commoners and merchant classes picking their way through the streets. She held her nose against the sharp sulphur smell of the coal fire burning only a length away in the steam chamber. Azure mists passed across the round boiling pot like clouds in a crystal ball.

The shipyards were a distance from the city center, unlike Alexandria which held its harbors close like a babe to its mother's breast. The western side seemed to be more industrious, less political, the opulent mansions replaced with sturdy workshops and tall stone warehouses.

It'd been half a year since she'd seen Hoth the Black. His starlight attentions during the trip to Syracuse had been a nice distraction from the monotony, but she wondered what kind of reception she would receive. Partially, she scolded herself for even agreeing to deliver the scrolls. Her place was in the domus for the discussion with Senator Silius.

Next time, she wouldn't let Heron talk her out of attending, but she wasn't worried. There were other meetings, other parties, and still she had not yet visited the Forum.

When the shipyards came into view, Sepharia found that the massive iron ship waiting in the harbor defied her expectations. She'd heard tales of the pleasure barges of the pharaohs, or the floating palace of Emperor Caligula, but neither stories did the ship Hoth the Black called *Jörmungandr* justice. Gawkers streamed towards the grand boat which dwarfed even the *Mars Valliant*, previously the largest ship in the world.

A three-banked quinquereme next to it, barely came up to the half-way point of the bow above the water. The phallic outlines of steam catapults lined the upper deck of the sailless ship. Four vertical cylinders with six paddles each sticking out from the center like spokes on a wheel were positioned on the rear of the boat. Even one paddle was larger than the *Grey Cetus* that they had taken from Alexandria to Syracuse.

Carefully stepping from the steam chariot with the scrolls under her arm, Sepharia strolled towards the gang plank. To her surprise, a pair of women were headed down toward her. Since the plank was barely wide enough for one, Sepharia waited for the women to pass.

At first she thought they might be envoys, or merchants, since some women ran their husband's businesses in Rome, but even before she smelled the thick perfume, she knew what they were by their togas and tousled hair. In Rome, only prostitutes were allowed to wear togas, a fact that made Sepharia wonder about the quality of the Senate when she'd first heard it.

The women gave her sly glances and conspiratorial grins. Sepharia watched them march confidently into the crowd. She sighed deeply.

Nearby, citizens gazed at her with wonder as she stepped onto the edge of the long wooden plank as if she were boarding the kraken.

Clinging tightly to the guide rope, Sepharia made her way up as the wood bowed beneath her feet, leaving her stomach queasy with vertigo. The gang plank was actually three sections connected together. The creaking and snapping of the wood as she neared the top made her wonder if she'd be swimming soon, but the gang plank held and she stepped to the upper deck.

"Hail, *Freyja*," said Hoth the Black as he took her hand, "welcome to the *Jörmungandr*, the Hyperborean Traveler, the floating Atlantis, the City on the Seas."

"What did you call me?"

"*Freyja*," he smiled and tucked her arm beneath his, pulling her along gently in a slow stroll, "it means Lady in the language of the North."

He was dressed as she'd never seen him before, she assumed in the manner of his people, but yet also, in a way all his own. The dark gray overtunic he wore appeared to be made out of the stuff of dusk, longer than the Roman tunic, hanging past his knees and lined with a woven ebony thread. Black leggings wrapped up his feet and around his thighs, held by thick cords. His hair, normally pale like moonlight, had been dyed midnight black. It wasn't until they were halfway across the deck that she realized he was limping.

"You're injured."

"A lucky arrow nicked my thigh."

She slapped his arm and the scrolls clattered to the deck. "Fighting? I thought the war was over."

"Pirates off the coast of Carthage," he smiled. "If only my old shipmates from the North sea could see me now."

"But why an arrow? Can't you just blast them from a distance?" she asked.

Hoth gave her a decidedly sheepish grin. "I needed to take their captain alive, so that I could know their hideouts. So we boarded them."

Sepharia pushed him away, punching him in the shoulder. "Are you mad? *We* boarded them? You mean *you* boarded them. You're a fool."

Laughing, he rubbed his arm. "What do you care if I do?"

"If you haven't noticed, we barely hold Rome. We need all the allies we can get, and this ship, or whatever you call it, will help keep it."

"I should have called you, *Hörnar-vé*, for troll-wife," he said with arms crossed. "I'm well aware of the risks. If you recall, I was doing this long before I came to Alexandria."

"Then why didn't you send your men and wait on the boat?" she asked.

He shook his head and his hair danced around his face. "That's not how it works when you're a captain. You wouldn't know that *girl*."

Sepharia punched him again, right in the middle of the chest.

"You punch like your father."

"Exactly!"

"Did you come here to abuse me? Or do those scrolls mean something?" he asked with an impish grin.

"Abusing you is just the payment I get for missing out on the meeting with Senator Silius," she said.

"We're enjoying Roman politics, aren't we?"

Sepharia scoffed. "Heron needs me."

"Well, then," he said, squatting down to gather up the fallen scrolls, "let's get to the delivery so you can hurry back and help him."

"Well, since I'm here," she said. "I can stay and catch up for a little while. By the time I get back, the meeting will be over." She tapped a scroll with a Greek 'H' stamped into the wax. "This one's for you, the rest go to Plutarch when you get back to Alexandria."

"Wonderful," he said. "I'm an errand boy."

"How appropriate," she grinned wickedly while he broke the seal. "Why did you name your boat *Jörmungandr?* What does it mean?"

"World serpent," he said, glancing up. "If I ever encountered another sea monster, I wanted to be riding the bigger one."

"Have you ever? Seen one, I mean," she said.

He had just begun reading, but dropped his arms down and let the scroll rest at his stomach. His eyes had a faraway look as if he were reliving a memory. "A few times. On the way back from capturing those pirates, I thought I saw the leviathan."

"What's that?"

"A twisted, coiled sea monster as long as this ship, or longer. Some say it's the child of the world serpent," he said.

"And you? What do you say?"

Hoth shrugged. "I don't. But I saw it one night when the moon was a scythe and the waves gentle like a woman in bed." The smile in his eyes went right through her. "It was moving through the water at great speed, like four great hills ascending and receding from the waves, going on like a steam chariot with white mist from its head."

"So you'd had too much wine then?" she asked.

"I had," he said, "but it was still the leviathan."

"And I'm a magical wind spirit that turns figs into gold," she said spinning around and waving her arms.

Hoth laughed as he dipped back into the scroll, his lips moving as he read the words.

When he was done, he spun the papyrus in his hands until it was a tight scroll, staring at her the whole time. His look was halfway between concern and impishness, the slight crook at the corner of his lips almost a question.

"What?" she asked.

Hoth put his fingers to his lips and a shrill whistle erupted. A sailor ran up, one of the Northern men, and Hoth spoke quickly to the man, glancing at her the whole time.

"What are you doing? I don't like this," she said.

She watched the sailor go running to the rear of the boat where a number of other sailors were painting the inside of the iron with a pungent black substance.

"What did the scroll say?"

"It was an instruction from your father," he said.

"I know that. What did it say?"

He tilted his head slightly. "Your father is the Consul of the Empire, right?"

"Of course."

"And my position is the Admiral of the Alexandrian navy, which reports to the Consul in Wodanoz's absence?" he asked.

"Yes, of course. What foolishness is this?"

When he frowned she knew she wasn't going to like what he had to say.

"Then know that I am just following orders when I say that I've been instructed to take you back to Alexandria with me," he said tight lipped.

Sepharia turned to run back to the gang plank when she realized what the sailors were up to. The six men were pulling the heavy wooden plank onto the ship. There would be no leaving the *Jörmungandr* now.

Her face was as hot as a volcano when she turned to Hoth. He held his hands up. "Apologies, it's the Consul's command. I know you want to be at your father's side, but trust me, Heron explained his reasoning in the scroll. You don't want to be in Rome."

Sepharia marched up to Hoth and pushed him with both hands. "You don't understand. My father needs me. Vestalis is busy with the army, you're hiding on this cursed boat, Agog is off chasing that old Roman general, and Jarngard is dead. There's no one left but me. I have to stay. You *cannot* take me."

"I have to," he said.

"My father disdains politics. They'll eat him alive. It doesn't matter how smart you are if you can't be coy and duplicitous," she argued.

"And you are?"

"More than my father," she said, balling her hands into fists. "Heron was building his pyramid or running off to Old Babylon with you when I had to deal with Ramses and Vima. And they'll underestimate me. Think I'm just a young girl who knows nothing of these things."

"They don't think that," he said.

"They'll kill him. Poison him, or something. You can't leave him here to die. You might as well be sentencing him to death," Sepharia pleaded.

"It can't be that bad, can it?"

She dug her fingernails into her palms. "It can. I've read the histories. The leading cause of death for a senator is assassination, usually by poison, but it could be anything. They killed Caesar in the middle of the Senate!"

Hoth looked momentarily sympathetic, but then he glanced at the scroll. "I can't. The orders and reasoning were clear."

"Then tell me the reason," she said.

"I can't do that, either."

They faced off for a while, matching stern looks, until Hoth finally shrugged and limped back toward his cabin. Sepharia's hands unclenched and her arms hung loosely at her side. When the deck began to hum and black smoke puffed from the stacks at the rear of the iron ship, Sepharia put her palms to her eyes and pressed until blue geometric shapes formed in the darkness.

The sailors moved about the deck, ignoring her as she stood like a statue. They feared to meet her gaze. When the giant steam mechanicals that rested in the belly of the iron ship gave their full throated roars, and the cylinders began a slow churning revolution, Sepharia bit her lower lip and watched the *Jörmungandr* pull away from the docks.

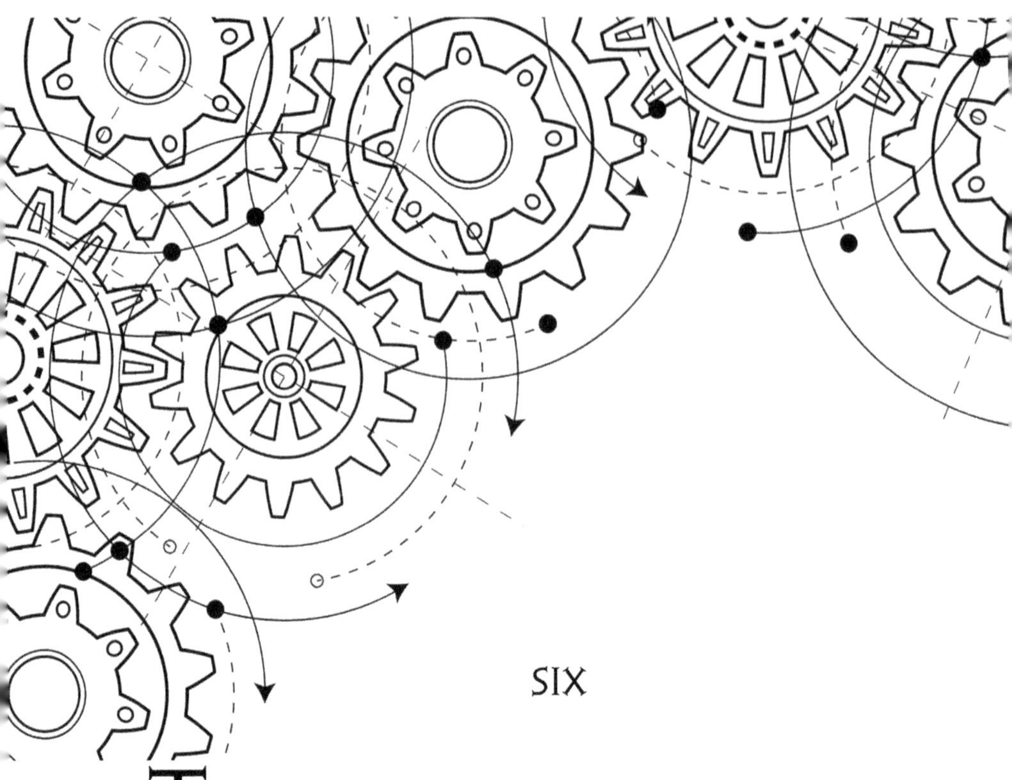

SIX

The hard bench wore a knot into her rear while the Senators chattered on like a great host of magpies. The scents of their musks and perfumes were so thick Heron expected to see a light mist hovering through the great bowl of the Senate chamber.

A Senator was speaking, Heron had no idea what his name was, only that he'd been droning on for a while, ignoring the clattering going on despite his impassioned oratory.

"...in the esteemed fashion accorded a member of the legates, it is our duty to make known that which is most important, the glory of the Empire, though changed, we still endure, and so I say..."

At the beginning of his speech, Heron recalled mention of a statue to be commissioned for Tiberius' role in brokering the peace plan, which she knew was a lie. Heron wasn't inclined enough to dispute the claim, deciding it would be more than appropriate to let the pigeons shit on his likeness.

Bored, Heron practiced the articulation of her metal fingers, tapping each one against her palm in succession. When she'd first come to the Senate floor, she'd expected to be gawked at like a lion in a zoo, but most of the Senators ignored her as they puffed up like peacocks showing off their colorful togas and flashy rings while spouting annoyingly long oratories about the glory of the Empire (with no mention of Alexandria in any speech.)

Heron dressed in the simple tunic she wore to the workshop each day, though this one was absent of ink marks or food stains, making her feel less than useful. She glanced to the far side of the bowl to where Silius and his side sat. The Senator's regal mane of gray hair had been copiously brushed and his toga barely had a scrap of white on it, a near traitorous choice of attire if he'd worn it while Claudius still ruled. The Senator caught her looking, and nodded, so she nodded back.

The other two groups sat to either side of the Wolves, neither one as large or as powerful as Silius' group. Heron expected some contact or overture from those groups, but neither had been forthcoming.

Heron sighed, silently wishing for the session to end. Moving her pointing finger, she noticed a hitch in the knuckle causing a delay in the movement.

She started to make a mental note to have Sepharia fix it when she got back to the domus, but then she remembered she'd sent Sepharia back to Alexandria with Hoth. At the time, it'd felt like the right decision, even though it made the domus quite empty each night, especially since the freedman attending her were put off by her mechanical limbs. Sepharia would be in Alexandria soon, the thought of which left Heron with an odd ache in her bones.

A great clatter rose up and Senators were standing. As the assembled filed out of the chamber, Heron waited. A strong hand grasped her arm, forcing her to turn.

"Ave, Senator Silius."

"Ave, Consul Heron," said Silius, "I just wanted to stop by and thank you for fixing that rule. An Empire runs on its laws and bad laws only impede its progress."

Heron stifled a yawn behind a cupped hand. "Of course. Glad to help in any way I can."

"Consul Heron!" came a voice from the other direction, giving Silius the opportunity to withdraw with a quiet farewell.

"Ave, Senator Messalina," she said to the tall, bird-like man approaching. He had a prominent Roman nose, almost too prominent, making it appear a beak, and Heron couldn't help but picture him as a lanky parakeet, especially with the mismatched colors of his toga.

"Consul Heron," said Messalina, out of breath. "Why do you not take your appointed position in the Consul's chair?"

"I'm not as familiar with the procedures of the Senate enough to take that place. I prefer to observe for now," she explained.

And hopefully Agog returns before I take that chair, she thought while smiling.

Smiling, already her cheeks hurt from smiling, a common enough greeting, coupled with a nod and with six hundred Senators in the same room, it left one with a tired jaw.

Senator Messalina thought for a moment before adjusting his shoulders which only gave Heron the impression of a great bird ruffling its wings. "A wise choice, but if you'd like I can give you the proper education on your responsibilities to the Senate. I think you'll find we're a necessary part of ruling an Empire."

"I agree, Senator, and so does the Emperor," said Heron. "Our intention has always been to maintain the order of the Empire."

"It warms my gentle heart to hear this from your lips," said Messalina, smiling. "For more than anything, the powers of the Senate must be preserved, and maybe, I dare say, even rolled back to the times before

Caesar gutted our powers?"

Senator Messalina looked on curiously, as did the group of Senators with him, waiting on her answer. Heron spied for an exit, but she saw no way to safely retreat.

"I cannot know the mind of the Emperor..." she began.

"Then why are you his voice for the Senate, if you cannot?" countered Messalina.

"Yes," she said annoyed at the interruption, "I am his voice, only on the workings of the Empire, but I do not dare to upset his powers. Remember, it was Alexandria that conquered Rome."

Messalina shrugged off her comment. "Trivial details. The Senate has never cared much for the infighting of the Roman military. It's a wonderful way to promote new Senators into our ranks, but the military is still made up of barbaric soldiers."

Heron frowned. "Senator Messalina, need I remind you that this was not a coup from within the military. Agog took Alexandria away from Rome, then with it as his capitol, defeated Rome's armies and took the Roman Empire."

"Well," began Messalina, "as long as Rome is still the capitol since this is where the power of the people lies."

Heron choked back a rebuttal since she knew it would do little to change his mind.

"Is there something I can help you with, Senator Messalina?" she asked through gritted teeth. "Otherwise, my arse is sore from these cursed benches and I'd like to get back to the domus to rest."

His eyes lighted with wonder. "I thought with your metal limbs you could work all day? Are the stories about you working through the night in your workshop to create your machines just a story?"

Heron was about to give a pithy answer when she remembered Vestalis advice to stay mysterious.

"Who's to say that I haven't been working all day and night on the machinery of the Roman government?" she said smugly.

"Consul Heron," said Messalina dryly, "Romans are not machines."

"Then what is it you want?" she said, tired of the game.

"To protect the powers of the Senate," said Messalina.

Heron closed her eyes briefly. "Specifically, Senator, specifically."

"There's a minor rule that we'd like to see changed," he said.

"Of course you do."

"A trivial thing."

"Aren't they all," she replied.

"The rule states that no man over the age of eighty may hold a questorship," said Messalina, "we'd like this rule stricken from the lists."

"And why would this rule have been once necessary?"

"A relic from a previous time," said Messalina, "when men in their old age were frail and senile, and the rule protected the Empire from poor decisions. Now, with new medicines and deft surgeons, men live longer and with their full faculties. They should be allowed to serve longer. Look to your metal limbs as an example of the miracles of our advanced times!"

She thought briefly of the potential repercussions, but could find none. What was the harm in men serving longer? They were already in the role. There could be no harm in that. She'd probably be long gone from Rome before the rule actually took effect.

"I will strike the rule from the lists," said Heron.

Messalina's face broke into a smile. "Your wisdom knows no bounds. I will leave you to your duties."

The Senator and his Senatorial companions withdrew and Heron was left with her thoughts, finally. Moving carefully to avoid any more encounters, she made her way to the steam chariot waiting outside and returned to the domus.

Heron gave the head of her servants the order to draw a hot bath only to be notified that a delegation from Senator Pallas' camp was waiting in the courtyard. With a heavy heart, Heron made her way there, the mechanical leg feeling like an anchor by the time she reached the courtyard.

Two figures stood by the lilac bushes speaking quietly to each other. The first had a soldier's stance, shoulders back, hand resting on the hilt of his gladius. The second, a woman, wore a silvery stola.

Heron summoned her resolve. A hundred miracles for the temples wasn't as tiring as Roman politics. She nearly had fond memories for the high priest Ghet.

"Greetings, friends," she said, shrugging off a snag of a rose bush. "Apologies that I was not here sooner and I'm afraid I don't know the pleasure of your names."

Heron moved toward the soldier, thinking him a Senator and his wife, but as soon as they turned, she realized her error, though not the reason for it. The soldier's smooth pink cheeks belayed his age, making him too young to be a Senator. And the woman held the countenance of an Empress with ebony hair coifed around her head like a crown. The creases at the edges of her eyes and lips hinted at her age, making her too old to be his wife, but her skin was strong and lustrous.

Heron froze as the woman's gaze shot arrows, not understanding the mistake until realizing the pair had similar green eyes. Part of her cringed at the realization that she'd automatically moved to greet the man and her embarrassment came out as a nervous laugh.

"Do you find us amusing?" asked the woman while rattling the silver bracelets around her wrist.

Heron wrinkled her brow. "Apologies, I mistook you for another."

The words felt brittle, but the woman seemed to accept the excuse. The soldier watched with wide eyes, his gaze firmly fixed on her mechanical arm.

"Your names, then?"

The woman shot a scathing glance to the soldier and he made a little jump, and cleared his throat. "Apologies, this is my mother, Aelia Octavia Paetina, and I am Sextus Octavia Paetina."

Even Heron with her limited knowledge of Roman politics knew it was unusual for a woman to give a *nomen gentile* and *cognomen* name. It was even more unusual that she'd been sent as the spokesperson for Senator Pallas, the person she'd expected to see in the courtyard.

"Excuse me for my ignorance, but you are Senator Pallas' wife?" asked Heron.

Aelia raised her chin high. "Does this bother you?"

"No," said Heron, trying to remember where else she'd heard the woman's name. "Not in the least bit. I'm still unfamiliar with all the players in Rome."

"You certainly had time for Senator Silius, helping him steal a large fortune from my family with that stricken law. I would say you know quite well who the players are and you've decided which side you're going to back."

Heron stammered for a moment. "Steal a large fortune? I'm afraid I don't understand."

Aelia stepped closer and a flood of old perfume nearly made Heron gag. The son, Sextus, watched mutely, his intelligent gaze bouncing between the two of them as if he were watching two gladiators square off.

"The lies don't become you, Consul Heron," said Aelia taking a slightly softer tone, "we could have been good friends in different circumstances. I suspect our goals align."

Unexpectedly, Aelia moved close enough to touch and her lips parted hungrily. She was a handsome woman and Heron suspected that many men desired Aelia, the thought of which led her to remembering where she had heard Aelia's name before. She'd been Emperor Claudius' former wife, until he'd set her aside for a younger one. That woman had died not long after Alexandria had taken Rome, and by poison, if Heron remembered correctly.

"But these aren't different circumstances," said Aelia as her coy lips abandoned their seduction and exposed the white teeth beneath. "Our copper and tin mines have had to shut down for lack of demand now that the Wolves don't have to go through us to do business."

"I don't understand," said Heron.

The withering gaze was brief and terrible. "Then you're a fool if this was done in ignorance, and that makes you even more dangerous than an enemy. Paying fines in Rome is the price of doing business. Some laws must be broken and the fine is levied as a kind of tax. My family and those of my faction own most of the copper mines and all of the tin mines, leaving us in a position of power when it comes to the payment of bronze coinage to the Empire. That little rule change neutered our family like a hot blade to a steer's balls."

Heron swallowed the word *apology* before it even dared her lips. She'd given Senator Silius a major advantage and had exacted nothing in return. Aelia was right, she was a fool.

"What's done is done," Heron said finally though the words felt ashy in her mouth. "But I offer the Emperor's hand in friendship. If you think we have similar interests, I would be inclined to speak of them with you. These other ways might serve to repair the loss of funds."

When Aelia surged forward, Heron flinched thinking she was about to be slapped. "You've made a grave mistake in siding with the Wolves. I would enjoy your mealtimes with great care."

Aelia swept from the courtyard while Heron looked on, too stunned to comment. The son, Sextus, who Heron had nearly forgotten, gave a little nod with an almost apologetic expression before he left.

A lonely bee nearly flew into Heron's face and she just watched it go past. Slumping onto a stone bench, she tried to take a deep breath and cleanse the claustrophobic feeling suddenly invading her bones, but the fragrance of the flowering courtyard had been annihilated by the meeting with Aelia.

Six months.

Agog had sentenced her to six months in Rome. By the time he came back, the city would be in ruins from her ineptitude. It was no wonder she preferred machines over people. Until it broke, a machine did what it was designed to do. If only she could peer inside their heads and see the gears that drove them, then maybe she might stand a chance.

Six months.

Six more months in Rome.

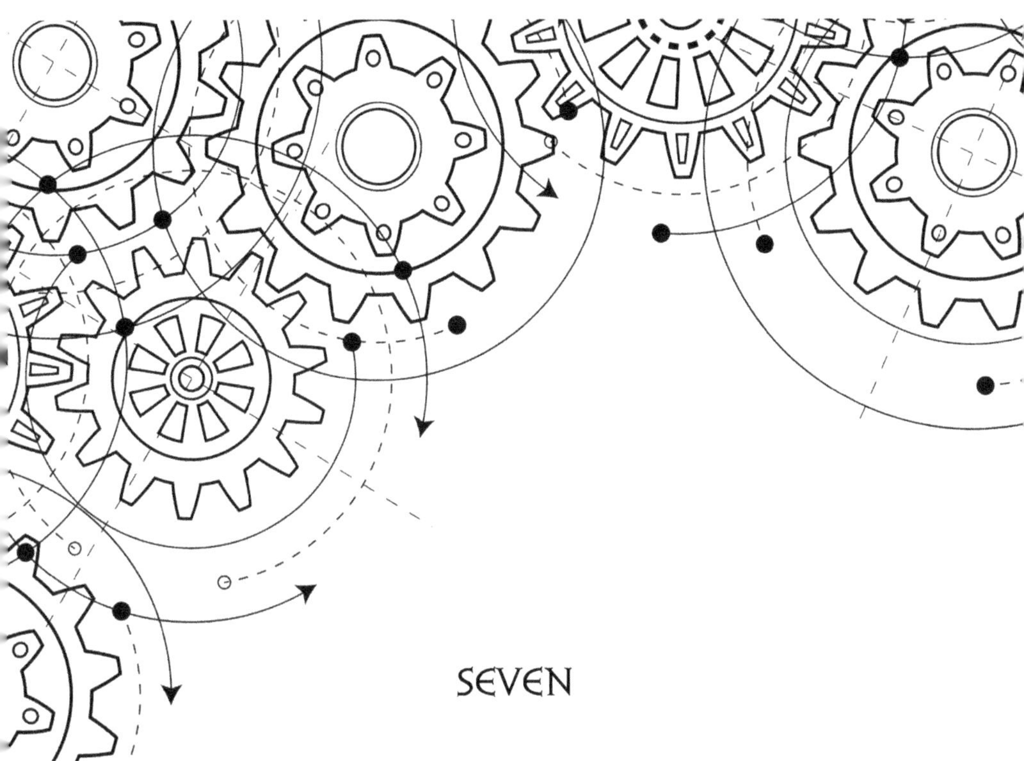

SEVEN

The candle light flickered with the opening of a distant door, but Heron scribbled on, determined to get the idea out of her head and onto the papyrus. After a practiced flip of the lid, she took a spoonful of the violet powder and shuddered in its embrace.

A plate of lark tongues waited nearby, long since cooled from the ovens. Heron ran an interested finger across the edge of the plate, before deciding better of it, and going back to her drawing.

A heavy knock sounded from the doorway.

"Go away. I don't need food. I'm not going to eat it anyway. Feed it to the dogs like the others."

"Afraid of poison?" asked Vestalis.

Heron whipped around, startled by the voice. "It's you."

"Last I checked," said Vestalis before he took a sniff. "How many days have you been in this room?"

Heron glanced to the table filled with barely touched plates of food. There had to be at least a dozen. "I haven't the faintest idea."

"A week," said Vestalis, "or so my spies tell me so. Surely you haven't been awake this whole time?"

A pile of finished scrolls were stacked just out of reach. She didn't remember working on them, but the stylistic 'H' in the wax seals were unmistakable.

"I'm certain I caught a nap here or there," she said, feeling a hollowness in her bones.

Vestalis raised an eyebrow, his jaw pulsing with thought. "There is much talk in the Senate about your absence. Conclusions, none beneficial, are being drawn."

"I'm afraid it's probably best this way," she said. "I can't make any political blunders from here and I'm getting a lot of work done." Though she hadn't the foggiest idea of what she'd drawn.

"Without your presence as a representative of Alexandria, the various factions are starting to doubt our relevance," said Vestalis with only a slight scolding tone in his voice. "It's better that they bicker with each other than to consider temporary alliances to remove the invaders."

"Then take my place," said Heron. "It's clear I'm unfit for the job."

"Your concern is understandable. Rome is no easy stage to make your first steps upon. But I cannot take your place, or we will lose the gains I've made with the Legion. We have no choice but for you to continue."

Heron shook her head. "Did you come here to taunt me in my stupor?"

The corner of his lips ticked upward. "Partially. And partially to check on the invention I requested last month." He paused. "And partially because we have another problem."

Heron sighed. "What is it?"

"The barrels," he said, frowning. "My spies tell me certain factions are growing interested in them. If they helped us take Rome from the

Empire, why can't they help take it back from Alexandria?"

She drummed her fingers on the table. "An excellent point. Where are we keeping them?"

"In a warehouse at the edge of the city," he said. "I have a garrison there, all loyal Alexandrians, but a garrison in a city this big is easy to overcome."

"Then we have to move them," she said, matching his frown. "Or hide them somehow."

"I was thinking we needed to split them up," he said. "Scatter them around the city in hidden locations that only we know about."

"Without guards?"

He nodded. "It would only point an arrow to them."

"How will we move them? And where?" she asked.

"I don't know," he said, "that's why I came for help."

She nodded again, the malaise lifting from her limbs. "We'd need a reason to be moving around the city. And locations to hide them."

"Good idea, but too vague. We can't make a plan without details," said Vestalis.

She glanced to the massive map on the wall. The city was a large place, there should be plenty of places to hide the barrels of sparkpowder.

"Could you help me put more light into the room? We need the map," she said.

"What a good idea," he said, grabbing a candle from a mahogany side table and sticking the wick into the one on the table.

Before long, the room was brighter, which had its downsides. The plates of old food looked quite pathetic in the light. She picked up one of the slippery lark tongues but decided against it, throwing the piece of meat back onto the cream terracotta plate.

Heron stared at the map with Vestalis by her side. She tapped her lips while searching for inspiration. "When I was making miracles for the temples, I had to hide the contents of my wagons, lest the believers get a whiff of our deceitfulness. We used grain wagons to mask our movement, even throwing bundles of grain on the tarped contents. When guards would stop our wagons, we would show them the workshop papers, and they would let us by, a problem here because most of the guards of the city are Roman."

"It would only give suspicion to the movements," he said.

"We need a reason to be moving about the city. One they will accept without question. The best illusions gave believers every reason to accept the lie. They should *want* to believe."

"It seems I've come to the right place," he said.

"But I don't have an answer!"

Vestalis smiled. "It sounds close."

Heron scowled and went back to studying the map. "Why would they look the other way from our wagons? What would get them to accept our ruse. What could we be doing?"

"Moving workshop supplies?" he offered.

"No." She shook her head vehemently. "Too obvious. We need something they want to believe...wait. I know!" The excitement running through her veins was something she hadn't felt in quite some time. Not since the search for Archimedes weapons, she realized.

"I assume you'll tell me eventually," said Vestalis dryly.

Heron marched before Vestalis and gave a deep bow. "Good Vestalis, thank you for waking me from my delusional self-pity. I am eternally in your debt."

"If you've solved my problem, then I am in yours. Have you?"

She nodded enthusiastically. "What would make Romans excited about seeing my wagons?"

"I don't know."

"Is there a shrine still outside the domus?" she asked hurriedly.

"Is that what that pile of junk is?"

She nodded again. "You said it yourself. They're fascinated by my metal limbs. Even Agog said so. It was why he wanted me at the negotiating table."

"Are you planning on moving yourself around the city? Seems impractical," he mused.

"No," said Heron. "Not me, but something similar. Automatas. Alexandria is known as the City of Wonders for the automatas on every street. I shall bring some of those wonders to Rome."

She felt out of breath and dizzy and considered eating for a moment, but thought better of it. It would only come back up.

"Will you send back to Alexandria for them?" he asked.

"That would take too long. I'll need to have them made in Rome. It will add to their importance and maybe ease the plots against me. If the plebs are on our side, then we stand a better chance."

Vestalis looked entirely too self-pleased, but she decided he deserved it.

"Thank you again, my friend." She bowed.

"Don't thank me, thank yourself, it's your head on the chopping block, too," he grinned.

She let out a sigh. "This is something I can work on, but the Senate. I have no answers for that and I'm afraid there's not enough time to learn on the job. I need someone who has experience with this sort of political intrigue."

"Would you allow your daughter to help?" came a voice from the doorway.

Heron turned awkwardly on her metal foot to find Sepharia leaning in the doorway with her arms crossed, wearing what had to be one of Hoth's black tunics because it hung well past her knees.

"Or do you plan on shipping me back to Alexandria again?" asked Sepharia.

"It appears it doesn't matter what I think, since Hoth failed to follow my instructions," said Heron. "I'm not sure I want to know how you convinced him."

"It was easy," said Sepharia. "I took over his cabin and made him sleep with his officers and told him that unless he took me back to Rome, I would make those quarters my permanent home."

Vestalis chuckled lightly. "Your daughter has become quite formidable. Surely she can help you with your Senate problem."

"It seems I have no other choice," said Heron, slumping into a chair. "Good Vestalis, explain to my daughter how I've turned Rome into a snarled mess."

He nodded and turned to address Sepharia, arms clasped behind his back with his shoulders square. Sepharia stepped into the room, fierce eyes studying the Alexandria general. For the first time, Heron actually saw what a woman Sepharia had become and noted that sending her back to Alexandria was a mistake. She needed all the allies she could get, even if it put them in danger.

"You are familiar with the three major factions of Rome?" he asked to a nod from Sepharia. "Then I will say this simply. The Wolves gained a major advantage over the New Aristocrats through a change in a law Heron removed which made an enemy of the New Aristocrats, while the Protectors were able to block the Wolves from gaining new Questorships when their members aged out of the position which angered them."

"And the Protectors? Are they on our side?" asked Sepharia.

"No," said Vestalis, "sadly not. Because Agog continued the position of Emperor and took more power from the Senate, they are our natural enemies."

"So we have a city full of enemies?" asked Sepharia coolly.

Vestalis nodded, a slight frown on his lips.

"See what a mess I've made of this?" asked Heron.

"These problems aren't insurmountable," replied Sepharia.

"Then what do you suggest, daughter?"

Sepharia crossed her arms and stared at the flickering candle. "What does each side want?" she asked Vestalis.

Vestalis raised an eyebrow as if to tell Heron that was the question she should be asking. She rolled her eyes at him.

"I can only hazard a guess, but in the end it's all different ways of obtaining power. The Protectors keep their power through the rules of the Senate, the Wolves through the glory of their families and vast coinage, and the New Aristocrats, they want what the other two have," finished Vestalis.

"You make it all seem so simple," said Heron with her head in her hands.

"And I look upon your machines and wonder the same thing. Did the temples not call you the Miracle Man?" asked Vestalis.

"It *is* simple," said Sepharia with a grin.

Heron glanced to Vestalis who only gave her a shrug, a gesture she didn't expect to see on the normally stoic soldier.

"It is?" asked Heron.

"Yes," said Sepharia, "we give them what they want."

Heron rolled her eyes. "That makes perfect sense."

"Actually, it does," said Vestalis, nodding appreciatively.

"No, it does not," said Heron, a little bit annoyed.

"It does, you'll see, Father. We just need to get them all into one place." Sepharia turned to the map and began searching across the hills of Rome with her outstretched hand hovering across its surface, ready to pluck the answer from its depths.

"Not the Senate," mumbled Sepharia, "we can't have all of them there, nor the Forum, or Circus Maximus. We need something more intimate, private. Ah, I found it!"

With a stab of her finger she announced the location, though Heron was sitting in the wrong spot to see anything but Sepharia's back.

"Well, where is it?" asked Heron.

"Here. You need to have a party and invite them all here. That way we can control how it happens."

Heron shook her head. "No. I won't. Not here, I can't escape them then."

She looked to Vestalis for support who only shrugged again.

"You wanted help," he said after a time.

"We must begin right away," said Sepharia, darting across the table to grab a scroll and quill. Vestalis followed her lead and took a seat, patiently attentive to Sepharia like a dignified uncle noticing for the first time that his niece had grown up.

When Sepharia reached toward the plates for a lark tongue, Heron snatched it away. "Let me be useful at least and get you something warm from the kitchens. Most of the food in here is days old."

Heron limped away, holding the terra cotta plate in her mechanical hand for practice. The newest design only broke plates when she wasn't paying attention. She made it to the back of the domus near the kitchens without even one lark tongue sliding off and opened the door to throw the old food to the street dogs that hung out in the alley for scraps.

Though the light was dim, the three forms were unmistakable lying on their sides with tongues plastered to the cobblestones. Heron pushed the nearest dog using her metal foot. It was a mangy critter with matted brownish-gray fur, but it didn't react. The half-eaten scraps from her previous leavings lay amid the dead dogs.

Heron glanced at the terra cotta plate in her mechanical hand and winced when it snapped in two. Poison. One of her meals had been poisoned. Only through her inattentive stupor had she avoided death.

She shook her head. Try as she might, it was hard not to want to be back in her workshop in that instant. Rome was a mess of political knife-fighting and deceit; and if Heron couldn't learn their game, they wouldn't survive long enough to make it back to Alexandria.

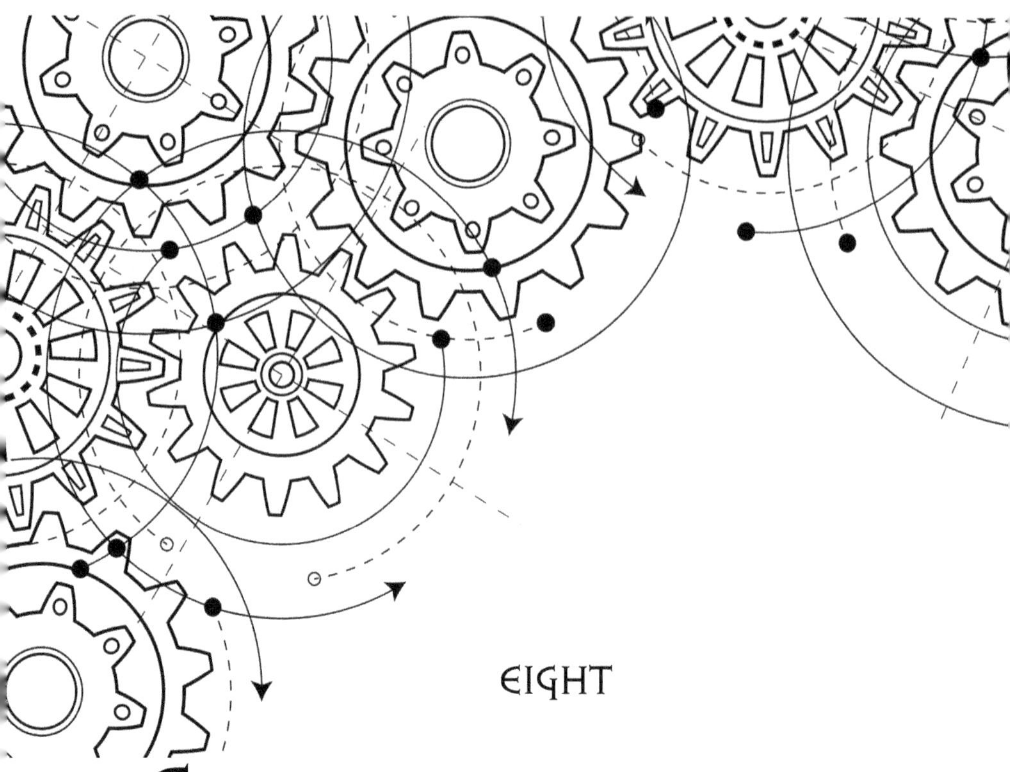

EIGHT

Sepharia caressed the fine strands beneath her fingertips before she set the wig of straight black hair aside. Her attendant, a plump woman with a scar on her chin, tugged on the ivory stola, fitting it around the waist to accentuate Sepharia's slender figure. The woman had been freed by Heron when they first moved to the domus, but Sepharia never quite felt comfortable around the woman.

"Young madam, I picked that one for you," said the woman with a considerable frown. "An Egyptian cut to remind the guests you come from Alexandria."

Sepharia took a deep breath. Like most Romans, the woman had a strange smell, something they ate, she guessed. Maybe it was the never ending supply of olives. Since she'd come to Rome, she swore she'd eaten olives fifty different ways.

"No wig," Sepharia said.

The woman made a noise of disapproval deep in her throat. "Young madam, all the women will be wearing wigs. It's the latest fashion of Rome."

Sepharia checked herself, straightening the purple sashes around her waist, and adjusting the silvery rings adorning her fingers and wrists. It looked like a silversmith had dumped out his cupola on her hands.

"Then what better reason not to wear one?"

The woman made another noise in her throat and Sepharia resisted a sigh. It made her uncomfortable enough to be attended to by the woman, especially since she couldn't remember her name. It seemed like every other woman in Rome was named Julia, Livia, or Claudia. Sepharia was certain it was one of the three, but she couldn't remember which.

From an ornate wooden box, Sepharia pulled out a brooch. It wasn't one she'd made, but the workmanship met her standards. She traced the Vergina sun with the serpent in the middle. It seemed a fitting symbol for her task in Rome.

"Fetch my sandals," said Sepharia, "I should be ready to greet the guests."

Instead of grabbing the sandals, the woman pulled a large bowl from the table and set it on the ground. A pale thin liquid sloshed around the wooden basin. It gave off a heavy ammonia smell that made Sepharia crinkle her nose.

"Pardon, but these hardly look like my sandals."

The woman returned a droll stare. "Luck, young madam. Dip your feet so that Tyche may bless your endeavors this evening."

Sepharia hesitated. The ritual meant nothing to her, but she could see it meant everything to the woman. For the sake of the evening Sepharia preferred that everyone, including the servants of the domus, believed that they would be successful.

"What is the mixture?"

"Fresh milk and horse urine," replied the woman.

Sepharia nodded and without delay stepped into the bowl, one foot at a time, before having her feet dried by the woman.

With her feet blessed and sandals tightly bound to her feet, Sepharia made her way down to the courtyard. There, Heron paced across the cobblestones, her gaunt cheeks fraught with worry. The tunic hung on her like a banner on a pole. She'd grown so thin, she barely had need of the wraps to hide her breasts. Between the attempted poisoning and the violet dust, Sepharia wasn't sure her father had eaten in two weeks.

Sepharia put a hand on Heron's shoulder. "Tonight will go well, Father."

Heron glanced back, eyes pierced with thought. "Tell me this will work, Sepharia. These are flesh and blood people and not machines, my mind cannot foresee how they will act and this makes me ill with thought."

"There's no need to worry. Everything is in motion now anyway. You've said it yourself before important miracles, *there's only time left for the doing.*"

"My words come back to haunt me," said Heron, wavering on her feet. Sepharia grabbed Heron's arm to steady her.

"Are you well?"

"I'll be fine," replied Heron, but leaning her weight into Sepharia.

"When was the last time you slept? Or ate?" asked Sepharia. "A slight breeze could knock you over."

Heron blinked slowly. "I couldn't tell you."

"Go eat something before you fall over," said Sepharia. "And certainly no wine tonight. You have the biggest part of this."

Heron steadied herself and looked up. "When did this happen? When did you start taking care of me?"

Sepharia smiled and hugged Heron and made her promise to eat something before heading to the entrance to greet the guests.

It was customary to give a gift upon arrival. Sepharia had designed and ordered the souvenirs herself, a small pin with a Vergina sun and a pair of wolves, Romulus and Remus, across the center.

The guests came at a slow trickle brought by the latest steam chariots. The choice of transportation had been deliberate to keep certain groups from entering the domus at the same time and also because it showcased the power of Alexandria. Even after many months in Rome, the smoke belching vehicles were an oddity.

Sepharia was waiting for the woman Aelia to arrive, and based on the order of the guests, she should have already. As she handed out pins, Sepharia kept glancing over the heads of the guests, expecting to see the distinguished woman's face.

The other two factions would come later, but Aelia had to come first, because if Sepharia wasn't successful at her part of the gambit, then the other two didn't matter. As more guests streamed in, Sepharia's stomach did back flips. If Aelia declined to come, they were lost before they began.

A line had backed up at the entrance, the bulk of the guests were waiting to get in. A ruddy-faced Senator wearing a toga that strained his girth blocked the way as he stared at the tiny tungsten and brass pin in his meaty hands.

"I will not wear this cursed Alexandrian pin, a symbol of our barbarian oppressors," he said, the words frothing at his lips. "You nor the gods can make me."

He was twice her size, but she stepped in his way as he tried to move into the domus without placing the pin on his toga.

"Apologies, citizen, then I will not be able to let you into the party," said Sepharia.

She knew his name, Senator Antonius, she'd memorized everyone that would be attending, but refused to say it.

"Citizen? Do not mistake me, I am a Senator," he blustered.

The line of people sensed the confrontation ahead and heads craned to see what was going on. Sepharia felt a sea of eyes upon her.

She swallowed her fear and spoke as calmly and as quietly as she could so the others behind could not hear, "You might have eaten a Senator before you came, but you certainly cannot be one, acting so improperly as a guest of the ruling Consul."

The heavy-set Senator's eyes went wide with rage, but before he could stammer out a response, Sepharia continued, "If you look over my shoulder to the alcove, you will see one of my *barbarian* friends waiting to make an example of someone."

She waited for him to look, noting the press of people behind leaning forward in hopes to hear. As the Senator's rage deflated and turned to concern, Sepharia continued, "If you would like to be that someone, try to pass by without that pin."

The Senator glanced behind him, clearly weighing the embarrassment of wearing the pin with being dragged from the party. To her relief, the Senator turned to the crowd and with his double chin raised high said, "I wear this pin in protest," before marching into the domus, staying away from the alcove as best he could.

Sepharia didn't have long to enjoy her relief when a servant notified her that the guest she'd been looking for was already in the domus and in the map room, no less, which was supposed to be reserved for Senator Silius.

She gave the servant instructions, changing the meeting locations with the other factions. The map room was the most distinguished location of the domus and Vestalis had suggested it as the best place to receive Silius since he would be the most difficult part of the evening, but they would have to make due.

Despite the urge to rush to the map room, Sepharia took her time, also because the stola bound her thighs together so she could only make small steps. Now she understood why Roman women powdered them-selves so liberally. It wasn't for the scent as much as the lubrication to keep her thighs from sticking together in the humid Roman air.

Sepharia paused at the swinging door and reminded herself that she had once wished to be involved with events like these. There was no point in having second thoughts now and as Heron said, *there's only time left for the doing.*

A thrust of her palm against the swing door and she was inside. Sepharia prepared to greet Aelia, instead finding a pair of brilliant green eyes staring back at her. The soldier from the wig shop was standing before the map with his arms crossed.

"You? What are you doing here?" she asked, glancing around the room. "You can't be here, I have to meet an important guest now." She paused. "In this room."

His eyebrow went up playfully. "You're the Consul's daughter? Here I thought you were just a soldier's daughter, or a…"

"Or a what?"

"Nothing," he laughed.

"You need to leave now. As I said, I'm waiting for someone." She paused again. "How did you get in here? I greeted everyone that came through the door. You're not wearing one of my pins."

He was grinning and behind that grin, she could see him laughing in his head. He knew something that she didn't, which bothered her.

She thought back to her preparation for this evening. All the lists of Senators and their guests whirled through her head like a spinning aeo-lipile. She wished she had Heron's gift for recall, but Sepharia's memory came with more sweat.

"Sextus," she said, the name finally clicking into place. "Sextus Octavia Paetina, son of Senator Pallas Julius Paetina and Aelia Octavia Paetina. And since Aelia's the former Emperor's wife, this was her domus once, so you came in through some secret passage."

A soft clap from the doorway startled Sepharia. Aelia stood there, looking resplendent in a flame-kissed saffron stola and red-haired wig, the same one Sextus had retrieved from the wig shop. She was a woman of grave beauty with a gaze cut by diamonds.

"Not so secret, but I applaud your understanding," said Aelia. "How is it that you two have met?"

"I mistook him for a wig," said Sepharia.

"A story for another time," said Aelia coldly. "Where is the Consul? Will you be fetching him now that I am here? I'm willing to listen to this *offer* he wishes to make, though I scarcely doubt it will be of any interest."

Sepharia prepared the answer in her head, an explanation about the needs of the party and her father's role in it, but she could see by the piercing gaze of Aelia, it would be woefully short. For all her preparation, Sepharia had forgotten about one important piece. She herself had no position of power. The Consul's daughter wasn't a title, but a happenstance.

Outside the room, the sounds of the party echoed like a flock of geese. Aelia's flowery perfume was strong enough to crowd out most of the other smells of the room, except for the musky odor of Sextus that Sepharia caught as she moved to the table to steady her nerves with a drink of honeyed wine.

The wine was sweet and Sepharia did her best not to let the shaking of her hand rattle the cup against the polished wood table, but it did, and the sound was as loud as a blacksmith at his forge. Sepharia shared a smile with Sextus, who was quietly studying her.

"My father has not received you because he does not need you," said Sepharia, squaring herself to Aelia, who was studying the map.

Aelia glanced over her shoulder and craned her neck sideways, appearing to be quite interested in something on the wall.

"When I was the Emperor's wife, I grew quite used to being ignored. Sometimes they would even forget that I was there in the room. While they laughed and planned their next conquest, I studied them, watching and learning, figuring out their weakness, ones they couldn't even admit to themselves and when my opportunity came, I did not miss it." Aelia brought her gaze around. "How are you and your father any different?"

The shaking of Sepharia's hands calmed and so too did her hurried breaths. Rather than anger, Sepharia felt understanding, compassion even.

"Are you saying you're too proud to deal with another woman?" asked Sepharia.

She knew she'd struck true when Aelia didn't answer right away. Sepharia continued through the opening, "As I said, we don't *need* you, but we *want* to work with you. There have been missteps, mistakes even, and we greatly apologize for these, but if you cannot even listen to our offer, then I can summon a steam chariot to take you back to your do-mus." Then after a thought she added. "And I wanted to be the one to meet with you, because I hoped to learn from you, but if we cannot be friends, I can learn from you as an enemy."

Aelia's lips pursed and the wrinkles around her eyes creased with thought. After a time, she spoke, "Fine, then. An offer. I will listen."

"First, we make a proposal for peace to general Magnus, if he should accept," said Sepharia.

Aelia feigned surprise, shaking her head disapprovingly, while Sextus cleared his throat and turned away to hide his reaction.

"Why would you say such a thing?" asked Aelia. "Magnus is an ene-my of the new Empire. I cannot answer any such offer."

"Fair enough," said Sepharia, "but if you, by the luck of the gods, encounter someone that does, please pass along this offer to general Magnus. We'd rather get on with the running of an Empire than fighting a war."

Aelia made a non-committal pursing of her lips. "Such a thing would be doubtful to happen."

Sepharia did not press further on that item, since she knew Aelia would never admit to it, though it was a poorly kept secret in Rome that Aelia and Magnus had been secret lovers in the past, a point that made her wonder about Sextus' true lineage. Also, her faction revered the former Consul as a symbol for Rome's lost meritocracy as opposed to the aristocratic stranglehold of the Wolves.

"On the second point, we would like to make amends for damaging your business by investing in your mines. A twenty percent stake, if you're agreeable," said Sepharia.

"With the loss of income, new capital would be quite agreeable, but why invest in a failing business?" asked Aelia.

"You will learn the reason soon enough tonight, my father has an important announcement at the end of the party, but know that both parties will benefit from this arrangement," said Sepharia.

"I cannot speak for all the families involved, only the Paetina's. I will need to gather them before we sign any such agreements," said Aelia.

"We expected as much. Tonight I'm asking only for your verbal agreement. We can work out the details at a later date, but know that there are other suitors we can work with if you choose not to agree," said Sepharia.

Aelia did not take long to make a decision, though a brief twitch at her lips suggested a hesitation. "Well, to this I can agree. We should all get back to the party then, I never miss an opportunity to remind my enemies I'm still alive."

A smile crept to Sepharia's lips, giving Aelia pause before she left the room. Sepharia began, "I was once to be married to the Parthian prince. He did not ignore me, though."

"He did not?" asked Aelia.

Sepharia wished that Sextus wasn't in the room, but if she was going to do it, she best get on with it, *there's only time left for the doing.*

"No," she said calmly. "He beat me and tortured me and killed my handmaidens and eventually gave me to one of his men as a slave."

She could see by the widening of both their eyes that they had not heard this story. Outside of a select few, it was not well known.

"And what did you do?" asked Aelia.

"I killed him," said Sepharia before she marched from the room.

And try as hard as she might, she could not help but notice that while Aelia gave her a nod of approval, her son Sextus reacted in mute horror.

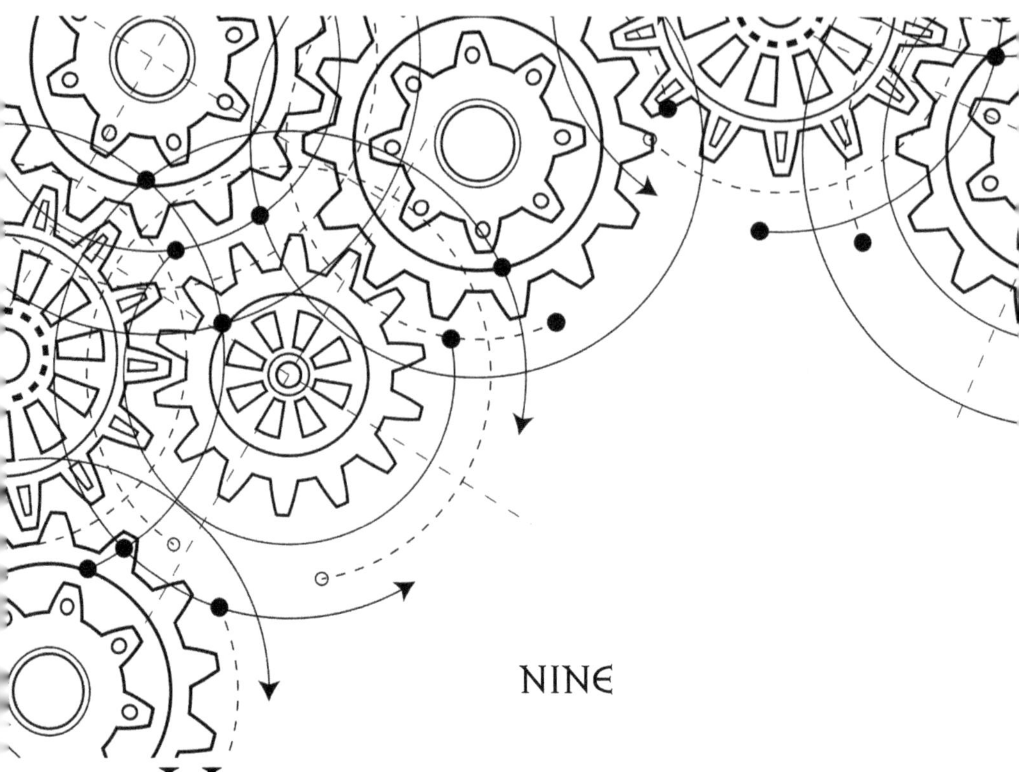

NINE

Heron shifted weight to her good foot, trying to concentrate on the Senator spilling his words out like a river. Her tongue worried at the back of her teeth, they felt looser, like they might shift out of place if she pushed too hard. Too little sleep and too much powder made her feel translucent, like a piece of leather scraped so many times that light shone through it.

Distracted, she found herself confronted by a localized bit of silence. Unfamiliar faces stared, waiting.

"Pardon?" she asked.

The quiet relief displayed on their faces once again reminded her of their view of her—a machine of flesh and steel. She could only imagine what they would say about that little pause, that her gears were turning, that she was waiting to be rewound by the gods, that a piston had gotten stuck.

"Can you really bend a sword with your mechanical arm?"

That one. She'd heard it before. Tales of her wading into the battle in Antioch, ripping Roman soldiers in half with her mechanical arms. Popping their helmeted heads like grapes between metal fingertips.

Part of her mind calculated the forces, considered the leverage of her bindings, the gear ratios inside the arm, and what it would take to make an arm that could do so and then tell them as much; and part of her mind remembered Vestalis' advice to stay mysterious and let them guess and wonder about her.

To the crowd's delight, Heron flexed her arm, letting the pistons wheeze as the elbow bent, fingers dancing like a spider on its back. As she opened her mouth to speak, she caught a glimpse of Sepharia motioning toward the back of the domus.

"Apologies," she said, inclining her head in semblance of a bow. "I must attend to the needs of the party. Long live the Empire."

She pushed through the crowd, which wasn't hard, most flinched away when they saw her. Like the previous group, they feared she might accidentally snap them in two, or so the stories said.

The truth was laughable compared to those stories. The mechanical arm gave her some function and usefulness, like being able to put on clothing without help, but it bestowed no godlike powers, which is what the superstitious Romans thought it did.

In some respects, Heron found the Romans more superstitious than the Egyptians. While the Egyptians were devoted to one set of gods, a pious relationship that went back millenniums; the Romans embraced any and all gods, taking the stance that each region might be blessed by the gods of those people, therefore they didn't want to miss out on any potential advantage. In the domus alone, there were eight shrines and five *larariums*. Before the guests had arrived, Sepharia had filled them with offerings and half-burnt candles to appease the expectations of the guests.

Beyond the first courtyard lay the *peristylum*, or private atrium, used for relaxation or receiving important guests. While the main courtyard sang a song to the sun and was filled with flowering bushes, the *peristylum* felt more like a private garden.

Mosaics covered the floor and walls, depicting the gods and mystical beasts of the sea. Heron stepped across a trident wielding Poseidon and a pair of frolicking mermaids to reach her guest.

"Ave, Senator Messalina," said Heron, "I am honored to receive you."

Messalina ambled forward, his head swaying from his long neck before ducking beneath a flowering cherry tree. "Ave, Consul Heron. I suspect you did not invite me here to chat about the weather."

Heron forced a grin. "Only if you wish, though I would prefer to talk about other more important topics."

"Straight to business, then?" asked Messalina.

"Apologies, the Empire has little time for rest," replied Heron, while remembering Vestalis' warning not to make an offer too quickly. "But...I would like to know how your son fairs in the Legion? An equestrian, right?"

"Yes and well enough. He marches with the new Emperor, so I do not fear for his safety," said Messalina.

"No worries about general Magnus?" asked Heron.

When Messalina shook his head, it looked like an apple being dangled from a long stick. "He was beaten at Antioch while he was in possession of a much larger force. The Emperor has the upper hand now in numbers and technology, so it's just a matter of time."

"Still, his army has done some damage in Gaul, turning some to his side there and destroying the garrisons that refused," said Heron, carefully watching for Messalina's real thoughts, but to his credit, the Senator gave a passionless shrug.

"Power is like trying to hold onto a fish snatched from the sea, grasp too hard and it slips from your fingers, hold on too lightly and it wriggles free," said Messalina. "The former Consul's position gives him a weak grip with few options. It's only a matter of time before the fish escapes."

"But he has turned some of the Gauls to his side," said Heron.

"Only out of loyalty, since it was he who had quelled their rebellions and brokered the peace with Rome."

Heron nodded appreciatively. "Wouldn't it be better to turn them to our side?"

"Of course," said Messalina. "How would you do such a thing?"

"Well," said Heron, trying to draw in his interest. "What is it that the Gauls want?"

"Power. It's what everyone wants, and what the Senate keeps balanced, by not letting too much power reside in any one set of hands." Messalina paused, seeming to recognize the intent of his words. "The Emperor notwithstanding."

Heron nodded. "But the Emperor does not want all the power. Only to change a few things in the Empire. It's why he kept the Senate, because that body provides stability to the Empire by giving the people its voice."

Senator Messalina narrowed his gaze. "What are you proposing?"

"Another one hundred Senate seats, split up amongst the provinces, and another one hundred and fifty for Alexandria," said Heron.

"But that would nearly double the Senate."

"Exactly," said Heron. "And in response, the Emperor would give back some of his dictatorship powers. Let the people rule the Empire."

The wheels turned behind Messalina's eyes. She knew what he was thinking because it was why they'd made the offer. Two-hundred and fifty new seats would diminish the Wolves influence while maintaining the power of the Senate.

Heron spoke again while Messalina was in the throes of thought,

"Do we have your support? Your side can deliver enough votes to ensure its passage. In return, the Emperor will return some of his powers."

She handed him a scroll, which he quickly unrolled and read, his lips moving as he did so. When he was done, he gave a solemn nod.

"I believe all this is agreeable," said Senator Messalina.

"Good then," she said. "Then if we are done, my humblest apologies, for I must go attend to another matter."

As she moved to the balcony to meet Senator Silius, she wondered how angry Agog would be once he found out what she'd given up in the name of politics. It would only serve him right for leaving her in this mess of a city.

But Agog wasn't her biggest concern now, that would be Senator Silius. He was a prickly man in the best of circumstances and already he would be put off by the less than honorific meeting location. Originally, she'd planned to meet him in the map room, but Aelia's appearance there changed that.

When she reached the balcony, Senator Silius was leaning against the balcony, his noble mane of gray hair swept grandly to his shoulders. Surprisingly, he wore a more subdued toga of pristine white with a sash of purple, more appropriate for a Senator.

The click of her metal foot on the marble made her approach known. He tilted his head slightly to the left.

"What a vista this balcony provides," he said. "All of Rome's great buildings lie in our view."

Emperor Claudius had not necessarily been an extravagant spender, but his choice of domus was particularly inspired. It sat across from Palatine Hill and through the valley, the white stone of the Forum glimmered in the fading light. To her right, Circus Maximus made a crown of raised earth, while further still, the Senate building towered over the rest of the city.

But Rome felt different than Alexandria. Rome was blinding white with marble and a sea of togas that filled the streets between. It was majestic and distinguished, like the statues of Roman soldiers, all discipline and crisp lines with effortless deadly efficiency.

Alexandria was messy and uneven, like a disheveled scholar with food stains on his tunic. While the streets were straight, and orderly, the people traversing them were varied and unique. It wasn't uncommon to bump into a scholar of the Great Library lost in his thoughts, or a trader from the southern jungles in colorful silks. While Rome seemed inevitable with its Legions and laws and roads, Alexandria was impossible with its Lighthouse and Great Library and mechanical wonders.

"A city of great energy, Rome is," said Heron, taking a place next to the Senator.

"Some day I would like to visit Alexandria," said Silius.

Surprised, Heron responded, "I could have one of the iron boats take you there. You'd only be gone a month, giving you a few weeks to enjoy the city."

Silius chucked. "You'd like to be rid of me that easily. Maybe have one of your barbarian friends throw me into the sea on the way."

She was going to protest, tell him that her answer was honest, that she truly wished to share the wonders of Alexandria with him, but then she remembered what kind of man Senator Silius was.

"I don't think a man of your resourcefulness gets removed that easily," she said.

"A battle avoided is better than the one fought. A lesson I wish I could have imparted to my son before he marched off to war with Consul Magnus."

This was new to Heron. "He wasn't...at Antioch?"

The lines in Senator Silius' face deepened. "Nay. My son died in the Britons when Consul Magnus sacrificed them for his victory and glory."

Her relief was palpable. If his son had died at Antioch due to her weapons, she would have little reason to continue their discussion.

Silius looked her in the eyes. "I've heard rumors that you're pursuing peace with our former general? I dearly hope this is not true."

The fact that he knew about their plans made the next steps more precarious. Vestalis had been quietly testing the waters with other Senators, ones not affiliated with the Wolves, but it seemed they were not quiet enough.

"It's a topic that cannot be avoided, despite our intentions," she replied.

He turned his back to the city and leaned on the iron railing. "Have you considered my request for reparations again?"

"It's why I asked you here," said Heron.

"I knew you'd come around. Without the support of my fellow Senators, you're finding it quite difficult to get things done, aren't you?"

"We're prepared to offer a bill on reparations, but one only valid while the Wodanaz is the Emperor, and only when the war with Consul Magnus is over," she said.

He gave her an appraising glance before wandering away from the balcony to take a sip of wine. She knew what he was thinking, but only because Vestalis and Sepharia had planned the encounter. The bill would give him what he wanted, but not right now, which would make him more hesitant to disrupt the new Empire. It would also make him more amicable should peace be offered to Magnus, though his earlier admission made her believe that he might oppose it for spite. The Wolves and Consul Magnus had never gotten along.

Mostly, they did not believe such a bill would come to fruition. The offer was merely to delay, since their other moves would only enrage him.

"We might be interested," said Silius.

"Interested or not, the bill will be brought up for discussion, whether or not you give it your blessing," she said.

"I see," he said, narrowing his gaze.

He took two steps toward her and seemed ready to say something when Sepharia appeared.

"We're ready for your announcement," said Sepharia.

The Senator hadn't realized she was back in Rome, and he smiled at first when he saw her, but then he seemed to notice what she'd said.

"What announcement?" he asked with a furrowed brow.

"You'll hear it along with the rest of Rome," said Heron as she walked past him and hooked her arm around Sepharia's.

As they marched to the courtyard, Heron whispered, "Good timing."

Reaching the courtyard, she found the attended waiting. With Sepharia's help, she stepped onto a simple wooden box. Vestalis had wanted a grand stage draped in crimson and gold silks, but Sepharia thought it best to keep it simple.

In front of the lilac bushes, a piece of cloth hid a painting. They'd hired an artist in secret and paid him extra to keep him from discussing his latest work, even though she didn't think anyone would understand it.

A sea of faces regarded her. Heron wobbled slightly on the box, but was able to stay mostly erect. She wished for her ivory cane for support.

"Ave and greetings, Senators and citizens of the Empire!" She waited until their responses died down. "As your Consul and the voice of the new Emperor, I bring you confidence that the Empire will live as long as Rome stays its heart."

She paused and looked to the many faces, smiling at some, nodding at others. Vestalis stood stoically in the back with a group of select Legates from the Legion.

While the delicacies of politics eluded Heron, the tools of oratory she held firmly in her grasp. Time in the Great Library arguing for the benefits of knowledge in practice rather than in theory gave her confidence to woo them with words.

"But the Empire is vast and nearly endless. As wide as the seas and as immeasurable as the heavens. At its heart, the Empire is ruled by laws, but laws cannot be enforced without a strong military and a strong military cannot bring its arms to bear without good roads.

"If the Empire is to expand—" She paused and waited for the murmuring to subside, "—then the time for new roads must commence. But not simple roads of rock and mortar. With the marriage of Rome and Alexandria, we can lift our sights higher, using new technologies devised in the Great Library, new materials, new methods, new ideas.

"So today I give you a new road, a new road for a new Empire, one that will first connect Rome and Alexandria, and then the Empire with the rest of the world. I give you the Iron Road!"

She gestured toward the painting and the tarp was pulled away, revealing a metal road with an elongated steam chariot racing along it. The artist only had her description to go on, so he made the chariot serpent-like with a tail extended into the distant hills, and the head reminded Heron of a gorgon.

She stepped down while the assembled broke into ripe discussion. There had been applause, but not as much as she expected.

Sepharia squeezed her good arm. "Well done, Father. I think tonight has been a success."

Heron opened her mouth to speak when a plainly dressed man interrupted them.

"My patron would agree," said the man. "You've done quite well to reverse the damage you so crudely engineered before."

Heron paused, but only because she recognized the man's voice, though she didn't know how. She glanced around for Vestalis, feeling vulnerable, and when she did not see him, looked back to take stock of the intruder.

Matching his clothing, he had a plain look: simple tunic with but the smallest of flourishes, dirty brown hair, a face that could be Roman or a Gaul or even Greek. He appeared to be a man that one could bump into on the street and not even notice.

"And who are you?" asked Heron.

He shrugged. "Who I am is unimportant. But if you must know, you can call me Juvenes. But you really should care about who pays me."

"And who pays you, Juvenes?"

"Senator Dominitus."

She didn't know the name, but the way Sepharia's eyes flinched told her he was important.

"And what does Senator Dominitus want?"

Juvenes grinned, which made the man suddenly less plain and more dangerous. "He wants to meet you."

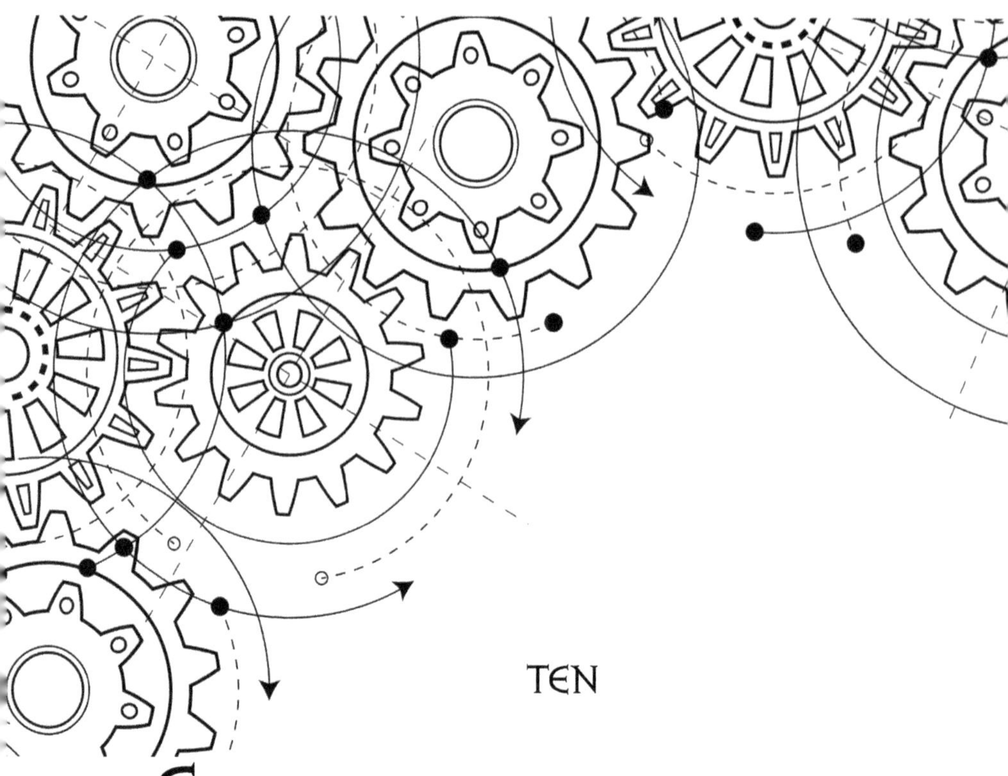

TEN

Senator Dominitus lived near the northern edge of the city on Quirinal Hill, overlooking the rest of the city from his high villa. Heron rode there on a steam chariot piloted by a loyal Alexandrian with a small guard following on two Manticores. The poisoning of her food had taught her not to trust anyone, as even Caesar had been killed by his fellow Senators in broad daylight.

Quirinal Hill overlooked the city's artisan district. They passed glass blowing shops, and smiths, and weavers by the dozen. Standing in front of one shop was a painted stone gladiator with a real bronze *galea* helm. The facemask had a fish on its crest, symbolizing the myrmillones fighting style. As they passed, the sounds of steel hammering could be heard over the steam mechanical. A sign on the door in Latin claimed it was the best gladiatorial armor and weaponry a deaneries could buy.

The paved road climbed the hill, snaking through a forest of olive trees. Tenders wandered through the straight rows, examining the hard green fruits as they passed with baskets under their arms. Heron had rewarded herself with a good night's sleep after the party and had awoken with a terrible hunger. She thought she'd sated herself with breakfast, but the smells of the olive trees only made her mouth water.

The domus rested on a plateau at the edge of the steep hill. Heron's shoulders hurt from holding on to the bench, feeling like she was going to slide off the chariot the whole ride up.

A well-dressed female servant greeted her with a moist towel to wipe the dirt from her face. Heron noted the simple cloth and sea shell jewelry which indicated a free woman. She led Heron to a brightly lit library and left. Heron surveyed the wealth of scrolls and bound texts, inhaling the delirious, musty smell of papyri that made her miss Alexandria.

"It's a small thing, but I see you approve?" came a voice from the corner. The man, Senator Dominitus she presumed, had been sitting so still and quiet she hadn't noticed. Or she'd been so enthralled by the books, she'd gone right over him.

"Apologies, Senator Dominitus, for my rude entrance," she said.

The Senator made a throaty, phlegm-filled cough and waved away her apology. "Call me Dom. All these titles and honorifics, Senator this, Legate that, are a waste of my time, and when your time is running out, you don't want to waste it on useless words."

He sat in the corner on a high-backed chair with a blanket on his legs despite the warmth of the day. He wasn't as decrepit as she thought he would be based on the description Vestalis had given. His skin was wrinkled and a deep scar traveled the length of his jaw, creating a smooth valley on either side and drawing down his right eye.

He was a shadow player of the Senate, or as they called him *occulta imperatore*, or the Hidden Emperor. Vestalis knew little about him except that he'd once held great influence, a position that had deteriorated with his health.

"Strange philosophy for a Senator," said Heron, intrigued.

Dominitus chuckled, a sound that emanated from his chest. "There was once a time I was in love with my own voice, thinking I was the successor to Cicero's legacy. Until an assassin's dagger nearly took my life."

"So you withdrew from the Senate?" she asked.

"After I was healed, I took a voyage east, fearing that I would die before I saw the Empire that we ruled. On my three year journey, I went farther than the boundaries of the Empire, as far east as the Indus river. I wanted to see the world Alexander had conquered. With my new disguise," he pointed to his scar, "I could go where Romans feared to tread. I saw the world as my fellow Senators will never see."

"Did you go to Alexandria?"

He cleared his throat, pounding his fist lightly on the armrest. "I meant to on my return to the west, but a mysterious illness felled me, and I was brought back to Rome in a litter."

"Alexandria would have welcomed you," she said, feeling that she knew the man. Previous encounters with the other Senators left her drained, but the burden of speaking with Dom, as she'd begun to call him in her mind, lifted from her shoulders.

Dominitus pointed to her right, to a shelf stacked with scrolls and trinkets. "Over there," he said proudly, "you'll find something of interest."

She moved cautiously, wondering what she would find, cringing at the way her metal foot clicked across the stone floor. On the shelf was a bronze device used for measuring angles. It fit comfortably in her hand and she flipped it over to find a delicate 'H' stamped into the handle.

"I've been following your work for a number of years, even before the war," said Dominitus. "I even purchased one of your automata plays, but some internal gearing has snapped and it doesn't work anymore."

"Show me to it," she said while rotating the bronze measuring tool in her hand. "I'm sure it could be fixed easily."

Dominitus gave a deep laugh, his eyes sparkling. "I would not dare to ask the Consul of the Alexandrian Empire to be my personal inventor."

"It would be my pleasure."

He waved her off. "It doesn't matter now. That's not why I asked you here."

She wanted to ask why, but thought better of it. She was enjoying the conversation and didn't want to move to business too quickly. Heron set the bronze tool back on the shelf and couldn't help but notice the label on the scroll rack.

"The writings of Eratosthenes, I see. Have you read all these scrolls?"

He nodded. "And Seleucus, and Aristotle, and Strabo, and well, look around, you'll see I have quite a collection here."

"You sound more like a scholar than a Senator."

They were interrupted by a servant woman with a tray of golden yellow flaky cakes. She set them by Dominitus and he motioned for her to take one.

She hesitated, but only until she smelled their sweetness. The Senator already had one shoved into his mouth, his eyes rolled back and he appeared to be quite happy as crumbs fell from his lips.

Heron was unprepared for the burst of almost tart honey that made her jaw tingle with pleasure. She found herself with a second almost as soon as the first had been eaten. When the tray of cakes was gone, Dominitus began speaking again.

"In my youth, I devoured every text I could find, testing my mind with ideas far greater than I could handle. It was this challenge that helped me achieve the position of Senator, despite my background. For how can a man not outwit his fellow Senators when their minds are so small they cannot understand that Eratosthenes proved the world is round by measuring the shadows in a well? Knowing makes a mind strong and nimble, and makes a man curious to what you would find if you had the courage to sail west."

"Maybe the Indus river," mused Heron.

"Maybe," smiled Dominitus. "But those adventurous days are behind me and now I am swayed by the simple pleasures of life."

His eyes twinkled with such intelligence and mirth that she was simultaneously drawn in and concerned. She reminded herself that they called him the Hidden Emperor, though his days of influence were supposedly past.

Heron spoke up, quietly, while she matched gazes with him. "You did not bring me to your domus to share in simple pleasures."

With a surprisingly nimble hand, he plucked a crumb from the tray and lifted it up before he deposited in his mouth playfully. "But were they not pleasurable?"

She nodded. "The cakes were quite good."

"Then let us know that we have enjoyed them." He stared at her with some unfathomable expectation.

Avoiding his gaze, Heron turned back to the shelves, looking for scrolls she could speak about that might spark a conversation. The Senator seemed to be waiting for something, or was subtly plumbing her for information like the presence of a vacuum would pull water up a long tube. She wished Sepharia was here, or had visited in her stead, an impossibility, considering she wasn't the Consul. Thinking of Sepharia reminded Heron of the servant who had greeted her with the cool towel.

"Your servants are freedman?" asked Heron.

"I gave it to them for their loyal service."

Heron feigned at examining a rack of scrolls, running her fingertips along the chunky edges. "Is this common in Rome?"

"Manumission? Aristotle suggested that slaves should be freed for their service, should it be loyal, in the idea that all men should have aspirations, even slaves. And in times of war, when Rome bulges with new slaves, it increases in fashion to free the loyal, but with the Empire in upheaval and no conquering wars to bring new ones, there has been little or no manumission."

"Then why did you?" she asked.

"An old man might die at any moment, and with my death, their sentence as a slave would be sealed. I gave them their freedom as a precaution," he said.

"A generous gift."

"No more generous than their leal service."

She felt his gaze upon her back and moved to match it, but in her inattention, her mechanical arm caught a piece of pottery and knocked it to the floor, shattering it.

"Apologies, Senator, I forget myself at times," she said, holding the metal arm to her chest as if it were an unruly child.

"It's Dom, and no need for an apology, it was a worthless piece of junk."

He smiled magnanimously, but she did not believe him, for across every shelf were items from far off places, valuable trinkets from his journeys. A warmth spread across her face and she wished in that moment that his gaze would not be upon her, but he studied every move.

Even though his face was weathered with time and the scar from his eye to his jaw gruesome, a lightness passed across it like the rays of the sun bursting from a hole in the clouds. But as quickly as it shone, the obfuscating clouds returned and the sun of his intellect passed into quiet contemplation.

"Why have you withdrawn from politics?" she asked.

An eyebrow went up. "Who says I've withdrawn?"

"The three factions battle amongst themselves and you don't seem to care one way or another," she challenged, hoping to draw out whatever he was thinking.

"Maybe they're doing exactly as I want, leaving me little need to interfere," he countered.

"Or maybe you're too smitten with the simple pleasures of life," she said, but as soon as the words left her mouth, she knew that wasn't true, "but then you wouldn't have asked me here, unless it was so that I might fix your automata play, which it wasn't."

Senator Dominitus adjusted the blanket on his legs, straightening the edge and smoothing away the wrinkles. "The dexterity you exhibited after your initial missteps was quite remarkable. I wondered if you might get gobbled up by the our proverbial Cerberus at our gates to the Under-world."

"Then are you Charon? The boat keeper on the river of Styx?" she asked hopefully.

His lips took on a playful cast, the wrinkles on his face deepening. "As you said before, I'm just an old man in search of simple pleasures."

She wanted to sigh, or curse, or something. He was playing a game with her, but she didn't understand it. Frustrated, she asked a question, "Why is it that you've asked me to your domus?"

Senator Dominitus shifted on his chair, shadows falling uncom-fortably across him in strict lines. "Maybe Charon is an apt description of my place in Roman politics in these days. I do not affect the mortal realm anymore, but sit on the edge of another place and offer passage for those paying the proper price."

"And what price is that?"

The old man tapped his chin, gaze upward, the scar making his smile almost cruel. "What is the coin called that Charon takes for passage? It's a Greek term and it escapes me."

"Obolus. An old name for halfpenny."

"Ahh...yes, an obolus. As your river warden, your Charon, I still hold some influence in the city, though it may not be what you expect, and offer passage at some later date." He paused. "For an obolus, of course."

She shook her head. "I don't understand. I don't have an obolus."

"Not yet, but when the time comes, you'll bring me one, it'll be nothing, just a trifle, to amuse an old man's curiosity," he said.

The understanding came slowly, making her irritated for not realizing it sooner.

"You want something," she said. "And when I bring it to you, you'll do me a favor."

"Yes."

She scowled. "But what if I don't need a favor?"

"Favors are the coin of politics, well, and death, but let's not trade that," he said. "I think you'll find it quite useful to have a favor from me. The politics of Rome is a terrible game and you never know when you might need a friend."

Not a friend, she realized. He'd never be a friend despite feeling some connection with him, but yes, she could see his point. A favor from such a man could be useful.

"Your logic interests me," she said. "What is this obolus you seek?"

He smiled and spoke with little inflection. "The death of Caesar. I must have knowledge of it."

"Caesar?" she stammered. "His is the most well documented death in the history of the world! He died at the head of the greatest Empire in front of three hundred Senators. What could possibly be a mystery about that?"

"Not how," he said, his smirk creasing wrinkles around his mouth, "but why."

"Why? Surely this is known. He was the dictator for life, and an affront to the powers of the Senate. They feared him as much as any man," she replied.

"Then why did every one of his assailants die, some mysteriously, after his death? If he was so hated, his death should have been rejoiced, but it was not. Nothing about his death makes sense."

"But I don't have time for this," she said honestly. "I have an Empire to hold together."

He sunk back into his chair. "Do or not do, it's your choice. But this is the obolus I offer, if you choose to take it."

"I'll think about it," she replied.

"As well you should."

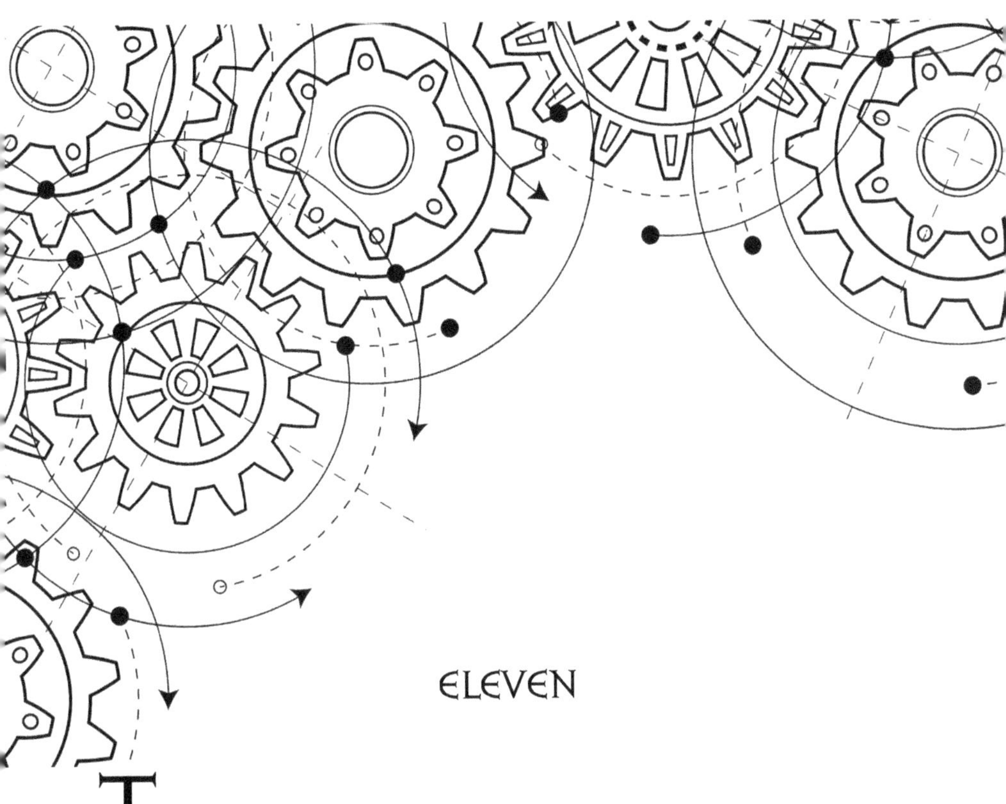

ELEVEN

The winds of early autumn came rushing through the streets, blowing leaves into eddies to be chased by sun-kissed children. Sepharia was enjoying the day, cool winds had washed the heat from the city and rather than stay at the domus, she snuck away to explore. It was Heron's command that she never leave the domus without guardians, but the day was bright and the streets were busy, so Sepharia decided to go alone.

The open-aired cafes were flush with Roman citizens attended by well-dressed slaves. As she made her way toward the Pantheon, she saw a commotion down a crossing street. A throng of people gathered around a central focus and their joyous cries could be heard rising and falling like waves.

Her lips peeled back from her teeth, for she knew the source of the crowd's interest: it was one of Heron's automatas. Sepharia hadn't seen her father much in the previous weeks, she was either buried into her drawings, sketching like a mad-woman, meeting with Senators about the dry workings of the Empire, or guiding the workshops in their endeavors including both the automatas and the Iron Road, which was the talk of the city.

There was little left for Sepharia to do since the party. Vestalis needed no help with the Legion and her father, after her initial problems, seemed to be performing her role well enough. The vote for additional Senators would come next week, leaving Alexandria and its new coalition in control. Like a sail without wind, Sepharia felt limp, and when reports of Agog's war against general Magnus came back to the city, Sepharia found herself disappointed that it was not over so she could go back to Alexandria.

The pleasant day, at least, washed away the bulk of her frustrations, or at least masked them long enough to escape the domus. When the Pantheon revealed itself from behind the rows of buildings, it made her gasp with delight. The strength of the Roman people could be seen in its towering walls and majestic dome.

Sepharia pulled the confining stola up and away from her ankles and swept toward the entrance. The portico soared above her head, suspended by granite Corinthian columns as wide as a horse. She hurried through the vestibule to the rotunda, the wide space beneath the dome. A pillar of light through the oculus at the center of the dome turned the temple of all-gods into an altar of the sun.

Standing at the edge of the light, she carefully placed her hand into the warmth, dust motes floating like stars through the luminance. Around her, men and women moved silently through the building, murmuring quietly amongst themselves, but Sepharia wanted to shout and laugh, buoyed by the immensity of the structure.

"It's typical for worshipers to attend the altars on the walls rather than the empty floor in the center," came a familiar voice in fluent Greek.

Slightly giddy, Sepharia whirled around to find Sextus Paetina strolling up to meet her, looking every bit like a soldier ready for battle, despite his toga and leather pointed headdress held on by a chin-strap. His green eyes flashed a smile and he gave her a little bow.

"Ave, Sextus," she said in greeting.

"Ave, Sepharia, daughter of Alexandria," he replied.

Though he stood a pace from her, she felt a tangible energy between them, pulling her closer.

"Do you come to the Pantheon often?" she asked.

He made a turning-hand motion and tilted his head slightly as if to say it depends. "When I am called by duty."

"Are you called by duty?"

He hesitated to speak, glancing around once. "Yes, I'm supposed to be on my way somewhere else, but I saw you enter the Pantheon and wanted to speak to you."

She narrowed her gaze. "You're wearing a strange hat and none of the artifices of a soldier, what is this other duty?"

He cleared his throat and glanced around once more. "As *flamen.*"

"A priest?" she asked perplexed.

"All Romans with ambition join the priesthood as well as the Legion," he replied.

She grinned wickedly. "Do you have ambition?"

Sextus scowled. "Any sensible Roman does. To seek glory for Rome is our highest calling."

She laughed. "I was only teasing."

Sextus pulled his shoulders back straight. "The priesthood is a noble profession."

"And it provides connections useful later in the Senate."

"You sound like my mother, Aelia," he said.

Sepharia crossed her arms.

"Why did you come to the Pantheon?" he asked.

"Curiosity. To see the architectural marvel. No place in the known world does a dome like this exist," she said, looking up to the oculus.

"Not interested in the gods?"

She detected a deeper meaning in his question. "I am." She touched her brooch, the one with the sunburst and snakes. "I follow Dionysus."

He flinched at the mention of Dionysus. "He's a peculiar one."

Sepharia could hear the disappointment in his voice, which in itself was encouraging, but before she could speak again, Sextus seemed to realize something.

"I'm afraid I've delayed too long. I cannot keep the Magister waiting," he said, but before he turned away, he glanced around again for the third time. When he spoke, he did so quietly so that only she could hear. "Tomorrow, Augustus the twenty fourth, is an important day in Rome, I would not wander without your guards, you or your father. In fact, I would stay in your domus if at all possible."

His sudden seriousness gave her pause. "But why?"

"*Mundus patet*," he whispered and left, marching away stiffly.

Sepharia was left with confusion and an ache in her chest. The last few weeks had been bland but at least predictable. Now the future seemed mercurial.

The lightness of the day had been banished and even the broad column of light seemed lifeless. Sepharia trudged out of the Pantheon, dodging around the afternoon crowd. The distance back to the domus seemed a chore where before it'd been a leisure.

A brusque soldier bumped into her as he hurried forward. The tingle of being watched formed between her shoulder blades and Sepharia did her best to dismiss it, owing the feeling to Sextus' sinister words.

Mundus patet.

Her Latin was decent enough that she had little trouble conversing with any citizen of Rome, including its highest-born, but the phrase Sextus had uttered gave her pause.

Mundus meant 'world' and *patet* mean 'open', but that made little sense to her. The phrase could be translated as 'open world' or 'the world is opening', but even that didn't help. Eventually Sepharia dismissed it as religious posturing. Every priest like to imbue a certain mystical danger to its rituals, just as Polyxena had taught Sepharia to use snakes to guard against nightly intrusions from Vima.

But the feeling of being watched did not subside, so Sepharia made a point of stopping on occasion, feigning interest in the buildings or birds flying overhead, to watch for followers. It wasn't until she was nearly back to the domus that she caught sight of him.

The bald priest stood some distance away, but the intensity of his gaze made her feel like he was right there, reaching out to snatch her from the streets. The moment was brief and then the priest seemed to disappear into the crowd.

Feeling like an antelope on the edge of the Nile, Sepharia hurried in the direction of the domus, holding her stola up so she could move with some alacrity. When she reached the threshold, she was doused in a light sweat and breathing heavily. Behind her, the streets had lost their menacing quality, but the memory of the bald priest was stuck firmly in her mind.

Sepharia found Livia, the servant whose name had eluded her, and requested a bath to be drawn. Livia gave her a scolding stare before marching in the direction of the bath house. The woman probably guessed that Sepharia had been away from the domus without guardianship, and she knew no amount of pleading would keep that knowledge from Heron, but any punishment from her father seemed miniscule compared to the implied danger of the bald priest.

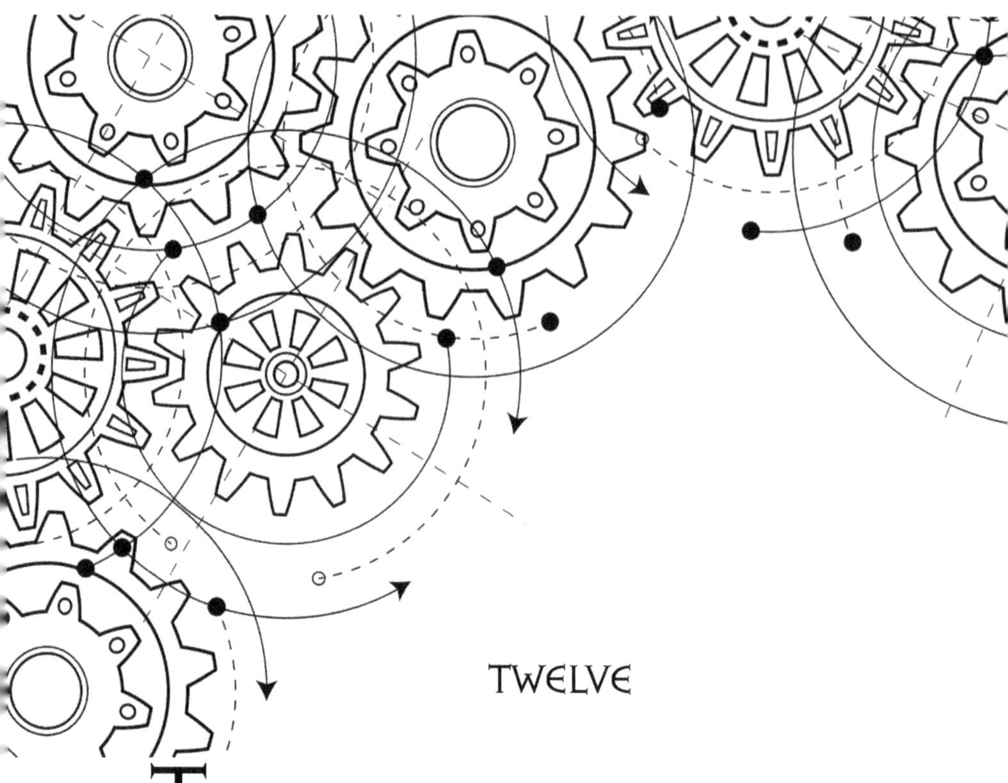

TWELVE

The broken scaffolding cradled the automata's fallen arm like a nest holding a baby bird. The foreman had called her into the workshop to review the wreckage, giving her time to compose herself. Wide, fearful eyes watched her approach the damaged automata. The fallen arm matched the one attached to her shoulder, except it was nearly ten times the size.

Dispersing the sparkpowder barrels around the city was taking too long. Each day brought new rumors about an assault on the warehouse where they were stored. Vestalis had tripled the guard, but they still didn't trust leaving them there. She'd instructed the workshops to build bigger automatas, larger than she typically constructed, except for the Kushite colossus, but that one had been built in her personal workshop. The Romans were excellent builders, but she had no connection with them. They carried out their jobs efficiently and with great haste, but lacked the creativity of Punt or Plutarch for solving issues as they arose. Each day she was called to a different workshop to answer questions left unanswered by her drawings.

"Sulla?" she asked to a nod from the foreman. "What happened?"

He appeared ready to shake out of his sandals. She could see him formulating his answer, most likely a deflection of responsibility, or an excuse blaming the gods or something foolish like that. The Romans were more disciplined than the Egyptians, but just as superstitious.

"There's no punishment for mistakes," she told him, knowing that Emperors had hung or quartered makers for failing their architectural duties in Rome.

He hesitated, mouth stuck half-open, so she turned to the rest of the workshop and called out, "There will be no punishment for mistakes. My workshops in Alexandria are free to make mistakes and make them often. It's the only way to learn." The faces didn't change. "I blew my roof off when I invented the steam mechanical, it nearly killed me and my foreman."

She saw a few mouths tick with a smile, but mostly they stayed silent. Sulla the foreman was still dancing on his sandals.

"What? Speak," she commanded.

Sulla muttered under his breath before clearing his throat and trying again, "*Di Manes*. The Day of the Dead. The workers, they try to pay attention, but their mind is on the dead. We should not be working."

Knowing all eyes were on her, Heron resisted a scowl. She'd thought the holiday an excuse not to work and had given orders that all workshops should ignore it, using her powers as Consul to override superstition, or so she thought.

"The automatas I commissioned are behind schedule, and so is the Iron Road. I thought you Romans were masters of all craft?" she said, hoping to spark their pride, but as she turned in a slow circle, partially to take stock in all their faces, and partially because her metal leg made her unbalanced, she realized their unearthly concern couldn't be assailed.

"Well, then," she said, realizing that no good work would be done this day. "I will honor this *Di Manes,* then. Take the rest of the day off to honor your dead."

There was little joy in the reactions. The workers meandered away from their stations as if they were in a funeral procession.

"Apologies," said Sulla the foreman. "I tried to make them work."

Heron shook her head. "No need for apology. The fault is mine. I forget myself in my haste to get things done. Not even the gods could meet the expectations I have for our progress."

Sulla made a hiss. "You should not speak of the gods on a day like today. The dead will become jealous and punish you for it."

She thanked him for his guidance and gave him leave. She was about to make her way back to the steam mechanical and her guards when a pair of men came marching into the workshop.

Senator Silius' mane of gray hair was unmistakable and she'd spent far too long on the winter journey with Legate Tiberius not to recognize him, though he was dressed in more finery than she'd seen him before. He had a strong jaw and golden wrist guards that matched his gold etched belt.

"Ave, Senator Silius, and Legate Tiberius," she said.

"Do not dare give me that tone of greeting when you have been avoiding me since your announcement," said Senator Silius, his face flushed and his proud toga slightly disheveled.

Tiberius stood by passively with a near impenetrable smirk. During the snow march across the mountains, she'd come to hate that twitch at the corner of his lips that signified how superior he thought he was. Whenever he spoke to Agog or Vestalis, he always regaled his accomplishments, even in defeat as he had at Antioch, owing it to Magnus' treachery rather than Agog's skill or his incompetence. In Heron's eyes, the only thing worse than a fool was a fool who thought he was a king.

"I dare because I am Consul," said Heron, trying to keep her voice calm, "and I have not been avoiding you, but busy in the affairs of the Empire. The Iron Road will benefit us all, if you've been paying attention."

"I don't care about your Iron Road," he sputtered. "Two hundred and fifty new seats in the Senate? This will obliterate my leadership of the Senate, a position I have upheld for nearly two decades. You cannot just take away the rights of our citizens!"

"Taking away rights? I'm merely offering them to those not represented by your system. That *is* the point of the Republic, if I've heard correctly," she replied calmly.

His face reddened a shade darker and his lips grew so thin they disappeared. "I won't allow this to happen."

"I have the votes, Senator," she said, glancing across the room to her two guards, who were slowly moving in her direction, sensing the anger from the Senator, but if he were to lash out with a hidden dagger, there would be nothing she could do about it.

He pointed a finger in her face, daring her to flinch. She stared back, unmoved, while her guards crept closer, hands on their hilts. Tiberius sensed their approach and pulled his gladius halfway out of the scabbard, causing her guards to pause. They looked from her and back to the Legate, clearly waiting for a command. Heron shook them off, so they stayed away, but tensed at the ready.

"Five days," said the Senator, "a lot can happen in five days. If this vote goes through, you'll find I make a dangerous enemy."

"It doesn't have to be, Senator. We can all win with the Iron Road. Imagine moving people and goods from Rome to Alexandria in a week rather than three months. Or Rome to Susa, or further east. It'll make the Empire the trade capitol of the world," she said.

"You haven't the slightest idea of what you're doing by opposing me.

How long I have labored for this Empire. Your ignorance will be the end of you," he seethed.

Heron almost reached out to close her metal hand around his throat, but thought better of it. She was trying to improve the Empire, not tear it apart.

"I hope you're not threatening me," she replied.

"I wouldn't dare," he said, bearing his teeth, before wheeling around and marching from the workshop.

Tiberius gave her a smug bow and followed the Senator out. When they had left the building, she let the breath she'd been holding out and leaned against the table.

"Take me back to the domus," she told her guards, "this day has been a disaster."

Settled on the steam chariot with one guard piloting the craft, while the other watched from the arrow launcher, Heron ran through the vote count again. With the factions of Aelia and Messalina on her side, the Wolves didn't have the votes to oppose her. And once Alexandria and the other provinces were added to the rolls, Silius and the Wolves would be diminished to the point of irrelevance. There would be new problems, but by then, Agog would be back in the city and she would be back in Alexandria.

A maudlin ache for the City of Wonders settled on her bones. Too long she'd been away. Too long since she'd seen Punt and Plutarch. The Festival of Nyx would dominate the city soon as revelers donned masks and practiced their pranks on strangers. Heron had never participated, and honestly, she'd never liked the festival much when she lived there, but she missed being annoyed by its frivolousness.

Heron held onto the seat in the back of the chariot as it turned a corner, a little too fast for her taste. Her mind was on anything but the present when her guard took an arrow to the throat. She didn't see it hit, only his slumping and the death gurgle as he reached for her as if she could somehow fix it.

Standing unsteadily as the chariot bumped across the cobblestones, she opened her mouth to shout at her pilot when she saw the flicker of movement from the side streets. Two horse-drawn wagons charged into their path, blocking the way.

The pilot pulled on the stopping mechanism and she flew into the boiler, searing her palm on the hot metal. The chariot swerved to the side and Heron almost flew out, avoiding a face first sprawl on the cobblestones by hooking her metal fingers on the steam piping.

The street was narrow and there was not enough room for the steam chariot to turn around without careful maneuvering. Men with pale white faces and wearing bronze and fur armor she didn't recognize came running towards them with swords drawn. The blades were longer than a gladius and thinner, but she had little time to contemplate the meaning.

Her guard drew his weapon and moved to engage the attackers, but there were six of them and only one of him. Two more ghost-faced attackers climbed down from the wagons. The first had a wide nose with flaring nostrils and teeth that would make a camel proud. The curved sword in his fist caught the sunlight, accentuating its razor sharp edge.

Heron stumbled off the chariot, nearly falling in the street when her metal foot caught a loose rock. She hobbled straight for the alleyway, searching for an escape. Running drove the buckle attachment into her thigh but she kept her legs moving.

A wooden door halfway down the alleyway resisted her initial attempts to barge through. She could keep going, but there was no way she'd outrun eight men. Behind her, the Alexandrian guard died with little noise, and she hoped she was not soon to follow.

Yanking on the door proved fruitless, so she dipped her shoulder and smashed against the door, nearly falling on her face as it gave way.

Men shouted behind her, so she fled into the building, which she quickly realized was a storage warehouse packed from floor to ceiling with transport boxes. Jagged rows ran through the boxed goods.

There was a second level, so Heron looked for a ladder or staircase, hoping she could hide amongst the boxes. Open windows let in faint light. Her eyes were not adjusted, but she kept running. Unfamiliar custom stamps marked the goods. The door behind her opened, turning it to a conflagration of whiteness.

She darted down a side passage, finding a wooden ladder going up to the second level. Quietly as she could, she climbed, finding her metal limb unhelpful in making the ascent. Each step she had to maneuver the bottom of her foot squarely onto the rung or it would slip off. She kept expecting her pursuers to curl around the corner at any moment.

Each breath sounded like a lion's roar in her ears. She flung herself over the top and rolled away from the edge as she heard footsteps. Lying on her back, she tried to determine if they'd seen her, or if someone was climbing the ladder to the second level, but her booming heartbeats overwhelmed everything else.

When no one stuck their head over the edge, Heron crawled forward on her belly. The ghost-faced man with the curved sword stood below the ladder looking around. The bronze helm he wore was unfamiliar. More like a cap with chin straps than a protective helm. The whiteness of his face was clearly paint, as his olive skin could be seen on the back of his neck through the smears. Foot scuffs warned her on the approach of a second pursuer, and she slid away from the edge.

"Have you seen him?" asked the man below in Latin.

"He must have escaped," said the second.

"Not likely," said the first. "There are only two doors and Levities came through the other, while I was the first on his trail. He's in here somewhere. We just need to look harder."

"This was supposed to be a quick kill," said the second. "We should just leave."

"A little bit longer. Better to be seen than to fail. *He's* not a forgiving man."

The second man wandered off and Heron couldn't tell if the first was still at the base of the ladder, so she moved back to the edge. Creeping forward, she tried to see over without revealing herself.

The bottom of the ladder was empty. Heron moved back and breathed a sigh of relief. If she could only stay hidden for a while longer, she might survive the assassination attempt. But there were no guarantees, so she started formulating a plan as a backup.

On both sides, wooden shipping boxes were piled high. The ones on the left were stacked like blocks while the other side sat in neat compartments keeping each one separate.

On her knees, Heron lifted the lid on the nearest box, hoping to find something useful. What she found was so unexpected she almost made a noise of surprise.

Inside the box were dozens of self-trimming lamps, the ones she'd first tried to sell in Alexandria to fund the war, resting in a bed of old hay. Heron examined the box for the trader stamp, finding the outline of a wolf's head. The mystery of who'd ripped off her designs would have to wait until she was safely back in her domus, but the presence of her lamps bothered her.

Heron pulled one out, finding it completely empty as expected, but with a dry wick stuck in the middle. A flint and steel cap hung from a sturdy chain.

Quietly as she could manage, Heron stuffed the empty lamp with hay from the box. Once it was full, she pulled the wick out and squeezed the flint and steel cap to make a spark. The scraping of the steel across the flint was a windstorm in her ears. She cringed with each try, until on the third, a spark flew out and nested in the hay like a bright red bird.

With a hushed breath, she fueled the little spark until it turned to flame. Her distraction would quickly draw notice so she had to act fast. Heron grabbed more hay, placing it carefully into the fuel compartment on the lamp, as not to put out the flame, and then moved to the edge. When she saw none of the ghost-faced men in the aisle beneath her, Heron lobbed the flaming lamp onto the platform across from her.

She quickly made a second lamp and started lighting it when she heard a cry of alarm from the other direction. With a second lamp lit, Heron moved the other direction and leaning her arm through a space between two boxes, she threw the second lamp onto the boxes below.

Turning around to get a third lamp, she saw a ghostly face with wide flaring nostrils appear over the edge of the ladder. Contrasted by the white paint, his mouth was a cavernous grin. The curved sword in his fist clanged against the wood as he started pulling himself standing. She was trapped.

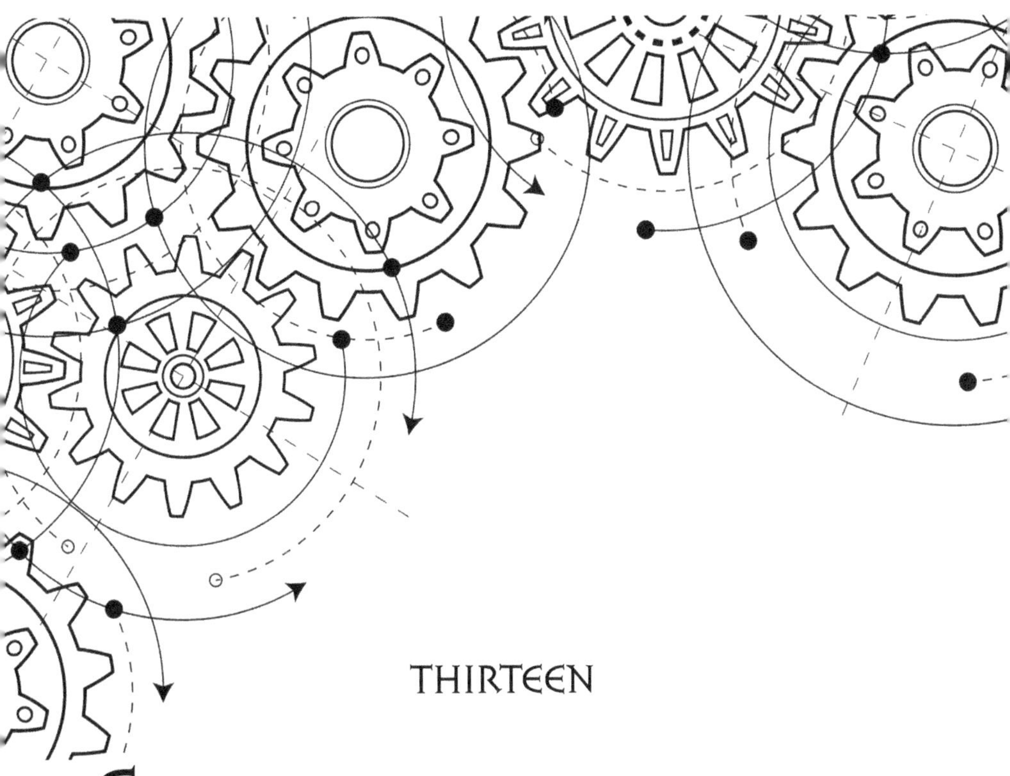

THIRTEEN

Sepharia was sitting naked in her room scraping the perfumed oil from her skin with the strigil when she heard the strange sound from the courtyard. The afternoon breeze blew through the window bringing the smells of sea air and the holly trees from the grove behind the domus making her shiver until gooseflesh sprung from her skin. Livia, the servant woman, had offered to clean her, but as much as Sepharia enjoyed certain rituals of Rome, she was not accustomed to personal grooming or the public bath houses that were common to the city.

The domus was empty since Heron had been called to the workshops and many of the servants went home for the day. She froze when she heard the noise again, the bronze scraping tool halfway down her thigh still glistening in oil.

She might have dismissed the noise as the wind knocking branches against the building had it not been for the warning from Sextus. She'd forgotten all about it until now and hadn't really taken it seriously even when he'd said it. In Alexandria, she'd spent her whole life watching the temples make their every action to seem important, when their only desire was to squeeze coin from the masses.

It was not so different for the nobles in Rome. Except it seemed the temples were a tool of the wealthy rather than a leach on the people. She hadn't really considered the difference until now, poised naked in her room with nearly no one at the domus. Sextus' warning in that light carried a sinister weight, rather than the dismissal she'd given it when first heard.

Mundus patet.

The phrase still meant nothing to her, but it must have something to do with the unofficial holiday—the Day of the Dead. No one was forbidden from working, but most declined to do so, for fear of upsetting their ancestors.

With an ear to the wind, Sepharia hastily finished scraping the oil from her skin and donned the saffron stola that was draped over the chair. She almost put on her tunic, the one she wore at the workshop in Alexandria, in case she had to move quickly, but decided against it. Livia had nearly fell dead from fright the first time she saw Sepharia in the tunic, so she only wore it privately in her room.

She kept the stola loose, so her ankles were not bound by the fabric. An onlooker would think she were a prostitute coming from her job by the disheveled nature of her clothing, but the ominous warning from Sextus made her wary.

Creeping down the hallway sharpened her hearing, but not in the way she would have liked. All the sounds from outside the domus came rushing to her: the steady clatter of a wagon wheel across the cobblestones, a distant bell toiling a mournful tune, the growling of a steam mechanical passing through a nearby street, a lone bird cawing from the grove. Only her heartbeat overcame the outside noise, and together they muted everything between, leaving Sepharia blind about what was around the next corner.

The courtyard at the center of the domus was large enough to hold a party and filled with enough flowery bushes and small trees to hide a dozen men. Sepharia peered from around the corner, pressing her face against the cold marble archway. Staying flat against the wall, she watched for movement, expecting to see a flash of bronze, or crimson through the bushes.

Sepharia was so focused on the way before her, she didn't hear the person coming up from behind until the final foot scuff against the tile.

"Good Sepharia," said Livia, "have the dead roosted in your mind and made you wander off?"

Sepharia spun around, a squeak slipping from her lips. "By the gods, no." She glanced over her shoulder at the courtyard. "I thought I heard something and went to investigate."

"You did hear something," said Livia with a disapproving purse to her lips. "You have visitors in the map room since Consul Heron is not here to greet them."

"Visitors?"

Livia gave her a droll look. "Yes, visitors. Are you sure the dead haven't addled your mind?"

Sepharia almost replied until she saw the hint of a smile at Livia's lips. "I shall attend to them immediately."

"Not until I've fixed your stola, good Sepharia," said Livia. "You look like a child putting on her mother's clothes for the first time."

Livia didn't give her a chance to reply, pushing Sepharia's arms out of the way and tugging on the fabric until she felt like a mummy in a cocoon.

"It's clothing," Sepharia gasped, "it's not supposed to be bonded to the skin."

Livia smirked and pulled tighter. When she was done, she gave Sepharia an approving nod and sent her to the map room.

There, she found Vestalis waiting with a few handsome Legates from the Legion. They were breathing heavily as if they'd just been running. The general gave her a worried glance, though he softened slightly when his eyes laid upon her.

"Greetings, Consul Vestalis," said Sepharia.

"Greetings, Sepharia, are things well in the domus?"

She glanced to the three Roman soldiers, and Vestalis nodded, giving permission to speak in front of them. "I thought I heard something earlier, but it's gone now."

Vestalis frowned. "We chased six men from the domus upon our arrival. Strange men with white painted faces and unfamiliar armor."

One of the Legate's stepped up. "It was armor from the early days of Rome when we were not yet an Empire. I've seen it before in the museums. I assume they did not mean you well."

"Thank you for your protection. It seems your arrival was fortuitous. Maybe the gods watch over this domus," she said, adding the last part for a little superstitious benefit.

"Where is Heron?" asked Vestalis.

"Visiting workshops, but he's safe, he took two guards and a Manticore." Even after she said it, she wasn't sure she believed her words and Vestalis didn't either, by his deepening frown. "May I ask why you came to see my father?"

Vestalis thought for a moment before speaking, "These Legates had once served under Magnus. Heron wanted to question them to learn more about the man."

There was something else, but Vestalis wasn't saying. Sepharia guessed it had something to do with the tentative negotiations with Aelia to bring Magnus back to the Empire. She knew her father's thoughts, if she could end the war early, then she could return to Alexandria. An inviting prospect, given the events of the day.

"We could go find him," offered Sepharia.

Vestalis shook his head. "Rome is a big place. There's no way we'd find him. Better to wait here. I'm sure he'll arrive soon enough."

"No," said Sepharia. "I know exactly where he is. He's been visiting the same workshop for the last five days..."

As soon as the words left her mouth, she knew her father was in danger. Vestalis ran from the room with the Legates close behind. Sepharia followed and as soon as they reached the outside, she saw the twirl of black smoke on the horizon.

"Fire," said Vestalis simply.

"It's been too dry lately. A fire could devastate the city," said the Legate who had spoken before.

When Vestalis looked to her, she knew what he was asking. "Yes," she nodded, "that's the way to the workshop."

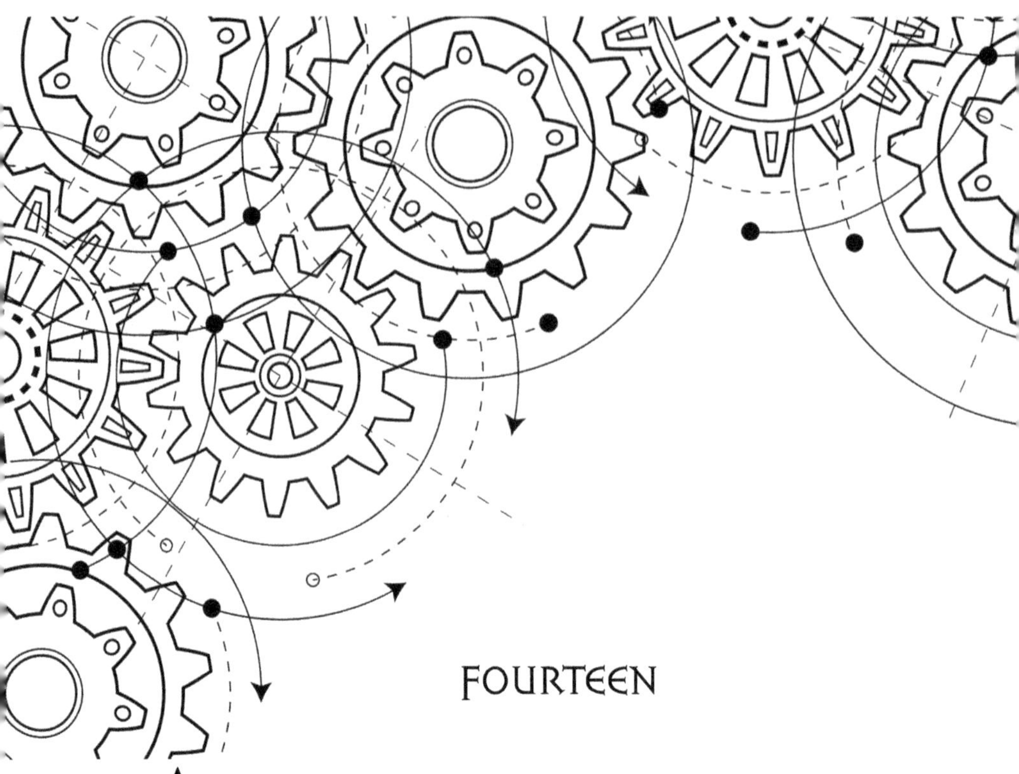

FOURTEEN

As the ghost-faced attacker climbed onto the platform, Heron threw an unlit lamp at his face and he knocked it out of the air with his sword hand. There wasn't enough room for his curved blade to maneuver, so Heron stepped in close and grabbed him around the throat with her metal hand.

The attacker put his weight forward, tripping her backwards into the boxes. She landed hard on her back, knocking the air from her lungs. The metal hand slipped from his throat and he tried to bring the sword around to cut her.

Light flickered up from below. The fire had grown, spilling flame and smoke into the empty air. Worried shouts filled the warehouse.

Her ghost-faced attacker had one hand on her face, gouging her nose and eyes with his fingers, while she flailed at his arms, using her metal limb like a hammer. She didn't have enough room to hit him with any force, so she grabbed the edge of the boxes and yanked down.

At first nothing happened, as the nearest box slipped out of her fingers, but she must have unbalanced them, because the pile fell on top of the both of them, slamming him on top of her and knocking the sword from his hand.

A corner of a wooden box caught her near the temple, causing bursts of blues and violets in her vision. It seemed the weight of the world was on her as she struggled to stay conscious. Each gasp was like her lungs were made of iron.

As she fought for each breath, she felt a wet warmth on her neck. Her attacker was slumped onto her, motionless, the buckle of his bronze helm cutting into her chin. Beneath the boxes there was little light, except the reflections of orange flickers.

Heron strained to push the man off her. He was either dead or unconscious and she wished he was neither. The floor beneath her grew warm and the crackle of fire could be heard above her laboring heart.

In a burst of energy, Heron thrashed against the weight like a wolverine caught in a trap. Her efforts barely moved the man or the boxes. Fear crept into her mind like a thief as she started to realize she might be burned alive.

Like living tendrils, black smoke snaked through the holes between the boxes. The first cough was like a punch to the chest, the second cough a sledge hammer.

Panic seized her limbs and she tried flailing again, but it only resulted in tired muscles. Being restrained only reminded her of the time beneath the Temple of Sobek. It took every bit of her will not to give into the fear.

With the floor growing uncomfortably warm and black choking smoke invading her space, Heron calmed herself and used the light from the hungry flames to see if she had a way out. To her right, she thought she might be able to squeeze out, her arm had a finger-length of room to maneuver. It was the left side that was completely trapped. The weight

of a heavy box lay on her mechanical arm. As soon as she realized that, she yanked back the fabric of her tunic and placed her fingertips against the buckles that attached the mechanical to her arm.

But she couldn't do it.

A fit of coughing woke her to action, but not to undo the buckle. She couldn't give up her arm, even if it was just a mechanical one.

But the fire had grown wild and the smoke pushed through her clamped lips and into her lungs, setting off a vicious fit of coughing. When she could finally calm her heaving chest, she started raging against the weight on top of her. At first, it did nothing, but then the metal arm slowly started working its way free.

With lips clamped and eyes squinting away the smoke, Heron heaved upward, trying to leverage her way free. Wiggling and turning as flame danced around the platform, Heron squeezed out from under the pile.

Free from the boxes, Heron allowed herself another fit of coughing as she held the crook of her elbow across her face to protect it from the heat of the flames. The whole building was raging with flame. Bands of heat rushed past like waves from an ocean, singeing her face.

Heron moved in the direction of the least flame. She pushed boxes off the level and jumped down, landing heavily as the mechanical leg jammed into her stump, bringing fresh tears. The way she'd come in was blocked by a wall of flame. She looked for the other exit, but her eyes could barely stay open against the heat.

A deafening crack made her jump. Heron stumbled forward, barely avoiding a collapse. Moving around what flame she could, she made her way through the fiery building, until at last she saw the glowing white light of an open doorway.

Heron surged through the door, stumbling into the street behind the warehouse. Away from the burning building, she collapsed on the street and drank at the delicious air. So fresh and pure it forced her into seizures of coughing.

A hand touched her shoulder and asked a question, but she was so focused on being able to breathe again she didn't understand. Only then she realized the streets were alive with men and women drawn by the fire.

Shouts of alarm and coordination sparked through the air, but could not match the intensity of the warehouse fire. Bucket lines formed, and two buildings over, men frantically hacked down a house to create a fire break. The other direction ended in an open street, so there was less danger the fire would spread that way.

A man and a woman in disheveled clothing, hastily donned, were screaming and crying, trying to stop the men. The woman held an infant in her arms. The man's face was as bright and red as the fire. Others dragged them away, much to their continued and fruitless protests.

Heron watched in muted horror as the men raced the fire. At least a dozen buildings would be consumed, even if they could stop it at the break. The water lines focused on the break, soaking the buildings next to it as protection, and removing as much of the potential fuel for the fire as they could.

Hands pulled her standing. Hands that belonged to Sepharia and Vestalis. Heron barely realized she was being led to a steam chariot until she was sitting on the bench.

As Vestalis piloted her away from the fire, Sepharia hugged her and told her how glad she was that she'd survived. Heron heard her, but not really. Her mind was back at the fire, watching the poor people who had done nothing having to deal with the repercussions of a battle far above their station.

That was the way of it, she realized. The nobles schemed and planned, ignoring or not even caring about the people they affected when they made war on each other. Her ire did not end with her enemies, she saw her own complicity in the fight as a maker of warmachines and unleasher of Archimedes' spark powder. Her inventions had led to the death of tens of thousands of soldiers.

Sacrifice. That's what she'd told herself when she'd done it. Progress required sacrifice. How else could you fight unless you were willing to make sacrifices? But if she fought their way, it would always end up like this. Lots of pointless destruction, but little actual change.

As the steam chariot carried her back to the domus, back to an implied but very tenuous safety, Heron vowed that before she left the position of Consul, she would change the game. Do something that gave power back to the people. What that was, she didn't know. But she'd figure it out.

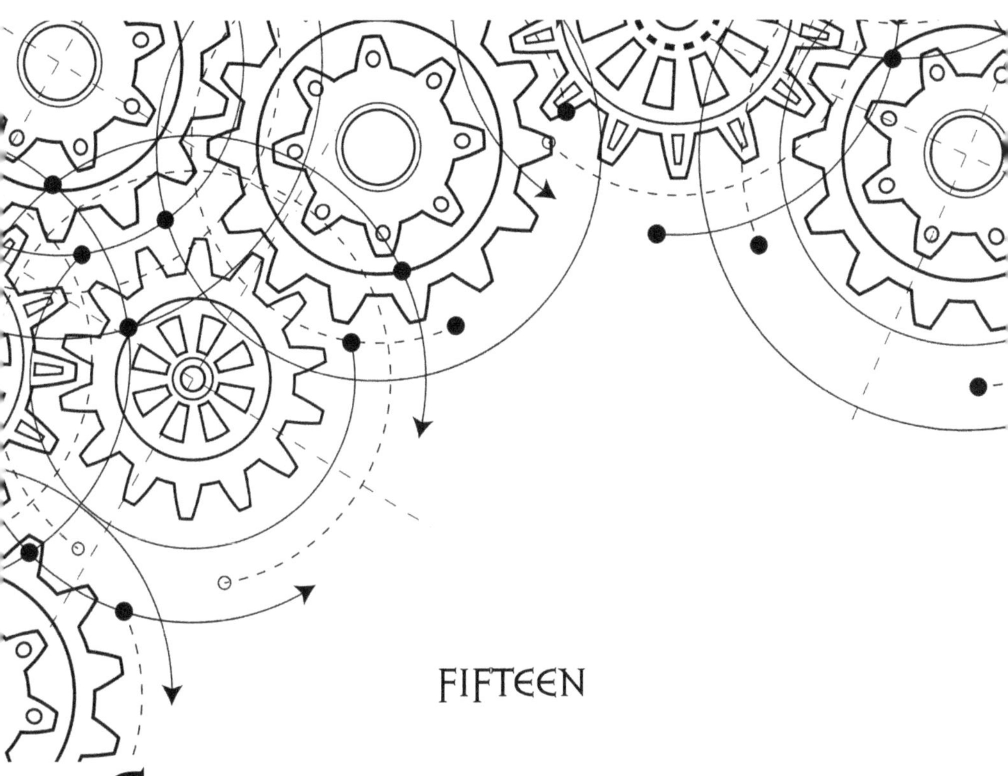

FIFTEEN

Sepharia adjusted the tiny silver wire in Heron's wrist, increasing the tension until it could be plucked like a lyre string. The connecting thread wound around a spool so small it could fit on her smallest finger with room to spare. Delicate gears, like brass snowflakes, tugged on the wire until the fingers yearned towards the palm. With the adjustment complete, Sepharia snapped the metal door closed.

Heron turned her arm back and forth like a rotating cylinder, testing the fingers one by one until she seemed satisfied, or at least what Sepharia thought meant satisfaction, which was mostly not giving further instructions.

"I'm glad you came back," said Heron, much to Sepharia's surprise.

The attack and near immolation had muted her father, not to mention burning off half an eyebrow. Heron's other hand rested in her lap, wrapped in bandages.

"I couldn't let you be alone in this place," said Sepharia.

The watered-down look in Heron's eyes, the gaunt cheeks, and almost gray skin, brought a tightness to Sepharia's chest. She was about to open her mouth and suggest Heron take a few days off to rest when Vestalis marched through the door.

"Good," said the general, giving Heron a quick once over before moving to the table to examine the array of stones displayed in three groupings, "it seems you're well enough to talk plans. We only have two days left until the vote."

"The vote will go as planned," said Sepharia, motioning towards the stones. "We have enough to pass."

Vestalis' lips creased with disagreement while his hard gray eyes washed over her. "Things never go as planned when it comes to the Senate." He pointed to the smallest pile of stones. "Those are the ones in flux, if all of those go against us, or if Messalina can't deliver his side as promised, we'll be lost. If we can't add the additional seats to shift the balance into our favor, we'll be forever blocked by Silius and his Wolves."

Sepharia shook her head. "I still don't understand why Agog just can't add the seats. He *is* the Emperor now, right?"

"Only if he'd made it a part of the treaty when we first took Rome," said Vestalis. "Once we agreed to keep the Senate, we agreed to follow their rules. And with the army out of the city, we can't afford to make enemies of everyone. Agog would surely take Rome back if they rebelled, but that would be little solace to our lifeless and probably headless bodies."

"The undecideds," said Heron, nodding towards the middle stones. "A group of them want the contracts for the steam wagons that will ride on the Iron Road in exchange for their votes."

"Then give it to them," said Vestalis.

"Two problems," said Heron shaking her head wearily. "One, those contracts are promised to some of Aelia's friends. Two, steam wagons that can ride on the Iron Road aren't yet designed and I don't have the time to finish them. There's only so much of me to go around."

"Do we have other contracts to offer?" asked Sepharia.

"Nothing," said Heron.

"We need to give them something," said Vestalis. "Does it have to do with the Iron Road?"

Sepharia smoothed an errant piece of hair away from her face. "Doesn't one of those Senators own a big quarry?"

Vestalis snapped his fingers. "Do we need any constructions completed?"

Sepharia couldn't think of anything, so she slumped onto the chair and picked up one of the 'Yes' stones to roll across her palm. When she glanced up, she caught a strange twinkle in Heron's eye.

"Father, you have an idea?"

Heron nodded slowly. "Do we have the funds to pay for another large project?"

"No, but it matters not," said Vestalis. "Once we have the votes we can worry about the cost. This law means more than anything else."

"Temples," said Heron. "We can build temples. The Romans love their gods, but unlike the Egyptians who seem beholden to them, these Romans expect the gods to work for them. We'll give the undecideds, and a few of our other weaker links, contracts on new temples built to honor this new Empire."

Coming from her father's lips, the idea seemed absurd. She knew Heron's view on the temples from their time making miracles in Alexandria. Sepharia might have thought Heron slightly mad from exhaustion, except for her completely sane and level gaze.

"But where?" asked Sepharia.

Heron smirked with a private joke. "We'll build great temples in Delos, Delphi, Dodona, Dium, and Amphipolis, and rebuild the greatest of all temples to Athena in Rome."

"Bold plans, but worthy of our goals," said Vestalis. "With those votes, the matter of the new seats should be settled. Now we must speak of the other issue. Do we know who was behind the attempted assassinations?"

"Assassinations?" asked Heron.

Sepharia shared a glance with Vestalis, before shrugging. "I didn't think to tell her. You chased them off without incident."

Heron shook her head. "It doesn't matter. We're all in danger. I just need to get used to it."

"Do you think it was the Wolves?" asked Vestalis.

"Like a piston and rod, they seem connected," replied Heron. "They have the most to gain by our deaths and I'd just met with Silius and Tiberius at the workshop. Maybe they'd only come to confirm I was there, so they could set their assassins on me. But why were they dressed in old armor and wearing painted faces? That's what I'd like to know."

"Only the gods know," said Vestalis.

Sepharia cleared her throat. "Because it was the Day of the Dead, that's why."

"But why?" asked Vestalis, his brow wrinkled with thought. "It serves no purpose. They could have worn Thracian armor, or simple brigand gear. Anything to hide their allegiance."

"I don't know why," said Sepharia. "But they wouldn't paint their faces unless there was a reason and that reason was the Day of the Dead."

Vestalis scowled away her comment, turning his back and facing the map. "What would a girl know about these things? It's one of the factions. Probably Silius and his Wolves, but it could be one of the others. One can never tell in Rome."

The rebuke felt like a slap across the face. She nearly retreated to her chair until she realized Heron was watching intently.

Sepharia swallowed her fears and spoke again, "It probably *is* one of the factions, but the Day of the Dead matters. A few days ago, I met Sextus Paetina at the Pantheon, and he warned me not to go out of the domus on Augustus the twenty fourth. The day of the attack. The Day of the Dead."

"Why didn't you tell us this before?" asked Vestalis, his grey eyes boring into her.

"I didn't think it mattered. He was wearing his priestly gear, flamen or some such word, which made me think his warning just a bloating of his religious importance. In Alexandria, every other day is a religious holiday and each and every temple claims the world will come to an end unless you give them your hard earned coinage."

His gaze softened, if only slightly, as he nodded. "In Rome, the temples are different. They're tools of the nobles, not a pantomimus dancing for profit."

"Were you a priest?" asked Heron suddenly.

"No," said Vestalis with his chin lifted. "My father was not connected enough. I earned my place through the army and the glory of battle and once I'd returned to Rome, my father sent for me in Alexandria to take over the business due to his illnesses."

Heron looked to Sepharia. "Could it be Aelia's side behind the attack?"

Sepharia clamped her lips tight. It was possible, but she didn't want to admit it.

"It very well could," said Vestalis. "It could be that Aelia wanted you in the domus so they could kill you here. That's why he warned you."

"But why?" asked Sepharia. "Won't they profit from our plans?"

Heron shook her head. "Once we set the plans in motion, we became irrelevant. Even the workshops could figure out how to make the steam wagons work, given enough time. And don't forget, we took a sizable stake in their mines. I'm sure they're not happy about that."

Sepharia was trying to imagine Sextus' face, to remember if he'd been truly warning her, or sending her to her death. It seemed hard to believe the latter. Envisioning his face reminded her of the rest of the conversation.

"There was something else he said when he warned me about the Day of the Dead. *Mundus Patet*. What does 'open the world' mean?"

Both Sepharia and Heron looked to Vestalis. He seemed to consider the word, even mouthing it twice before frowning. "Mundus Patet. It means what you say it does, but I don't think that's what he meant. That's an older usage of the words, not common these days. It might be something I've heard once, but I can't recall where. It's been decades since I lived in Rome. It's not the city I remember."

"Just ask him," said Heron.

"Ask Sextus?" she asked.

"Yes. Plan a meeting with him, make an excuse to the reason, but ask him. If it matters he'll tell you, or if he's against us, he'll try to avoid it," said Heron.

"A wise course," said Vestalis. "I'll see if I can learn anything else about the word. And the Day of the Dead."

"Good," said Heron, "we all have work to do. Me, most of all."

"Father, you should rest. You look terrible," said Sepharia.

"I've felt worse and there's no time for idleness. Our heads depend on it." Heron paused, metal fingers articulating, fingertip to palm, one after another. "I have one more job for you. An important one, I think, though I cannot tell you why, and I have no time to pursue it myself."

Both Sepharia and Vestalis looked on perplexed.

"I need you to find out about Caesar's death." Heron held up her hand to stave off questions. "Not how he died, but why."

"What? I don't understand," said Sepharia.

"And I can't tell you. I just need you to do it," replied Heron.

"Where will I start?" asked Sepharia.

Heron sighed wearily and before she could speak, Sepharia offered, "I'll figure it out. You have enough to do, considering the vote."

"Good," said Heron with a weak smile.

"Good, I hope," replied Sepharia.

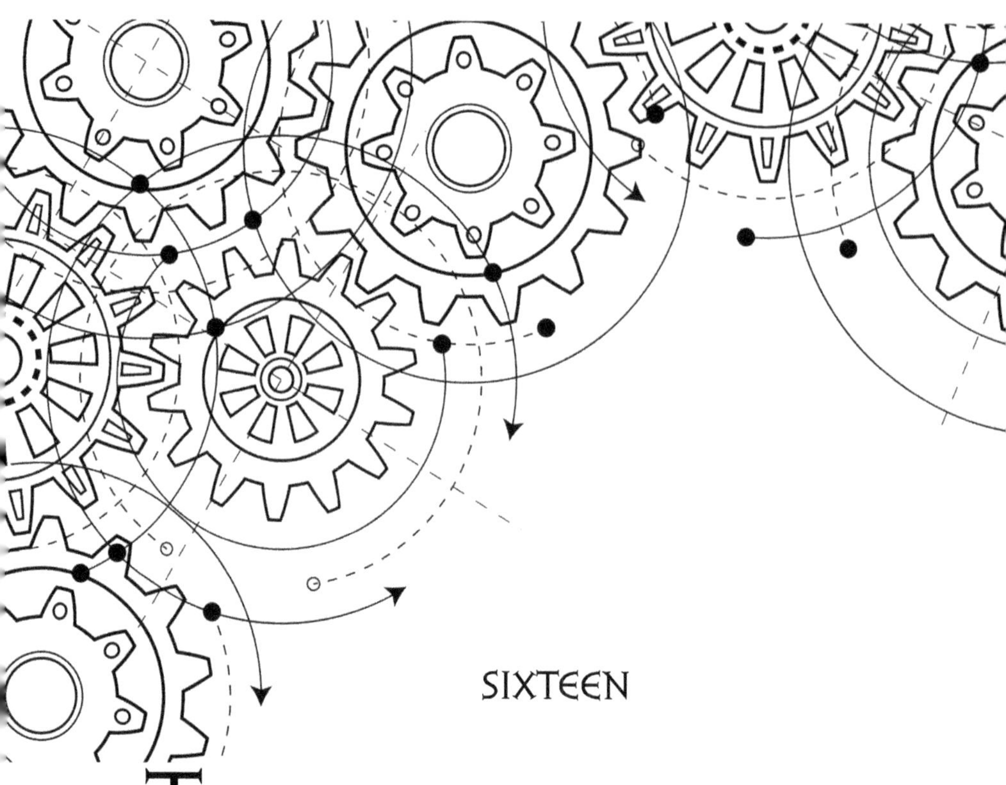

SIXTEEN

The panic she felt waiting on the steam barge to disembark was nothing short of torture. Heron kept a stern façade, lips clamped together and chin held high, while the lesser Senators strolled past in their formal togas. Every passing eye blew away the shroud of protection she'd built up in preparation for the vote like the Lighthouse burned through a foggy night.

She hadn't expected there to be a line outside the Senate building when she arrived. Something inside had delayed the traditional procession, leaving Heron to be gazed upon like a zoo animal on the back bench of the steam barge.

While every Senator was capable of feigning a passionate opinion about the laws brought to the floor, today their feelings were unmasked. The addition of two hundred and fifty seats changed the balance of power within the Senate. Everyone was affected, no matter how powerful or powerless.

Rather than engage in a staring contest with every Senator that disagreed, Heron turned her gaze to the tarnished brass statue of the babes Remus and Romulus suckling from a she-wolf, set upon the high colonnades. Heron sympathized with the gaunt she-wolf, her ribs exposed to the elements, as she provided nourishment to the two founders of Rome. Those infants tugged hungrily on the teats of the she-wolf, teeth gnashing tender skin, much like the cities of Alexandria and Rome to Heron.

Why the wolf mother would choose to take in such ravenous beasts seemed irrelevant under the circumstances. Much as Heron had become tied to the two cities irrevocably. There had been a need and she'd stepped in. Now she had to care for them until they were old enough to care for themselves.

Heron knew the legends that went with the twins. Their mother, Rhea Silvia, had been raped by the god Mars, as gods were prone to do. The supposed half-divine children were ordered to be drowned, so as not to oppose the king, who had taken his brother's place through treachery. Saved and raised by the she-wolf, the twins returned to avenge their father and retake the throne, thus begetting the empire.

The twins also fought each other, with Remus dying to Romulus' hand in later years. Heron hoped the same would not be true for her two children: Rome and Alexandria. But judging by the bitter glances, the marriage of these two empires was not going smoothly. Even if the vote went as planned, which she had every expectation that it would, it would not resolve all their problems.

"Planning on sitting out here all day?" asked a familiar voice.

Vestalis stood at the edge of the barge, his shorn head gleaming in the morning sun, jaw clenched in a grim smile, while his gray eyes watched her solemnly. His were the eyes of autumn clouds, dark with cold winds and the promise of winter.

"Damn the traditions," said Heron, using the ivory cane to pull herself standing.

Climbing down from the steam barge was never an easy task. The passing Senators seemed to sense her impending failure and she felt their eyes warming her face. Holding on to the stamped shielding, while lowering herself to the cobblestones, Heron made her exit from the craft. Not at all graceful, but without incident and that was enough for her.

Inside the Senate, a towering automata in the visage of Caesar in his younger conquering days saluted them with a gladius in his fist. The smooth motion made no sound, though Heron could feel the vibrations of the gears inside the massive marble base.

"A remarkable resemblance," said Vestalis.

Heron smirked, "It's not the first time I've made Caesar's automata."

"I thought it would be outside." His voice dropped to a whisper. "How will we retrieve the barrels if it's in here?"

She shrugged and waited for a trio of Senators to pass before responding in a hushed whisper. "It wasn't intended to be inside the Senate, but when the curators saw it, they demanded that it be placed inside. It took some working to power the automata with the opening and closing of the outer door rather than the wind, but it'll have to do."

Vestalis made grumbling noises under his breath. "More problems we don't have time for."

"How many barrels do we have left to hide?" she asked.

"Too many. More than three-quarters. I've taken to storing some at the armory, marking them as nails and other similarly innocuous supplies, but it's still too many."

Heron repressed a sigh. She was hoping to get some sleep tonight after the vote. "I'll double the workshops' load."

"Good," said Vestalis. "And I'll see if I can move more barrels out of the city. I've been staging mock battles north of the city to drill the integrated troops. I should be able to keep some safely there."

"Word from Agog?" asked Heron hopefully.

"Magnus is a cunning foe. I would not like to face him. He's drawn Agog across the north, through Gaul and other lands," said Vestalis.

"But he has the advantage of the chariots?" asked Heron.

"Magnus keeps far from the roads, moving through the forests and across swamps. The chariots cannot follow and Agog rightfully fears to fight with his infantry only. It looks to be a long war."

"Six months," growled Heron. "He promised me six months."

Vestalis nodded towards the open doors leading to the Senate chamber. The cacophony grew inside, like a flock of geese readying for flight. They moved towards the side of the chamber only to be blocked by Tiberius.

"What are you doing here, Legate?" asked Vestalis.

"The same as you," said Tiberius, looking much too smug for the circumstances. "Watching history." He gave a perfunctory bow to Heron. "Burning down any other parts of the city today?"

"Plato have pity, I was attacked," said Heron.

Tiberius made a noise that announced he was pleased with himself. "The city is a dangerous place. I would not recommend traveling with so few guards and no slaves. Especially since the plebs are quite rattled by your careless use of fire in such a dry time. You could have burned down the city."

Heron swallowed her words and studied the man's face instead. He seemed calm, slightly gloating in his presence, not at all what she would have expected from one of Silius' faction.

"Have you ever been to the Nile?" Heron asked Tiberius in a moment of inspiration.

His brow creased. "No. Why would I? Nothing there but superstitious fools from a long dead empire. May the sands rot their bones."

"What a tragedy. For life along the Nile is an instructive place. The river brings food and life to the world, feeding even Rome in its bounty.

The river is a source of power to those who control it. But in the river there are great scaly beasts, huge crocodiles lurking in the water." Heron gave him a sinister grin, her lips cracking in dryness. "Be careful not to get too close and become mesmerized by the cool waters and idyllic reeds."

The smugness on his face soured at her words as he glanced to her mechanical limbs. Tiberius looked almost ill. He swallowed and stamped off, dragging his entourage with him, looking back over his shoulder more than once in retreat.

Vestalis gave her a questioning gaze. "What bit of darkness was that?"

Heron examined her bony wrist and imagined how gaunt her face had become. "By all things whole and true, I do not know. It came to me all at once and was out my lips before I considered it."

"Well," said Vestalis. "It's sure to give Tiberius pause the next time he wants to intimidate you."

"His tone worries me," said Heron. "Not at all like someone who has lost."

Vestalis nodded grimly. "I sensed the same thing. But we should have the votes necessary. Tiberius is known for his false bravado. Sometimes when a man is afraid he acts bravely, if foolishly."

"I'll feel better once I see Senator Silius' mood," said Heron.

They pushed through the throng around the bowl of seats, the heat from the masses bringing a trickle of sweat to her back. The conflicting scents of a hundred perfumes and oils made the space noxious to pass through. The outer ring was packed with plebs and equites and even well-off freedmen. A huge marble pillar with etched names of famous Senators spanning its girth blocked her view.

Heron leaned around the pillar, careful not to chip the stone with her metal hand, searching for Senator Silius on his side of the bowl. She

found him right away by the thick purple sash he wore, a signal of his
self-importance compared to his fellow Senators.

He smiled and waved to her, as if he'd been waiting for her to notice
him. Tiberius' smug attitude could be dismissed as bravado, but on Silius
it was a threat. She'd expected him sullen or angry, not smiling as if he
were cheering on a winning chariot at Circus Maximus.

She muttered a few curses against the gods and moved further
around the pillar. She needed to see her coconspirators.

Near the dais on which Senators sometimes came to give their oratories, she found Senator Pallas, the husband of Aelia. He was a wrinkled
bag of flesh a few decades older than his wife. He would be the Senator
to bring the vote to the floor when the session began. It was an important, but largely symbolic position for the aging Senator, who was clearly a
puppet for his cunning wife.

A little further she moved, leaning on the back bench of the highest
seats. The Protectors positioned themselves opposite the dais, because
that's traditionally where Emperors sat when they attended the Senate.
The gilded throne waited unused, for Heron declined to use it, even as
Agog's Consul.

Try as she might, Heron could not find the tall, slooping Senator
Messalina. Panic rose in her breast and she scoured the area, noting that
the remaining Senators did not appear to be concerned by Messalina's
absence.

Heron tried to allay her worry, telling herself that the Senator had
not yet arrived, but then she heard the formal calling of the doors to be
closed.

"Clausus Curia!"

The call brought sharp pains through her stumps as if her limbs had
suddenly woken and realized they were no longer there. Vestalis, standing at the edge, looked similarly worried.

Once more she scanned the bowl, looking for a misplaced Messalina. Back at the Protectors, she realized a different Senator stood in his place, one of his lieutenants, one who controlled one of the sub-factions within the Protectors. His name was Antonius and his size made him hard to miss.

Heron circled the bowl, stabbing her ivory cane forward, leveraging onlookers out of the way as the formal proceedings began. Senator Pallas would bring the vote to the floor almost immediately, so there was little time to spare if something was wrong.

She grabbed one of the Senators on the back bowl, digging her fingers into the bunched up fabric on his shoulder, and whispered, "Where is Senator Messalina?"

The Senator at first appeared to be offended by the rough handling, until he saw who had him in grips. "M—Messalina?"

"Yes." The words seethed out of her lips, drawing stares from nearby. "Where is he?"

The nameless Senator glanced to his compatriots, nervously mumbling a nearly unintelligible apology. "A—a...apologies."

"Apologies? Why are you apologizing?" she asked, tugging so hard, he was nearly falling backwards over the bench. Other Senators in the area were coldly watching her and every one of their glances felt like betrayal.

"He's dead."

A shard of dread lodged itself in her breast. Upon the dais, Senator Pallas moved at a languid pace, carefully climbing up the steps to announce the vote.

Senator Antonius, the one in Messalina's place, smiled at her with half-lidded eyes. He was a portly man with pink cheeks and thick fingers. When his lips peeled away from his teeth, exposing them in a grimace, Heron knew they had been betrayed.

Heron lunged toward Vestalis. "We have to stop the vote! We've lost, we've lost."

She hobbled past Vestalis, but the distance was too great. Even the feeble Senator Pallas would make the dais before she got even halfway around the bowl. Heron moved to the back bench and cupped her hands around her lips.

"Stop the vote!"

Her shout echoed through the chamber which had been solemnly observing Senator Pallas, but once her words had pierced that silence, the whole floor erupted in shouts. Heron tried a second time, "Stop the vote!" but her words were drown out by the Protectors and the Wolves, all calling for the vote.

The aged Senator Pallas moved to the front of the dais and pulled a papyrus from a pouch and began to read, oblivious to the mayhem in the chamber. His words were drowned out by cacophony, but it didn't matter. Once he began, there was no way for Heron to procedurally stop the vote. Not that they would hear her.

When Senator Pallas wrapped up his speech, the vote was called for and it didn't take long for the counting to be done. An overwhelming voice vote sealed the fate of the law.

As Heron felt the strength go out of her limbs and she leaned heavily against the ivory cane, the Senate crier called out the fate of her bill.

"The law does not pass!"

SEVENTEEN

Sepharia fingered the edge of her stola with unease, the soft fabric doing nothing to reduce the tension wound into her bones. Ever since the fire and the lost vote, the domus had felt besieged.

Waiting outside the Museum of the Legion with a dozen Alexandrian guards in attendance, Sepharia drew the disapproving stares of passing citizens. By way of courier messaging, Sextus had agreed to meet her at the Museum. Before the vote, the meeting only had the purpose of information. Now, they must use it as a banner to test if Aelia's winds still blew their way.

An autumn zephyr ruffled the hem of her stola, bringing goose-flesh and shivers. She'd been waiting long enough that her guards, led by Donar, a broad-shouldered Northman with a mane of reddish hair and a bushy beard of the same color, avoided her gaze so not to further her embarrassment.

It seemed the whole city knew the repercussions of the vote. Since that day a week ago, Vestalis had stationed dozens of loyal guards at the domus. Often, when Sepharia entered a new room, the men would hush their whispering. She knew they were talking about going back to Alexandria. Vestalis had admitted as much in their discussions afterwards for they feared they would not be able to hold the city much longer without Agog's army.

But there was another reason that fed her disappointment at Sextus' absence. She'd hoped to see him once again. While she didn't entirely trust him, as no one was above suspicion in Rome and her past experiences with Ramses and Vima had been quite instructive, she found his presence intriguing.

"Your man, not coming," said Donar in halting Latin.

Sepharia smiled wistfully at Donar's choice of words. He'd used the possessive term reserved for a husband, rather than the generic term for a male.

"I'm afraid you're right," said Sepharia. "Let's go back to the domus. Heron won't welcome the news."

A strong male voice sung out behind them. "Nor will Aelia, if she finds out that we didn't meet."

As her guardians reached for their weapons, Sepharia spun around to find Sextus standing at the entrance of the Museum. With his lanky arms crossed over his chest, he smirked, the corners of his summer green eyes creased in humor.

"I didn't take you for a sneak," called Sepharia, raising a questioning eyebrow to Donar who blushed as red as his beard. "How did you get past my guardians?"

Sextus flashed a wicked grin. "Secrets, good Sepharia, should be earned, not given freely."

She gave him a playful scowl. "Or maybe you arrived well before us and had been waiting inside."

"Ha," he exclaimed. "You unmask me. A simple soldier loses to the guiles of a cunning woman every time."

"Well, then," she responded, the weights on her heart lifting. "Let us examine this Museum with great leisure."

As she moved to join him, her guard flowed with her, until he frowned and she stopped. "I'd hoped we could walk alone."

"It's a dangerous time in Rome."

Sextus nodded, while glancing at Donar. "The Museum is safe enough at this time of the morning and I will take responsibility for her safety."

Donar grumbled, "I will stay with her."

Sextus looked to her, conflicted. She could sense his reluctance and so made an offer of compromise. "What if the others stay outside, while Donar follows at a distance, so we can talk freely."

"Heron will not like," said Donar.

"I won't tell if you don't," she said.

Donar nodded and Sepharia moved to join Sextus. He put his arm out for her to take. She placed her fingertips along the inside of his wrist, caressing softly as they strolled across the marble floor.

"A strange place for a meeting," said Sextus. "Are all women of Alexandria interested in the artifacts of war?"

Sepharia tried to ignore that his breath smelled of mint, but his words at this close distance set her cheeks and lips to tingling.

"No. Only those that grew up in Heron's workshop. When I was a young girl I would help Plutarch, the workshop foreman, fire the cheiro-balistras to test them."

A surprised laugh slipped out of his lips. "And I thought my child-hood odd. When I was a young man, my mother brought me to the Senate to listen to the oratories and made me memorize the best lines."

"Do you practice the art of oratory?"

"Practice? Yes, but I'm no Cicero. I'm better at regurgitating old speeches than improvising during a debate. I'm afraid, much to my mother's dismay, that I'm a better soldier than a future Senator."

Distracted by his presence, Sepharia hadn't realized they'd moved into a new room, until she was standing before the suit of armor. The gilded breastplate displayed twin griffons and a winged cherubic face while the loincloth appeared to be golden fish scales over a crimson river.

"The inscription says this was Caesar's armor when he crossed the Rubicon," said Sextus leaning forward and squinting down.

"He was quite the titanic figure in your history," said Sepharia, hoping to draw out information.

"Most say that Caesar was the end of the Republic and the beginning of the Imperial Empire," said Sextus, frowning.

"Do you disapprove?"

His voice lowered in volume. "The Republic had been lost a century before when a man required large amounts of coinage to become a Senator. When only the rich can be a member of the Senate, the Republic is lost."

"But isn't your family wealthy?" she asked, suggesting a new topic.

"Our fortunes only came in the last fifty years, when we discovered copper and tin mines on our ancestral lands. We are the new elite and the old guard resents us," said Sextus. "Only this new found wealth has allowed us to compete for influence."

"So your ancestors disapproved of Caesar?" she asked, trying steer the conversation back to the old Emperor.

"Not at all," said Sextus, gazing wistfully at the armor, "Caesar was beloved by the people. He championed causes agreeable to the plebs. It was the entrenched interests that murdered Julius Caesar."

Sepharia pulled Sextus toward another room. She wanted to keep speaking about Caesar, but didn't know the direction to take the conversation. She suspected that Sextus wouldn't know what Heron needed.

Aelia's son could only provide background on Caesar, but not the real reason why he was murdered.

To Sepharia's surprise, she recognized the ancient armor in the next room, if only by description. It was the brass and fur armor worn by the men Vestalis chased from the domus and by the men that attacked Heron.

"Does this armor frighten you?" asked Sextus, clearly perplexed.

"Why do you ask?"

He nodded towards his wrist. "You're digging your fingernails deep."

"Apologies," she exclaimed, pulling back her fingers and leaving crescent shapes indented into his wrist. "And yes, that was the armor worn by those men that attacked us on the Day of the Dead."

Some flicker of recognition passed across his green eyes and his hand flexed as if grasping for a weapon.

"Is that why you warned me? Did you know I would be attacked?"

Sextus pulled away from her suddenly, leaving her limbs cold by way of absence. He glanced around and then leaned forward conspiratorially. "I should never have spoken about that. I was not meant to hear even what I did. I thought to say it only because..."

The implication hit her boldly in the chest, but she had little time to consider it. His fingers reached hungrily for her, but she had to know more about this Day of the Dead.

"Does it have to do with your priesthood? As flamen?"

Sextus kept glancing nervously around despite no one else being in the room. Donar standing guard at the entrance didn't count, of course.

"Not mine, but another I cannot speak of. To even say the name would invite mine and my mother's death. It was a mistake for me to speak so freely."

His green eyes had turned gray and he seemed to shrink upon himself.

"Dare to speak, I implore you," she said. "The lives of my family depend on it."

"I have told you enough, should you wish to explore further, but leave me out of it," said Sextus, his voice hissing out. A great weight hung on his brow and all traces of their earlier closeness was gone. Sextus looked upon her like a poisonous snake.

"Apologies," she said. "I didn't know."

His revulsion diminished slightly. "No, your apologies are unnecessary. It was only my foolishness to impress that let those words slip my lips."

Her response was stolen from her lips. The silence was held mutually between them.

"Tell me more about Caesar," she said.

He shook his head. "I told you everything I know. Visit the Roman Bibliotheca if you want to study our history."

She moved close, tasting his minty breath on her lips. "I want to hear it from you."

He sighed apologetically. "I should go. I've made a mess of our visit."

Before she could protest, Sextus pulled away from her. He was strides away before she darted after him and grabbed his wrist, spinning him around. She pressed her lips against his, feeling their warmth invade her mouth, tingly with mint. She felt his hesitation and then he pressed harder, smashing his body against hers, hands gripping her shoulders tightly.

All the techniques that Polyxena and her friends had taught her fled from her mind, as she dug her fingers into his tunic. If not for the public place, she might have unclasped his belt and slid her hands beneath his tunic.

An autumn breeze stolen through the marble hallways, came between them, as Sextus stumbled away. He seemed distressed by the moment, bewildered as he shook his head and staggered towards the exit.

Sepharia watched him go, conflicted on the meanings of the visit. There was no denying his lust for her as his lips crushed against her, but the troubled glance he gave her as he left the room only confirmed her fears that their last allies were slipping away.

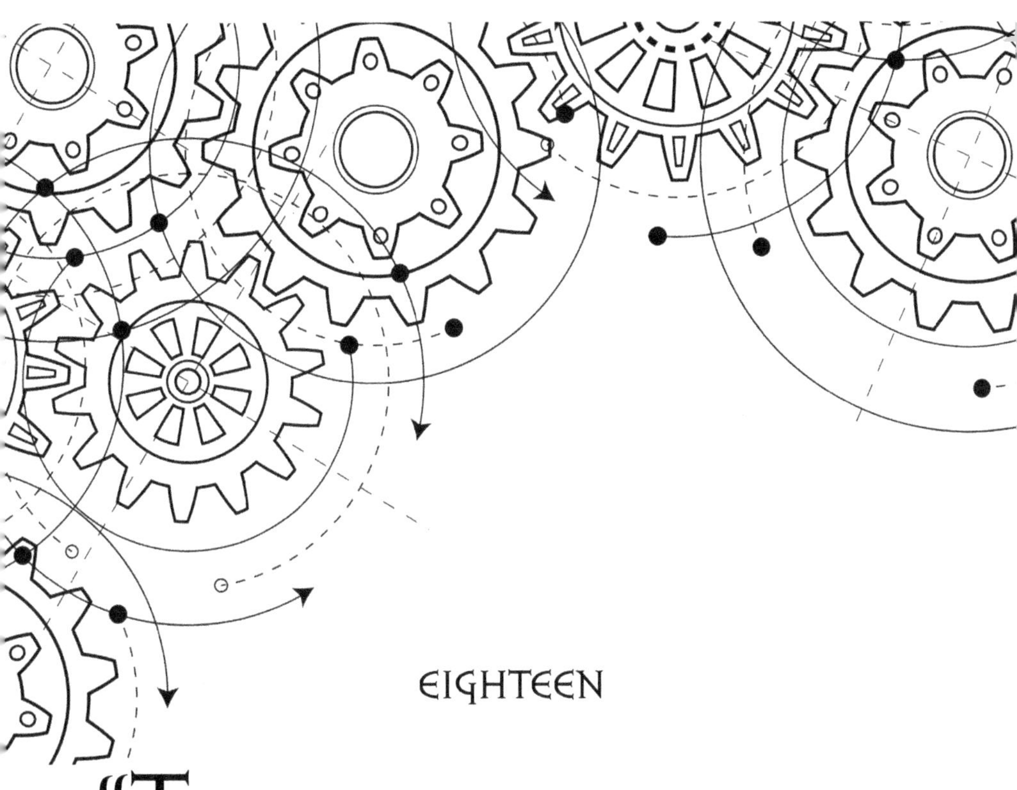

EIGHTEEN

"This infernal device born of the underworld will not work, no matter what you say!"

The foreman, Attia, threw the rolled papyrus onto the ground at her feet. His nostrils flared in distress and crimson rose to his cheeks. He was a thin, bony man with a high forehead and a sloped chin.

Heron carefully considered her words. It didn't matter she was the Consul of Rome, or the Voice of the Emperor. It didn't matter that she could, given enough time, figure out how to fix the steam wagon, or make it move along the proposed Iron Road. It didn't even matter that she had the power to have the man whipped and beaten for his insolence, for daring to raise his voice to someone far above his station. It didn't matter, because if he couldn't figure out how to fix the machine, he was useless to her.

When Heron leaned down to pick up the scroll, Attia flinched. Then she hobbled to a table and carefully cleared a space to place the drawings. She didn't have time to explain everything to Attia, and she was to receive visitors from the merchant guild this evening at the domus. Any delay would be an insult, but she couldn't leave Attia without giving more direction.

"Come here," she said as calmly as she could, patting a spot on the table next to her.

Attia hesitated and then joined her, leaving a sizable gap between the two of them as if she had an infectious disease. Behind them, the sounds of hammering resumed. When Attia had made his frustrated declaration, the workers had frozen in fear. Some Consuls might have punished them as well as the foreman.

"What are you having a problem with? Are my drawings not detailed enough?" she asked.

Rather than meet her gaze, he stared at the drawing. With a trembling hand, Attia indicated a section of the steam mechanical.

"When Vulcan heats Neptune's breath, and it travels through these pipes, its journey does not make sense. If the breath goes out here, then the how will Mercury make this piston move?" he asked.

The mystical explanation gave Heron pause. If she would have known Attia was superstitious, she would have given the drawings to a different workshop, but she'd been told he was the best in Rome and had built versions of her steam mechanical just from seeing a sketching of one.

But despite mention of the gods, Heron heard a vein of truth in his explanation. She traced the pipes with her fingertip and tried to remember why she put them in that location, but try as she might, she couldn't remember. She'd made these drawings in a haze of sleepless work.

She turned to review the assembled steam mechanical on the workshop floor, careful not to move too close to Attia. If her metal limb touched him, she was certain he'd run screaming from the building.

The monstrous steam wagon looked like a hippopotamus without legs, or a metal spider crouched on a wheeled platform. She intended the mechanically propelled wagons to travel along a guide rod while the wheels kept it from tipping over. The rod would be suspended on a metal fence and sit at the center of the wagon when it was moving.

Heron saw the error of her drawing, a pipe was directed into the wrong steam chamber, but she declined to explain. If she'd made this one mistake, she'd probably made others, or there would be unforeseen problems due to different materials, or building practices. So rather than explain what to fix, she had to get him to understand what she was trying to do, otherwise she'd be called back to the workshop again and again.

"I can see why you were recommended as the best workshop in Rome," said Heron. "A lesser foreman would have built the steam wagon to drawing, complete with my error."

Attia recoiled with a look of horror, leaving Heron confused. She hadn't expected him to react in that manner. A compliment usually left a foreman beaming with pride.

Heron restrained a sigh. It'd been a long time since she'd had to speak in this manner. Not since her last miracle with the high priest Ghet. Heron calibrated the words in her mind, careful to use the language that would be understood by Attia.

"The pace of the piston must work to Saturn's beat, thus giving Mercury the speed he needs, straight from Vulcan's..." she paused, searching for the right word, "armory? And so Neptune's breath must drive the gearing."

She wasn't sure she'd said anything intelligible, but even from the first word, Attia seemed to brighten, and by the last he was nodding.

"By Neptune's boots, I understand," said Attia.

The forced smile was held long enough for her to collect her ivory cane and leave the workshop, nodding to the workers as she hobbled out. Slumped into the back of the steam chariot, Heron rode away from the workshop, surrounded by a guard of thirty Alexandrian soldiers.

Heron was busy ticking through lists in her head like a great counting machine, confirming that all of Rome's workshops were working towards her goals, when she saw the bald priest. He was standing in the olive grove, beneath the dappled sunlight, a distance away from the road. Their eyes met and she felt a shock of recognition. Memories of a damp, dark place and scales shivered through her bones.

"Stop the chariot!"

She had to scream it a second time before her pilot stopped the vehicle, skidding it to a halt on the road and almost causing the Manticore behind to crash into her. With wide eyes her soldiers waited for direction, glancing around to make sure there were no threats incoming.

Once the dust had settled, Heron had a horrible thought. That the bald priest had been a mirage. But when she remembered that the last time she'd seen him, he'd had a head full of dark, listless hair, that he had to be real. He'd been waiting for her, too.

"Stay here," she told the soldiers. "I saw something I must attend to in the olive grove."

"But Vestalis gave us strict instructions to stay with you at all times," said their commander, an Egyptian with a strong jaw.

"You may follow at a distance, but not too close. I think someone wants to speak to me and I'm afraid your presence would scare him away," she said.

The commander looked boldly into the grove. "Then let us retrieve him with force and you can speak to him at your leisure."

Left without an answer, Heron stared at the grove, wondering why she did not give the command to retrieve Lysimachus, the priest of Sobek, the one who had taken her hand from her. She found herself staring at her brass arm, remembering that Lysimachus was also missing a hand.

"He won't speak that way," she replied, knowing it for truth. "I should get moving before he decides to leave."

"Consul Heron, know that Vestalis has threatened me with decimation if I fail in protecting you," said the commander.

"And I'll have you fed to a Nile crocodile if you don't let me speak to this man alone." The venomous words came as a surprise to even Heron. A darkness cultivated by the months she spent in Lysimachus' temple.

Warily, the commander backed away, giving a disappointed bow. She mentally sighed, wishing she'd treated the man better. He was just trying to do his job, but she did not let herself linger long on these thoughts, for Lysimachus was a dangerous man. Dangerous enough, that as she limped toward him, using her ivory cane to navigate the uneven ground beneath the olive trees, she wondered why she did not just have him killed.

But that was an easy answer. Killing him would acknowledge the darkness he'd stirred into her soul. And it would prove the argument Lysimachus made under the temple, that it was Sobek that made her and provided inspiration for her inventions.

She caught a glimpse of his white robe between the gnarled trunks. Behind her, the soldiers waited at the edge of the road, if she went much further, they wouldn't be able to see her because of the curve of the hill. Resigned to follow Lysimachus, Heron pressed on.

Deeper into the grove, the dusty rich scents of the trees created an otherworldly ether, as the twisted trunks with silvery green leaves and tart fruits beckoned her onward. Despite the afternoon sun, she walked in shadow, as this was an older grove, less tended, with wide canopies that connected the tops of the rows.

His white robes moved between the trees ahead, tantalizingly near, but yet far. She sensed her soldiers nearby, but not close enough to reach her before Lysimachus could, if he turned and advanced on her. Heron pulled the blade halfway out of the cane as a comfort that she was not completely defenseless.

The hill sloped upward and Heron followed, using the occasional flashes of white to follow. The distance she'd gone into the grove began to worry her, but not enough to make her turn around. Though if he left the grove, she would go back, which was soon, as the hill ended in rough terrain, a rocky cliff that she couldn't climb without difficulty.

Standing in an eerie calm at the base of the chalky stone wall, Heron looked around for her former torturer. The cliff bathed her in shadow, sending a shiver through her spine. When she could not find him, she pulled her blade.

"You need not fear me," said a voice from above.

Lysimachus stood on the edge of the cliff, arms hanging at his sides, with one ending in a stump. His calm demeanor bothered Heron as if he felt completely in control of the situation.

"Our history suggests otherwise, Alabarch."

She held up her mechanical arm, but regretted it when a fevering grin appeared on his lips.

"That man is long gone. Scrubbed from the earth by my master's former priests. And now you are left with a gift from Sobek. The crocodile god shines his light on you," said Lysimachus.

"Your god did nothing. It was you who took my hand. Only a fool believes his destruction can create," she spat.

Lysimachus bowed. "Apologies, O' Broken One. I know we two see things differently, but eventually you will come around to see the wisdom of Sobek."

"What do you want?" asked Heron, growing annoyed. "My soldiers wait just beyond those trees. One yell and I can have them capture you and we can speak at our leisure about these things."

"Oh, I would be most pleased to speak with them. What would they say if they knew that their Consul was a woman?"

Her stomach clenched. Heron glanced behind her to make sure the soldiers weren't close enough to hear. She couldn't see them, but that didn't mean anything.

"Yes," said Lysimachus. "Your secret is safe with me. Man or woman, if Sobek has decided to make you his vessel, then I will not argue."

"What do you want?" she asked, cringing at her own timid voice. In coming to confront Lysimachus, she'd hoped to silence the nightmares that woke her in the middle of the night sometimes, dreams of the pit beneath the temple of Sobek and the horrors inflicted on her there, but her heart made raucous drum beats in her chest.

"The selfish me, the part that is still proud Lysimachus, and not the humble priest of Sobek, wants to see you dead." He gave her a tooth-filled smile. "But my creator has other designs on you. Things he has told me in the darkness. He sent me to Rome to protect you, for while you live, Sobek's vision can come to pass."

Heron grew angry at her own fear. "Tell me what you must and be gone with you. I grow tired of this game."

Lysimachus chuckled. "Would you be so quick to rid of me if you knew I had twice stopped assassins from preying on your daughter?"

"Curse you," she said. "Leave her alone."

"I'm afraid, I cannot. Sobek has plans for her, too, you see. He tells me much in my dreams," said Lysimachus.

"Your dreams mean nothing," responded Heron.

"I can see you do not believe that. If you'd been listening, you would remember that he's been speaking to you for quite some time. Showing you the path on which he wishes you to tread, the path that will change the world. That is why he sent me to Rome, to protect you and your daughter, to creep amid the mud and snap off the limbs of those foolish enough to attack you. But I am only one man, and so I can only do so much, so I knew it was time we met, so I can give you Sobek's wisdom revealed in the dark."

Heron could not bring herself to speak, instead gripping the ivory cane tightly, the blade pointing limply at the earth.

When Lysimachus spoke, his words fell upon her like ash. "Beware the dead, *Michanikos*, Cerberus hunts you."

Heron's forehead warred into a knot. "What does that mean?" she asked, looking up, but only pale fronds bobbed with the eddies of passage. Lysimachus was gone.

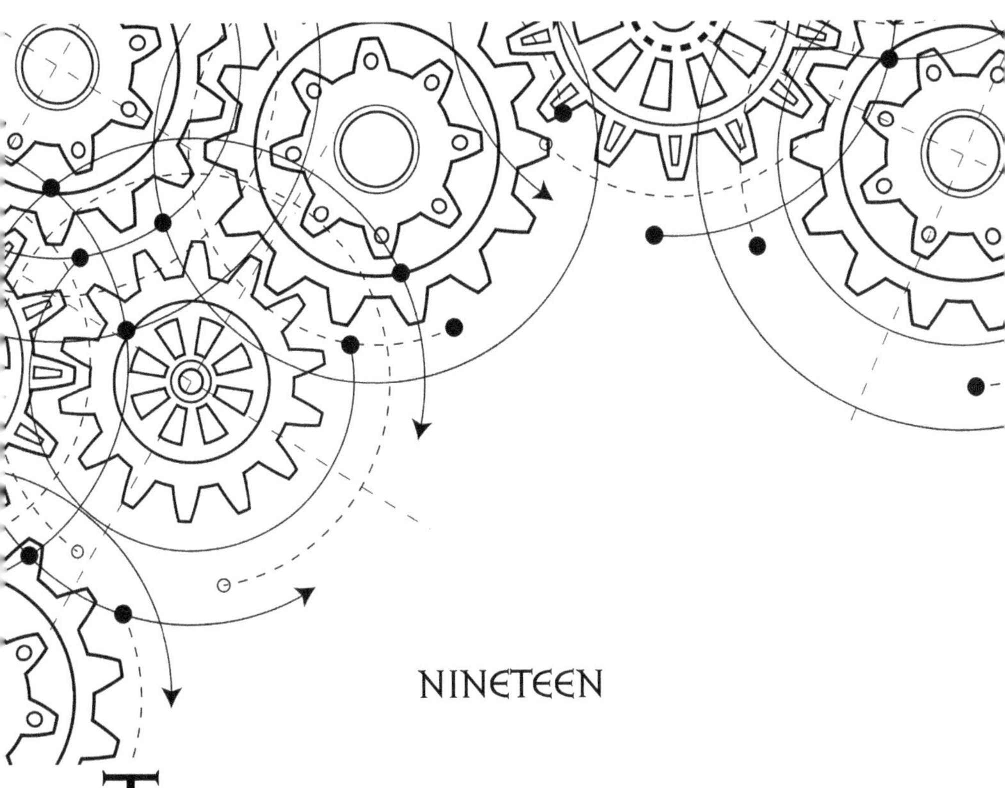

NINETEEN

The wig fit snuggly around the crown of her head, leaving a curtain of dark hair hanging at the edge of her vision. Sepharia had picked a curly mop of hair, so it might hide her blonde tresses beneath. Without a polished mirror, Sepharia did the best she could to fix the wig, so that she appeared to be a man of small stature. The tunic she wore was one from the workshop and the stamped leather wrist guards were the latest fashion in Rome.

With a carryall over her shoulder, Sepharia moved to the courtyard of the domus, where Heron was entertaining a large delegation from the merchant's guild. She needed to avoid the servants, especially Livia, who would surely recognize her in the disguise. Keeping an eye over her shoulder, Sepharia bumped into a man coming around the other way.

"Apologies," Sepharia muttered, trying to remember to keep her voice low.

"No need," said the merchant, a scowl hung on his lips, clearly intended for the meeting still going in the courtyard. "This farce nears an end."

He appeared to be thoroughly Roman, prominent nose, keen eyes, and strong jaw. He might have been called handsome except for the purple blotch of skin that went from his right eye down to his neck.

"Can you relate the short of it?" asked Sepharia. "I had some difficulties with my meal earlier and missed most of the meeting."

The merchant stared at her as if he were trying to figure out if she belonged. The moment before she thought she'd have to escape the man or be discovered as an imposter, his brow softened and he continued speaking, "This metal man, he thinks we are gullible Alexandrians, ready to believe his *miracles* will help us. This Iron Road is nothing but a ploy to steal our business. I don't care how much faster these steam wagons might go on the Iron Road. If we don't have control over our caravans, we might as well be enslaved."

Sepharia opened her mouth to explain that the steam wagons would be designed to be used on the Iron Road and off, but then she remembered she wasn't supposed to know this, having come late. She glanced over the merchant's shoulder to see a sea of faces similarly cast in disagreement.

"I miss the old Empire," said Sepharia in a conspiratorial voice.

"Truer words were never spoken," said the merchant, matching her volume.

Leaning in close, the man's perfume made her nose twitch.

"While I was no supporter of Claudius," he continued, "at least he didn't interfere in our business. Shame that Mars abandoned him in the war against the barbarian and his metal man."

Sepharia was saved from having to respond, when the mass of merchants moved like a herd towards them. Shuffling out of the domus with the rest of them, Sepharia kept her head down. Once on the street, she walked briskly in a southern direction. She wanted to make Caelian Hill by nightfall.

After her meeting with Sextus, she did as he suggested and went to the Roman Bibliotheca for research. The library had little information about the Day of the Dead, and she found no mention of *mundus patet*. So she plowed into the religions of Rome, specifically those associated with the nobles and the powerful.

As Sextus had indicated, the priesthood was one of the many paths to power in Rome. Julius Caesar, himself, had been a Pontifex Maximus, or the high priest of the College of Pontiffs, the most important state religion of the Roman Empire. They served as keepers of important rituals and advisors to the leaders of the Empire.

Nothing in any of the texts tied these religions to the Day of the Dead, but that's not why she was researching them. If Sextus had heard about the attack through the priesthood, then someone within the ranks was suspect.

Sextus was a member of the Sacris Faciundus, the keepers of the Sibylline Books, which were ancient texts from the early founding of the Roman state, even before the Republic, that were consulted in difficult times of upheaval. The other two major priesthoods were the Augures, in charge of reading the signs of the gods, and the Septemviri Epulones, the priests in charge of public feasts. Either of the four could house their enemies, and each of them had the means to influence the Senate using the artifices of their priesthood.

As Sepharia took long strides toward Caelian Hill, keeping an eye out for the slim possibility of being followed, she found herself longing for the simplicity of the Alexandrian temples. The priests of those religions were not members of the elite, nor did they control the levers of power within the government. There, they only performed expensive tricks to encourage coin from the masses.

The problem, she realized, was that when power was hidden behind a religion, it was difficult to see how or why things worked. And maybe this was what Heron needed to know about Caesar. But that also didn't make sense, because Caesar had been a part of the priesthood. Unless he hadn't been a member of the right college. The Pontifex Maximus was supposed to be the most powerful of the four, in charge of all priestly colleges, both major and minor, but other secretive organizations had been hinted at in the texts. It could be that he was not a member, or that he'd run afoul of them during his rise to power. But all this was speculation, as she had no facts to go on, other than a few tenuous phrases that led to no further insights.

Sepharia paused at a street corner while a steam barge chugged past, coughing black smoke from its brass pipes. The vehicle was hauling a pair of wolf automatas. It seemed that if they stayed in Rome much longer, the city would resemble Alexandria, as every important building in the city would display one of her father's miracle machines.

She waved away the sulfurous smoke drifting onto her. The coal used here north of the Mediterranean seemed to have more odor than what they procured in Alexandria.

Joining a crowd of craftsmen leaving their respective halls, Sepharia let their presence act as a shield, so that she might further consider her charge, without having to be alert. The men carried woven bags with well-worn wooden handles sticking from them and they chatted merrily amongst themselves, smiles creasing their faces as they marched home-ward. Sepharia stayed with them until the crowd dissolved, leaving her exposed to the wind that had whipped itself up as the sun dipped toward the horizon, casting long shadows, and bringing an autumn chill.

Sepharia worried that her own experiences with the Cult of Ur might influence her negatively. It was easy to see a hidden force behind the attacks, especially when the religions of the state created a curtain of mistrust. The real truth was probably the obvious answer: that Silius and his Wolves had sent the assassins, using the Day of the Dead as cover.

But without further clues, Sepharia decided she needed more first-hand knowledge of these priesthoods. So without telling her father, she decided she would investigate the Sacris Faciundus, the priesthood Sextus was a member of, in hopes of furthering her knowledge.

Caelian Hill, the location of the college of Sacris Faciundus, had once been a vibrant part of the city. It still housed museums and shops, but mostly it consisted of ancient estates from noble families. While the marbles of Palatine Hill shone brightly in the sun, the stoneworks on Caelian Hill draped themselves in thick carpets of ivy and hid behind gnarled olive trees as wide as a chariot and as old as the Empire.

With day only a nimbus on the horizon, Sepharia climbed the winding avenue that brought her to the college of Sacris Faciundus. As the temperature dipped, Sepharia pulled a dark woolen cloak from her carryall. She took a wide circuitous route around the three story college, looking for guards or priests. Flickers of lamplight shown through the open windows of the upper floors, but otherwise, the place seemed unattended.

Sepharia carefully climbed over the wrought iron fence, making her way onto the grounds. Keeping to the shadows she reached a side door with a key hole and crouched down to examine the lock.

While she'd never broken into an unfamiliar lock, Sepharia had on many occasions designed and built locks for her father, and so understood the concept, which wasn't particularly difficult. A key had to trip tumblers inside the key hole, thus removing the bolt from the door.

After selecting a couple of tools from her carryall, Sepharia pushed them into the hole and felt around until she found the correct tumblers. With a deft turn of her wrist, the lock popped and the door swung open a hair.

The ease at which she'd bypassed the lock startled her. She'd expected it to be more difficult. Either the lock was exceptionally simple, or her experience with delicate tools and knowledge of lock making made her an accidental expert.

Sepharia crept into the pitch black building, making measured steps and keeping her hands out in front of her. The heavy curtains on the windows made seeing difficult. Even after she let her eyes adjust, only the outlines of large objects like scroll shelves could be seen.

Realizing the futility of stumbling around in the darkness, Sepharia made for the stairs in search of a lantern or candle. She didn't quite know what she was looking for, but knew she would need light to find it.

The sound of footsteps growing louder froze Sepharia. A dim, orangish light filled the stairway and Sepharia used that precious luminance to find a place to hide. She stood in a wide room filled with couches and divans. A few shelves were stacked with scrolls and the occasional bark bound book. It appeared to be a meeting room and Sepharia could imagine it filled with the *flamens* in their strange conical hats, drinking wine and trading influence.

There seemed to be no obvious places to jam herself into and no time left to sprint from the room without being seen. Whoever was coming down the stairs would be in the room in moments.

In a fit of haste, Sepharia shoved herself into a nook between a sturdy scroll shelf and the etched marble fireplace that commanded one side of the room. She pulled the cloak around her face and body, hiding as much as she could, minus a thin opening to see out. There wasn't much room, even for her slender figure, and the carved rump of a stone pegasus from the mantle dug into her back.

The priest, a heavy set man with rosy cheeks, entered the room cradling an open book in one hand and a gilded lamp in the other. The lamp was made in the shape of a hippopotamus and the light flickered across the priest's face, who was too busy reading from the book to notice her. Sepharia recognized the priest immediately, Senator Antonius, the Protector she'd antagonized at the party and the one who'd taken Messalina's place upon his death.

Antonius seemed enraptured by the text in his grip, lips moving rapidly but without sound. He glanced up once and upon seeing his location in the room, made for a shelf one over from Sepharia's hiding spot.

She held her breath as the lamp's circle of light fell upon her. Antonius slapped his book closed and shoved it into a hole on the shelf, before beginning a search for his next book. He walked his fingers across the shelves, gaze flitting from location to location. He moved to the shelf Sepharia was hiding behind. He was standing so close, she could smell the wine on his breath and see the way the conical hat sat crookedly on his round head. Antonius lingered before the shelf, pulling a scroll out and briefly digesting its contents before pushing it back onto the rack. He repeated this a half dozen times, each time deciding the scroll was not the one he wanted. Each time he pushed one back in, Sepharia expected him to reach for a scroll right next to her head and in doing so, discovering her. She prepared herself to knock the lamp from his hands and sprint for the door should the need occur.

Antonius pulled another from the shelf, this time a bark bound book, and laid it open against the flat surface. As he read, his lips moved and faint words slipped from them. Sepharia closed her eyes and tried to will the man away. Every second he stayed, she was convinced he'd find her.

Trembling with anticipation, Sepharia jumped when something sharp bit into her leg. It was like a row of needles was pushing themselves into her calf. She choked on the curses she wanted to let loose.

Looking down without moving her hood, she found the source of her agony. A tabby feline was stretching its claws into her leg. It released them and made a *mrrowr* noise before rubbing its side against Sepharia leg in repeating circular motions.

Sepharia thanked the gods that Antonius was so engrossed by his book that he hadn't noticed her slight movement, or the unwanted attentions of the feline at her feet. She wanted to kick the cat away, but she couldn't dare with the priest so close.

Ignored, the cat moved to Antonius and repeated the ritual, first putting its claws into his leg in a full-bodied stretch and then rubbing past his thick calves with a pitiful *mrrowr*.

Still cradling the book in his meaty hand, Antonius crouched onto his heels and ran his hand across the back of the feline. "Little Lucius, are you hungry again? I already fed you some of my *garum*. Shall we go up and find you something more substantial? I could use a treat, myself."

Antonius shoved the book he'd been reading back into its home and made for the stairs with the feline bounding behind. Once the light had fled the room, Sepharia moved to the shelf and grabbed the book Antonius had been reading for later examination. She shoved it into her carryall and moved to the bottom of the stairs.

Creeping upward, one step at a time, she stayed vigilant, preparing to flee if necessary. The second level, she found, was made up of many smaller rooms. Antonius' light had gone in a different direction, but there was enough moonlight coming in through the windows for Sepharia to move around without fear of knocking anything over.

Through a long hallway, Sepharia saw a lamp indicating the presence of another priest. She stationed herself right outside the room, finding it filled with colorful robes and headdresses. The priest in the room was working on something at a table. Sepharia was about to leave when she saw the glow of a lamp covering the entrance to the hallway. Trapped, Sepharia slipped into the room ahead and hid behind a shelf containing various sized scepters with what appeared to be fake jewels glued on.

Antonius appeared in the room, munching on a piece of hard bread with a pungent substance smeared across it. "Ave, Sextus, working late will certainly impress the high priest."

"Ave, Senator Antonius, while the crowd values glory and entertainment, the high priest values industriousness, though I suppose if I were better at these tasks, I might have been done before evening," said Sextus.

Sepharia shouldn't have been surprised to find Sextus at the college, given that he was a priest. And based on the exchange, it appeared he was new to the position. She stood on her toes to get a better view, but the shelves were positioned in a way that she could only see the back of Antonius' broad back.

"What keeps you here this late?" asked Sextus.

"A bit of reading," replied Antonius. "Though I'm afraid my eyes cannot take another word. I think I'll take my leave and retire to my estate."

"May your sleep be restful," said Sextus.

Antonius cleared his throat. "Please pass along to your mother that I'm considering her offer. It's hard to turn down, considering the circumstances, though I feel I'd be giving up too much."

"She will be pleased," said Sextus.

Antonius left and Sepharia was confronted with her concerns. Inside the Senate, it seemed the factions were furious foes, but within the confines of the college, they turned agreeable. Sepharia suspected the priesthoods had more to do with the power structure of Rome than she'd first considered.

She snuck out the way she'd come in and made it back to the street without incident. The walk back to the domus would take a couple of hours, but it would give her time to consider the exchange between Sextus and Antonius. It appeared there were other alliances between the various factions, making their task of wrangling the Senate even more complicated. And while she didn't find anything of note about Caesar -

assuming the book she'd stolen would bear no fruit - she'd learned a little bit more about the politics of Rome and that her first instinct not to trust Sextus had been correct. She just wished she'd learned this before she'd kissed him.

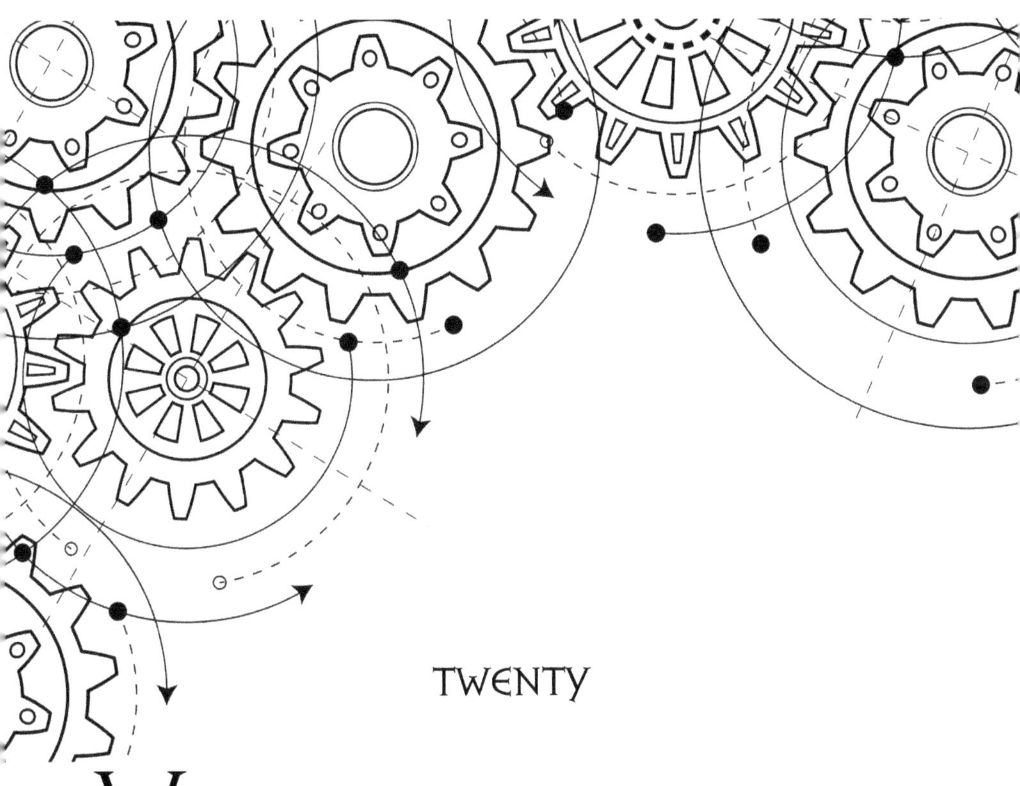

TWENTY

When Heron arrived at the workshop, the same one she'd attended only two days before, she found Tiberius waiting outside with his arms crossed and a smirk on his lips that would rival the gods. He was dressed in finery, silken tunic and gold etched belt, while still appearing to be a soldier, if that soldier was performing a play rather than fighting a war. She climbed down from the chariot carefully, but once on solid ground, marched over to Tiberius, stabbing the ground with her ivory cane at each step.

"What manner of interference is this, Legate?" Heron barked. It would be so easy to reach out and choke him with her mechanical hand.

"Apologies, Consul Heron. The needs of the Empire dictate a change in direction for this humble workshop," said Tiberius.

"Change in direction? What do you speak of?" she asked, while craning her head to find Attia, the foreman. There was no sign of him, nor the steam mechanical to be used on the Iron Road that had been in the middle of construction the last time she'd visited. Instead, wooden scaffolding formed around a steel assembly that looked similar to her cheirobalistras, except there was no slot for a javelin and there were two spring mechanisms instead of one.

"This workshop was given contracts by the Senate for equipment to help with the war effort versus the traitor Magnus," said Tiberius.

"But I need them to be working on the Iron Road. And I already have contracts with the workshop. How can this supersede them?"

"Apologies," he said without a trace of regret, "but the Senate laws dictate that contracts may be voided in a time of war, prioritizing the war effort over useless and vain constructs like the Iron Road or these silly automatas that you're placing all over Rome."

Heron leaned heavily on her cane. She'd been outmaneuvered by Silius once again. This change would weaken the few allies she had left, if she even had those allies from the start.

"I assume the lion's share of the contracts for raw materials will go to Silius," said Heron.

"Oh no," said Tiberius, relishing his role as spokesman, "Silius is a generous man and has spread this wealth around. He wants everyone to benefit from the war effort, rather than just a few families."

The barb was meant for her and the way they'd distributed the contracts to Aelia's supporters. Some had gone to those within the Protectors, but she thought the concessions for keeping Roman laws would have swayed them more. Either Antonius was a more fervorous spokesman than the rest of his faction, or she underestimated the lure of wealth. Probably both.

"I assume there were votes on these new contracts," she said, regretting her frequent absence from the Senate.

"Of course," said Tiberius, holding a wounded hand to his heart. "We wouldn't dare pass rules without consulting the representatives of the people. And we were rewarded for our patience, as the bills passed almost unanimously."

Heron stared at the Legate in his silken tunic and gold etched belt. Her nose caught a hint of his perfume, a sickening sweet scent; and she almost swore he had a bit of rouge on his cheeks. He was exactly the type of soldier the commoners of Rome cheered, assuming they did not get too close.

She looked to her own shabby tunic, smeared with ink stains along the hem. Then she moved her gaze to the dingy mechanical hand, marked with scars from bumping unceremoniously into everything she passed. Even as she balanced herself standing, the knee joint wheezed and clicked like an old man stumbling up a tower. Despite their initial curiosity, she knew that she was everything the people wouldn't love. Even the barbarian Agog, a foreigner, would draw more adoration from the people of Rome because they admired his warrior ways. While she was a trick and a miracle made flesh, illusions did not rule Empires.

If they were somehow overthrown, Heron could imagine the people choosing Tiberius as Emperor rather than Silius, because he was too old, and he preferred to rule from behind the scenes.

"How did Senator Pallas vote?" she asked eventually.

"Don't worry, Consul Heron, you have a few loyal dogs left in your kennel. Though it's certainly possible Senator Pallas just got confused. He'll soon rival the stars in age. Pretty soon that wife of his will have to find a new husband, maybe even one quite younger and with many more prospects."

Despite the fact that Tiberius was completely unarmed and she had a guard of twenty Alexandrian soldiers and two Manticores behind her, Heron felt completely neutralized. She knew that even if she pulled her hidden blade and tried to shove it into his heart, he would somehow survive or turn the blade on her, and claim appropriately, that it was self-defense.

"Good Tiberius," she said after much thought, "give my apologies to Senator Silius when you see him next, which I assume will be soon by the tugging of that leash on your neck."

Tiberius gave her a cold smile. "And what shall I apologize for on your behalf?"

"For being as stubborn as Athena. As I have learned in the workshop, each failure is not a failure, but only instructs us to the possible solution."

"And what if your failure ends in death?" he asked.

"Then may Rome burn to the ground."

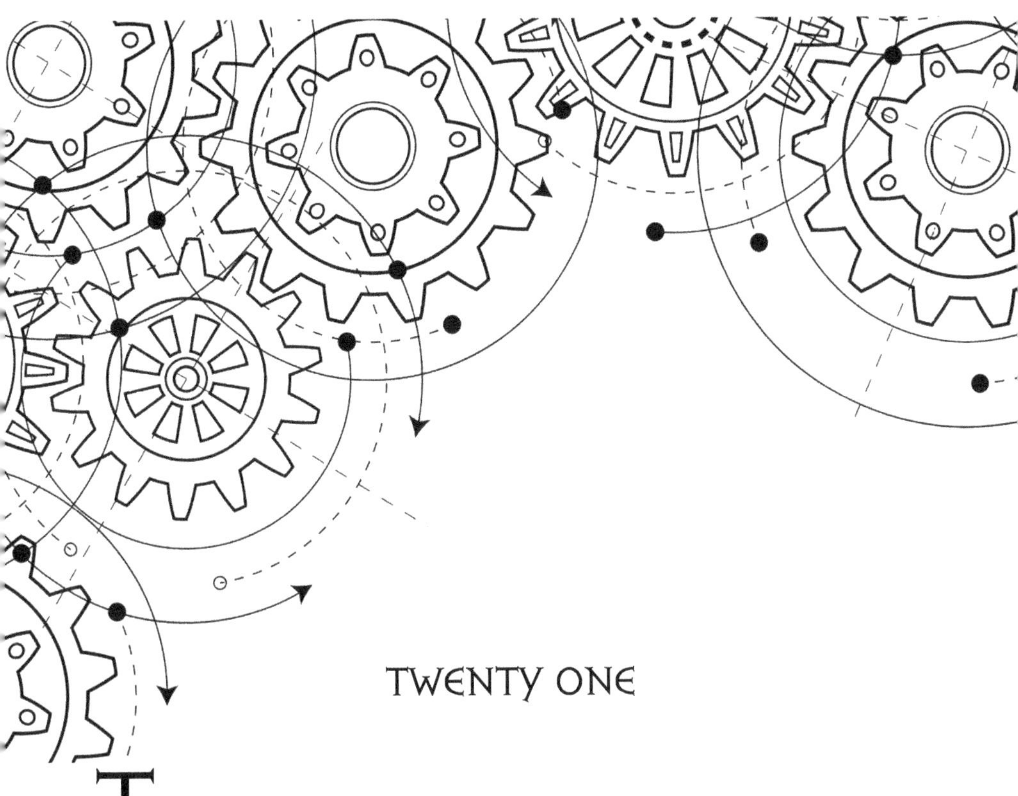

TWENTY ONE

Tiberius lounged in his personal bath, gazing upon the painting he'd commissioned after returning from Rome. As steam curled around his glistening body, he tilted his head, admiring the way the artist had added the symbols of Venus and Mars to his likeness. In the tree on the hill, a lone sparrow indicating Venus' favor looked on, while a wolf for Mars sat at his sandaled feet.

While the public baths provided him with an opportunity to interact with the lesser peoples of the city and listen to their trials and foibles, Tiberius enjoyed quiet solitude almost as much. His bath house was tiled from floor to ceiling, paying homage to the god Neptune. At the bottom of the wide bath, a mosaic depicted the watery god riding a pair of hippocamps across an emerald sea.

He let his lips caress the goblet, spilling ripe honeyed wine into his waiting mouth. He'd been saving the vintage for a special occasion and this one seemed special enough. Everything Senator Silius said would happen had happened. The Alexandrians were all but neutralized and with the instructions he'd just given to his favorite problem solver, their enemies would be wiped from the stage, being the poor players they were.

And though Silius had never promised it directly, Tiberius thought there might be a considerable reward for his part in the game, especially this last bit that kept Silius' hands clean. Maybe even a chance to replace Claudius as the Emperor (and he only thought of Claudius as the last Emperor, because he did not consider the barbarian Agog to be a credible successor.) And with the inventions of the traitor Heron, the Roman Empire would be reborn. They would find no enemies worthy enough to defy them, especially with the Parthians still in turmoil from the loss of their young King.

With the spark powder and steam chariots, the Roman Empire would stretch as far east as the Indus River, as far south as the Kushites, and as far north as the barbarians. He, Tiberius the Great, would rule an Empire larger than anything even Alexander the Macedonian had conceived.

Tiberius drained the goblet and called out to the slave girl who should have been waiting by his bath, ready to refill his cup.

"Quinallia! Attend me, girl. I need more drink and your mouth," he said, sitting up and cupping his hand around his hardening cock.

Before he could call out a second time, a rope slipped around his neck and was pulled tight. His goblet clattered to the tile, bouncing and spinning, making a raucous noise that should have brought his slaves running.

Tiberius flailed against the rope, trying to turn and face his assailant, but a heavy pole was pressed against his neck and the rope kept him from drawing breath. Water fled the bath as he kicked and struggled. A cry for help was strangled into a gurgle. Spots formed in his vision and as the darkness closed in, he could not figure why none of the servants or guards of his domus had not come to his rescue.

He clawed at the rope, but it was pulled too tight, so in an attempt to pull the catcher's noose from his attacker's hands, Tiberius charged forward through the bath regardless of the pressure on his neck. He made it two steps before he was yanked backwards. It felt like his throat had been crushed and the spots began to connect while the heavy drumbeats of his heart played loudly in his ears.

Tiberius slapped at the water, wishing he had just one breath to offer his attacker anything in return for his life. This one thought formed a loop in his head until the spots claimed his consciousness for their own.

#

Tiberius woke to a throbbing headache and a dull ache in his throat. It felt like an apple had been lodged there and each breath had to wheeze past the obstruction.

He came to enough to realize he was sitting in his library, strapped to the chair he used for writing letters, except it had been dragged to the middle of the room. A moldy rag had been shoved in his mouth and bound there with a thin string. His wrists and feet were bound by more ropes, tight enough he could hardly flex a muscle. Whoever had restrained him, knew their craft.

He also realized he was naked and his cock was surprisingly semi-hard. This seemed to disturb him more than the other aspects of his bondage. He'd never been shy about his body in the baths, but felt helpless and his cock seemed ready to embarrass him when he needed to be ready to negotiate his release. For that had to be the reason he had not been murdered while unconscious. An assassin would have killed him already, but as a ransom, he was worth a hefty sum. He would pay anything to get out of this alive.

Turning his head was difficult. Bunched up cloth had been bound around his neck, so he could only move slightly to the left or right. A sudden and irresistible fit of coughing turned his whole body to an agony and drool leaked past the earthy rag in his mouth and dribbled onto his chin.

What distressed him more than the bondage, or his erectness, or even the pain, was that he was still in his domus. What had happened to his guards or his slaves? Had they been killed? Or had they revolted and hired an assassin to enact their revenge? If so, though it would be little solace to his dead body, a hundred slaves would be killed in Rome for each one of his that had joined this rebellion.

Tiberius froze when he heard a footfall. His captor approached from the left and Tiberius strained against the bindings to see in that direction, despite the pounding headache.

The bald man with sallow skin surprised him when he walked into view. Especially when Tiberius noted the stump at the end of the bald man's arm. He wore priestly robes and had black, beady eyes like a crow.

"For a big man," said the priest, "you were surprisingly easy prey. I've caught some half your size that gave twice the fight."

Tiberius struggled against the ropes, throwing his frustration into a fleetingly meaningful frenzy. The priest watched him interestedly like a cat observing an injured mouse. Tiberius could not sustain his rage, so he allowed himself to relax, defying the priest's gaze with his own.

"I've given dogs to He Who Dwelleth Amid Terrors like you," said the priest. "They growl and bear their fangs, trying to make me believe. But believe, I do not. And in the end, when the waters rise toward them, eyes full of teeth, they succumb and whimper and go willingly to their grave."

The priest retrieved a bag from the table and dumped it onto the floor. Knives and other sinister implements clattered onto the marble in a pile. Tiberius found he could not keep his eyes from the barbed hook that had landed near his right foot.

The priest leaned into his vision. "I see your eyes and know what you are thinking. You are wondering, who is this man? Why has he come here? These thoughts should be banished from your mind. I am just a humble priest to the crocodile god and it is not me who you should be thinking about."

Mention of the crocodile god brought bile to Tiberius' throat. He gave his coin freely to the gods of Rome, and sometimes those of Egypt. But to the one called Sobek, he gave nothing. To him, Sobek was a vile pretender and his priests, worshipers of pain and death.

"What is that?" asked the priest with glee. "What do I see in those eyes? Ah yes, you have heard of Sobek. You know him. I smell your fear of him, but you do not respect him, I see. I'm afraid today we must change how you think about He Who Dwelleth Amid Terrors. Yes, today you will believe."

Despite all efforts otherwise, Tiberius' gaze drifted to the barbed hook near his feet. The handle of the tool appeared to be quite old, the carving of a crocodile smoothed with time. The black metal seemed imbued with the blood it must surely have letted. The priest picked up the tool and held it before Tiberius' eyes. It seemed there was nothing else in the world than this barbed hook.

"My Lord Sobek has your attention, I see. Now, all I ask, is that you tell me the truth. When you tell me lies, I will use his hook," said the priest. "Nod and tell me you understand."

Tiberius nodded vigorously.

"I am going to remove the gag from your mouth. When I do so, it is only so that you may reveal what it is I want to know. If you say anything else, I will use the hook. Nod again."

Tiberius nodded.

"Well, then," said the priest and released the string holding the restraint with one deft pull of the knot. Then he tugged the cloth from

Tiberius' mouth and he gagged as the cloth tickled the back of his throat, unraveling on its way out.

The priest let him cough a few times and before the priest could speak, Tiberius wheezed out, "I'll pay you anything, give you anything, just—"

The rag was stuffed back in and the hook was held before his eyes. The priest let him watch as he moved the tip to his chest, right above the nipple and pushed it into the skin. Like a bolt of lightning had passed through him, Tiberius tensed and strained against the ropes, screaming muffled prayers to the gods until the priest removed the hook.

When it was out, it glistened with dark fluid. Warm blood ran down his chest and into his pubic hair. Before he could bring his gaze back up, the priest grabbed Tiberius' cock and squeezed.

"Next time you dare to beg or offer me *anything*, besides what I ask for, I'm putting the hook here."

Tiberius swallowed and nodded vigorously again. The priest retrieved a chair and sat down across from him with the bloody hook resting on his lap. He leaned forward and pulled the gag from Tiberius' mouth.

"Now," said the priest as if the two of them were sitting down for a nice chat over pickled olives and spiced wine, "what I wish to know is this: what are your plans for Heron and her—" The priest smiled. "—his daughter? And tell me nothing but the truth."

"I—I...I," stuttered Tiberius.

The priest held up the hook. "My Lord Sobek knows many paths to pain and has taught me many of them. We can explore the extent of my knowledge for as long as you're willing to resist."

Tiberius glanced to the doorway, wishing for one of his guards to come bursting in to save him. The priest looked to the door and tittered.

"Oh, you don't have to worry about them. My Lord Sobek has

already taken their offerings."

The priest's grin made Tiberius slump against the ropes.

"Now, tell me what you know. Everything."

Tiberius took a deep and trembling breath. "They will be poisoned tonight. One of the servants will put the poison in their dinner. If all goes well, it will kill them both."

Letting the truth out released a weight from Tiberius' shoulders. A weight he didn't even know he had until the words had left his lips. He took a second breath and found his headache had lessened.

The priest seemed to be considering his words and then after coming to some internal conclusion, nodded and smiled. Maybe the priest would leave him, or at least go out of the domus to warn the Alexandrians, giving him enough time so he might escape. The priest had to be an agent of Alexandria, sent by Vestalis. Silius had warned Tiberius that Vestalis was the one to be wary of, but once Heron and his daughter had been eliminated, his death would be simple.

Because the priest wasn't moving, and to help spur him into action, Tiberius added, "It should be happening as we speak, the poisoning, that is. That's why I'd gone to take a bath, to celebrate our victory."

When the priest didn't move, Tiberius' heart skipped a beat. And when the priest smiled, Tiberius shrunk against the ropes. And when the priest lifted the metal hook, Tiberius prepared to beg.

The priest shoved the rag back in and stood triumphantly over Tiberius. The pink, cracked stump was caressed across the curve of the hook.

"My Lord Sobek thanks you for your offering and for your part in this great test." The priest's eyes were alight with inner flame. "For now I know that tonight is the test of all tests, and should the Broken One survive, then I will know that all he has shown me will come true. That a new Empire, not Roman and not Alexandrian, will rise up and cover the world. An Empire devoted to my Lord Sobek."

The priest set the hook against the tender flesh above Tiberius' other nipple.

"But first we must finish with your offering."

He pushed the hook in.

TWENTY TWO

"I don't think they're going to come," said Sepharia, looking out from the entrance of the domus. The street was empty except for a merchant on his wagon passing by, snapping his reins and calling softly to his lead mount. The leaves had fallen from the olive trees along the street and she could smell the fires burning near the Forum for the Festival of Ceres.

Heron replied from the atrium. "If Aelia doesn't come then we'll know we're friendless."

Sepharia thought about Sextus' lips pressed against hers and grew warm, the feeling starting in her chest and traveling to her face. All this despite what she'd heard on the night in the Sacris College. She took a deep breath before joining Heron. She didn't want her father to know that she'd kissed Sextus or done any of those other things, at least until she determined if they were important or not.

"They'll come," said Sepharia confidently, even though she had doubts.

Heron limped to the table in the courtyard. Its surface was covered with terra cotta plates of various dishes: spiced lamb, pickled duck eggs, pomegranate sauce, and at least four kinds of breads.

"What a waste," said her father, looking at the spread. "I should have known we're alone."

"You should eat. You're wasting away to nothing. By the time we get back to Alexandria, you'll just be a bag of skin and a few loose bones," said Sepharia, trying to make a joke, even though her father's gaunt frame worried her. Heron had begun to go without the wrapping on her chest, since her breasts had long since disappeared. Only ribs and bony shoulder bones stuck out the front now.

Heron's hand drifted over a plate of fresh olives drowned in a lemon brine before coming to rest on the edge of the table. "I cannot eat with such worry in my head."

Desperate to take her father's mind off their lack of dinner guests, Sepharia spoke up, "I found something interesting about Caesar. If it still matters."

"Go on," said her father, "though it might not mean anything now."

After gaining Heron's attention, Sepharia hesitated. She hadn't yet told her father about the incursion into the Sacris College, nor the book she'd stolen, or the ominous conversation between Antonius and Sextus. She planned to do so after tonight, but had only delayed in hopes that the evening's dinner with Aelia and Sextus would clear up their possible guilt.

"You asked me to find out why Caesar had been killed. Caesar was loved by the people, but not by his fellow nobles. When the people called Caesar, King, the nobles objected." Sepharia paused trying to judge if this information was helpful, but Heron waved in a manner that said 'I already know this.'

"Some historians find it hard to believe that they murdered Julius Caesar. He'd been hugely successful in his Gaul campaign and they had every expectation that the next war against Parthia would go similarly. Many, including the revered Plutarch, believe it was simple jealousy that gave them cause for murder," she explained.

Heron gave her a severe look. "And after your time here in Rome, do you think these nobles are motivated by simple jealousy?"

"No," said Sepharia shaking her head.

"Is there anything else?"

Sepharia bit her lower lip. "He was the head of the Pontifex Maximus at one time. Though, when I checked the records, it seemed that the conspirators came from every one of the Colleges." She thought about explaining her idea of a secret cult within the Colleges but decided against it, since nothing in the book or her research seemed to indicate it.

In the intervening silence, Livia entered with a silver platter covered with bowls for dipping breads. She set the tray down, gave Sepharia a sour look, and exited the room.

"There was one thing I found, in this book, which I—"

Sepharia let the words die in her mouth when the sounds of footfalls on the marble alerted them. Led by one of the guards, Aelia appeared, dressed in a sapphire blue stola with her hair bound by a golden net. Sextus entered behind his mother, dressed in a soldier's tunic and wearing a gladius at his side; and behind him Senator Pallas hobbled in last when he should have been first. When Sextus smiled at her, she didn't respond.

"Greetings, Senator Pallas and wife Aelia," said Heron. "Your presence is quite welcome beneath my humble domus."

Aelia gave Heron a searing glance. "Maybe a little less humility and a bit more competence would be in order."

Heron forced a diplomatic smile and led them to the table. The son took his father's arm and led him to the table. Then Sextus quietly took his place at his mother's side. None of them reached for a plate, though

Pallas looked bleary-eyed rather than defiant.

The silence made itself an awkward guest. Aelia's lips pressed tightly, disappearing to thin, pale lines while she glared across the table at Heron. Sextus found something interesting in the lilac bush nearest his location and fidgeted like a boy at his first party. Her father's emaciated form and sunken chest looked almost comical before the table of delicious fare. Visibly conflicted, Heron seemed to wrestle with an internal dilemma before giving a heavy sigh and scooping a ladle of pickled olives onto her plate.

"Has there been news from the war?" Sepharia asked tentatively, hoping to draw out information about the negotiations with Magnus.

Aelia collected herself and a flush of color returned to her lips. "I have heard through sources that the former Consul Magnus might be interested in having discussions."

It was the same thing Aelia had been telling them for months, never once letting the negotiation go a step further. Everyone knew that she and Magnus had been lovers, and everyone knew she had nearly direct contact with him, despite the general waging an effective guerilla war against Agog. The subterfuge had begun to draw angry evocations from Heron each time the subject was brought up by Vestalis.

Sepharia was quick to watch for her father's reaction and she didn't disappoint, as Heron's brow tightened. "If by discussions, you mean—"

"Father!" interrupted Sepharia, drawing everyone's gaze. She gave a telling glance towards Senator Pallas to remind her father of his presence. "Would you pass me the lemon-brine olives, I know those are your favorite, and I'd love to hear more about those concessions you were willing to make in order to end the war, and I'm sure Aelia does, too."

Heron redirected her ire to Sepharia, which suited her fine, because it gave Aelia an opening.

"I would like to hear more about these concessions," said Aelia cautiously, while taking a hunk of bread from the tray and setting it on her plate while never once looking away from Heron. Sextus ladled out some berries onto his father's plate, and the old man picked one up with an arthritic hand and pushed it into his mouth.

Before Sepharia could reach for a plate, there was a clicking of gears and a sudden crack. Something wet hit Sepharia's face. Everyone looked a bit stunned - except Pallas who was busy working the berry in his mouth - until they realized that Heron had broken the plate in her metal hand. From beyond the room, the servant woman Livia came running and began cleaning up the mess with a cloth rag.

While they were corralling escaping olives into a bowl, and handing shards of the terra cotta plate to Livia, Heron shared an intense glance with Sepharia. She knew what her father was trying to say. Heron hadn't intended for those concessions to be known, but had only confided in Sepharia during a late night discussion.

"Tell them," Sepharia whispered while handing over an olive she found by her foot. "We have no other options."

"The concessions?" asked Aelia when Livia left them.

Heron dropped her hands into her lap. "Apologies, my thoughts are not well organized on the matter." She shot a glance at Sepharia. "But I think we might be able to get a full pardon for Magnus if he can end the war. I'm sure we'd all like to get back to the business of running an Empire."

Sepharia caught Sextus gazing intently at her, and looked away. Aelia tore off a piece of bread in her fingers and rolled it around like a ball, back and forth across her forefinger and thumb.

"But why would the Senate approve such a pardon? Silius would never let it pass and by keeping Magnus as an enemy of the Empire, he keeps the Emperor out of the city," said Aelia.

The implication of her father's incompetence in the matter of politics was clear, but it wasn't anything she hadn't already said upon entrance. Her father took the insult well, nodding slightly after a moment of thought.

"It's true I'm a better inventor than a politician," said Heron.

Aelia seemed to sense the degree of her insult and her hard features softened. "Apologies, Consul Heron. Do not despair your troubles within the Senate, for even Julius Caesar could not keep the wolves at bay forever."

The two shared a smile and Sepharia breathed a sigh of relief. They needed all the allies they could get, though she wasn't sure if Aelia was trustworthy.

Sextus spoke up, "Do not worry, Consul Heron, if the gods gave you the gift of politics as well as invention and war, we might all believe you were a son of Jupiter."

They all shared a laugh and a tension seemed to break. Sepharia grabbed an olive and put it up to her mouth, when Aelia asked a question.

"My son tells me you have an interest in war and the Legion. A strange occupation for a beautiful young woman," said Aelia, her eyes sparkling with thought.

Sepharia set the olive down. "I learned at an early age in the workshop that such weapons have an elegant poetry, though I recognize my naiveté on the matter since these tools are used by men to kill other men. Still, the weapons and armor are beautiful. Especially the ones worn by Julius Caesar."

Aelia smiled and glanced meaningfully at her son. "I do like the parades during a tribute. It seems the gods always favor Rome during a tribute, bringing good weather and sunlight that makes the armor gleam like the sun." She paused reflectively. "When Consul Magnus left Rome, every citizen in the city thought he would come back in tribute. Especially me." Her eyes held a distant sadness at bay.

"What if we were to offer something in return for Silius' vote?" asked Heron.

"What could you offer that would make a man like Silius give up his superior position?" asked Aelia.

"What if Senator Silius was the Consul? And I gave up my position to return to Alexandria, but only while Agog was back in the city," said Heron soberly.

They each grew quiet, contemplating how an offer like that would be received by Silius. Sepharia was hopeful. It was a way out of Rome for her father and back to the workshop in Alexandria where she belonged.

The more Sepharia thought about it, the more she thought it sounded like a good idea. She could see the eyes of the others widening, as if they were coming to the same conclusion. It might be an offer that Senator Silius would agree to, because it gave him a position of power greater than what he held currently.

Sepharia lifted the last brined olive, gave it a once over, and popped it in her mouth. The lemony tart hit the back of her throat, followed by the salt across her tongue. Her teeth crushed into the soft fruit and an acrid taste exploded into her mouth. Something unexpected and awful tasting.

She glanced to the others, and quickly decided that spitting out the rotten olive would be rude under the circumstances, especially with Sextus' green eyes smiling at her from the other side of the table. As unobtrusively as she could, Sepharia swallowed the olive mash whole, grimacing as it went down.

A smile hid her immediate discomfort, but she couldn't maintain it very long as an itchy burning sensation traveled from the back of her throat down to her stomach. Suddenly, she felt flush with warmth.

Sepharia opened her mouth to speak and the faintest breath of air across her throat turned it to burning agony. Her distressed gurgle brought the table's attention.

Sextus stood, reaching for his gladius with one hand and reaching out for her with the other. "She's poisoned!"

Hands held her and the ceiling swam overhead. As the fire spread from her throat to her chest and down her limbs, she realized that someone was shouting. Lying on the ground, Sepharia witnessed a fleeing Aelia, dragging her son behind like an uncooperative wagon.

Tears pooled in Sepharia's eyes from the pain that, like hot knives, went sliding across her forearms and thighs and down to the arches in her feet until her toes were curled in rictus. She felt flayed by whips and doused in lava. It went on and on, growing like a forest fire until even her fingernails screamed.

And then it didn't.

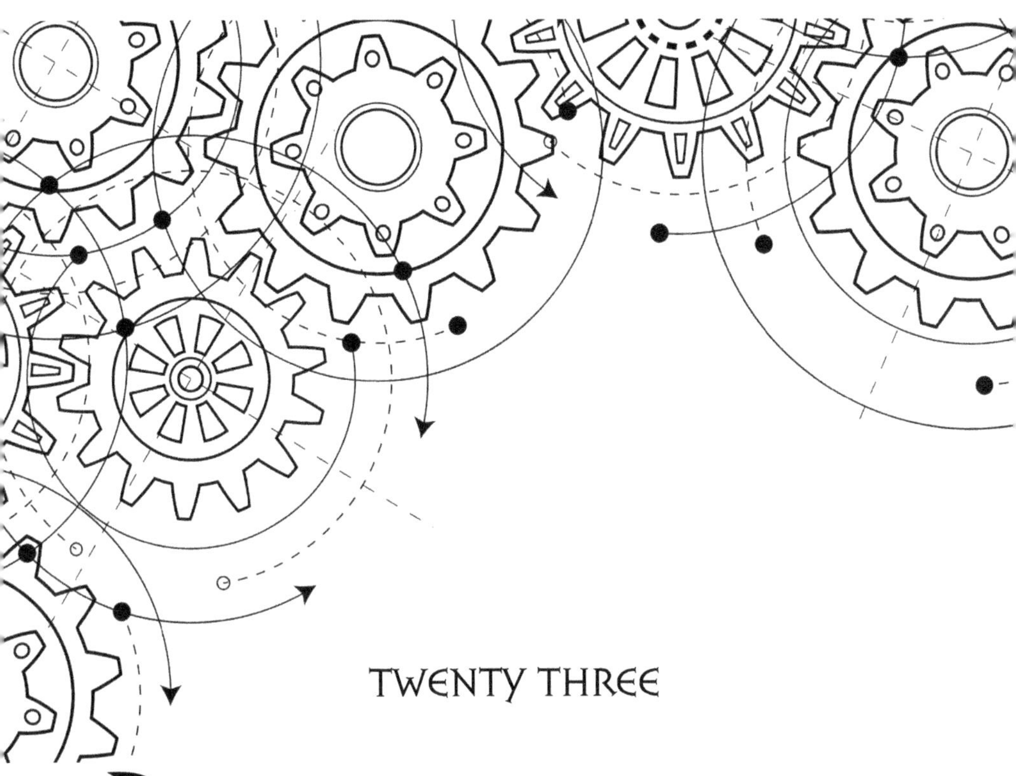

TWENTY THREE

Dominitus gazed across the hillsides of Rome from the graying stone outbuilding. The building stood on the edge of his olive grove, catching the breezes that flowed across the city. The building had once been used by his workers to store their equipment during the picking season, but now he let the fruits rot in the soil, or be eaten by the big, black birds that frequented his domus. He'd converted the building into a sitting area, though he wished he could stand, as much as it ached his knees.

The old Senator pulled the blanket around his shoulders tighter for the breath of winter could be felt in the whispering winds like a thread of ice. Already his bones ached with the anticipation of cooler times and if it weren't for the pressing needs in Rome, he might plan a winter in Catania on the coast near Syracuse, relaxing in the warm winds that blew across the Mediterranean and enjoying the company of the fine dark-skinned women who would feed him salty figs and laugh at his horrible stories.

A footfall sounded on the stone and Dominitus smiled. That insignificant noise had been made only so he wouldn't be startled.

"Ave, Cultri," said Dominitus.

"Can you see the inner workings of the Empire from here?" asked Cultri. "I expected you in your courtyard, enjoying your mealtime surrounded by beauty rather than hiding out in this, how should I say, glorified shit house."

"Do you know what this building is?" asked Dominitus.

Cultri made an amused noise. "Normally, I make it my job to know everything, but even so, there are some details too pointless for even my mind to worry upon."

"Ahh...bold and direct Cultri. This is why I have enjoyed employing you all these years. But in this case, you are wrong. This building is not an insignificant detail. In places much like this, slave revolts have been planned. Minor revolts that led to the murder of their owners and major ones that led to wide scale wars, if you know your history."

"And what does this have to do with the current situation?" asked Cultri, still standing at the entrance to the building.

Dominitus tugged on a strand of ivy escaped from the wall until its tendrils broke from the worn stone. He could pull the whole vine away, but it would only grow back. Dominitus let the ivy dangle and went back to staring at the city spread out before him.

"While most slaves meekly serve their masters," began Dominitus, "many thirst for freedom. In times of war, slaves are plentiful and the freeing of those who have served for many years through manumission releases the tension that might otherwise build up. It has been many years since we've seen new slaves in Rome. The Briton campaign, while eventually victorious, provided no new slaves to replace those who ache to be free. And even if it had, the fleet was destroyed, so they couldn't be transported south. And now, with the Alexandrians in charge, and no victory slaves brought forth, the slaves with ambition are beginning to grumble and plot."

"How do you know this?" asked Cultri.

"Because I am a student of history. During the last two major slave rebellions, not including the one led by Spartacus, which was a different sort of revolt, they occurred after long periods of no manumission. This Empire requires a steady stream of human flesh to keep operating. And now the machine is dry."

"So this is why you freed your slaves. Not in a fit of generosity," said Cultri, clearly amused at the revelation.

"When have you ever known me to be generous?" asked Dominitus.

"Apologies," laughed Cultri. "But now I see your interest in the *Michanikos*. Machines that might free the need for slaves might release the tension."

"Your eyes are clear now."

"Yes," said Cultri, "but now this Heron is neutralized. Silius has all but buried the man and has at least buried the daughter. My sources tell me that Heron has not left the domus in a week. Silius rules unchecked."

Dominitus gazed across the city, his weakened vision turning the distant buildings to pale smudges, but he imagined the domus that contained Heron, saw the man sitting in the dark contemplating his options. He knew the feeling because he had once been there after his wife and son had been poisoned while he was speaking on the Senate floor. He wept in his room for weeks and only when he reappeared in Roman life, did the assassin try to finish the job that the poison couldn't do. Dominitus ran a wavering fingertip across the scar that marred his once handsome face.

"Silius is an idiot who can't see the bigger picture at hand," said Dominitus. "He's waging a war in the shadow of a volcano. We need the Miracle Man."

"But he won't leave his domus. He's still grieving," said Cultri.

"He's not grieving," said Dominitus. "The girl did not die and he sits at her bed side praying to the gods that she might awake."

"She lives? How?" asked Cultri incredulously. "I know the poison they used and it does not fail in its task."

Dominitus shrugged. "It was some remedy from the North that saved her, though her fate is not completely known. She may still die, or if she eventually lives, might be so damaged from the poison that she might wish it."

Still, Dominitus wished he'd had this remedy for his wife and son when they were poisoned, and had been there to administer it.

"Then what task do you need me for?" asked Cultri.

"Heron needs a nudge in the right direction," said Dominitus.

Cultri chuckled lightly. "I specialize in nudges."

"Carefully, Cultri. Carefully. Silius cannot see my hand in this. It is much too early to alert him to my presence. He thinks me all but dead," said Dominitus.

"How can he not? Even I expect to find you dead in your chair upon each visit," said Cultri.

"I feel much better than I look these days," said Dominitus.

"You must feel terrible, then," replied Cultri.

Dominitus let out a small laugh. "Bold, bold, Cultri. How you amuse me. But the time for amusement is over. Now is the time for nudging, and if that goes well, a little more. But remember, good Cultri, we grapple on the edge of a cliff and one misstep will be the death of us all. There's a scroll on the table with no seal. It's for you, explaining my instructions. In the future, do not come to my domus unless called, but I expect things will move quickly and there won't be time for that. And remember, if we're not bold in our plans, we might see the end of the Empire, Roman or Alexandrian."

TWENTY FOUR

Heron threaded the copper wire through the hole in the folded piece of leather. Her mechanical hand clamped onto the tan material and the other pushed through while holding the excess wire in her teeth.

This was her third try. The first two had resulted in cursing and scrambling under Sepharia's bed to find the fallen wire. This was work better suited for Sepharia, making a harness that would keep her daughter's head up, but obviously she couldn't make it.

Heron had lived her life sleepless, but never like this. Before, her mind whirled like the stars above, creating machines that eventually made their way to ink-stained papyrus. This sleeplessness was like trying to hold a heavy rock over her daughter's head without dropping it. The longer she held it, the heavier it got.

A gurgling noise alerted Heron to the danger. She dropped the harness and carefully pushed Sepharia's head back onto the pillow and then wiped the drool from her cracked lips. The rolled cloth that had kept Sepharia's head straight had slipped. Heron repositioned it before returning to the harness which lay in pieces at her feet.

Not feeling at all ready for a fourth attempt to finish the harness, Heron grabbed the bowl from the table and pulled the rag out. She squeezed the rag with one hand until it was only mostly damp and then held it over Sepharia's mouth, patiently letting droplets make their way to the bottom tip and then release into her waiting mouth.

Heron had seen baby birds in the Great Library, raised by scholars in an attempt to learn about them. The young birds yawed eagerly at the damp cloths desperate for water. Heron wished that Sepharia would make some effort toward the rag in the same way the birds had. Instead, she lay there, face sunken from no food for a week with only water to sustain.

The pair of them would become skeletons before long. But while Sepharia lived, Heron needed to keep her strength, so she grabbed a hunk of bread from a nearby tray and shoved it into her mouth, chewing it like an automata, without a trace of enjoyment.

At least she did not have to worry about poison. There were only Northmen in the domus now, not even Alexandrians who could be corrupted. The quality of food had suffered, but when had she ever cared about that?

After the poisoning, Vestalis had interrogated the servants and not long after, the body of the woman Livia hung on the crosstrees near the Forum. Heron felt little solace from the swift justice. The woman had only been acting on behalf of someone else, the identity of that someone she didn't reveal because she did not know and had only taken coin for the deed. They had guesses on who might have paid the woman to poison the olives, but no proof. Even Aelia was suspect, which left Heron without trustworthy allies.

Heron picked up the strange bark-bound book from the table in an effort to distract herself. On first glance, she'd assumed it was a tome from Sepharia's research into Julius Caesar, but upon reading, she found it to be a play of sorts, but none she'd ever seen or heard about. Her best guess to the meaning of the text was that it was a religious ceremony. Heron had been present at enough of them in Alexandria to know when she was reading instructions.

The rituals revolved around the keeping, reading, and presenting of the Sibylline Books when requested by the Senate. These texts came from ancient time when Rome was still a young kingdom. The rituals told little about the Sibylline Books themselves, only giving the context of when they could be read, by whom, and the assorted gestures and words that had to be enacted before an interpretation could be uttered.

Why this book mattered to the investigation of Julius Caesar's death was a mystery to Heron, as much as the mystery of the death itself. It still puzzled Heron as to why Senator Dominitus would make such a request. At the time, it seemed innocuous, but now, after dealing with the other members of the Senate for the last few months, she saw sinister motives within everything.

But they needed allies, so being choosy in their current circumstance seemed self-defeating. The bigger question was could Dominitus deliver with credible help? In all her dealings with the Senate, his name had not been uttered once, leaving Heron to conclude that the Hidden Emperor was long past holding the reins of influence.

As Heron sped through the text a second time, she noted a section that mentioned the *mundus cerialis*, or World of Ceres. It wasn't the same as *mundus patet*, but she'd seen no other mention that came close. Ceres was the goddess of agriculture and fertility, which were both important to a fledgling empire.

The mention of Ceres only came once in the book and Heron could not make sense of any connection with Caesar. Or maybe the book was not about the investigation into Caesar, but Sepharia was trying to figure out who had tried to kill them? Her daughter had mentioned that she found something interesting in a book, and that had followed a discussion of Caesar and the religious colleges of Rome. Could it be that Sepharia believed they had something to do with his death? Caesar had been the head of the Pontifex Maximus, which oversaw the others. If he was its leader, how could he not be privy to its mysteries? It might even help if Heron knew where the book had come from and her frustrations only deepened as she considered what Lysimachus had told her. At the time, she'd pushed his warning from her mind as the ravings of a lunatic, but now the words echoed resolutely in her mind, haunting her thoughts.

Beware the dead, Cerberus hunts you.

It was not the first time she'd heard mention of Cerberus, but the source of that memory was faded and dim. She'd remember if she'd read it, but hearing did not stick it into her memory the way reading did. And that assumed it had some real meaning? She was chasing will-o'-wisps in the fog.

She worried it might have something to do with Tiberius' death. While she had no love of the man, that his slaves would turn on him so mercilessly and leave his body in such a mutilated state surprised her. The talk of the Senators had been that the tiled bath had been filled with his blood and even the hanging bodies of the offending slaves had not calmed them. But it was probably unrelated, and her thoughts cleaved to Senator Dominitus and his request.

None of it made sense, either because she was exhausted and couldn't think rationally any longer, or because it really wasn't connected. For all she knew, she was wasting her time trying to garner the help of a man with no influence, and listening to the warnings of a priest who had taken her hand and tried to feed her to a Nile crocodile.

Heron closed the book, running her fingers across the bark covering, taking solace in the rough texture, for her mind was as tangled as a knot.

She would read longer, but her bladder had other intentions, so after fixing Sepharia's head upon the pillow, Heron made her way from the room in a limping trot.

She might have missed the folded parchment on the floor had she not been watching where she placed her mechanical foot, so not to slip on the smooth marble flooring. Using the wall to steady herself, Heron picked up the note and examined the outside of the chunky parchment. There were no markings or identifications that clued her to the author, so she unfolded it, expecting it to be a message from Vestalis or Aelia.

To her surprise, it was neither. There wasn't much writing at all, except for one line, written neatly in a tight Latin script. Even if she didn't know the language, she could have read it with ease. That was because it was an address for a place at the edge of Rome's border on a hill noted as Monte delle Piche and directly to the right of it was the name of a god—Ceres. She didn't know the meaning of the address, but she had the suspicion she should visit the location soon.

TWENTY FIVE

Heron hugged the cloak around her shoulders, keeping the heavy cotton fabric draped over her arm. With a corner tucked into her metal fist, she smoothed the wrinkles away from the blanket across her thighs.

"You fidget more than a Thracian boy on Children's Day," grumbled Vestalis from the spot next to her on the bench. The stern soldier snapped the reins, spurring the pair of nut-brown work horses forward. A cloak hid his face, but she sensed his thinly pursed lips that would be pale as milk.

"You might have grown a beard to hide your well known jaw, but I cannot make my limbs simply disappear. I travel nowhere in Rome without bringing heavy stares," she seethed.

A portion of his hood dipped away as he turned his head toward her. There was an unexpected softness in his gaze that felt like pity to her.

"Apologies. I meant no insult. You're worried about your daughter."

Heron blew a breath out her nose. "No, the apology should be mine. The events of last week should give me no excuse to act the tyrant. When Donar bumped into Sepharia's bed when he was bringing a tray of food, I threw him out of the room and made him move a table outside the door, so he could put the tray there rather than risk Sepharia's life again." She paused. "Don't look at me like that, of course I know I'm a fool. Her life was never in danger. I was right there to push her head back up and if I hadn't, I'm sure Donar would have done the same. Still, he slunk away from her room like a great wolfhound with his tail between his legs."

They rode in silence a while longer, except for the bumpity-bump of the merchant wagon across the cobblestones. The clay pots in back, though packed around with loose straw, sometimes clicked as the lids loosened and snapped back on. Inside each pot was a pinkish paste called *garum*, a fermented fish sauce that was eaten with most meals in Rome. It gave off a rich aroma that reminded her of brined sardines.

As Vestalis was a merchant prince of Alexandria, he had wagons to spare, a useful disguise if they wanted to examine this house on Monte delle Piche. Both of them had snuck out of their respective abodes. Heron had done so by riding under a tarp in a wagon driven by one of the Alexandrians bringing supplies back to the army camp north of the city. Then, she and Vestalis had taken the *garum* wagon from there.

As they neared the outside of the city, the streets widened and the houses were more spread out, giving the homes a country air, a breathing space not commonly enjoyed in the city except for the wealthier inhabitants. Olive groves were being harvested by slaves in tunics and carrying baskets. It was the only agricultural industry still in the city, because the olive trees lived for centuries, so residents were loath to cut them down, even when there was want for space. Foremen called out commands to the slaves, who moved methodically through the neat rows, collecting the green fruits.

Vestalis yanked the reins suddenly, stopping the wagon and forcing Heron to grab the bench or slide forward.

"We near our destination. Just over this hill. Is it really important for us to see this villa?" asked Vestalis.

"I wish I knew," said Heron. "I've been asking myself the same question this whole ride. It depends on how badly we need allies."

A cloud of thought passed across Vestalis' face before he spoke, "So you think Dominitus left you the note?"

"I can think of no other," said Heron.

"Unless it's a trap."

Heron shook her head. "Who would know to leave this address? Without the request from Dominitus, an address is meaningless. It can only be him. He wants us to find something. I just wish I knew if I could trust him."

"Trust is a strong word," said Vestalis, "especially in Rome."

"My meaning of the word should not escape you. I trust no one now, except those of us that came from Alexandria," said Heron.

Vestalis raised an eyebrow. "Livia?"

Heron frowned at him. "I trust you."

The old soldier inclined his head. "For that I thank you. I know the Northmen don't always see me in a good light."

"If they don't then they're blind. If it weren't for you, we would have never won the war," said Heron.

"Many people had a hand in that victory."

Heron shook her head. "And all of us would be dead if we'd lost each other's trust."

"This doesn't solve the mystery of Dominitus."

Heron sighed. "I wish we knew more about it."

"I cannot help," said Vestalis. "I've been too long from Rome, and when I was here, I was never privy to his machinations.”

Heron looked away toward the olive grove. A small boy followed behind a pregnant woman, carrying a basket for her to drop plucked olives into. Heron bit her lower lip and considered the options going forward.

“What's your decision?” asked Vestalis.

“We cannot trust Dominitus.” She paused and Vestalis tilted his head curiously. “But for now it seems our paths align. He's using us in some way, but I'm willing to let it go if it gains us an upper hand against Silius.”

Vestalis grunted and snapped the reins. The wagon lurched forward and he drove it a ways until they came upon a small estate surrounded by iron fencing. Vestalis had arranged for the building to be available as a destination so they would have a reason to be in the area. The residents of the estate had been given a generous allowance of deaneries to vacation in the south.

As Heron struggled down from the wagon, she regretted not bringing her ivory cane, especially as she spied the uneven ground they would have to traverse to gain a closer vantage point on the Piche estate that lay on the other side of an olive grove. Vestalis led the way, moving methodically through the trees, his sandaled feet crunching the fallen, dead leaves. He paused occasionally to let her catch up and she could sense his impatience by his thinly disguised scowl.

The trees grew in width as they passed, until the pair of them were surrounded by twisted sentinels as wide as three men around. The larger olive trees looked like thick sailing ropes, knotted and entwined. The pale greenish leaves were falling as the wind shuttled through the trees. A particularly massive olive tree marked the edge of the estate, its trunk a grotesque mass that almost looked as if it'd absorbed human bodies into the wood. Vestalis seemed unmoved by the impressions and leaned his hand against a section that had the shape of a screaming woman as he gazed across the field to the building on the hillside.

Heron shook away her impressions and concentrated on the Monte delle Piche. It was a grand villa unlike the structures in the city: three stories tall and arranged in a circle with parapets spread evenly on three sides. Nearly obscured by the lengthening shadows and next to a stable, carriages and steam chariots waited. At least one steam chariot leaked black smoke into the sky.

"That's the steam chariot of Senator Antonius," noted Vestalis. "I'd know it by the crimson banners he flies."

"Do you see Silius or Aelia? Or Senator Pallas?" she asked. "Anyone else who might make this visit worth our time?"

"I can't tell from this distance." Vestalis glanced to the sky, judging the angle of the sun with a slight tilt to his head. "But it should be dark soon. We could move closer if it's important."

"It is."

"Maybe the gods will smile on us and we'll see who haunts this villa without having to risk discovery," said Vestalis.

Heron smirked. "Despite all I've done for the gods in their temples, I doubt they will be smiling on us any time soon."

The wait was interminable. By the time the shadows had stretched across the field, grasping at the stone house that was the object of their interest, Heron's knee ached like a piece of steel being bent on a hot forge. At best she felt tired, like a well-used saw worn down to the nubs, at worst the tip of a dull stick jabbed into a hornet's nest repeatedly. This whole business of ruling Rome was a waste of time. Her inventions created progress, moved things forward. Roman politics made as much sense to her as requesting to take Sisyphus's place rolling that boulder up the hill. But yet, here she was, staring at a villa on the outskirts of Rome on the instructions of a folded piece of parchment left beneath her door, only because it offered some way out, back to Alexandria.

Heron was about to call the whole thing off when Vestalis spoke, "I think it's dark enough."

She nodded and they moved across the field, keeping their profiles low. Halfway across, a bright flame erupted in the field behind the villa. A bonfire grew to a fiery rage. They hesitated in the weeds, crouching behind tangled bushes. Shapes moved before the fire. Nearer the villa, they were able to make out men in togas with colorful masks wandering around. Heron stayed Vestalis from moving closer by squeezing his arm.

Every short while, one of the masked men grabbed a stalk of wheat and threw it onto the bonfire creating a conflagration of sparks like a bucket of fireflies being thrown into the air. They weren't close enough to hear over the crackling wood, but the men grouped together, clearly chatting and waiting for something to happen. Eventually that something happened, when from the darkness behind the house, a woman was led out by two masked men. With her eyes adjusted to the dark, Heron could tell the masks were ornate and distinctly male.

The woman wore no mask and she moved sluggishly as if she'd been drugged. Her hands were bound before her. A priest appeared from the far side of the fire and greeted the woman. He wore a toga and a mask, same as the others, but also wore the conical hat that marked him as a *flamen*. He took her arm and began leading her around the bonfire. The priest had made one revolution when Heron heard a crunch of dead grass behind her. She froze, turning slowly, and looking out of the corner of her eye. Vestalis had heard it as well and when they made eye contact, he nodded towards her metal arm. Even from a distance, it glowed reflected light from the bonfire, so she cradled it against her chest and kept turning.

Behind them by only a few lengths, stood four soldiers clearly on patrol. They didn't wear the livery of the Empire, but the cut of their breastplates and the way they carried their swords marked them as a personal guard. The four soldiers had paused to watch the events near the bonfire, until one of them mumbled 'we should move on' in Latin.

When the soldiers were gone, Heron turned her attention back to the ritual. The slight breeze shifted toward them and suddenly, the voices of the men could be heard above the crackling. At first, she couldn't make out the individual words, but then she could hear clearly.

"He who plows, offers his sacrifice."

"He who prepares the earth, offers his sacrifice."

"He who plants seeds, offers his sacrifice."

At the speaking of each phrase, one of the men stepped forward with a stalk of grain, laid it gently on the woman, and then tossed it into the fire.

"He who traces the first plowing, offers his sacrifice."

"He who harrows, offers his sacrifice."

"He who digs, offers his sacrifice."

The woman seemed unmoved by the attention, head bobbing lazily to the side.

"He who weeds, offers his sacrifice."

"He who carries the grain, offers his sacrifice."

A cool touch startled Heron. It was Vestalis, nodding back toward their wagon. She shook her head, determined to see the rest of it, hoping they would unmask themselves.

"He who stores the grain, offers his sacrifice."

Vestalis tugged insistently on her arm, a look of concern weighing his brow.

"He who distributes the grain, offers his sacrifice."

As familiar as Heron was with rituals and offerings, she was unprepared for what happened next. Normally, the end of such offerings would signal a time for revel and drink. In Alexandria, religion had been a carnival of competing attractions with each priesthood trying to out-perform the others. If the believers did not enjoy the experience, their gods would shrivel and die from lack of coin.

The priest's voice carried loudly and as he turned his head to face the woman toward the fire, she could see a mane of hair flowing from the back of the mask. He began walking forward with measured steps and the woman went with him, stumbling like a newborn foal.

"To Dea Dia, we offer this woman so we might bring the Empire back under Rome's guidance!"

She found herself standing even before she'd realized it. This was her Empire, born on the back of her machines. How could she let this woman be sacrificed by a bunch of power-hungry old men? Wasn't she the Consul of the Alexandrian Empire?

Like a captain in battle, the words roared effortlessly from her lungs as if she'd never been tired before, "In the name of the Empire! Release that woman!"

But as the words left her lips, doubt flooded in and the stupidity of her actions became abundantly clear. The masked men scattered, thinking they were under attack, which was probably the only thing that saved them from capture right away.

Vestalis was yanking on her arm, forcing her to stumble into the darkness behind him. She ran as if she had two perfectly good legs, arms wheeling to keep balance when scrub grass tried to pull her to the ground. There were shouts of confusion and all the while, Heron hoped her metal limbs couldn't be seen. To her left, lanterns appeared like wisps, bobbing madly in pursuit.

The field, which had seemed a short distance across while they crept, now appeared infinite in the darkness. With only the darkest blank spot ahead to mark their destination, they ran. Vestalis could have easily outdistanced her, but he stayed within sight, constantly and silently urging her on.

When at last they reached the olive grove, Vestalis cried out in pain. Heron found him on his knees, an arrow sticking from his side. Lanterns converged on their location, so she helped him up and they limped to the wagon, remembering that they'd unhooked the horses when they'd arrived.

Heron was able to help Vestalis onto one of the horses. He was an accomplished rider, but wounded he could barely sit and leaned heavily to one side. Using the fence to climb on, Heron made the spot ahead of Vestalis and using the reins, turned the beast toward the road.

Soldiers appeared out of the darkness and Heron kicked one in the face with her metal foot. The horse galloped past two men who tried to grab the reins and at each bounce, Vestalis moaned in her ear. After a brief moment of panic, they burst past the soldiers and flew down the road. Heron kept at a frantic pace until they were sufficiently away that she felt safe enough to check on Vestalis.

"Are you well?" she asked, fearing the worst.

"It passed through my ribs," grimaced Vestalis, "but I bleed too much. Get me to the Alexandrian camp."

"I'm a fool," said Heron wiping the sweat from her eyes, "I should have never thought to stop them. They'll kill that woman with or without us and now you're going to die."

"I won't die unless we stay on this road unmoving," said Vestalis through gritted teeth.

"We move, we move," she said, kicking the horse's sides.

"Gently," cried the old soldier, "gently!"

The pair rode through the streets, making their way north to the Alexandrian camp. They reached it without incident, Heron enduring the penance of Vestalis' strong grip digging into her side the whole ride. When they pulled him carefully off her mount, she let out a tortured breath knowing that whatever pain she'd endured was only a small fraction of his. Sitting alone as broad-shouldered Northmen carried Vestalis to the physician's tent, Heron wondered how much more pain she would inflict on her friends before this whole thing was over.

TWENTY SIX

Heron's arm wheeled in a circle, twenty revolutions, tightening the gear until it shrieked. All around her, the sounds of industry rang: hammer blows, saw yawns, the grunt of effort. A single bead of sweat hung from her nose, tickling it until she wiped it free by shoving her face into the crook of her good arm.

It might have been any workshop in Alexandria, or Rome, but it wasn't. Heron stood in the transformed courtyard of the Alexandrian Domus. Well-tended trees had been ripped out, bushes hacked to kindling and used to heat the kiln, hastily erected near the marble colonnades. Trapped by Sepharia's illness, Heron had brought the work home, employing the soldiers stationed at the domus as her workers.

She looked up from her work to see Donar about to smash a row of pipes with a hammer. "Donar! Not there! I said to tap them into place, not smash them. They're brass pipes for carrying steam, not heads to be broken open."

The broad shoulders of the Northman slumped and he tugged at his mane of reddish hair in frustration. Heron left the project she was working on.

"There." She pointed to the base of the pipe. "This pipe has to seat tightly or the steam mechanical will never run on the Iron Road. And use a wooden hammer, not an iron one, less chance of damaging anything."

"Can I remind you that I'm a soldier, not a worker, Consul Heron," said Donar.

She raised her chin. "And I'm an inventor not a ruler, yet here I am. These times whip about us with furious winds and we can either be impeded by them or hang sheets and catch sail."

Admonished, Donar reluctantly nodded and leaned back over his work, comically so, for his shoulders had to hunch so he could tap delicately on the pipes. Heron spied a second accident in the making and made a stiff legged limp over, ignoring the ache in her hip. A dark-skinned Egyptian soldier was tugging fruitlessly on a wrench.

"Twist the bar this way." She rotated her hands like a farmer turning his butter churn.

The soldier scowled and moved his hands the opposite direction.

"No, no. Not that way. This way." She repeated the gesture, but still he went the wrong way, his jaw pulsing with frustration. He looked ready to snap the bar right off the side of the platform which would only set her further back.

She closed her eyes and tried to remember what Plutarch would do. He always moved effortlessly through her workshop, saying just the right things at the right time. He had a gift for tailoring his message to each worker, which was not her gift at all. She knew her occasional outbursts had their purpose to motivate, but not without Plutarch's guiding hand.

When she opened her eyes, the Egyptian soldier was still staring at her. What could she say to him to get him to understand? She glanced around at the haphazard work. Her idea had been to bring the work to the domus so she could oversee it while not being too far away from Sepharia. Any major problems could be fixed later by real workers, but if the soldiers destroyed the equipment, they'd be further behind. But she needed the steam mechanical for the Iron Road to work. Without it, she'd have little to offer reluctant Senators in the way of business.

The Egyptian soldier frowned, sensing her indecision. The raucous noise around her sounded nothing like a workshop. It had more in common with children beating each other with sticks and reeds than actual work in a workshop. She was about to send them all back to their other duties when she noticed the ankh on the soldier's neck. One more try to get him to understand wouldn't hurt, would it?

"The pipe needs to go in this direction." She moved her hands again and he moved the wrong way. She closed her eyes momentarily, remembering that the Egyptians were typically superstitious.

"You need to think of it like a drum for Anubis." His eyes brightened at the mention of his god. "Right hand must always be going down like it's beating a drum for Anubis when you want to tighten. If you want to loosen, then the left hand must move down and beat the drum."

He nodded and moved his hands the correct direction. When she was certain the soldier knew his task, she moved to another who was struggling to build a small scaffolding. It took a bit longer than the others, the task was something she'd forgotten over the years how to do. And the instruction didn't end there, she moved from place to place in the courtyard, hauling her metal leg along, guiding the soldiers in tasks they'd never performed before. It was barely managed chaos and by the time she'd made it back to her project, she was drenched from sweat which made the fake genetalia chaff along the inside of her thighs.

She wiped her forehead and muttered, "If ever I should return to Alexandria, I shall double Plutarch's pay. How he deals with this day in and day out, I shall never know."

A sing-song voice from behind startled her. "No need to wait until Alexandria, you can pay me double starting today."

Heron shook her head, daring not to turn, fearing that she'd gone mad in her exhaustion or had been drugged. Heron checked to make sure her metal arm was still attached. If it were a dream, it would be flesh and blood.

A deeper, rumbling voice followed the first. "And what about the blacksmith? Doesn't he deserve double, too?"

"It couldn't be," she whispered, still facing away. None of the soldiers had startled, so maybe these voices were just her imagination.

"Of course, double of a pittance is really not that much," said the first voice. "Nektam would pay us five times more if we were to work for him."

A grumbling laughter followed. "Or ten times! But then we wouldn't get the pleasure of getting yelled at for our slowness."

The first voice tittered. "Or have to create items that while seemingly functional on the papyrus, can no more exist in the real world as the sun can sprout wings and fly into my pocket."

"Have I gone mad?" she asked.

"Gone mad?" countered the first voice. "Or always been mad? But that may be what drew us to your workshop."

Heron couldn't take it any longer and spun around, nearly toppling in her haste. She grabbed onto the table before stumbling forward, almost into Plutarch's arms.

"You're here? How can that be?"

Plutarch gave a dramatic sigh, leaning on the table in his aquamarine tunic and necklace of shells. He looked like he'd stepped out of the halls of Poseidon.

"I seem to recall a month at sea, which I thought would be dreadful, but on Hoth's *Jörmungandr* the journey was almost pleasant. Of course, if you say that it's not possible, then I suppose it was a dream and we really rode on a ship of air, which I suppose is possible since Hoth told us about your adventure."

"Plutarch!" she exclaimed and had to restrain herself from throwing her arms around him, both for the impression it might give the soldiers and so she didn't wound him.

"I, for one, did not enjoy the ship and hope that your metal road works by the time I return to Alexandria," grumbled Punt. "I spent far too much time feeding the fish from the railing."

"With you two here, that might happen," she beamed. "But how? Or should I say why? A month long journey? Who's doing was this?"

"Vestalis," said Plutarch. "He sent for us months ago. It seems the need in Rome is greater than Alexandria."

Heron paused, putting an incredulous hand to her forehead. "There's so much to tell you."

Plutarch waved her off. "No need. We met with Vestalis in the camp first and he explained the situation in Rome. Though his description did not quite relay the severity that you would use these soldiers as craftsmen." Plutarch tilted his head. "In the name of the gods, what are you building?"

Still slightly delirious from the shock, Heron gazed upon the efforts of her soldiers. While it held a passable shape as a steam wagon, it was clear that the construction as a whole would never work. Pipes snaked upward without direction like whiskers on an old man. Wheels were off-center and listed drunkenly to the side. The steam chamber had holes and gaps and dents like a boulder after it'd rolled down a mountain.

Heron chuckled. "Be kind to them, their efforts are my doing."

Plutarch glanced curiously at the drawings on her table and the pieces of armor she'd been working with. Gears and pistons connected the sections between the overlapping metal sheets.

"And what is this? Are you still trying to make metal soldiers that can fight?" he asked. "Did you solve the problem of a steam mechanical small enough to power it?"

"No," she said. "But I had a different idea recently when I nearly got Vestalis killed."

Quietly, Punt spoke up, "How is Sepharia?"

A heavy mood overtook them like ink dumped into bright waters.

"She lives yet," said Heron. "She has strength in her, but does not wake. Sometimes she speaks as if someone is right there, though her voice is changed from the poison."

"We should visit her," said Plutarch, to nods from the bald blacksmith.

"My heart sings that you have come," said Heron, holding her hand across her chest.

"It seemed you were having all the fun," laughed Plutarch.

Heron responded with a maudlin smile. "I should warn you. We're in grave danger here. Rome is against us and I am a feckless politician. We should have burned the place to the ground when we took it rather than ruling it."

"No different than it's ever been," said Punt. "We'd rather die by your side than feel helpless from across the sea."

Plutarch gave a solemn nod of agreement.

"Let's hope it doesn't come to that."

Plutarch raised an eyebrow. "What of this work? Shall we put an end to it?"

Heron watched a soldier trying to figure out which end of a wrench he needed to use on a gearing. "Agreed. The work for the Iron Road can return to the workshop. I assume Vestalis has a place for you?" They nodded. "But leave my work here. I need something to occupy my time while I wait for Sepharia to awake."

They left her after gripping forearms and Heron felt a great heaviness lifted away. These were terrible times and still she had no idea how they would counter the stratagems of Senator Silius, but at least she would do so with her friends. Now, she just needed allies and without the needs of the workshops to delay her, she could resume the investigation into Caesar's death. It seemed this dance upon the stage of Rome was two-fold: one, the actors said their lines, marking the play with bold declarations and promises; the other, a shadow of the first, but the truth obscured behind those twice-meaning words hidden within the artifices of power. If they were going to escape alive, and keep their fledgling Empire from being absorbed by these shadowy puppeteers, she needed to understand who they were really fighting against. Heron ripped a section of papyrus away from her drawings and quickly scribbled out a note. She needed a lesson in Roman politics and she needed one quick. Heron sent a messenger away and then slumped against the table, letting a bit of exhaustion claim her. If she was wrong about this next step, she might doom their fragile efforts, but if she did nothing, they would surely lose anyway. Heron just hoped the note she sent wouldn't get her killed.

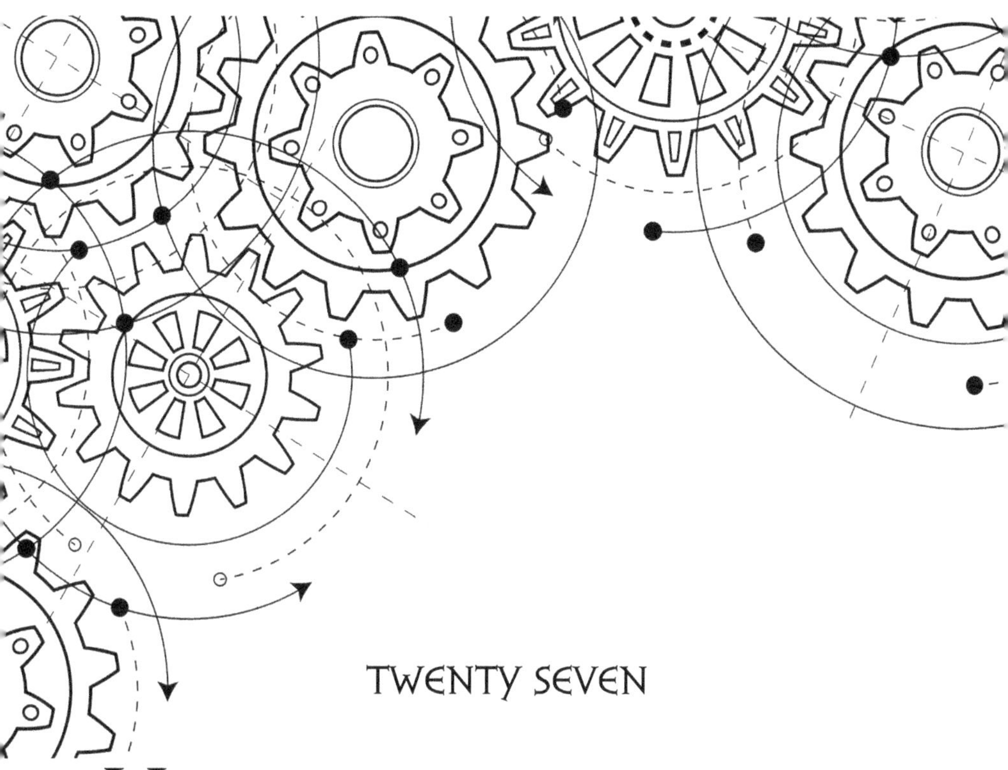

TWENTY SEVEN

Heron felt the fraud within the forest of marble colonnades outside the Senate house, despite being empty of its charges since it was a festival day for the Goddess Minerva. Her tunic was fresh and clean and smelling of faint lemon. She'd bothered to acquire the stamped leather wrist guards that were the fashion and a belt marked with faint hammers, a subtle nod to the god Vulcan. Yet, by all their rules, she should not be here among them as women were forbidden from holding office and were little more than property.

She placed a hand on the cool stone that had captured the evening's chill. Winter would come soon and if she couldn't fix things, she'd be stuck until springtime. She shook her head, trying not to entertain those thoughts and focus on her intentions on the day.

Below, on the avenue leading up to the Senate house, men and women milled about, oblivious to her presence in the atrium. Donar and a few other soldiers stood guard nearby, but she doubted anyone would assault her here under the auspices of power.

Then she chuckled, realizing her foolishness. They'd killed Julius Caesar in the Senate building, stabbed him sixty-two times in front of the assembled Senators.

The waiting ended when she saw Aelia on the far side of the square and knew it was her, even before Heron could see her face. Aelia marched across regally, her presence fit for the surrounding grandeur, despite their restrictive rules. She wore a stola of the deepest azure, almost violet in its richness, accented with pale blues within the folds that created a sense of weight. The matching palla that rested on the crown of Aelia's head and draped around her shoulders framed her strong features. By the time Aelia reached her, Heron felt that she should be the one climbing the marble steps to greet Aelia, not the other way around.

"Ave, Aelia Octavia," said Heron, pressing her lips against Aelia's cheek in greeting. The woman smelled of lavender. The questioning glance was brief as they pulled away.

"Ave, Consul Heron. I came at your request."

Judging by Aelia's dress and makeup, she'd guessed to the purpose of the visit. Heron planned to let her wonder for a while and extended her good arm and led them on a stroll into the Senate. Aelia wrapped her fingers around Heron's wrist and began massaging the soft flesh on the inside subtly, like a cat flexing its paws.

"Do they hurt you?" asked Aelia.

Heron startled. "What?"

"Your limbs? The missing ones. Do they hurt you?"

Heron replied after glancing at her arm and flexing the fingers, creating a brief symphony of gears and pistons. "Sometimes, especially when I'm not wearing these." She held her arm up. "When I wear them, it helps me forget that they're gone."

Aelia leaned in close, her lips parting slightly, "Did the crocodile take any other parts?"

It was a valid question, one that Heron didn't mind answering, but she didn't want to have to start lying to Aelia, yet.

"Nothing that I needed." Heron kept her expression neutral. "But I didn't ask you here to discuss my old wounds."

"Your note implied an important request." Aelia's gaze searched her own. The Senator's wife was trying to figure out what it was, but Heron didn't think her guesses would strike true.

"I do," said Heron, "but not yet. First, I would like a lesson on the politics of Rome." They stood beneath the shadow of Caesar's automata, the one she'd designed and that hid barrels of spark powder in its base. "I don't want to end up like him."

Aelia raised an eyebrow. "You would ask a woman for advice on games that men play?"

"I would," said Heron, trying to repress a smile.

It was clear Aelia didn't trust the request, but she seemed to come to the conclusion that to refuse to answer would be more rude than offering advice. This behavior might have seemed odd, given Aelia's forceful demands during previous encounters, but then Aelia had been speaking on behalf of her husband, a Senator of the Empire. By way of the request and by greeting Aelia with her full name minus the family name, Heron had made it clear this was a private matter.

When Aelia responded, she did in her woman's voice, the one Heron noticed women used when they wanted something from men. It was softer, more gentle, and closest to the voice they might use in bed. "Certainly."

"Are you familiar with Caesar's death?" asked Heron.

"As any leal Roman should be. Especially if they wish to wield power in Rome," replied Aelia, matter-of-fact.

The truth of Dominitus' request hit her soundly in the chest, so much that Heron paused, resulting in a questioning look from Aelia.

"Are you alright?" she asked.

Heron shook away the question. "Only a realization to the extent of my blindness."

"Do all Alexandrians speak so plainly? My fellow Romans would never admit fault, so much that even if they'd dropped a valuable gem into the ocean during a voyage, they would claim they were giving an offering to Poseidon."

"In my line of work, as an inventor, I must have a strong grip on the truth, and failure is only proof of a way that it cannot be done. I think I begin to see the way of my troubles in Rome," said Heron.

It was more than that, too. Senator Dominitus had asked her about Caesar as a lesson in Roman politics. He was giving her advice. She remembered his praise of her handling of initial problems with the Senate. He was sizing her up as a political ally, for what, she couldn't guess. But he'd called what she needed to learn an obolus and had even mentioned Cerberus, much as Lysimachus had when he'd said 'Cerberus hunts you.'

When they found themselves outside of the empty Senate chambers, Heron nodded inside. "So this is where they killed Caesar?"

"No." Aelia shook her head lightly. "They killed him in the east portico. They intended to kill him in Pompey's theatre during a gladiatorial match, but their plot had begun to unravel, and Mark Antony moved to warn him, so they ushered him into the portico and fell upon him."

"And then all those that murdered him came to unlikely ends in the years after," said Heron.

"It had to be done," said Aelia, much to Heron's surprise. "Even though Caesar had gained too much power, those that killed him publicly had to pay a price, or such murders would become more common place."

"You say it as if you know?" asked Heron.

"Only as a student of politics," said Aelia. "The worst crime in the Empire is to garner too much glory, too much power. And Julius Caesar was a bonfire, drowning out the faint candles of the Senate. The people adored him, he held dictatorial powers, and he planned to invade the Parthian Empire. If he would have succeeded, he would have been untouchable, as the second coming of Alexander the Macedonian."

Heron nodded soberly. "Then I see my crimes clearly now. When I changed those rules by fiat, the ones that affected your family, I marked us as above the law."

Aelia squeezed her arm comfortingly. "Do not worry about such mistakes. By the nature of your conquest, you were already a subject of their ire. The only way you could have avoided becoming mired in politics was to have eliminated the Senate upon arrival and started anew."

"A mistake too far past," said Heron.

Aelia leaned in conspiratorially. "It's never too late." Her lustrous brown eyes sparkled with intrigue. Even while she was offering lessons in politics, she was practicing the craft.

"Even if Agog wished it, he would have to be back in Rome, and the war with Magnus over," said Heron.

"That is attainable," she replied.

They treaded on dangerous ground. If a plot like this was to reach the ears of the Senate, it would cause a riot and plunge the Empire into an internal war. Heron chose her words carefully, speaking under her breath.

"Theoretically, if such a thing happened, how would the Empire be managed? The Senate provides the mechanism on which the Empire runs," said Heron.

Aelia frowned, like a teacher disappointed in a previous star pupil. "The purpose of the Senate is to acquire wealth and power for the Senators. The magistrates of the Empire make it run, the Senate just siphons off what it wants."

Heron paused, reeling from the insight. "But the people would revolt? They love their Republic."

"Then reform another that includes the additional seats you want. You can allow certain Senators to keep their seats, ones more amicable to your cause, and find reasons to exclude others. As long as the people see a resemblance to the previous Senate, they'll be satisfied."

Despite her nimble mind, Heron found the whole thing hard to grasp, only because it seemed so fundamentally self-serving and dishonest. "But can we do such a thing?"

Aelia shrugged. "You won the war. You beat Rome on the battlefield. I would think it's your right."

"Your words persuade me," said Heron reluctantly.

"And would they persuade the Northman?" asked Aelia.

"If I presented it, I think it would. He listens to my counsel, though in this, I fear he shouldn't," said Heron.

"Caution is admirable," said Aelia, "but boldness is necessary."

"Would your husband be agreeable?"

Aelia smiled. "If I told him so. He takes my advice without complaint." She was about to say more, but paused, seeming to catch herself. "How odd. I should not be speaking so freely with you, but I find you make me feel at ease." Aelia lightly danced her fingertips across Heron's arm, bringing goose bumps.

Heron ignored the comment. "And what reward would you want for your place in this?"

A coy smile spread across Aelia's lips. "If I were a younger woman, I might desire to sit at the Northman's side. But I am older and wiser and know such titles bring danger."

"And that he is married," added Heron.

Aelia shrugged, as if to say that such things can be dealt with. "But I think I would prefer the arm of a different man, one more intriguing than all the rest." She stared directly into Heron's eyes, making her feel uncomfortable in their nearness.

"What about your husband?" asked Heron.

"He's old and getting no younger." Aelia put a hand on Heron's chest, her fingers kneading into the tunic. "I make a very formidable and attentive wife. If you prefer to stay outside of politics, I could be a liaison for you." Aelia paused and Heron sensed a bit of honesty from the woman. "I think I might actually enjoy standing by your side and I'm afraid my current marriage comes without certain benefits."

"I...I'm not..."

The words were kissed from Heron's lips as Aelia pressed against her. It was not a chaste or friendly kiss, but one normally given in the full lust of passion. The softness of it was markedly different than the rough, hard lips of Jarngard, but not at all less pleasurable. Heron felt her knees weaken and could do little about it, until Aelia pulled her closer, keeping her upright. The kiss went on for a while until Heron remembered where they stood, right at the threshold of the Senate chambers and though currently empty, a page or attendant could wander through at any moment.

Heron pulled away, feeling delirious from the attention. Aelia looked positively wanton and ready to press against Heron anew. Her lips were parted eagerly and her tongue wetted her teeth.

"I cannot..."

She had no time to get the words out when Aelia pulled her close, their lips clashing and tongues tangling. Heron let herself succumb for only a moment before coming up for air.

"It would not work," she got out quickly.

Aelia looked on, concerned. "The crocodile...did it?" She nodded downward.

"No." Heron shook her head. "But..."

"What?" asked Aelia. "I have to admit. My interest was purely political at first, but your kiss was remarkable. So different than I've enjoyed before."

Heron could sense a growing understanding, so she pulled away from Aelia. "Our plans, we should continue them, but this, I'm afraid, it wouldn't work."

Aelia looked on despondent. "Could we not be as paramours? My husband does not attend to my needs."

"I will write to Agog, if you will contact Magnus. If they both agree, we can make plans for the rest. And we should do so quickly, before winter sets in and strands the armies in the north," said Heron, slowly backing away.

Aelia's brow was wrinkled with thought. "Are you not inclined toward women? No, it could not be, your kiss was not unmet. I felt your passion."

Heron limped away with Aelia in pursuit. "By letter, we should converse. So no one can know our plans."

When Aelia stopped in her tracks, fingertips held to her lips, there was a bright beacon of understanding on her face. Heron stood a few paces away, waiting for the accusation.

"I know..." whispered Aelia, her eyes both searching for further confirmation and widening in comprehension. "I understand..." She seemed enraptured by the truth, while Heron felt reduced.

"You cannot," pleaded Heron. "They would kill me."

Aelia stared back with an unreadable expression. Heron prepared to lean on their shared womanhood, when Donar came running into the Senate building, cutting the debate in two. Heron spun around, teetering on weak legs.

"A message has come," said Donar, out of breath, his cheeks rosy with the effort of sprinting up dozens of steps, matching his bright beard.

"Out with it then," said Heron.

"About Sepharia," he said, between breaths.

Heron's heart nearly split. She knew what it must mean. Her knee nearly buckled.

"She's awake."

TWENTY EIGHT

Sepharia knew it was a dream by the iron rods connected to her arms and legs. She stood atop the pyramid once again, surveying the whole world as it curved away from her in the distance. Even from a great height, the colors of the landscape below were vivid: vibrant greens, flashing yellows, scintillating blues. It seemed the fire of life burned brightly in every tree and field and stream. The city, Alexandria, churned with industry, great tendrils of black smoke tickling the clouds, gears as large as buildings turning, driving some great machine beneath its soil. She'd dreamed of this land in the past and the iron serpents that undulated into the distance took on more shape than before, so much that she could see the clouds of steam burst from the pistons driving the wheels. Each rotation hissed out the puff of mist, leaving a haze around the Iron Road like a necropolis at midnight. She reached out toward the steam mechanical, like a child might pick up a toy, but found her reach restricted by the iron rod connected to her wrist held with a rust-tinged manacle. Glancing over her shoulder, she saw a man with no hair and desolate eyes, controlling the other ends of the iron rods like a puppeteer. Vestalis appeared on the platform, merciless gray eyes making stern accusations as he approached. Sepharia tried to speak, but her lips were bound by clamps that she hadn't noticed before. She tried to put her arms up to tell him not to move closer, but her arms disobeyed. A knife found its way into her hand and her arm lurched forward, pushed by the iron rod, driving it—

"—the priest," she blurted out as she shot up straight in bed.

"What?" said the voice beside her.

Sepharia turned to find a pair of wide green eyes brimming full with worry.

"Sextus?"

He smiled, which created a tiny dimple on his left cheek, a detail she'd never noticed before. "I'm sorry it's taken me so long to visit since you've woken, but things have been moving quickly lately."

Seeing him reminded her of something, but she couldn't remember what. She hid her confusion behind a clearing cough, which only made her grimace due to the pain.

"Is your throat not healed?" he asked, somewhat tenderly.

"Better than when I first woke. I was sure my throat was choked with sand when I tried to ask for water. The physician thinks my voice will always be deeper now," she lamented.

Another emotion passed across Sextus' face, far too quickly for her to capture, or she was still too tired to notice such things. At least she didn't want to sleep all the time like she did when she first woke. She could almost imagine a walk down the hall in a few days.

"It sounds...pleasant," said Sextus, but his heart didn't seem into it. In fact, he looked on with an expression of concern tugging the corner of his lips. Something had happened to cause him to doubt her, but what she couldn't think of.

"Has Magnus agreed to the terms?" asked Sepharia, hoping to change the way he was looking at her. It bordered on disgust.

"Yes." He nodded solemnly. "Both he and Agog are hurrying back to Rome, secretly, of course. The plan is to announce the change in the government on November the 8th, right when they arrive."

"And what day is today?" she asked sheepishly.

"The 27th of October. Time is as short as Mercury's breath now. The whole thing has to be choreographed so Silius and his side doesn't know it's coming. If we surprise them and have a replacement government ready, then the people won't revolt," he explained.

"I've slept through everything," she said, staring at her hands.

"Not slept," he replied. "You nearly died."

On that mention, the image of Aelia and Sextus fleeing the domus came back to her in full. He must have sensed her sudden change, because he started looking around the room.

"I have to know something," said Sextus. He seemed hesitant to speak, and his jaw yawed a little as he stared at the wall. "Are you...are you like your..." He shook his head, the words seemed too difficult to speak. "I should go."

He got up and she reached out towards his back. He paused at the doorway, his green eyes full of dark clouds.

"What?" she asked.

"I don't know," he said. "The things my mother told me. Are they true?"

"Is what true?" she asked.

He frowned slightly and left, leaving her filled with questions. She slammed her hand into the bed, feeling dizzy for the effort. None of it made sense. She felt like she was supposed to be questioning him, not the other way around, but she couldn't remember what for. The weeks before the poisoning seemed to have been wiped out, like an ink spill spreading across papyrus, wicking through the chunky grains until she could remember nothing.

And what had Aelia told him? Nothing Sepharia could remember. She vaguely remembered the dinner conversation, only that they had spoken, nothing of the content. It felt like a serpent had crept into her head and swallowed her memories whole. Sepharia put her head in her hands and willed her memories to return. It seemed like something was important, something that she'd been ready to tell Heron. If it had to do with Sextus or Aelia, she wasn't sure, but it felt that way, only because his nearness had triggered that feeling. Sepharia kneaded her hands into the blankets with frustration, hoping that whatever it was she was forgetting wasn't important.

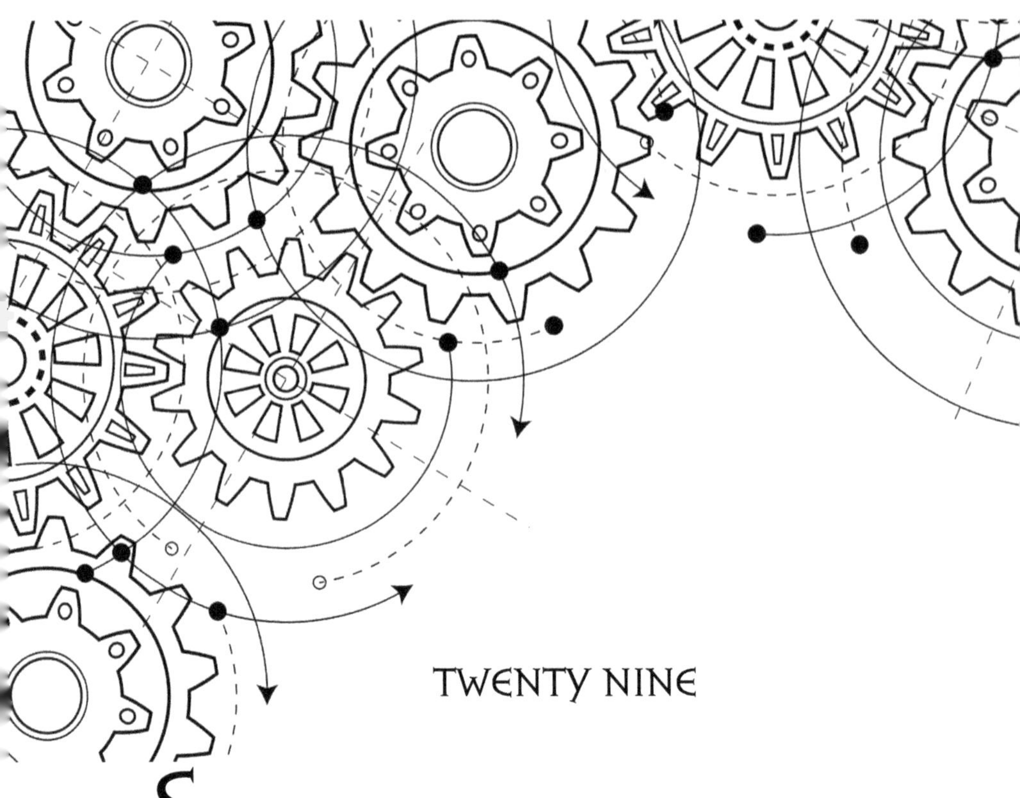

TWENTY NINE

Senator Julius was a stick-thin, frail old man with skin like old papyrus. He teetered on his knobby knees like a couple of stilts, and his disheveled toga seemed more bath robe than formal attire. He stared intently at the brass pipes of the steam mechanical, while Heron looked on.

Plutarch, who'd been standing next to the Senator, cleared his throat to catch his attention. "Senator Julius, apologies for my disagreement, but the pipes do not *inhale the breath of babes* to run, nor do they carry dragons in their bellies that breathe that black smoke. It's simple coal, you see, that's burned and the puffs of smoke are water turned to steam, like a pot boiling."

The effeminate foreman gave a warm, but helpless smile, while the Senator sucked at his teeth and squinted at the steam mechanical like a venomous snake. If the outcome of this meeting wasn't so serious, Heron might have laughed, but the future of the Empire depended on finding enough Senators to support the reformation of the Senate, all the while not letting them know what was going to happen. Heron stepped forward, slightly into the Senator's view, distracting him enough that he split his attention between Heron and the steam mechanical with a few uneasy glances.

"How it works matters less to such a stalwart of the Senate," she said, after placing her hands behind her back. "What matters is that the Iron Road will require great mountains of materials, including the forging of iron rod for which your foundries are renown. We wish to offer contracts for your foundry to supply three hundred and seventy-five stadia of iron rod as thick as a man's arm. That length would be the first leg on the route north to Volsinti."

The Senator frowned and spoke in a slight toothless lisp, "I thought your road went to the sea? How can I supply iron rod for that?"

Heron tried not to sigh since it'd be the third time she'd explained it. "The Iron Road going from the eastern hills to the docks on the Mediterranean are already done. That contract was completed and we don't need any more. What we need is iron rod, three hundred and seventy-five stadia worth, for the road north to Volsinti."

"Volsinti?"

"Yes."

The wrinkles on the Senator's face deepened. "Not the sea?"

"Volsinti," said Heron, hoping the repetition would sink in. Over the Senator's shoulder, Plutarch was turning a light shade of crimson as he held back laughter.

The Senator nodded appreciatively and sucked on his teeth some more. When he ran a shaking hand through his wispy gray hair, it left half of it sticking straight up. He turned to Heron and smiled, showing all the remaining teeth left.

"Explain again, why you need this the iron for the route to the sea?"

Heron bit the inside of her lip rather than scream. "Maybe it would be best if Plutarch took you on a tour of the workshop. He can show you the small scale Iron Road that demonstrates how the steam coach will move from Sea to city and back."

His wide eyes and head shaking were quickly curtained behind a generous smile as the Senator turned to Plutarch. The Senator began wobbling in the wrong direction. Plutarch looked helpless as he tried to corral the Senator in the right direction, much to Heron's amusement.

"This way, Senator. This way, this way!" Plutarch's voice rose with each word until it floated across the ceiling. "Senator, watch out for the nails. Senator. Senator!"

With the Senator mercifully removed from her presence, Heron turned only to find Aelia standing near the wooden timber that held up the roof. She wore a stola the color of lemon, looking like a bright flower within the soot-dusted workshop. In her gaze, Heron caught the thread of worry before it was banished behind a formal nod. This had been the way of it since that day at the Senate.

"Don't worry about Senator Julius," said Aelia. "Much like the god Dionysus, he acts the fool on purpose. I've seen him slice a man wide open with his sharpened wit. He knows what you have to offer, he's just hoping to extract a bit more before he leaves your workshop."

Heron glanced in their direction. "As long as he doesn't guess why. How does your half of the list fare?"

She made a sound—half a laugh with a hint of exhaustion. "Well enough, these Senators are like pigs at the trough. Pile enough rubbage for them to eat and they won't notice you're lining them up for the slaughter."

"That reminds me," said Heron. "Vestalis wants to set some surprises for Silius and his Wolves in case they resist too strongly."

"What kind of surprises? And shouldn't the soldiers and the vote be enough?" asked Aelia.

Heron calmed her heart and said the words as neutrally as possible.

"They wouldn't be surprises if too many people knew."

Aelia didn't flinch, she was much too strong a politician for that, but Heron detected the slightest waver in the woman's eyes.

"You still don't trust me," said Aelia.

"I never said that, but the more people that know a secret, the more those secrets can be lost. Even my own workers didn't know the most important tricks of my Temple miracles," said Heron, looking around to make sure the two of them were alone. "And you know the most important secret already, at least to me. If I don't trust you now, then there's no point in going through with the rest of it."

Aelia was a stern and beautiful woman, she tilted her head, exposing a long and lean neck, much like a queen might do before passing a sentence. "Why do you go on like that? In their world."

The implication was cold steel across Heron's heart. "I had no choice if I wanted to practice my trade." She paused, trying to carefully choose her words, but in the end not caring enough to censor herself. "You think I've cheated somehow, or defied the gods, don't you?"

"You haven't had to go through what I've gone through," replied Aelia coolly.

"I make no apologies," said Heron. "I've lived my life in fear. Fear of discovery. Fear that my inventions would become heretical if it were found out. Fear they would burn my writings and erase my name from history."

"So much pride that you believe you're their equal," said Aelia.

Heron tried to make a fist with her flesh hand, but the accusation had stung her like a thousand bees and she reeled with pain, stretching her fingers. "How can you say that? I thought you, of all people, would understand? Of course, we're their equal. And in some respects the greater."

"If the gods wanted it to be different, it would be so now," said

Aelia with a wounded sharp gaze. "And maybe I'm a fool to trust you in your defiance, and in the end, this will only end in smoke and ruin."

Heron's metal limbs weighed like anchors, dragging her down. She was angry, perplexed, numb. "Then why do you carry on trusting us, trusting me?"

Aelia looked to the ceiling, as if she were acknowledging the gods. In that moment, Heron thought she saw the real Aelia, the one beneath the fineries, the gold bracelets, and silken stolas. It was an Aelia older than her appearance suggested, aged by her responsibilities and burdens.

"Hope." Aelia shook her head lightly, grimacing with sadness. "Foolishness. When I kissed you, I thought I would seduce you, I seduced myself, but then the truth, and I went back to my villa and my servants attended me and all the while I was thinking. They asked what was wrong, more than once. I don't know if I gave them an answer. I could not decide if I were mad at you for tricking me, mad at myself for not seeing it sooner, or mad at the both of us for having to live under these circumstances. How do you survive it?"

All at once, Heron thought to move close to Aelia and take her in her arms and comfort her. It seemed like what she would do, what she, in the place of a man, should do. But was that her? She'd never questioned herself like that before, at least not in a long time. Maybe she had at the beginning, when she was first learning to move among them, to ape their tendencies, their speech patterns. It wasn't too hard, and it never felt uncomfortable, but it was always full of fear. Fear of being caught.

"I do what I can," said Heron. "Are you still on our side?"

Aelia smiled, and not a politician's smile, but one that went all the way to the little wrinkles around her eyes. "I am, along with my son and wrinkly old bag of bones for a husband." She paused. "It is a shame you weren't really a man. We'd make a formidable team."

"You'd quickly become annoyed by my devotion to my work," replied Heron.

"It doesn't matter now. We have too much work ahead of us. Even after the government is reformed, there will be much to do," said Aelia.

Heron nodded, but did not say what was on her mind. As soon as Agog was back in the city, and Silius and his Wolves dealt with, she would be on a ship back to Alexandria. She'd sent messages to Hoth to be ready for her on November 8th, the day Rome would be remade. Once Agog arrived, there wouldn't be anything he could say that would keep her in Rome. She'd done her duty, given him six months and more, and survived the cesspool of politics that Rome was. She deserved to go home.

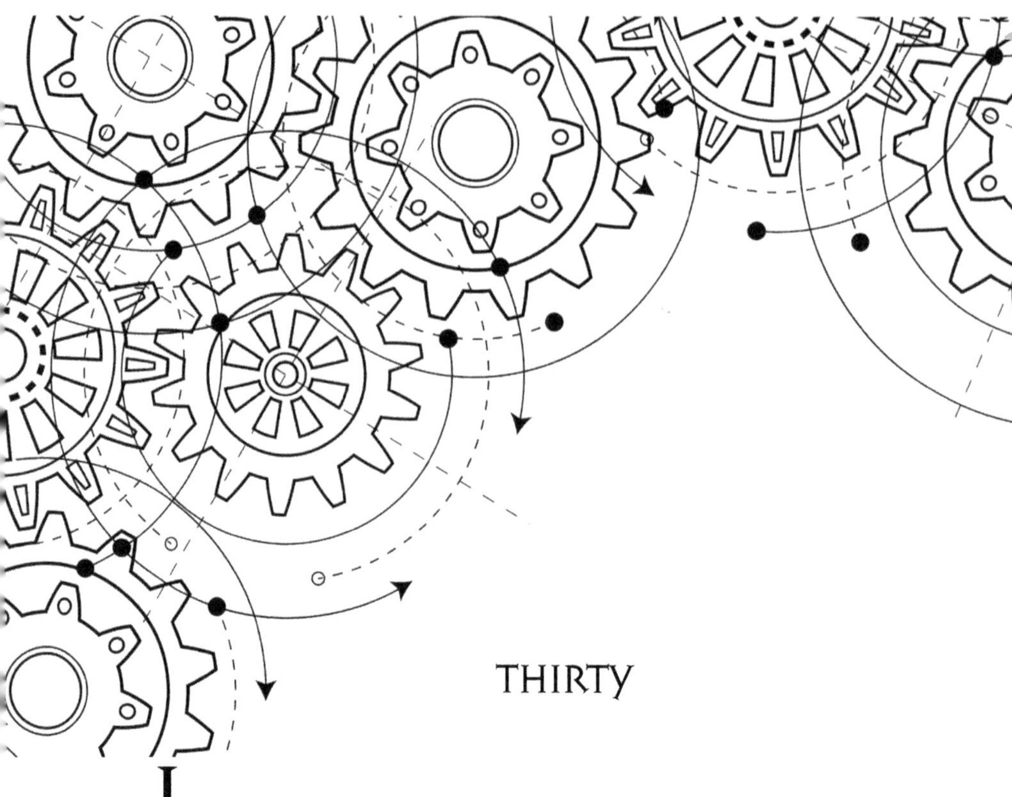

THIRTY

It seemed the gods had blessed the day with balmy, salt-scented breezes west from the sea, unnaturally warm on the eve of winter. Sepharia moved gingerly to the window and stretched her neck. It'd been a long time since she'd felt the urge to get up and move. Most days she just wanted to sleep away the aching muscles and scratchy coughs that plagued her.

The morning had an air of false peacefulness. The domus made its home on Palatine Hill and beneath her window, the white stone buildings battled with each other for space. In Alexandria, the criss-crossing streets left travelers at ease as they moved deliberately through the city, knowing they could easily find their destination. The buildings of Rome, though starkly beautiful with their heavenly colonnades and thundering arches, bone-white in their coloring, seemed ill-at-ease with their compatriots, jammed together like a crowd gathered for an execution.

The question that perched in her mind like a raven in a high tree, was if she should return to Alexandria with Heron tomorrow after the reformation was complete. Home had its benefits, she could return to the workshop and throw herself back into making jewelry and delicate gears for Heron. She could even attend the Palace with Polyxena and play at politics from time to time.

But the summer green eyes of Sextus had a window to her soul. During the long hours in bed, between the fits of raw coughing, she imagined his body against hers. But these desires were like Icarus trying to catch the sun. If she stayed, and Heron left, then beyond simple at-traction, Sextus would have little need to see her, and she would plummet to the earth. Sepharia knew all too well that Aelia would want to match him with a woman of considerable influence. She was not one to waste the fruit of her loins on love. Not that Sepharia had any delusions that it was love. Her childhood illusions had been shattered with Vima. Love was a myth, just like the stories. But stories were nice to hear once in a while, and that's what Sextus represented, a story she'd like to hear, even if it were only for a little while.

With the walls of her room closing in, she wrapped a comfortable stola around her body, noting the way her ribs stuck out from the weeks without food. With her throat still raw from the poison, she'd found it hard to eat enough to regain the weight she'd lost.

She found Heron alone in the demolished courtyard. Piles of dirt from the upended bushes still sat on the cobblestones. Dead leaves crunched underfoot. Her father hunched over the drawing table, ink-smeared tunic hanging like a curtain over her body. Like a pair of ghosts they'd become. The area gave the impression of a necropolis to Sepharia with its chthonic smells.

Sepharia stood silently to the side, waiting for Heron to notice her. And when she did, it was with a warm smile. Somewhere else in the domus, the baritone voices of Northmen carried.

"Have you made your decision?" asked Heron.

"Not yet. That's why I came to see you. What would you do?"

Heron shook her head. "We're different people, you and I. I just want to get back to my workshop. You, I think, have other ambitions."

The ends of her fingertips felt soothing against her cracked lips. "It's hard to say. At times I feel like Athena, filled with wisdom and ready to go to war, but then I remember in these games, you can only lose once. Rome is an awful place."

"Then come back to Alexandria with me," said Heron, smiling wistfully. "Tomorrow evening, Hoth's ship leaves for Alexandria. Punt and Plutarch will be joining me and we'll go home."

"You're right when you say I have other ambitions. I want to be in the middle of events, but once I'm there, I realize how terrible they are. Is that the price of having your name etched into history?" asked Sepharia.

"Every path is difficult, for different reasons. Mine as a simple owner of a workshop has never been simple," said Heron.

"Simple?" Sepharia raised an eyebrow. "You're right, it's never been simple. But I feel like we're on the edge of a calmer time. With Rome conquered and you free to practice your trade in Alexandria, there will be no intrigue, no secret plots."

Heron laughed. "You really are made for this. I just want to be done with it and you want more."

"I'm a fool for thinking so, I think," said Sepharia.

The quiet filled in between them, and beyond the domus, the sounds of the street trickled in: a wagon clattering across the cobblestones, men shouting greetings to one another, the distant sounds of steam mechanicals echoing off the buildings.

"Will it really be calmer after tomorrow?" asked Sepharia.

Heron looked uneasy for a moment, before she took a sip of water from a cup. "Both Agog and Magnus wait outside the city with their retinues, ready to arrive at the Senate at the appointed moment. We have enough Senators ready to reform the government, though they themselves do not know our plans. The first leg of the Iron Road, from the city to the sea, though untested, waits ready to transform the Empire. And finally, Vestalis has prepared our loyal Alexandrian troops to ensure this all goes smoothly."

"Won't their presence in the city alert Silius to the danger?" asked Sepharia.

"Maybe, though it'd be too late, even if they figure something was happening," said Heron. "By the time I move to the Senate floor to announce the reformation, they will have no more power. But, as a precaution, Vestalis disguised his non-Northmen troops as merchants, so they can get near the Senate without alerting Silius. If you see men in gray tunics with crimson edgings, know they are Vestalis' soldiers."

A different question formed in her mind, one she had not considered for a while. "And what of the quest for Julius Caesar and the *why* of his death? I recall that I was researching that before I was poisoned. Does it still matter?"

Heron looked distracted for a moment, rearranging the quill and inkpot on the table. "It might, and I mean to find out tonight."

"Why *was* he murdered?" asked Sepharia, feeling an itch in the back of her mind that something about this was important.

"He grew too powerful, took too much glory from the others in Rome," said Heron, simply. "A lesson we failed when we first took the city."

"I recall..." The words trailed from Sepharia's lips, "that phrase, *mundus patet.* Open the world. Did you ever find out what it meant? It still bothers me that I do not know."

"Nothing," said Heron, shaking her head lightly.

Sepharia recalled that she'd heard it from Sextus, and that it had something to do with the priesthood.

Heron frowned. "Or have I? My mind has been too weighed down by our plans to remember. It has to do with Ceres, the goddess of agriculture. I witnessed a ritual, one involving Ceres, or so I think. Silius was there, and Antonius, and some others. I never heard her name, but the man who sent me there, made mention of Ceres."

It seemed her father was quite distracted, so Sepharia sounded out her thoughts. "I cannot think of why Ceres would be important? The goddess of agriculture would be necessary, except Rome cannot even feed itself anymore. It gets its grain from Egypt. Probably it means nothing. These Romans use gods for power, not the other way around like in Alexandria."

"I've noted the same thing," said Heron, glancing up. "And I would say it interests me further, but it does not. I am sick of battling these gods over the affairs of men. It seems that they are made real by our actions. But yet, if I ignore them, I do so at my own peril, since others are ruled by them."

"Only another day," Sepharia comforted her father. "Only another day and we can return to the simpler gods of Alexandria."

Heron's face went soft, hopeful. "You'll return to Alexandria?"

Sepharia searched her thoughts. "Yes, it seems that's my truest desire, that I would speak it, unbidden."

"I am much pleased, daughter," smiled Heron.

"November the 8th," said Sepharia and when she did, a slight jolt went through her, "the day we shall return."

The piston on Heron's leg wheezed awake as she stood. Heron looked down at her ink spattered tunic. "All this talk has reminded me that I have one more task before our plans are set. One more ally to confirm before the momentous day. I shall put on less dreadful attire and take a steam chariot away."

"Bring a sizable guard with you," reminded Sepharia. "Better to be safe with so little time left."

"I will," said her father, as she hobbled from the room, brass arm glinting in the morning light.

Sepharia, feeling tired for the effort, returned to her room after grabbing the hunk of hard bread left on Heron's table. Breaking sections of crust away and slipping them into her mouth, she let her saliva soften the bread before attempting to swallow.

When she reached her room, and plopped onto the bed, Sepharia was struck by a nagging remembrance. She glanced to the table, expecting some memory to come rushing back, annoyed triply that it stayed just beyond her grasp, when at last it came to her like a coin spotted in a fountain.

At first she paused, reeling with remembrance and then she looked frantically around the room. She'd been awake in her room for weeks and she had not noticed it all this time, but she desired to look upon it and reconnect with those memories that would not come back to her, knowing that if she could, she might discover if she knew anything that might put their return to Alexandria in jeopardy.

"Where is that book?" she whispered.

THIRTY ONE

The wind rattled the dying leaves like bones. Her steam chariot voiced its power mutedly, the surrounding olive groves seeming to take offense by its presence and annihilating its normally throaty roar.

As they climbed Quirinal Hill, Heron looked backwards into the city. Autumn had been brief, coloring the landscape in vivid yellows and purplish-reds, before plunging into decay. It'd been months since rain had fallen and the city had a desiccated feel to it, like ancient papyrus from the oldest sections of the Great Library. Heron had signed three laws just the day before: one on the diversion of more water down the aqueducts from Trastevere, another to collect funds to build a sixth major aqueduct into the city, and the third a ban on public fires. And though she could not see it now since it flowed behind Palatine Hill, the Tiber River had become a brackish, polluted stream as herders to the north took their livestock to the water since their ponds had dried up. It was a noxious flow, even in the best of times; now the physician halls were filled with those ill from taking their drink from the Tiber.

The steam chariot rattled to a stop and the same servant girl with the wet towel greeted her upon arrival. The soothing cloth was a luxury, to wipe the dust from her face, and clean the corners of her eyes of the gunk that had collected there. The air was alive with dust from the farmers gathering their crops east of the city.

Upon entering the domus, her nose immediately caught the scent of fire and alarm bells went off in her head, until she remembered his fireplace. Standing right inside, having come from the courtyard, her backside felt cool, while her front was warm.

"The Warrior of the Senate returns," said Dominitus, his voice carrying through the dimly lit room.

Heron stepped further into the room and blinked hard, to clear the light from her vision. Senator Dominitus sat on a simple wood chair before the fireplace, warming his hands on the crackling fire. The flickering flame cast shadows across his wrinkled face. He smiled at her and she could see what a handsome man he'd been at a younger time.

He motioned her over and she moved to join him on a chair set near him, facing the fire. Had he been waiting for her? A scuffed foot from the corner made her turn her head, but she saw nothing and dismissed it as her imagination. The closer they got to the fruition of their plans, the more she worried.

"Expecting me?" she asked, standing next to the chair, feeling the warm wood beneath her hand. The mechanical arm, she let hang at her side, she'd damaged enough of his personal effects on the previous visit.

"Always," he said, staring at her arm. The firelight reflected in his eyes. "Such beautiful workmanship. Have you ever figured out how to make a mechanical man?"

She shook her head. "Not yet. And it might be beyond my talents. He would have to be a big as a house to contain all the parts I find necessary."

"Shame," he said, his lips curling and his wrinkles gathering shadows, "it would be a boon to the world to have such servants."

So close to the end, she did not take solace in his like-minded thinking. Maybe in Alexandria, she could reconsider the problem, but not now.

"I worry that some folk cannot live without having people beneath them. Rather than use these mechanical servants to make their lives better, they'd use them to lord over the others," said Heron.

"And this surprises you?" asked Dominitus with an eyebrow arched.

"No, I suppose it does not."

Dominitus cleared his throat. "Yet, you seem disappointed."

"I have not fully embraced my cynicism, it seems," replied Heron. "But in all my time making miracles for the temples, I saw this truth over and over."

"So some men are meant to be lorded over, want to be lorded over?" Dominitus asked in a way that made her feel like the question was a test. Much as the previous visit, she felt like there'd been an additional layer of conversation that she'd been missing. If this were a set of gears to be calculated, to determine the best ratio for driving a wheel, she could do it in two heartbeats, but the unknown machine of man's intellect and drive eluded her.

"I do not propose how men feel," said Heron cautiously. "But I am a realist and do know that sometimes it works best to act as if men want to be ruled, though it is not me that wishes to rule."

From his seated position, he gave her a surprisingly deep bow, hinting to an unexpected limberness for the old man. "Spoken like a true politician. Maybe in a few years, you'll be usurping the Northman and leading us into an enlightened age."

"It's not my desire," she said, leaving out that she would be leaving tomorrow evening.

The wrinkled skin around his eyes creased, ever so slightly. Judgingly, if she'd read him right. He loved his games, she could see. The way his lips parted like a lover before a kiss, the glint of his teeth in the firelight. But she was tired of them, tired of sparring, tired of subtext.

"Do I pass your test?" she asked.

Dominitus reacted as if slapped. "What?"

"Your test? The obolus, the questions. Do I pass?" she asked.

"But you haven't even told me why they killed Caesar? By the gods, I didn't even know you still remembered my request." He smiled coyly.

Heron let the words flow from her lips, not caring if she coached them in the oratory styles of the Great Library: "He was too successful and by my recollection, it was simple jealousy that killed him. By the adoration of the people, his ambitious Gaul campaign, and the warping of the Republic around his mantle, he sucked the life from their glory. Glory is everything in Rome, right?" Dominitus nodded. "That is the real coin of Rome. Glory. The dream of every Roman is to be cheered during a parade through the Via Sacra, leading up to the Forum, to be crowned with glory eternal. To be remembered like the myths, to have their name etched into history, never forgotten, to be spoken fondly of, or even cursed if that is the way of it, like the gods. By Julius Caesar taking all the glory, and threatening to invade Parthia, which he would have certainly been successful, after which, he would have been untouchable. They had to kill him before his death caused the upheaval of the Empire."

"You call that simple jealousy?" he asked.

"Simple? I suppose not. Wretched jealousy, maybe." She stopped, fearing she'd said too much.

They held their silence amid the crackling fire. Senator Dominitus seemed at ease with it, while Heron felt slightly ill.

"The city is ripe," said Dominitus. "Look what happened to Tiberius. His slaves turning on him. They said the scene was gruesome, but I don't think the hanging corpses of those slaves will dissuade others if they think they have no way out."

"I cannot say I am saddened by his loss and his death was the talk of the Senate," replied Heron. "But I think those concerns would be lessened if they freed them like you have. The elite have the coin to pay their workers, they just prefer absolute control."

A slight *tick* of metal on metal in the corner drew her attention. She looked deeply into the darkness between the two grand cabinets filled with books and trinkets, but saw nothing.

"So why did you come to visit me?" asked Dominitus.

"I feel you already know," she said.

He shrugged ambivalently. "I still prefer to be asked."

"I want your support, no, I want your leadership," she said.

He frowned. "A pointless exercise. Silius controls the Senate. He has the votes."

"He won't after tomorrow."

Senator Dominitus perked up, sitting straightly in his chair. The fire popped sending an ember onto the stone before his feet. He stretched his foot and squashed the bright spot until it was a soot smear.

"Intrigue," he said, tasting the words on his lips as if it were a delicious meal. "I'm quite pleased to hear this. Can I hear more?"

"No," she said. "But you'll understand after tomorrow. If your health is up to it, please attend the Senate proceedings. I think you'll find them quite interesting."

"And do I have a part to play?" he asked quizzically.

"You will, but not yet. Your role will be to get the Senate back to work after tomorrow, get them back into governing rather than extracting wealth from the Empire," she replied.

"I shall be there." He smiled, all the way up to his eyes. "It seems you've brought me more than an obolus. You've brought me the whole River Styx. You've blossomed into quite the player in Rome. I tremble with curiosity on the matter of your play tomorrow. I'm sure the gods will be watching with much interest, too. And what an interesting and significant day to strike, oh, how Senator Silius will be wrathful."

Heron tilted her head. "And why would he be wrathful?"

"You've picked the Ludi Plebii to strike."

She wrinkled her forehead. "The Plebian Games? It seems every other day is a festival in Rome."

He spoke proudly with fervor in his voice. "But it is also the third and final Day of the Dead before winter. The last day of harvest historically and the last day before the world descends."

It meant nothing to her, though he confirmed that it'd been Silius who'd sent his men after her on the first Day of the Dead. "Apologies that my visit must be short, but there are last minute plans to make. We are agreed?"

"By Jupiter, I will be there," he smiled.

Heron felt a wave of relief. Though she had given him little idea to the nature of their plans, it gave her solace that Senator Dominitus would be on their side. More so, that he could advise Agog when he returned, giving him a safe voice. The Senator's return to power, coupled with the reformation, would leave him beholden to the new government. He was also the man least likely to have ties since he'd been out of power for so long. Even her occasional inquiries to the status of his name was left with wonder that he was even alive. Most Senators had forgotten his existence as he secluded himself in his domus like it was a fortress.

Heron turned to leave when she remembered the note he'd left her. She gripped the chair tightly as she pivoted. "Why did you send me to the Monte delle Piche?"

In her brief dealings with Senator Dominitus, she'd never detected even a hint of surprise. His mastery of their encounters seemed never in question, but her mere mention of Monte delle Piche brought an unmistakable flinch in his eyes, a look of deep worry, but true to his nature, it was gone in a blink.

"Why would I send you to that place?" he asked sternly, the wrinkles on his forehead making deep valleys. "How did you even hear of it?"

"What do you know of it?" she asked.

"Only that it is a place of power."

She paused, feeling cracks form in their agreement. "A place you were once a member of?"

He nodded. "Did you witness anything?"

She shrugged. "A ritual with a woman, Senator Antonius, possibly Senator Silius, the others we couldn't see. Can you tell me of it?"

"They wore masks?" he asked and after she nodded her head, he stared into his wrinkled hands. "Did they see you?"

"No," she lied, feeling that it was important to do so. "Can you tell me of this place."

"It will not matter after tomorrow."

"And you did not send me there?" she asked.

He shook his head with great exaggeration and she believed him wholeheartedly. "I would not risk your life to do so."

She wanted to stay and ask him more questions, but she could see by his gaze that to do so, would damage their agreement. There were other threads that this revelation brought to light, but she had no time to think about them.

"It doesn't matter," she said, moving toward the courtyard. "At least not after tomorrow."

He nodded solemnly and as she turned, she thought she caught a glimpse of something in between the cabinets. Maybe a person, or maybe just a trick of the light. She dismissed the thought quickly, for she had other concerns: the Senate, the reformation of the Republic, the moving of their troops into place, and now it seemed, the identity of who had sent her to the Monte delle Piche.

THIRTY TWO

"The conspirator hides in her domus."

The voice startled Sepharia and she grabbed the dull knife that she used to pry wax seals from letters. She spun, brandishing the flimsy blade with both hands, ready to defend herself from the intruder.

Sextus Paetina leaned in the doorway with a thumb hooked into his gold-leaf adorned leather belt. A mercurial grin formed on his lips as he eyed the weapon in her trembling hands.

"A vicious arm-cleaving weapon, that one," said Sextus.

Sepharia threw the letter opener at him and it bounced harmlessly off his chest. "You should not startle me like that. I was busy." She picked up a lemon stola and began folding it, glaring over the fabric as if it were a field of battle.

He whistled softly and glanced around the room. "I see it's true, you're preparing for a long journey. The return to Alexandria, I assume."

The traveling chest was stuffed full with silken stolas and delicate pallas. A smaller box of jewelry lay on the bed, gold glinting in the afternoon sun, streaming through the window. Her tools had been packed away already, along with Heron's equipment, sent to the ship ahead of them. Her personal affects would ride with her on the final journey from the city.

"I wanted to tell you," She looked deeply into his green eyes, "but I couldn't. It seemed easier to just leave."

He stayed in the doorway. "That's why I came to you."

"Doesn't Aelia need you at the Senate? The announcement's in a few hours."

He made a gesture with one shoulder that belayed his interest. "The real work's already been done. There'd be nothing to do and I'd prefer to have my farewells."

Sepharia finished folding the lemon stola into a neat square and tucked it into the box. She was glad she'd packed the tunics earlier, since Sextus would wonder why she owned such garments. Once she was on the iron boat, she would change into her normal attire, but for now, she wanted to honor Rome with a cream stola with crimson accents.

"Then have your farewell," she taunted.

He marched up to her and gently took her wrist in his callused hand. She gave him a petulant frown. "You Romans say farewell oddly."

He appeared confused and dropped her wrist. She could still feel the warmth of his hand, even after it was away. Sextus backed up one step. "Apologies."

"Ha," she laughed and stepped up close. "The farewell I wanted was this." She pressed herself against him, biting his lower lip and sucking on it. When he let out a whimpering moan, she removed her teeth from his lip.

"Where did you learn such things?"

She could have told him it was with Hoth the Black, but she didn't think that would help the mood. "Alexandrian women are taught such practices at an early age."

"Lies. You just want me to visit you in Alexandria," he said.

"It's crossed my mind."

He smiled wistfully. "You never know if the gods might find reason to bring us together, but my duty to the Empire will grow after today. Once Magnus is pardoned, I will join his retinue, and we'll be sent out to quell the minor rebellions in the Empire."

"Half of them started by him," said Sepharia.

He nodded. "Making our success nearly assured."

"And giving you marks for glory."

"It's the first of many steps towards a place in the Senate," he replied.

"Like your priesthood," she said.

It was only a playful barb, but when he flinched, she remembered the book she'd taken from the Sacris Faciundus. "The book, you took it back, didn't you."

"How did you come to possess it?"

His face grew gravely serious and she decided to confess since she was leaving. "I stole it from your priestly college."

"But why?" he asked, visibly hurt.

"Because you would not tell me about the *mundus patet*, or why those men attacked us on the Day of the Dead," she said.

He flinched at the phrase and glanced worriedly toward the open window. "I told you, our lives would be in danger if I mentioned where I heard it."

She hit him in the chest with an open palm. "So you would let me die rather than break a vow? What kind of friends are you and your mother?"

He shook his head. "Leave her out of this, she knows nothing of it." He appeared to want to say more, but could only gnash his teeth.

"I'm leaving Rome. You can spare just one drop of your secrets, otherwise I will remember you the villain."

"By the gods, it doesn't matter since we know who our enemies are," he said forcibly. "But if it matters to you, I overheard Senator Antonius one night late at the College, speaking to another man about how *things would be different* after the Day of the Dead in Rome. And if I wanted to let you die, I would have said nothing. I only refused to tell you where I heard it afterwards and in the middle of that very public museum."

The name sparked a memory, like a bubble from the depth bursting on the surface. "I remember, when I was in the Sacris." She glared at him accusingly. "I heard you, conspiring with him, and your mother."

Sextus' forehead wrinkled with confusion. "I do not know what you speak of and if you should, be careful of making false accusation, especially when you should not have been there!"

Sepharia searched her memory then spit the words back at him: *"Please pass along to your mother that I'm considering her offer. It's hard to turn down, considering the circumstances, though I feel I'd be giving up too much."*

He frowned with remembrance.

"If I recall," she continued, "you said *she will be pleased.*"

Sextus tilted his head, and Sepharia couldn't understand why he wasn't either outraged or in full denial. When he started laughing, she felt unnerved.

"Yes, yes," he said, "I remember that conversation." He grinned, looking into her eyes. "We were talking about a horse. My mother wanted to purchase a horse from Senator Antonius for the chariot races. In the end, the deal couldn't be consummated, since she'd heard about a bit of lameness. Not long after, the horse broke its leg on the Circus Maximus and had to be killed. A nice bit of luck for the Paetina family."

"A horse?" she asked, relieved.

"Yes, a horse," he responded.

She took a deep breath. If there'd been some truth to it, what she thought she'd heard, then they couldn't trust the Paetina family and she'd have to race to the Senate and stop Heron from going through with it. After having the soldiers at the domus deal with Sextus, of course, which would have been difficult, considering their previous flirtations.

She smiled at his bright green eyes and thanked the gods, old and new, that it hadn't come to that. The relief took the edge off her nervousness and she placed her fingertips against his arm, letting them drag down playfully with just a hint of fingernail.

"The luck of the gods must be on our side," said Sepharia. "Had I not been poisoned, I would have revealed that overheard conversation to Heron and today would be an entirely different day."

He gently brushed the hair away from her shoulder. "But the poisoning did wonders for your voice, though I scarcely believed it could be improved."

"Do not jest," she said, digging her nails into his arm.

"I do not lie. Your voice has a quality now that I might expect from the goddess Minerva, deep with authority, while still warm and delightful. Like honey poured over steel," said Sextus.

She let her tongue touch the tip of her teeth. "I think I am done speaking now."

"By wha—?"

She kissed the words from his lips, pushing him against the wall. He pulled her in and hungrily returned her kisses. She slid her hand across his bare thigh, trailing upward until it traced the edge of his groin. She moved slower the closer she got, and the slower she drew her seductive line, the more a guttural moan escaped his lips. When she cupped him, he gasped and thrust against her, his fingers digging into her stola, trying desperately to unravel it. She toyed with him, letting his desire build. She wanted him to remember her for a long time.

When he found the edge of the fabric, he tugged it away, and the sheet slid across half her chest, exposing her taut nipple. He sucked hungrily at her breast and she gasped slightly for the stubble against her tender flesh.

She pawed at the door trying to close it, to hide their tryst, when she heard the scream. At first she thought it might have been her imagination, but then she heard it again. Not a woman's scream, but a yell of pain, of death. The world went cold and she pushed him away.

"What? Why?" he asked, clearly enraptured by her attentions.

"Listen," she whispered.

The clash of steel below carried to their level. There was no mistaking it. Sepharia tugged her stola back over her shoulder and together the two of them crept toward the balcony that overlooked the courtyard. Beneath them, five men in white face paint, bronze armguards, and leather breastplates battled two Northmen, and the Northmen were losing badly. Two corpses lay on the far side of the cobblestones with axes laying impotently in their cold grips.

When she looked in Sextus' eyes, she saw his fear, and knew that this had not been planned, at least by him. If she had needed any confirmation of his allegiance, this was it, but it might not matter if she only lived another hour.

THIRTY THREE

A flock of ravens scattered at the approaching steam chariots. Gray-bottomed clouds rolled over the field, pushing dead leaves into the sky. Titus Vestalis gave the signal, a lean muscled arm held skyward, bringing the ten steam chariots to a halt. He eyed the leeward angle of the back vehicles, leaving his scathing comments unsaid, for now was not the time to reinforce discipline

The field west of them had been stripped bare except for scattered piles of wheat stalks. He marched to the edge of the field and sniffed the air. A few hearth fires burned in distant homes, but otherwise, the air had a sharp bite to it, like the breath of winter exhaled. The red-haired Northman, Donar, joined him near the fence line.

"Where's Magnus?" asked Donar. "He should be here."

The big man surveyed the fields in searching patterns, lips partially hidden by the scraggly beard, but cast in a frown.

"Do you sense it?" asked Vestalis, feeling an itch crawl down his spine.

Donar tugged at his bushy red beard. "I don't like it."

"Neither do I. This is the farm where we were to meet," said Vestalis. "But even before we got here, after we left camp, something felt wrong."

Donar grunted. "You're a hard man, Vestalis. A kind of man who'd thrive in the North. I never thought you one for gut feelings."

"A gut feeling's just your experience telling you the truth without words. Just have to reason out why it feels that way," said Vestalis.

"Ever worked?" asked Donar, still surveying the field. The rest of the soldiers stayed to their steam chariots. A few were taking a piss by a lone olive tree on the fence line. It was old enough to look like three trees twisted together.

"A few times," said Vestalis. "Once on a campaign, I got sent out to find a rebellious group of Thracians that had slaughtered a messenger on the road back to Rome. It was only supposed to be a half-dozen of them, but Consul Odrii wanted the messenger avenged and the roads to be kept clear. On the way, we came upon an old woman trying to get her horses and wagon out of the mud. The wagon wheels had sunk deep and she was whipping the poor beasts and screaming at them in a tongue I'd never heard before. She was halfway pretty, and not terribly old either. There were twenty of us on horseback and we'd been riding for two days. A few of the men offered to use their mounts to pull her free, but I declined, on account of the suspicion I had upon finding her. In fact, I kept the men back and we watched her struggle, while I tried to work out what I found wrong."

"What had you seen?" asked Donar. "Was it the woman that gave them away?"

Vestalis gave a curt shake of the head. "Not the woman. It was the horses. They weren't farm horses, but the sleek fast traveling mounts the Thracians preferred, when they rode."

Donar grunted in appreciation. "And the Thracians? Where were they hiding?"

The stubble on his jaw felt soothing to rub. It felt like only yesterday he'd been that young. How time had passed, but not all together changed. "If we'd stopped to help that woman, who it turned out was a prostitute they'd brought with them, we would have been dead, every one of us. The Thracians had dug ingenious pits near the road, covering themselves with hunks of grass. And there were ten of them, not six, and that would have been enough by ambush to wipe us to the man."

"And you have that feeling again?" asked Donar.

Vestalis closed his eyes briefly, feeling the tingle of warning against his back. "I've had it since we left the Via Nomentana."

Donar took two steps away and turned one full revolution. "Maybe your feeling's not right this time. There's no one within a few stadia."

"And no Magnus, either," said Vestalis.

"Maybe he's late," replied Donar.

"He's never late."

Donar put a hand on his hilt and squeezed it. "Betrayal?"

"Not him, I think."

But Vestalis wasn't so sure. Magnus had signed the agreement with Agog, but it wouldn't be the first time an agreement had been broken, especially when there was a huge advantage to be gained.

"Shouldn't there be farmers gathering crops?" asked Vestalis.

The red-bearded Donar fruitlessly swiped the hair from his face, blown there by the wind, and unsuccessful, growled at it. "You're right. We haven't seen a soul in a single field since we left the Via Nomentana."

Vestalis climbed over the fence and started walking across the harvested field. Dust kicked up at each step, trailing away from his feet, carried by the steady wind. The piles of wheat stalks reached higher than his head. There were at least twenty of them scattered. Vestalis looked to the field and then back at his men, milling about the steam chariots. They were disciplined enough not to wander off, but they were hardly attentive. The Northmen were fearsome fighters, but not at all disciplined like the Legion. If it weren't for Heron's weapons, they would have long ago been put to the sword by Rome.

He walked back to Donar, who was still rubbing his beard. "Maybe I'm imagining things," said Vestalis.

One of the men gave a shout, and three of them were pointing in the opposite direction, toward a place two fields over. Vestalis didn't see it at first, but then he saw the glint of weapons lying in the dirt. There were at least three bodies, or at least from this distance, what appeared to be bodies.

Vestalis gave the order to investigate, but they did so together, all ten steam chariots with men at the arrow launchers. He massaged the hilt of his gladius the whole way over.

There were more than just three bodies. At least twenty men had perished in a pitched battle.

"Is it Magnus' men?" asked Donar.

The dead man nearest held a black shield with a crimson eagle. "That's the Black Legion, the legion he filled with his best soldiers. It was their bravery and skill that helped him cut his way out of Antioch and flee into the mountains."

"Is Magnus here?"

Vestalis walked among the bodies until he found him, or at least what had been Consul Magnus. They'd cut his head from his body. Though it been a long time, he knew the man enough to recognize his face.

"It wasn't treachery, at least by him," said Vestalis. "Died with a sword in his hand, at least."

"It's all any of us can ask for," replied Donar. "But no sign of his attackers.”

“They must have taken the bodies.” Vestalis pointed to the ground. “You can see the trampled grass and hobnail boot marks. Whoever did this brought at least thirty men.”

Donar grumbled. “But thirty isn’t enough to slaughter twenty.”

“Unless they thought they were friends.”

Vestalis spotted something shiny amid the grass. Surprise escaped his lips as he held up the finger length object.

“By Freya’s tits, what’s that?” asked Donar.

“A mechanical finger,” said Vestalis, as he tried to make the finger bend, but there were no gears in it. Just a hollow tube. “They ambushed Consul Magnus using someone disguised as Heron to get close. Even from a distance Heron’s mechanical limbs are unmistakable. Magnus must have thought Heron had come to greet him.”

“And paid for it with his life,” said Donar, shaking away the red hair from his face as he looked into the wind. “But only someone familiar with our plans could know we were going to meet with Magnus.”

The truth was as plain as the sky above and though Vestalis had never been one to shy away from truth, this time it pained him, since they’d invested so much. “It can only be that bitch, Aelia, or her son, Sextus. The Paetina family’s the only one that knows about this meeting.”

Donar’s eyes went wide. “This isn’t the only meeting they know about.”

A chill struck through his body like a frozen bell. “Agog should be in the city now, on the Appian Way. To the chariots!”

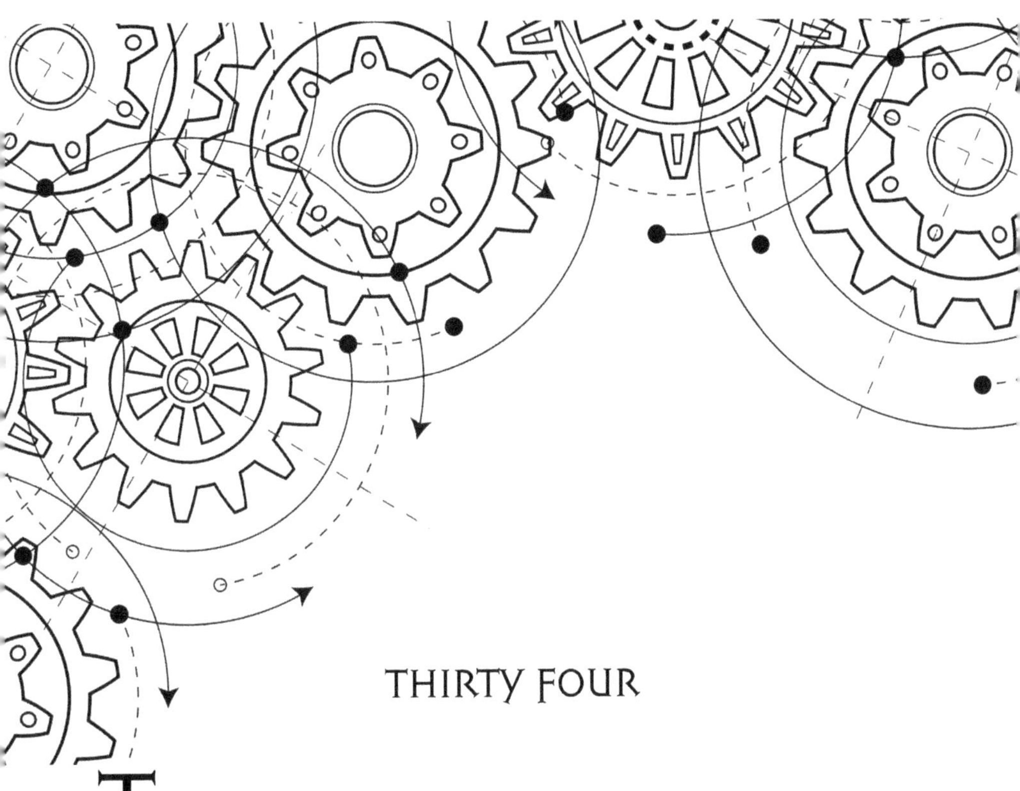

THIRTY FOUR

There were some battles in life worth fighting. Taking Alexandria from Rome, that'd been one of them. Killing the beast of the wood for Aurinia, that'd been another. But Agog's heart had never been engaged in taking down Consul Magnus. Agog would have been happy to have forgiven the battle master, and welcomed him with open arms back to Rome, but the Senate had been adamant about dealing with Magnus in the negotiations. At the time, Agog had thought it a simple task, given his superior armaments and backing of the Empire, but the Consul had proved a difficult foe. So Agog was quite pleased to be returning to Rome and putting the war behind him. Given everything that Heron had written to him about Senator Silius, Agog now understood why the Senators had wanted him to take on Magnus. They wanted him out of the city. Hopefully returning and the reorganization of the government would put an end to Silius' machinations.

He scratched his belly, what was left of it, and slipped past the brass piping that tugged on his hips as he stepped off the steam chariot. Even a year on the road couldn't make him that thin.

His closest guard formed around him, mostly Northmen, but a few Alexandrians who had gained his trust, and even one Kushite, a tall angular fellow who wielded a spear as long as two men and could throw it a dozen strides to stick in a man's eye. Battles were won and lost on small details and it was good to have men like these around him in the thick of things.

They moved in silence, everyone knew the plan: they would hide the steam chariots in a stable northeast of the city, a place Vestalis had chosen, and move to a warehouse not far away to take merchant wagons into the city to the Senate House. They wore simple tunics and cloaks for warmth, russet and gray woolen, nothing a soldier would wear. As a precaution, they brought weapons, and once on the wagons, it would be easy to hide them.

Agog glanced around him and smirked. Anyone looking closely at them would see them for what they were, there was no denying it. They walked with a hungry purpose, men used to throwing themselves into battle and their lives to the whims of the gods.

The Northman by his side, a tall blond warrior named Svarn with a twice-broken nose and a scar that crossed his lip and curled it into a permanent smirk, nodded grimly when they made eye contact. It was good to be home, or at least what his home had become. Agog looked forward to sitting by a warm fire and sharing stories with Consul Magnus, a man he planned on embracing upon first meeting.

He smiled fondly at a passing memory, one of a long ago winter battle, when the midnight wind could freeze a man solid three steps from his door. Night was falling and the battle was just getting started. The waist deep snow had turned their battle to a farce. Agog remembered the moment he locked gazes with the warrior who led the other side, a man named Bëorn, who was as wide as a bear and could bend a sword in his fist. It only took one look at the sluggish blows of the two sides and they both nodded in unison and ended the battle, retiring to the hall and drinking the winter away rather than fight. They resolved their dispute with a contest of stories, a contest that Agog handily won when he told the tale of his battle with the beast of the wild, the creature he had to slay to win Aurelia's trust (not her heart, since that took much longer and required less sword swinging and more herb picking.) Agog couldn't remember why they'd started the battle, but the ending proved memorable.

As he crossed the street, his hackles rose and he felt himself hurrying just a little bit. When Svarn raised his wine skin to squirt down a taste of the tart drink they'd liberated from the Thracian farmers, Agog shook his head and Svarn stopped himself mid-squeeze, letting the purple liquid dribble onto his tunic rather than into his mouth.

"When this is over, not before," said Agog.

He could see the disappointment, but he knew Svarn would understand. Never start celebrating until the battle was over, a lesson he'd had to learn more than once. They didn't have much of a part to play, Heron and Vestalis had set everything up, but every step was fraught with danger.

The warehouse was a sturdy wooden structure with wide timbers and a clay roof. They were still on the outer portions of the city where stone was less common for building. The wealth of marble near Palatine Hill made Agog wonder if there was any stone left in the world.

A chalk mark had been left on the door they needed to enter. A circle with two lines hanging beneath it, a rough translation of Yggdrasil. He touched his fingers to the chalk, smearing the trailing end of one line, before pushing open the door. The sun was not too bright outside, but his vision took a few moments to adjust. A hallway stretched out before him and he checked to make sure his guard was with him before he forged forward. Ahead, and inside the warehouse, there would be three wagons waiting for them, with tarps in the back to hide the extra men.

He took a deep breath and stepped forward, before Svarn put a hand on his shoulder to stop him. One of the men from Alexandria, a slight almost child-size man named Izzet, who'd proved to be an invaluable scout, pointed back the way behind them.

Three streets down, standing in the middle of the street, was a priest in white robes, the kind he was used to seeing in Alexandria. He was bald and standing as still as death. If the others hadn't seen him, Agog might him thought a mirage. At least until he noticed the priest was missing a hand.

"Should we send one of the boys to bring him in?" asked Svarn.

Agog frowned. "It's like he was looking for us."

"Won't take but a few seconds with a knife between his legs to get him to spill his secrets. Nothing loosens a man's tongue like having his seeds threatened," said Svarn, much to the amusement of the companions.

Izzet started moving down the street when Agog called him off.

"I know him," said Agog. "I think."

"Friend of Heron's?" asked Svarn.

"No," said Agog. "The worst kind of man, if I'm right."

Svarn looked ready to send Izzet. "Then let's pay him a visit."

"No."

It was all he said, and the men were disciplined enough not to disobey him. It just didn't make sense that Lysimachus would reveal himself to them, unless it was a trap. But he wasn't completely sure it was him either, though it was hard to fake missing a hand.

He flexed his shoulders, letting the huge sword on his back shift into a more comfortable position. Why would Lysimachus set a trap? Or even could he? There were no temples to Sobek in Rome, that was for sure.

Lysimachus raised his hand-less arm and pointed the other way, jabbing his stump twice in that direction. An indication to go that way.

It didn't feel like a trap at all. It almost felt like a warning, but why would that man, the one who'd tortured and maimed Heron want to warn them? And what was he warning them from?

Agog looked back down the hallway. They really needed to get moving. Heron's announcement would come soon and he needed to be there to ensure the change over happened smoothly.

Lysimachus indicated the other direction again and then turned his back and started walking away. In Agog's eyes, it was the worst ambush ever, but he still couldn't bring himself to give the command.

"We need to go," Agog told his guard. "Heron and the Senate awaits. It's going to be a new day in Rome."

A few of them looked disappointed, they were always up for a fight, especially with overwhelming odds, but they came along quietly enough. Lysimachus was on his mind the whole way down the hall, he worried at it like a bear trying to get into a hornet's nest and each time he tried to make sense of it, he got a sharp sting of worry.

Inside the warehouse, the three wagons hitched up to three pairs of draft horses waited for them, just as the note had told them. The men shared smiles and started moving toward the wagons, ready to make the final journey home. A huge tarp hung over the exit to the building to keep the cold out. Lining the walls were packing boxes, goods that had come from far off places like Indus or Kushite, or wherever Vestalis was doing business these days.

Agog took the lead wagon, testing the reins, feeling the warm leather in his hands, almost like someone had just handed it to him. The horses snorted and stomped, ready to go. The one directly in front of him took a crap on the stone floor, but that would be a mess for someone else to clean up, he was the Emperor, after all. As the men were situated in the back or at the lead, Izzet moved to the tarp and readied to open the way.

There were cries of alarm and weapons pulled from their sheathes in silent anticipation before Agog could look up. On the other side of the tarp, four Manticores were pointed at them and at this close range, they'd be easier to hit than grapes in a mash barrel. The soldiers on the other side of them didn't appear friendly at all and Agog didn't guess these were Vestalis' men.

"Stand down, men, stand down," Agog told them.

As Agog stared across the short space at the wall of arrows pointed at them, he couldn't help but wonder if Lysimachus had truly been warning them. But he didn't think he was going to get to find out anytime soon.

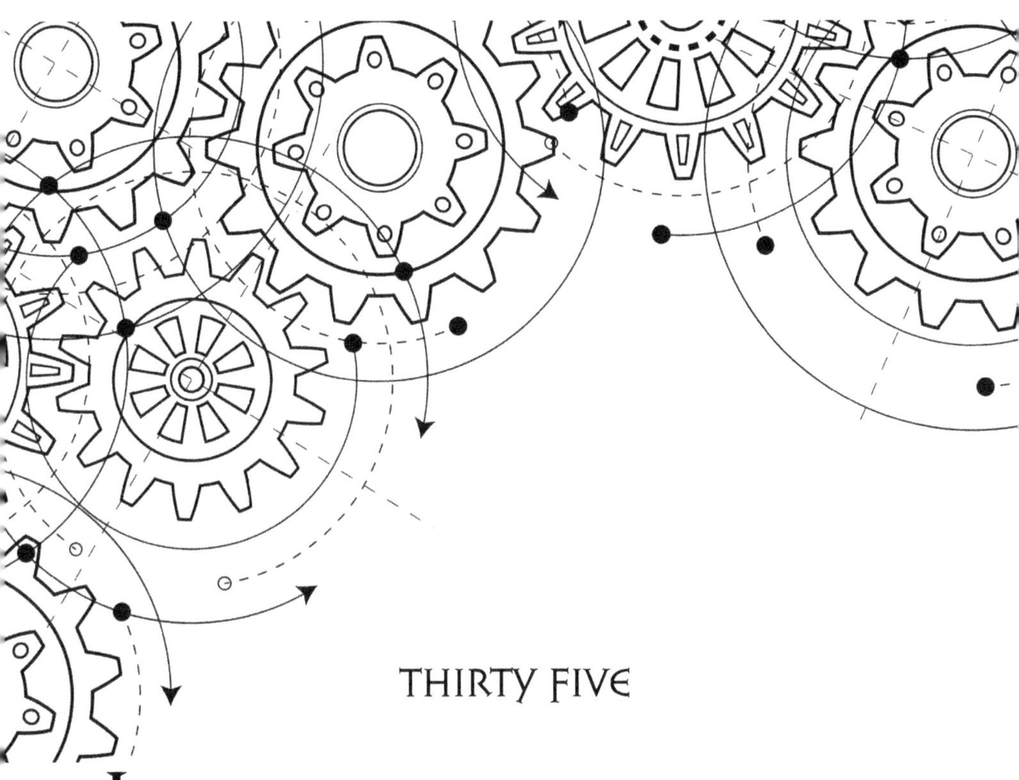

THIRTY FIVE

Leaning heavily on her ivory cane, Heron looked out the window of the Senate House, searching for signs of Agog, while behind her, inside the Senate chamber they gathered and their voices rumbled like war drums. She tried to swallow away her heartbeat, but it took residence in her eyes, in the back of her throat, in her fingertips.

It wasn't the art of oration that concerned her, she'd spoken in the Great Library numerous times, lecturing on the physics of air, or how to construct a gear train, or on the importance of parabolas. She knew and practiced the tricks of speaking, the inflections, counterpoints, how to turn another's argument against them. But in the Great Library, and in the matters of scientific thought, she was their superior. It was rare, if ever, that she was surprised with a clever thought or an answer to a problem she hadn't already solved. When she spoke on a subject, she already knew the answers, and no one could dispute the figures she used to construct them.

In this game of politics, there were no proofs, no calculations to confirm reasoning, no treatise on the underlining math. If there was a calculation, it was only as simple as alive or dead, powerful or powerless, ally or enemy. What she was about to do felt like drawing water from the Nile with nothing but a cracked bucket in hand. One might feel completely safe, no sign of crocodiles as far as the eye can see, only to realize there's one lurking steps away as soon as your feet sink into the mud.

"He'll be here," said Aelia, from behind.

Aelia and her husband Pallas walked into the room, a side area off the main chamber. The old Senator shuffled forward with feet always touching the marble, arm draped around Aelia's, more like a daughter leading her father than husband and wife. He wore the traditional toga of the Senate, in a deep crimson that bordered on purple with golden edgings, while she was wearing a modest stola the color of egg shells with only a simple silver necklace as adornment. It seemed she thought prudence more important on the eve of upheaval.

"I would prefer to see him with my own eyes before we begin," said Heron, digging a fingernail into her palm. "But either way, we must."

Senator Pallas sucked on his teeth and looked at her with age-addled eyes. The right one had a slight haze to it, like morning fog. "Apologies, I must prepare my role in this."

"You'll be ready to offer the new government charter when I'm finished?" asked Heron.

"Always ready, I am," he replied.

Aelia gave him a patronizing smile. "Don't forget to wait until Heron's finished and the soldiers have helped enforce order."

Pallas gave them a toothy grin. "I won't disappoint you, my beautiful wife."

Aelia kissed him on the cheek and patted his hand. He gave a perfunctory bow and shuffled out of the room.

"He wouldn't remember his toga if the servants didn't put it on him," sighed Aelia, as she brushed a strand of hair from her shoulder.

"I feel more nervous than a scribe at his first lecture," said Heron.

Aelia strode toward Heron, long deliberate steps like a Queen walking to her throne. Her eyebrow raised as she stopped, glancing over her shoulder before she spoke, "The great Heron nervous before the Senate? If the stories are true, she doesn't have a heart?"

"Don't use that," hissed Heron under her breath.

By the rounding of Aelia's eyes and the sudden slackness of her lips, Heron saw that the mistake had been accidental.

"Apologies," said Aelia, reaching out and running a fingernail down the mechanical arm, tracing the crease on the elbow that hid the gearing. "I cannot lie, I've been thinking about you constantly, reevaluating what I said to you in the workshop. By the gods, I think I was jealous, jealous that you haven't had to live like I have. Which is unfair. You were only doing what you needed to do."

"We're both doing what we need to do," said Heron.

Aelia gave her a maudlin smile and they stared into each other's eyes for a while. Heron had never had a woman as a friend before, and though the two of them had been at odds, she felt like they could be friends.

"When this is over," said Heron tentatively. "You should come to Alexandria with me. The city's not so stifling and you'd have more freedom. Polyxena's been running the city while Agog's been here."

Aelia's eyes sparkled with mischievousness. "That sounds tempting. Enticing, even. We three women could rule the city like a preverbal Cerberus."

While Aelia was reveling in the idea, Heron was reeling. Cerberus. The word gonged in her head like the all the bells in Alexandria, every tower and parapet, ringing and ringing, until her teeth were sore from the vibration.

Aelia narrowed her gaze. "What's wrong? Did I say something?"

"Cerberus," whispered Heron. "The guardian of the underworld, three heads but one body. Both Dominitus and Lysimachus warned me. Cerberus hunts, that's what he said." She paused, other memories coming back. "No, that's not all, *beware the dead, Cerberus hunts you.* The dead, as in the day of the dead, the painted soldiers that Silius sent against me."

Their hands gripped, Aelia stepped close, her voice down to a hushed intensity. "Should we fear this...Cerberus?"

"Cerberus, not the mythical beast, but a political partnership. I saw Silius and Antonius at a priestly gathering, they must be two of the heads. It's why the Protectors turned against us when Messalina was murdered."

"Silius and Antonius?" the words trickled from Aelia's lips. "They are members of different colleges. Silius from the Pontifex Maximus and Antonius from Sacris Faciundus."

"There must be another, then," said Heron. "I witnessed it. They were chanting to..." She paused, trying to summon the memory, there'd been a name, but she'd forgotten in the flight away, "...Dea Dia, but I'm unfamiliar with that god."

Aelia was about to speak when they heard announcements inside the Senate chamber. The session would be coming to order soon. They were running out of time.

"Goddess," said Aelia, the words rushing out of her mouth like a deluge. "Dea Dia is a goddess. Some say she's the same as Ceres, or Demeter."

"The address!" said Heron, feeling the pieces slowly connect. "Whoever sent me there put the name Ceres next to it, but why?" She tapped her fingers on her leg as she glanced at the door, expecting a Senatorial acolyte to summon her soon. "*Mundus patet*, does that mean anything to you?"

"The world is open," said Aelia.

"Could it mean anything else? Quickly, this could be important."

Aelia bit her lower lip. "I don't know. But I've heard it before."

Heron closed her eyes. "Your son said this phrase to Sepharia, as a warning. Something he'd heard in his priesthood."

Eyes opened with alarm. "The priesthoods. I remember something Sextus told me once when he first joined the Sacris Faciundus. About a secret priesthood that only the most powerful were allowed to join, and it was made up of members of all of them, something whispered about by the other members deep in their drinks, or at bath times. He called them the Arval Brethren. He wished to join it, but asked me how I thought they might be picked. Since it's from the side of politics I cannot tread, I had no advice for him, but I do know this Brethren is associated with Ceres."

"So many connections," whispered Heron. "But I don't know what they mean."

"Mundus patet," Aelia continued. "There's another way to interpret world. That can also mean the underworld, the underworld is open. That's why it's the day of the dead."

"Dominitus," breathed Heron. "He called himself Charon, the boat keeper on the River Styx." She flexed her hands in frustration, hearing the clicking of gears. "Or did I call him that?"

"Dominitus? Senator Dominitus?" asked Aelia.

A sense of dread settled onto Heron. "Yes, Senator Dominitus. I asked him to join our new government. Have I made a mistake?"

Aelia's eyes shot to the side. "When I was younger and still married to Emperor Claudius, he spoke to me about Dominitus often, complained, or cursed his name would be more like it. The Senator vexed the Emperor at every turn, though he could never prove it. Called him Dis Pater at his most angry, the Lord of the Underworld."

"Plato have pity, I've invited a monster into our midst," said Heron.

"And if he's a part of this Cerberus, then he knows something is happening today, and if he does, so do the others, and if they know, then there could be plans to thwart ours."

"By Minerva, I think you're right," said Aelia.

"Iam Clausus Curia!"

The doors to the Senate would be closed soon. It was the last warning before the final call. They were down to a few minutes at best.

"What should we do?" asked Aelia.

Heron glanced quickly out the window. Near the bottom of the cascade of steps, a merchant wagon had set up. Workers with arms much too large to be commoners were hauling boxes from the back. One of them in hood and long cloak, had to be a Northman by his size, but it was hard to tell without seeing the pale hair that so many of them had.

"What could they do to stop us?" asked Heron. "With Agog outside, ready to burst through the door after my speech, can they do anything?"

"An assassin could strike," offered Aelia. "Killing him upon entrance."

The missing hand throbbed in memory, forcing Heron to pull her metal arm to her chest. She marched to the door and pushed it open slightly to gaze upon the Senate chamber. It was packed with men, the outer ring swollen like the Nile, overflowing. A tension vibrated in the air, like a lyre string ready to be plucked. She quickly found her opponents, Senator Silius, proud like a lion, looking pleased as his lesser companions hung on his every word. Senator Antonius, plump and pink cheeked, was whispering conspiratorially into the ear of one of his fellow Senators. One and two, she found them, but where was the third? It took a bit to pick him out in the crowd with so many at hand. Senator Dominitus had not yet taken his seat, he stood near the entrance to the Senate with few men around him. In his domus, he'd seemed frail and brittle, but inside the Senate, he was rejuvenated. He spoke quietly with one of his men, making short nods and glances, clearly giving direction.

"I see them," hissed Aelia. "They plot!"

The man he'd given direction to, a plain man with no features that Heron could take note of, not even a nationality, drew away from Senator Dominitus, moving to the edge of the bowl near the entrance. With directions given, Senator Dominitus began the journey to his seat. Heron noted the way the other Senators gave him a wide berth, his reputation still standing.

"Get the Senate guard, have them remove that man from the chamber before we begin. If they cannot kill Agog, then we are safe."

Aelia squeezed Heron's hand, kissed her on the cheek, and hurried into the chamber. Aelia quickly commanded a group of guards and though at first they seemed hesitant, once they looked to Heron and she gave them a nod, they moved to intercept the assassin.

Heron split her attention between the door wardens and the advancing guard. If they got the man out of the room before the doors closed, Senator Dominitus would never know he was neutralized since his position in the bowl left him with his back to the door. It wasn't far from Senator Silius either, who when he saw Dominitus, gave him the slightest of bows.

The three Senate guards approached the assassin from behind, locked their arms around his, and marched him from the room over his protests which were lost amid the cacophony of chattering. Heron let a sigh of relief escape her lips. A moment later, the call for the door closing rang out, silencing the Senate chamber so suddenly it was as if the whole of them had fallen dead.

"Clausus Curia!"

The doors clanged shut, the echo hanging over the assembled like a cloud. The silence could not hold against so many and murmuring began in earnest, while sandals whisked against the marble on the outer ring.

As the call to order was cried out, a lump formed in her throat, like a peach pit. The only thing she could hear was a heartbeat: *boom, boom, boom*. It reverberated even in her tongue, and on the pink flesh of her stumps, down to the tender skin on the back of her knees.

She'd nearly forgotten her part in the play, until the whole chamber turned towards her like a field of sunflowers. She began the slow walk to the dais, stabbing the ivory cane with a trembling hand. Every other step clanged against the marble like a blacksmith hammering swords. The grinding clicks of her arm, swaying at each step, followed her almost musically.

When she reached the dais, the eyes of the whole Empire were upon her. Her words, when spoken, would reach out and touch every one of them, from Parthia, to the Britons, to Alexandria and beyond. The world was a machine and she stood at the controls, ready to throw the lever, letting the gears spin out her plans until that shining City of Wonders stood like the beacon she hoped it would.

The speech she prepared vaporized upon the heat of all their gazes. Her careful arguments that would slowly ascend until they became a towering pyramid seemed too gaudy, too garish for the moment. Part of her knew keenly how these words, however spoken, would be remembered in history. She leaned on the cane, raised her chin, and summoned a resolve that had served her well in the workshop.

"Friends, Countrymen, Senators, the Empire has ended. Let a new Empire reign!"

The words had little time to sink in when a ferocious banging thundered into the chamber, startling them to turn towards it. A fist soundly struck the door, in three heavy blows.

BOOM! BOOM! BOOM!

Before she, or anyone else could do anything to stop it, the inner warden slammed the lock open and the heavy door began to swing.

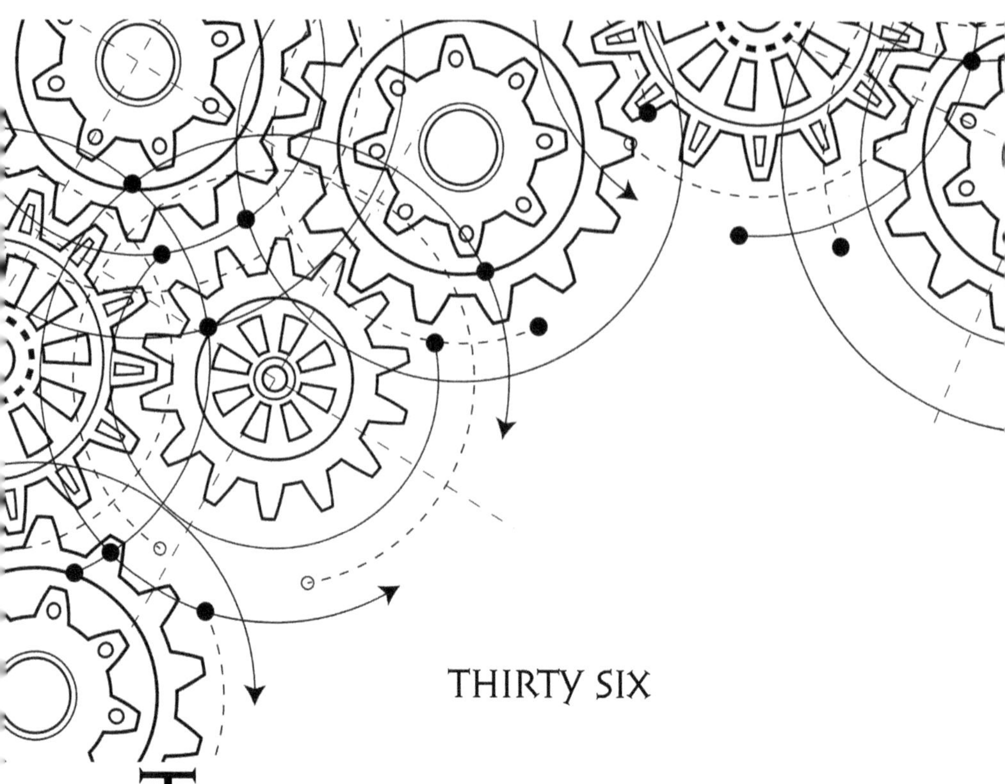

THIRTY SIX

The death scream of the man in the courtyard assaulted Sepharia's ears until she clamped her hands over them. She couldn't tell if it were one of the attackers, or the Northmen, but by his scream, she could almost picture the way the sword had entered his chest, piercing his lungs and filling his bawling with bloody gurgles.

Sextus leaned into the hall, his gladius still in the scabbard. From her crouched position on the floor, his trembling hands were evident. All traces of the confident Senator's son were lost and Sepharia could see he would need direction, so she took a deep breath and made for the back of the domus.

"Come on," she whispered as she tugged on his arm.

As he hesitated, still staring down the hall, slack-jawed, she eyed the clothes chest in the room and thought briefly about changing into one of her tunics, but the sounds of swords clashing had silenced, which meant the ghost-faced assassins would be coming after them.

She tugged again, "We have to move."

He shook off his daze and followed. She led him through the hall and down to the *peristylum* at the back of the domus. The private garden was filled with mosaics to Neptune and only had two exits, one that led deeper into the house, and another that led outside. The outer door had a bar that she set into the cradle.

"How many men can you kill?" she asked in a whisper, once the outer door was blocked.

"How many men? What?" His green eyes had lost their luster, almost gray like the cold sea.

"If it comes to fighting, how many can you fight at once?" she asked.

"I've never killed a man," he said in a little voice.

She banged her fist against his chest. "That's not what I'm asking. How many can you fight? This doorway's a nice bottleneck, can you hold it?"

His brow bunched up. "And what do you know of fighting?"

"Remember who my father is? And what does it matter, you're little more than an automata at this point," she said.

"I can hold it if I must," he said, the words sounding dreadfully resigned, but at least acknowledging the necessity of the task.

She looked around the dimly lit hidden garden for heavy objects to move in front of the inner door, but there were none. The stone table was built into the flooring and the chairs were metal with ornate cushions. She wished for a lantern or torch, since day was fleeting and a heavy cloud cover blocked the remaining sunlight.

"Keep watch of that doorway," she said, while searching for any other ways they could be attacked. There was a window above them, from the servant's quarters, but she doubted they would think to look out of it.

"Why don't we escape out the back?" he asked.

"We don't know how many are in the domus. We could very well walk right into their arms, giving up our defensible position," she responded.

"But they could climb over the walls." He nodded above them.

"True. But there are metal spikes up there and I can always throw a chair at them when they try to come over," she said, shrugging. "But honestly, I think our best bet is to survive as long as possible, give time for the others to rescue us. Unless you're up to fighting five men at once."

"By Jupiter, no, I've never fought even one, except in training," said Sextus.

"You might get your chance today," she said.

He glanced back, frowning. "Easy for you to say, you've never killed anyone."

Her palms grew sweaty with remembrance. "I have...twice. Much preferable to being killed."

He looked at her strangely, and Sepharia could sense what they had between them was changed. He focused his attention down the hallway, gripping his sword as he leaned against the door frame.

Without turning he spoke, "What do you think is happening to the others?"

The stone that had been rolling around in her stomach, jumped, and Sepharia felt sick. "Hopefully, the attack is just against us."

"Your *father*," Sextus hesitated on the word, "picked a bad day for this. It's the third and final day of the dead until the new year."

"It wouldn't have changed anything to pick another," she said.

"The gods think otherwise, it seems."

His voice had turned cold to her, and that hurt more than she expected. Her limbs ached. She knew she should be thinking of ways to get out, but she could only think about how it would change between them if they survived.

A flash of white drew her attention upward. Sticking from the servant's window, one of the painted men was staring down at her. He leaned back into the room and yelled to the others. The stone walls hid the message, but Sepharia didn't need to hear it to understand.

"We've been seen," said Sepharia. "Stay or run, which do you prefer?"

"I don't know," he said.

"Decide quickly, we haven't much time."

Sextus banged his fist against the vine covered stone and his face paled. Suddenly doubting his ability to kill even one attacker, Sepharia made the decision.

"We run," she said. "If we make it to the stables, we can escape through the back alley."

The bar clattered onto the stone floor and Sepharia prepared to flee. It wasn't very far to the stables, only a dozen lengths or so of mostly dirt where Emperor Claudius, when he'd lived in the building, like to stage gladiatorial battles. But even in the dim light, she could see three men standing beneath the clay-tiled overhang of the stables, faces painted into the rictus of the dead. They advanced. And from the other direction, through the secret garden and down the hallway, the other assassins made their slow approach.

THIRTY SEVEN

Betrayal had become as common as coal smoke over Alexandria. She'd grown rather used to it, expected it almost, going back to the times she made miracles for the temples and her ideas were routinely sold to her rival Philo. Ramses. Vima. Everyone in Rome, except those closest to her. Betrayal had become a vinegar poured into every drink, every meal, until she expected that bitterness at every taste.

So it was to her considerable surprise that the inner doors of the Senate chamber swung open and she was not immediately sunk by an overwhelming feeling of betrayal. In fact, she was dumbfounded by its absence.

Standing beneath the marble frame, the massive automata of Julius Caesar looming behind them, while the whole of the Senate looked on, was: the Emperor, Consul Vestalis, and the red-haired, bushy-bearded Northman Donar, looking like they'd just come from a fight. Other Alexandrians stood behind them, while the Senatorial guards saluted.

A quick glance to Silius told her everything about the day's events.

His jaw hung low, and his fist grabbed the toga of one of his lesser companions. Equally, Antonius looked winded by the figures in the door. Only Senator Dominitus appeared unaffected, almost pleased by the events, which only confused Heron further.

Concerned there were other plots grinding through the darkness, Heron slammed her cane onto the dais, the awful snap of it breaking bringing the attention back to her. Heron gave the gift a brief frown before lifting her chin, the cane had served her well, after all.

"Senators of the Empire," said Heron in her loudest voice, "today we have been betrayed. Seize Senators Silius, Antonius, and Dominitus!"

The room erupted as Senators started yelling and crying out, "Treason!" and "Lies!", depending on their allegiance, as the Senatorial guard pushed through the bowl toward the trio with gladii drawn. Silius was grabbed first and as he tried to speak, Heron yelled, "Silence them!" The guard clamped his mouth closed.

Senator Antonius tried to waddle out of the bowl, but three guards intercepted him and quickly subdued the large man, who succumbed quickly and was reduced to a quivering blob kneeling on the marble.

Only Senator Dominitus did not fight, as he looked to her with his head tilted in what could only be curiosity. When the guards reached him, he stepped into their grasp willingly and made no attempt to shout.

"Good Senators! Good Senators! Lend me your silence!" she shouted. "Good Senators! Please!"

The jostling crowd absorbed her shouts like the sea absorbed the rain. She was about to try again when there was such a volume of noise bellowing into the chamber, the shouts were ripped from the air, blown away like dust from a greater wind.

"Silence!" said Agog, and when he was done, the Senate had been reduced to a low murmur, like a spinning coin on its final rotations.

"Many of you Romans," began Agog, "believe I am just a barbarian, too war-hungry and dim-witted, like a trained bear ready to dance. Believe that to your peril. I left the care of the Empire to the Senate only to learn that it believes itself above the people." He paused, menacing the Senators from the edge of the bowl. "No longer! Today we begin again, this time in a way befitting an Empire, and without the troublemakers who have plagued us like locust." He paused again, giving the crowd a good long glare, while a dissenting voice cried out, "But the Empire!"

"Empire?" he shouted back, while a group of Senators jostled, clearly not wanting to be the one identified as who'd spoken. "It became my Empire when I took it and by the laws of force, it's mine to do with what I want. Remember, I could have had the lot of you killed, but I choose mercy instead, in hopes that the good of the Empire could continue."

He stomped his foot and a Senator along the top row of the bowl nearly toppled over backwards trying to get away. Only the pressing hands of the Senators behind him kept him from going over the bench. Heron suspected they only helped him to keep one more person between them and Agog.

With one fluid motion, Agog pulled the great sword from his back and jammed it downward, exploding stone from the tip. Senators in the front cried out and the whole bowl shuffled backwards.

"I cede the floor to Consul Heron, who will explain the changes I have already approved," said Agog.

A sea of bloodshot eyes turned to her. As a group, they seemed either only barely subdued, like a rabid dog on the end of a frayed rope, or completely frightened and would collapse at the flick of a finger. She hoped it was the latter.

"Good Senators, do not be afraid. For most of you, today will be just like any other day." She paused and let the *for most of you* line sink in. "When we took this Empire, we intended for the Republic to continue as it serves the people and the Empire simultaneously. It seems a small group of Senators, led by these three men," she gestured with her brass arm, "thought the Empire was only in existence to enrich their coin purses and continue their hegemony."

The area vacated by Antonius murmured in approval. It seemed large disagreement still lingered from the pudgy Senator's usurping of Messalina's former domain. The Protectors were back on their side, or so she hoped.

Heron continued, "No more! Today we give the Empire back to the whole Empire, not just a select few. Today we will reform the government, with laws mostly the same as before, expanding the number of Senate seats so representation can reach all ends of the Empire, and removing the special protections a select few used to their unearned benefit."

Her heart was a cannon in her chest and she felt dizzy, as if she stood on a mountainside and looked over the gnarled edge at a golden landscape spread out before her. Some of the bloodshot gazes seemed introspective, not as many as she'd liked, but enough to give them a promising start.

"In tradition of the former Empire, and in welcoming of the new, the Alexandrian Empire," she paused, expecting rebuttal but hearing none, "Senator Pallas will now read the charter of the new government, including those Senators who will, because of their leal service to the people, retain their seats."

Heron stepped to the side and tried not to topple, forgetting she had neither two good legs, nor a cane to steady herself. Senator Pallas made his slow shuffle forward, hunched over like a tired oxen, his progress too slow for Heron's benefit, since eyes were still on her and she wanted desperately to let out a heavy breath.

At the front of the dais, Senator Pallas made a great show of unraveling the scroll, and Heron wasn't sure if it were a show, or his age.

Then, almost unfathomably, he straightened, and she expected to hear a great cracking of his bones, like a bucket of rocks rolling into a ditch.

He stood as straight and tall as she'd ever seen him, shoulders pulled back, chin lifted high. He was rising to the occasion, she decided. A worthy moment for a worthy Senator.

"Good Senators, All-Knowing Gods, hear me speak." He held the scroll near his waist and Heron supposed he must have memorized it, a feat considering his poor memory, though she didn't remember the section honoring the gods. Still, she thought he might know better and superstition had served her well in the past.

"Today the Empire has fallen. And a new one will take its place." This definitely wasn't in the scroll, but she decided he was speaking extemporaneously. "One owing its creation to the gods. Remember good Senators, that Remus and Romulus created this city of the seven hills, brought it out of the darkness, fed it when it would have otherwise starved, opened the world with its arms!"

The speech was quite good, and Heron looked to Aelia, to see her reaction, since it *was* her husband. But the look on Aelia's face drained Heron's optimism of the moment, filling it with unrelenting doubt. Aelia was shaking her head at Heron, saying something, but not loud enough that she could hear.

"Remember the gods watch us! They hear us and see us and keep us warm because we honor them!" shouted Pallas, shaking his fist to the crowd vigorously. He seemed a man half his age.

Heron looked to Aelia to determine what was wrong. Heron glanced behind, almost expecting the assassin they'd removed from the chamber to be sneaking upon her with knife drawn.

"Remember that this Empire cannot stand without their blessing!" he continued.

Heron looked about, and then to Agog, who seemed to be coming

to some conclusion. Vestalis as well, since the both of them were looking around the Senate chamber.

Pallas was only two steps away. She could move to him and clamp a
hand over his mouth if she must, but he had the attention of the Senators, and they needed Pallas to sway them if they wanted the transition to
go smoothly, but he was well off the scroll they'd written for him. She
decided to politely interrupt him, so she stepped forward, right by his
side.

"Senator Pall—"

A lanky arm from the Senator swept her backwards, with a strength
that suggested a man much younger than his wrinkled exterior.

"Remember, it's one thing to let a barbarian from the North rule us,
but the gods will destroy this city if we are to be led by a woman!"

With her hand reached halfway towards him, she froze. Her shock
was such that she failed to move as he turned, slowly and with deliberate
menace. Her protest disintegrated under his cloudless gaze. Both his
eyes were as clear as a newborn, the fire of his intellect burning on his
brow.

"Beware the ills of the feminine!" He grabbed the bottom of her
tunic and lifted it up, and producing a short blade, cut the strap from her
leg, leaving the wooden genetalia to slide down the other side. Warm
blood ran down her thigh where his blade had touched skin. She moved
to cover herself, but it was too late.

The chamber erupted like a volcano. Senators rushed the dais and
she was quickly overwhelmed by clawing, punching, grabbing hands. The
sounds of swordplay rung out from the sides. Agog battled a group of
guards, his sword swinging in wide arcs, blood spilling freely. As a fist
connected with her jaw, Heron swiped her hand across, feeling the heavy
crunch as her mechanical arm knocked teeth from a Senator's mouth.
Her victory was short-lived as she was pummeled into a ball on the dais.

In the back of her mind, as she was kicked and punched, she realized her mistake. The third head of Cerberus hadn't been Senator Dominitus. It was Senator Pallas. Aelia's husband. He'd feigned old age, and withstood his wife's barbs quietly, while plotting with the others. He'd been in their midst the whole time.

Someone stepped on her ankle and she was afraid it was going to break, when heavy hands pulled her from the pile. The punches still rained down on her face and chest, but she was gradually dragged away until at last the attacks ceased.

She expected to see Agog, or Vestalis when she lifted her beaten head, but instead she found Senator Silius staring at her with a grin that could have cut glass.

"Bag her," said the Senator.

A hood was jammed over her head, bending her ears roughly. She struggled briefly, but too many hands held her. The darkness of the hood suffocated her and she started breathing more deeply trying to get one more gulp of air. And then someone punched her in the head so hard the hood was filled with a million stars crashing to the Earth.

THIRTY EIGHT

"Close the gate!" screamed Sepharia.

The gate rattled upon impact, but it wouldn't hold, since the bar was on the inside.

Moving at a predators' pace, the three ghost-faced soldiers approached from the stables. The wind ripped dust streamers from each step and she swiped away the hair from her face. Sextus moved to block them with sword drawn. His weapon drooped as the men moved closer.

Spying a broken limb from an olive tree, Sepharia shoved it between the curved handle. The door rattled seconds after, as the men inside tried to pull the door open.

"This way!" she tugged on his arm, and ran toward the back of the domus. Two archways later, they were in the mangled courtyard. Looming in the shadows, since the sun was setting and only a dim lantern gave light, was the suit of mechanical armor Heron had been working on.

It was larger than an automata, though not as large as the likeness of Julius Caesar in the Senate house. It had been constructed from heavy scale armor, with attachments bolted on, including a pair of javelins that stuck from either arm. The whole contraption was connected to a steam mechanical by a series of bronze tubes. The mechanical sat on a small wheeled cart behind the suit of armor like the back legs of the mythical centaur. Heron had meant it as a test piece, to see where there might be flaws in her design, but Sepharia needed it to work right now.

She put a testing hand to the steam chamber, the belly was still hot. Heron had been working on it up to the last second, and the servants had only just banked the fires.

"Hold them while I get in," said Sepharia.

"By Jupiter's balls, what's that suppose to do?" asked Sextus.

"Just hold them!"

Sepharia slapped the lever into the position that fed air into the burning chamber, then she hurriedly scooped a ladle of coal dust into it, spilling half while glancing over her shoulder.

As she climbed into the armor, the two ghost-faced assassins appeared out of the dim, moving deliberately toward Sextus. He seemed to regain a bit of composure, or his training had kicked in, and he straightened, holding his gladius in an angled defensive position.

Heron had built the armor for a person her size, so Sepharia fit easily, but the straps and connections took time to assemble. As the assassins neared Sextus, she realized the presence of the mechanical armor was keeping them from attacking as they eyed it suspiciously. Sepharia just hoped it kept them at bay long enough for the steam mechanical to gain power. Right now, it was just a useless piece of armor that could only move through her muscle power. The arm guards sat in a cradle, and they might be light enough to move, if she had the strength to wield them, but the legs would have to wait until the mechanical gave them power.

The attackers, seeing that the strange armor hadn't moved yet, advanced on Sextus. The third man appeared at the edge of the courtyard, having let the others out of the secret garden.

The first, his face hidden by the white paint, lunged forward with his sword, but Sextus beat him back, the smack of metal on metal echoing loudly in her armor. The second assassin timed his strike, hitting as Sextus blocked, but Sextus jumped away. He seemed competent enough, but she knew he wouldn't stand a chance when the others arrived.

Groaning audibly as she labored, feeling the muscles in her chest and arm strain against the weight, Sepharia lifted the left arm and aimed the javelin at the two men. The result had an immediate reaction. Rather than press their advantage, they both hesitated and avoided the aimed javelin.

"Come on, you stupid mechanical, heat," she muttered under her breath, while hoping she hadn't turned a lever wrong, or forgotten something that would make the mechanical work.

When the third attacker joined the others, they lost their fear and moved in again. Sepharia was stuck facing one direction and couldn't see if the others had entered the courtyard, or if they were coming in from behind. Sepharia tried to move her legs, but the armor and attachments were too heavy.

The ghost-faced men made a series of lunges and when Sextus failed to block properly, a blade got through and cut him on the thigh. Sextus had a noticeable limp and tried to examine his leg, but the men pressed again, forcing his blade up.

Sepharia strained every muscle in her arm and chest and lifted the javelin arm, aiming towards the leftmost attacker, but he ignored it. She shook the armor, willing it to start. She felt foolish for climbing inside, deciding she should have run, rather than to try to fight.

"Sextus, if you can, run," she told him. "They want me, not you. You don't have to die here."

Between parries, he yelled over his shoulder. "I'm staying and I want to see that thing work."

"I do, too," she said and then muttered under her breath, "but I'm beginning to think it's not going to."

As if Heron herself had heard Sepharia disparage her work, the steam mechanical began a slow beat and it didn't take long before it was churning fast enough to shake the armor.

"Now we'll show them," said Sepharia, but when she went to lift the arm, she had no assist from the mechanical. "Curse the gods, why aren't you working?"

The men, brought on by her admission, began swinging earnestly. Sextus was forced to defend himself from their onslaught. They appeared to get through twice, but he kept the defense up despite the cuts. Out of the corner of the helmet visor, she saw two more men creeping through the darkness. Even if he could survive the three before him, the additional two would spell his certain defeat.

Stuck inside the armor, Sepharia searched around, trying to find a lever or switch that she'd forgotten, something that would let the steam power reach the mechanical limbs, so she could help Sextus. Right now, it was only serving to restrain her until Sextus fell.

She craned her head left and right, up and down, searching, until she saw it, at her left hip—a lever in the down position. Sepharia snaked her hand out of the arm guard and engaged the lever. She felt the surge in the armor as the arms and legs lifted like a boat at high tide.

Moving her arm still felt clunky, and it over-traveled at each adjustment, but it moved with enough alacrity to get the ghost-faced men's notice. As the fourth and fifth attackers joined the fight, Sepharia decided to even the odds. With a careful aim at the unsuspecting fifth man, she pulled the lever in her hand grip and the javelin flew from her fist.

At first she thought she'd missed, as he stayed standing, but then he stumbled to his knees and fell forward onto his chest, sword rattling onto the cobblestones. It seemed the javelin had gone right through him.

The threat of the second javelin was enough to force the attackers to move as she swung the arm around. Enough that Sextus got in a few attacking swipes. Nothing dramatic, but enough to create some space.

Feeling the urge to move, Sepharia leaned her hip and upper thigh into a forward walk. She'd watched Heron use the mechanical armor the day before, so she had an idea. The whole structure surged forward, and on the second step, she had to jam the metal foot down to keep from ramming into Sextus' back.

"To my side!"

Sextus moved to the right of her, keeping the mechanical armor to his back. The ghost-faced men didn't know what to make of her and one of them stepped forward to stick his blade into the unprotected portion of the chest. Sepharia reacted, swiping her right arm to the left, smacking the heavy metal fist into the man's head, crumpling him to the ground.

When one of the attackers appeared stunned by his companion's death, Sepharia aimed the other javelin and pulled the lever. This javelin got stuck in the man's chest cavity, and he held the haft and stumbled into the dirt where the cherry tree had been, before falling onto his side lifelessly.

With the odds even, Sextus lunged forward and struck the attacker on his right with his gladius, knocking him backwards in a spray of blood. It might have been an acceptable maneuver had there not been a second opponent. The second soldier used the opening to slash his blade across Sextus' chest. He fell like a marionette with its strings cut.

With rage as her fuel, Sepharia took one step forward in the mechanical armor, but the soldier was too far away to strike. He took one look at her and fled into the darkness.

She heard a heavy moan to the side. Sepharia scrambled to get out of the mechanical armor, fingernails catching the rough buckles, angled bits of the interior levers catching on her arms as she struggled free like a newborn foal.

Dropping onto the cobblestones, and ignoring the shock of pain through her knees, she found Sextus and cradled his head in her arms. His bloody fingers still held onto the gladius, but he was shaking from head to toe.

"It's not too deep, it's not too deep," she told him. "You'll be fine. I'll stitch you up."

In truth, she wasn't lying. It didn't look fatal, though it didn't look good either. His chest was a bloody mess, the tunic peeled away from his skin, white lumps of bone showing through the cut. She'd fixed wounds in the workshop before, none as bad as this, but she could do it.

"Just be calm. Just be calm. I'll get my things from my room and come back and fix you," she told him. He gave her a shaking, "Yes," the word coming out amid teeth rattles.

She was about to let his head down onto the cobblestones when a flash of white surprised her. The one who had fled came running into the courtyard and before she could even scream, he stabbed Sextus right through the chest. The tip of the blade cut her leg and a great gurgle of blood erupted around the steel.

The attacker gleefully pulled his sword free and raised it for another strike, this one at her, and there was nothing she could do to stop it. Sepharia just stared, waiting for the blade to pierce her chest. She didn't even have time for regrets.

Right as his arm thrust forward, a bit of rope appeared out of the darkness behind him, slipped over his head and yanked the man backwards. Suddenly, the man was on his back.

Like a crocodile out of the Nile, the bald priest, wearing dark robes and carrying a catcher's noose, appeared and knelt next to the man, slipping a knife into his neck. The priest deftly pulled the rope from the dead man, and as quickly as he'd done it the first time, he placed it around Sepharia's neck. The rope cinched around her throat until she could barely breath. She didn't try moving, since Sextus' dead weight was on her thighs. Trying to grasp the staff from which the rope was ejected proved futile and only earned her a rope burn as the priest pivoted to the side.

From behind, the bald priest let his warm, fetid breath spill against her neck.

"I've got you now."

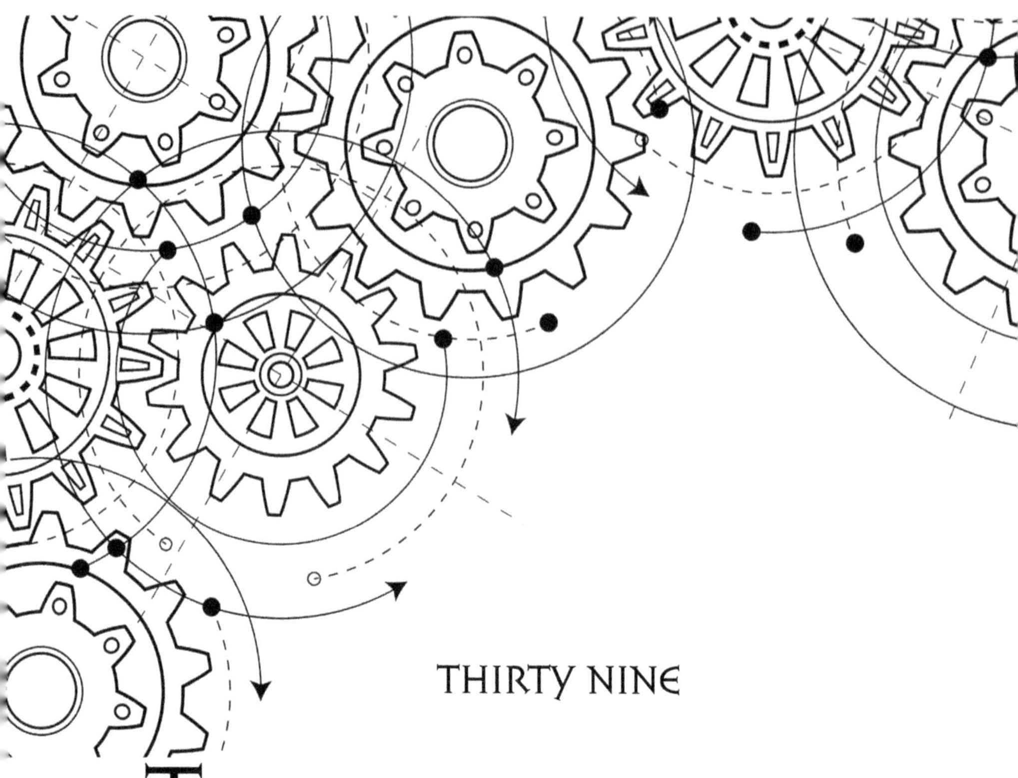

THIRTY NINE

The hood was scratchy. It was made from a thick, matted material that rubbed on the tip of her nose, the ridge of her eyebrows, and the tips of her ears. It muffled the world around her, at first the battle in the Senate house, and then the traitorous thuds of a steam mechanical, and finally their hushed whispers as they carried her into a building of some kind, down a flight of steps into a cold, dank room that smelled of mold, before a gate wheezed shut, clanging into place and then a key rattled out of a lock.

The darkness was complete. Not a flicker of a lantern or torch played against the thick fabric of the hood. She was chained to a wall, sitting with her legs splayed out before her. The chain was short and kept her arms, both flesh and mechanical, in a raised position.

Heron shook her head, trying to get the annoying hood from rubbing her nose. She strained against the chains, hoping to pull it away, and then realized her stupidity and leaned her face forward towards her hands, tugging a space for her nose. She felt around the bottom of the hood, but it was tied tightly in the back and she didn't feel like rubbing her neck raw just to get it off.

Besides, it gave her something to think about. Thinking about the hood was better than thinking about what might happen next. She'd been entombed in places like this before, chthonic pits that delved into human depravity. Could almost see the water seeping down the wall, looking like an oil slick surrounded by green algae. She knew too well how the rats would come out when the people were gone, exploring fearlessly, even across your leg; and even if you were screaming and trying to shake them off.

Yes, the hood was annoying, feeling like the tip of a feather stuck into her nose, making her want to sneeze or wrinkle it in frustration, but it was better than the alternative. Better than thinking about the darkness and what it contained. Better than remembering the months in the tomb of Sobek, under the tutelage of Lysimachus. Anything was better than that.

To her relief, a door opened somewhere above and she heard men carrying someone, but she couldn't make out who. A door near hers opened and she heard the rattle of chains and then locks and then they left.

"Ave?" she asked tentatively.

"It's me," said the voice. "Dominitus."

"Ah...apologies. I was wrong. I thought you were the third head of Cerberus," she told him.

"Do not feel bad for this," he replied, "he fooled me, too. Fooled everyone, it seems."

"What happened? Wait. Let me get this off my head. I cannot hear so well."

As expected, rotating the hood left her neck raw, and the knot was a struggle to untangle. So she leaned forward and with only one good hand tugged it off her head.

"That's better," she said. "What happened? I was taken so quickly. Is Silius in control? Or Agog?"

Dominitus hesitated, and she wondered if it was because he now knew that she was a woman. She'd never had to consider that before and it wasn't any consolation that she might not have to consider it for very long.

"They took me," said Dominitus finally, his voice weary with age. "Not long after you. They had soldiers amid the crowd and weapons hidden behind the statues in the alcoves."

"So it was true," said Heron. "You would have helped us reform the Republic?"

He chuckled. "I guess there's no harm in the truth, sitting here waiting for Charon's boat. I had hoped to take back my old place within the Brethren. I had a hunch that you would eliminate my old adversary, Silius, and with the influence you'd gifted me, I'd be able to take my place back."

"So you didn't get wanderlust when the assassin attacked you? You were forced out?" she asked.

He made a noise the old make when they're remembering the past. Wrapped inside that noise was a deep sadness. "My wife and son were both poisoned during that time. Silius, I can only assume."

"He was a member of this, Brethren?"

"Yes, the Arval Brethren. The true keepers of power in Rome, since the very beginning, even before the Senate, even before the Republic," he said. "Silius and I had a disagreement about power. We both wanted to rule and he struck first. I'd grown too complacent with my reputation. *Occulta Imperatore!* The Hidden Emperor! No one would dare to touch me, especially not a fellow member of the Brethren. Oh, how wrong I was."

"What is this Arval Brethren? What purpose do they serve?" she asked.

"What purpose does any organization have? To gather and hold power. But this one did its best from the shadows. Twelve men, dedicated to our god," he said.

"Ceres?"

He laughed, a short and cutting sound. "Yes and no. Ceres is the goddess of fertility. The reason the Brethren came together so long ago was to encourage the growing and harvesting of crops. When Rome was young, she needed food to grow. That was our official reason for existence, back before the Republic became an orgy of power. No, our god was not Ceres, but Dis Pater, the Father of Riches. When I was *occulta imperatore,* I held the position of Dis, the head of the Arval Brethren, but now that is Silius."

"The god of the Underworld," muttered Heron. "So when I called you Charon, I wasn't too far off."

"I should've just enlisted your help from the beginning, but I wasn't sure if I could trust you. It seems I was wrong and now that mistake will cost me my life, though at least it comes after a long and comfortable existence," he said.

She was about to speak when the door at the top of the dungeon banged open, flooding in piercing light, forcing her to squint. Shapes passed before the light, and then it was blocked out completely by a hulking presence. Heron knew who it was even before she could make him out.

"Agog!"

"Heron," he said, before getting hit on the back of the head with a sword hilt, driving him to his knees at the bottom of the stairs. He was wrapped in chains and two soldiers held swords to his back.

"No talking unless I give permission," said the man with the key.

Heron tried to get a glimpse of the man through the bars, but she couldn't quite make him out. Looking over, she noticed Dominitus glaring, chewing on his anger.

"It didn't take long for you to betray me, Cultri," said Dominitus.

"And I shall live a little longer for it," he said, and Heron recognized him for the one who they'd corralled and sent out of the chamber.

"You were the assassin," said Heron. "The one we interrupted."

Dominitus looked to her with bloodshot eyes. "Cultri was my insurance for Silius. He was to kill him if anything happened."

"So if I wouldn't have stopped him, we might not be here?" asked Heron.

Dominitus shrugged. "It might not have stopped the fighting. Remember, it was Pallas who betrayed you. Silius was always your enemy." He looked to the man beyond the bars. "And now you are mine."

"I'll shed no tears for you old man," said Cultri, as the soldiers were chaining Agog to the wall in a cell two over from Dominitus. "Your time was done. It's better this way. Had I killed Senator Silius in the middle of the Senate, I might have been killed myself."

"I didn't choose your line of business," said Dominitus coolly. "But now the hearts of Remus and Romulus go cold by your betrayal."

"And now the hearts of Remus and Romulus go cold," replied Cultri, with a smirk.

Dominitus laughed and glanced over to her. "My time hastens quick." And then to Cultri. "He wouldn't have sent you down unless he wanted you to kill me."

"No, he wouldn't have," said Cultri, slipping through the door. "It was part of the deal."

Dominitus nodded solemnly.

Heron had a better look at the man about to kill the Senator, but she couldn't quite pick out any details that distinguished him. Cultri crouched down like a lover moving in for a kiss, the blade held before him, and whispered something in Dominitus' ear. A last farewell, or a final barb for ill-led service, Heron couldn't tell, but the blade went in quick and the old man slumped against the bars.

"Soldiers," said Cultri, "come get the body. Senator Silius wanted to piss on the body before we buried him."

As Cultri turned, he looked to her, just a moment of eye contact between the bars, and she noticed a tiny scar over his right eyebrow, a childhood pock mark maybe. The soldiers collected the body and marched up the stairs and once more she was shut into darkness.

Heron blinked away the purple square of leftover light against her eyes and called out to Agog: "Are you well?"

"Alive," he grumbled. "That counts for something."

"What happened in the Senate? Are the others dead?" she asked tentatively.

"Vestalis lives, I think. We got split up in the fighting. When the soldiers overwhelmed us, Vestalis and a few others fought their way out. I was too busy trying to get to you, after, after the..."

"You're not mad, are you?" She felt the fool for asking, but she needed to know. They'd been through so much together.

"Mad? No. Surprised. Yes. And maybe a little disappointed you never told me." He paused. "It was you and Jarngard, then? That's what was between you."

"Yes."

"I could never figure it out. I didn't think he was like Plutarch. Just thought he'd bonded with you while building the pyramid," said Agog.

"Bonded," laughed Heron. "That'd be one way to put it."

Agog joined her laughter, and for a moment, the stone echoed with the pair of them. This was a place unused to laughter, and the sopping walls tried to swallow it, but they kept laughing, until it hurt. Heron bent down to wipe the tears from her eyes.

"Aurinia would have liked you," said Agog, suddenly.

Heron smiled. "I would have liked to meet her."

"Maybe you will soon," said Agog.

"Seems no maybe about it," she said quietly.

Whatever brief warmth she enjoyed was gone and the cold stone leached at her, leaving her with the slightest of shivers. At least the chamber beneath the temple of Sobek had been warm.

"Any regrets?" she asked.

"Regrets? No, I'm not a man for regrets. I had my chance and now it's gone. But I think the historians will remember us."

Heron grunted lightly. "Historians are fools. Only the winners get to decide the truth."

Agog made a non-committal noise. "I didn't do this to have my name splashed over a few moldy papyri."

"I know."

"There is one thing I wish though, not a regret, but a desire," he said, his voice strong and true.

"Our time is short, don't keep me waiting," she said.

"When the war was over, and things settled, I'd hoped to take one of Hoth's iron boats back north, see the lands one more time." His voice grew quieter. "I'd hoped to take you and Sepharia, as well. You've been through so much with us. Show you the snow covered mountains, the great mead halls, maybe Aurinia's walking hut, if I could find it. Though it probably wandered off after she died."

"You're a strange barbarian," she said.

He chuckled. "Any regrets for you? Any secrets held back? You're not really one of the gods here on earth to test me?"

"Like you, no regrets, no secrets." She leaned forward itched her nose. "Wait. There is one, one I'd forgotten about in all this."

"Keeping more secrets, eh? Athena's secret daughter?"

She laughed. "No. The heir of Alexander the Macedonian. I found out the truth later, after I told you what I thought was the truth."

A slight vibration put pause in her words. She knew that frequency. It had to be more steam chariots returning to the villa. Moments later, she could hear voices near the top of the stairs.

"It was me," she said.

"You?"

"Yes, me. The old book the priest of the Alexandrian Temple gave me linked my family to his, through the lineage of the Amazonian Queen Thalestris."

He made an interested noise, and he seemed to be gathering himself to speak when light burst into the room, brought by soldiers with lanterns. In no time, they had them out of chains and were leading them outside.

A cold wind whipped across the fields, rattling her teeth with shivers. Beneath the massive olive tree behind the house, a circle of men in masks waited. A rope had been hung on a thick branch, but only one. When they pushed Agog forward, Heron knew that fate was not for her, but she feared she'd get to learn hers sooner than she wanted.

"Bring forth the invader," said Silius, from behind his painted mask. Before, when Heron had crept upon the villa, she'd been too far away to see the details. Up close, she could see the visage of the Underworld in the strong black lines etched across his pale face.

They maneuvered Agog beneath the rope and as the circle expanded, shedding light across the field, Heron saw the rectangular hole hacked out of the ground that must contain the body of Dominitus. At sword point, they made Agog climb onto a box and one of the masked priests slipped the rope around Agog's neck.

Silius stepped forward to speak and before he could, a great wind blew from the north, frigid cold with ice in its teeth. The olive tree shook, its bare branches quivering under the gale winds. The men in the circle shrunk their shoulders and pulled their cloaks tightly, and for a moment, Heron imagined Agog using the distraction to knock away his captors and sprint into the darkness, free from Roman rule. But the wind shuddered to a stop and the ritual resumed.

"He who plows, offers his sacrifice."

The words were immediately familiar, though the men did not speak slowly, ritualistically, like they did before. This time they stepped forward and said their words quickly, as if anxious to be rid of the Northman.

"He who prepares the earth, offers his sacrifice."

"He who ploughs with a wide furrow, offers his sacrifice."

"He who plants seeds, offers his sacrifice."

A heavy man who could only be Senator Antonius stepped forward, "He who traces the first plowing, offers his sacrifice."

"He who harrows, offers his sacrifice."

"He who digs, offers his sacrifice."

"He who weeds, offers his sacrifice."

"He who reaps, offers his sacrifice."

"He who carries the grain, offers his sacrifice," said Pallas, standing strong.

"He who stores the grain, offers his sacrifice."

"He who distributes the grain, offers his sacrifice," said Silius, who swung his hand in a downward motion.

Agog was faced toward Heron and she kept her gaze on him as the soldier moved behind him. Agog gave her a nod and she nodded back before the soldier kicked the box from beneath his feet. He strained against the ropes, his face bright crimson, his feet kicking wildly.

A heavy push made her stumble forward and she fell to her knees. Arms lifted her up and she was led to a spot before Agog as he hung from the rope. A spear was shoved into her hand, the mechanical one, and before she could do anything to stop it, they pushed her arm forward to pierce Agog's side. Blood flowed darkly from the wound.

Before she could utter a farewell, they dragged her back the other way, marching her around the villa to two large piles of wood set out for a fire. At the center of each pile was a timber set into the earth and chains hung from the timber. The nearest pile was unoccupied, but the further one held a limp shape, hanging against the chain. Aelia straightened slightly as Heron came into view, but then she slumped back down onto the wood.

The mask of Dis Pater was suddenly in her face, bloodshot eyes leering out from behind the painted porcelain. Rough hands grabbed her sides and a vial of liquid was poured down her throat. Heron coughed and spit, trying to get it out, but she swallowed some of it.

"You'll regret that," said Silius. "But not for long." A gust of wind blew his cloak around the both of them. Tusk-like clouds streaked against the sky. "This barbarian invasion is almost put to rest, and the Roman Empire will resume its place in the world, and with the gifts of your inventions, *Michanikos*. Iron road, iron ships, soon we'll be racing through the sky. What a world you've left us." He glanced over his shoulder. "Chain her."

It took some maneuvering by the soldiers to get her onto the pile of wood, she felt like the timbers beneath her feet were about to shift. The manacle bound her wrist, but not too tightly. Her metal arm was stuck fast with no gap between iron and brass.

Silius stood before her and raised his arms. "To Dis Pater, Father of Riches, we offer the sacrifice of these two women, to bring back the glory of Rome, to spread its wisdom across the earth!"

The first masked priest stepped forward, "He who prepares the earth, offers his sacrifice," and then he threw a bundle of grain on the pile.

As the second masked priest moved forward, a trio of soldiers at each pile thrust torches into the wood. The flames were stretched long by the wind, and caught at the dry wood quickly, sending sparks and smoke away from the fire.

"...ploughs with a wide furrow, offers his..."

Her stomach gurgled and she shook her head, feeling the first tendrils of the drug they'd given her creep into her vision. Part of her wanted to succumb, to let the drug carry her away, so she could avoid the worst of the pain, but part of her wanted those last precious thoughts before she was consumed.

Glancing over her shoulder, she saw Aelia, limp against the chains, even as the flames licked around her feet. Her fire was catching faster.

As each priest stepped forward, Heron felt her heart double its pace. Between the in-breaths of the wind, smoke rose into her face, and she was soon squinting it away. Flames licked around her, crackling and shifting the wood beneath her feet as it was consumed.

Heron coughed, spitting away the smoke and fear. At her feet, the flames whirled in the wind like a dervish, hypnotically. The world thudded in her ears and no longer could she hear the priests, chanting away her life.

Her good foot rested on a log, but it was slowly sliding down, as flames curled around it. Sparks danced across her legs and she bit her tongue crying out. The heat was becoming unbearable.

Above the din of fire, a womanly scream pierced the night, shredding the tentative hold the drug had on her. To her right, the bonfire consumed Aelia, stola and hair aflame, wrapping the woman in a cloak of bright crimson, her funeral garb.

Heron took one last breath, before the smoke would burn her out from the inside and she would follow Aelia into the flame. And through the haze of heat and darkness, she saw embers in the distance and felt a vibration in her wrist. Around the circle, the masked men turned outward, facing toward some unknown threat.

Whatever threat it was, it was too late. A patient murmuring beneath her feet grew to a snarl. A gust of wind swirled sparks around her in a maelstrom. Her tunic caught fire along her hip and an ember caught in the dimple of her shoulder blade, searing itself into her skin.

In her last moments, she saw shapes moving rapidly towards them in the darkness. Soldiers moved with swords drawn. The masked priests moved away from the bonfire and toward the villa. And then the sky ignited in white fire, a thousand bright lions roaring an inferno from their mouths, heat and wind wrapping around them all, knocking the priests and soldiers to their knees while thick embers escaped from the bonfire and tumbled across the field, setting it alight.

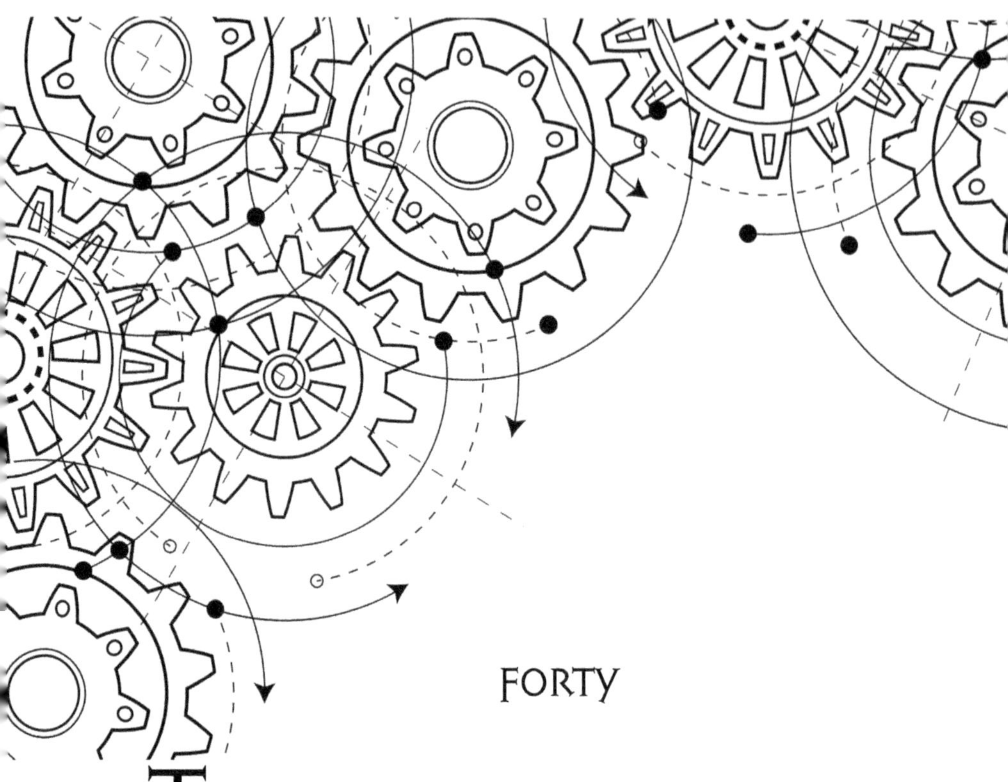

FORTY

The drug held her in its mute embrace. Heron felt no pain, no fear, as the battle raged around her. Dying was not as terrible as she thought it would be. By some gift of the drug, she felt no flame, where moments before, it felt like her skin was dry papyrus ready to curl into a char.

The air was as bright as daylight. Somehow the fire had escaped, by the wind, or whatever that roaring had been. A line of flame raced away to the west, headed toward the little villa Vestalis and her had taken brief shelter in when they'd come to spy on Silius, and if it escaped beyond that—Rome.

Though it wouldn't matter much longer, Heron worried about the fire. Rome was as dry as the scroll rooms of the Great Library. There hadn't been rain in months and the Tiber was a muddy brown stream.

She craned her head, to see it moving other directions. The field to the north rippled with oranges and reds, like a sidewinder snake flowing across the remnants of the harvest. It was when she turned her head the other way that she realized something was wrong. The place where the villa had once stood was mostly empty. Only a few structural timbers leaned together at a corner; the rest was a smoking hole.

Then, Heron realized why she hadn't been consumed by fire. Beneath her feet the bonfire had been scattered, though it wouldn't save her much longer if she couldn't get free of the chains. The perilous stand of wood her feet rested upon was gathering flame, climbing hungrily toward her.

On the field, men fought and slowly hearing came back in sharp cries and steel clanging. Of the Brethren she saw none, except the body of one lying not far from the scattered timbers. The mask had been blown off his face, and a piece of wood, like a giant splinter, stuck through his chest. Heron shed no tears for Senator Pallas.

Heron tugged on the chains, but they wouldn't budge, even when she put her full weight on them. Then she tried folding her hand into a cylinder and pulled against the manacle. Her knotty wrist bone caught on the rusty iron and wouldn't slide past. Heron grunted, pulling as hard as she could, even as the iron dug into her flesh. When she was finished, her wrist was still bound by the manacle and she was left with a bloody wrist.

As she gathered strength to try again, the wood beneath her feet shifted and she fell hard against the chains. Now she struggled, held in the air by her wrist as the fire, fed by the wind, climbed like quick red vines.

Rotating her wrist to spread the blood, Heron pulled again, hoping to use her blood as a lubricant. She strained and it felt like her hand was going to pop off at the wrist and then it was free.

Heron hung from the chains by her mechanical arm, held there by the straps and harness that went around her shoulder. Fingers coated with blood, she shoved her hand under the tunic to work at the buckles that held her in place. The fire burned around her and as she swung, flames seared her legs, but she stayed focused on the latches, having to wipe her wet fingers on her leg more than once.

The last buckle came free and she was released from her limb, falling into the burning wood, her knee landing in a pile of embers. She rolled away into the dirt, screaming as it burned her, saved from the worst because the leg that had gone deeper into the fire was the metal one.

With her tunic put out, Heron crouched in the dirt and surveyed her surroundings. The battle had moved, steam chariots glinted in the fire light. Across the field she could hear the echoes of their shouts: "Vestalis!" and "For Rome!" and "For the North!"

The battle wasn't the worst of her problems. Fire raged unchecked in multiple directions. She guessed that Vestalis had blown up the villa with a barrel of sparkpowder, which had saved her when it scattered the wood beneath her feet. But it'd also scattered the flames and with both sides engaged in battle, there'd be no one to fight the fires, especially with the winds gusting heavily towards the sea.

But she didn't want to linger long. In pockets of darkness between the flames, she saw men moving, soldiers from both sides. She needed to get away.

Crouching low, as low as her mechanical leg would allow, Heron moved towards the stables behind the house. Each step bent her burnt knee and she grimaced away the pain. If she could find a horse, or other means of transport, she'd ride back to the domus and get Sepharia. At the very least, they could escape to the docks and board Hoth's iron boat.

She came upon a dead soldier, eyes glazed over as he stared into the ashy night sky. Heron took his gladius, clutching it in her fist that still ached from its liberation from the manacle.

The scene behind the destroyed villa was worse than she imagined. The massive old olive tree had been knocked over. A flicker of hope kindled in her chest for Agog, until she saw that it'd fallen onto the side that he'd hung. Even if he had somehow survived the hanging, he'd have been smashed and run through by the branches.

The olive tree had partially crushed the stables, breaking the eastern wall. Even with only the distant glow of fire as her light, Heron could see that all the horses had escaped. She prepared to hike away from the destruction when she saw the glint of piping on the other side of the stables.

With the gladius held before her, Heron crept through the darkness. She heard the sound of a single voice, cursing and hammering at the metal with his fists. It wasn't hard to identify Senator Antonius' portly frame. He was trying to turn the correct levers on the steam chariot to make it work, but having no luck.

Heron was able to move right next to the steam chariot without being noticed. She was about to stick him with the gladius when he turned.

"By the gods!" Antonius recoiled from her. "Who are you?"

"Heron of Alexandria."

He recoiled further, practically climbing onto the bronze pipes, despite the heat. The glow of the coal chamber lit the back of his head.

"But you're dead," he said incredulously. "You burned in the fire."

She was covered in soot and dirt; her tunic was charred at spots. "I've come back from the Underworld to claim you for the gods."

Whatever fight Antonius had in him, it fled and he fell to his knees. Before he could muster a defense, Heron thrust the sword into his chest, killing him. He toppled over, his head hanging from the edge of the steam chariot. Stabbing the gladius into the dirt, Heron tugged the body off to thud resoundingly into the dust.

After retrieving her weapon, she struggled onto the vehicle and turned the correct levers to give power to the pistons. The mechanical chugged to life and she moved to the steering mechanism when four steam chariots appeared out of the darkness.

"Antonius," called a familiar voice. "It's about time you got..."

The voice, which she identified as Senator Silius, trailed off as he noticed the body on the ground. Lantern light spread across her, forcing her to squint, but she could see the Senator at the lead of the second chariot, his mask on a chain around his neck and his mane of gray hair dotted with soot. The look of horror on his face, relayed her state of being, as she must have looked like a body dragged from the grave.

A moment of insanity bubbled to her lips: "You are no Dis Pater, you pretender. I've come back to reclaim the city for my own."

As disbelief spread across their faces, Heron jammed the lever into position and the steam chariot surged forward, nearly knocking her into the hot piping as she had no second hand to hold on.

Her words only held them for a moment and then she saw the lights sway after her. On the steam chariot, she raced ahead, flying fearlessly into the dark, bouncing over the field knowing that a hole or tree stump could end her escape in an instant.

The cold wind made the burnt flesh of her knee cap cry out in pain as she pointed her craft towards the Via Cassia, or at least the direction she hoped would take her that way. Steering the vehicle with only one hand was made even more difficult by the uneven terrain. Each bump forced an overcorrection that erased her precious lead. The four steam chariots on her trail seemed to be catching up with each turn of the wheel.

Heron avoided a large rock in the field only because of the dim light provided by the fires. Though she could spare no attention towards it, the city burned, bright colors painted against the gray clouds overhead. Distant screams and shouts announced the city's awakening and fight against the moving flames.

Buildings reflected the glow not far ahead and she leaned into the steerage, willing it to move faster. If she could reach the Via Cassia ahead of them, she could lose herself in the streets, which she knew well because they'd laid the Iron Road near it.

A distant explosion in the city startled her. A fireball rose into the sky and even from a distance, the blocks and bricks sailing through the air made dark shadows against the crimson.

"Plato have pity," she muttered, remembering that they'd hidden the spark powder barrels throughout the city. Too busy contemplating the effects of that decision, Heron did not see the rock wall directly ahead and plowed into it.

FORTY ONE

The momentum of the steam chariot carried it through the stone wall, but the impact threw her into the steerage and she lost control of the vehicle. Onto the Via Cassia, the steam chariot bounced, snapping the gearings and cracking two wheels in half.

Heron was a bug in a jar, shook by an unruly child, careening against the levers and piping that surrounded the steerage position. It was only luck that kept her from flying from the vehicle, but it didn't feel like luck when the whole thing came to a stop and she lie on the warped floor, the pistons still hammering away fruitlessly, and at least two ribs in her chest broken.

A cough sent waves of pain and nausea through her trembling frame. Only fear kept her moving as she struggled to her feet, expecting to see Senator Silius' chariot bearing down on her. Her steam chariot had traveled a ways past the stone wall, nearly coming to rest against a stone building on the other side. She'd smashed a few clay jars sitting outside, their contents puked onto the cobblestones.

The lights of her pursuers turned north, as they searched for a way around the wall. Fearing that she might have pursuers on foot, Heron struggled from the destroyed vehicle and limped down the street, trying to figure out exactly where she was.

Every step was a knife to her side where the ribs had been broken, but she kept hobbling. Halfway down the street, she remembered the gladius still on the steam chariot, but it wouldn't do her any good now, and would only slow her down.

When she found an alleyway, she cut across, glancing behind to see lights entering the cobblestone street from the north. On the backside of the buildings, she found the Iron Road. It looked like a fence with a metal bar stuck on top. Heron crouched at the base to find the distance markings. They'd stamped the location of each rail onto its base so they'd know where to put it and where each post was in relation to the others.

Once she found the number, she knew exactly where she was. Her-on turned east and began hobbling along the Iron Road. Unless they'd moved it, the steam barge that would traverse the Iron Road shouldn't be too far ahead. She just hoped that Silius wouldn't cut across, otherwise she was headed right into his arms.

The ink spot of darkness was so thick that she nearly ran into the dull metal shielding on the front of the barge. After climbing on, she paused to listen, hearing the pursuing steam chariots racing down the Via Cassia past her. They hadn't found her yet, but once she started up the mechanical, she wouldn't be hard to find.

Using licked fingers, she tested the boiling chamber, finding the water was still hot and the fire banked. She spit the taste of burnt from her lips before dumping fresh fuel into the chamber and stoking it until the glow intensified. She turned the air supply on full, to give the fire the air it needed to grow hot and waited, glancing every direction, expecting her escape to come to a sudden end.

The skyline glowed in the distance as wind blew the fire west into the hills and the heart of the city. Two more explosions arced across the sky. Heron grimaced as she thought of the dozens of automatas with spark powder hidden in them. She couldn't even imagine the destruction if the fire reached the warehouses.

As the first tapping of the mechanical began, Heron's heart jumped, fearing that they would hear it. The growl of steam chariots raced up and down the street looking for her, but so far they hadn't thought to look to the Iron Road which was hidden right behind the row of houses.

Heron thought she might escape cleanly as the ticking pot of boiling water fed power to the mechanical, but then a steam chariot turned alongside the buildings, shining a lantern directly at her.

She engaged the lever immediately, cursing that she wouldn't have much power, and as the barge lurched forward, she cursed again, realizing that the sections of wagon behind were still attached. She should have used the time waiting for the water to boil to unhook them, so her section could move faster.

Men were shouting as the steam chariot raced to catch up and to her relief, they had to head back onto the road when they ran out of room, but it wouldn't hold them long as the Iron Road ran parallel to the Via Cassia most of the way through the city to the docks.

Without the need to steer, since the barge ran on the Iron Road, Heron moved to the steam mechanical and adjusted the levers, trying to coax more speed from it. Once it got going, it would go faster than the steam chariots, but until then she was vulnerable.

As the steam barge burst out from behind the buildings, her pursuers were right there. Crossbows were pointed in her direction and she barely ducked behind the steam pot in time as the bolts ricocheted into the darkness.

She heard Senator Silius shouting, though she could not see him as she crouched behind the pipes. The thump of feet landing on the wagons at the back of the barge alerted her to new dangers. At least three men had boarded her steam barge and were slowly working their way up to her position.

She'd gathered enough speed and was slowly pulling away from the steam chariots. Silius was screaming and pointing at her and to her surprise, she saw him leap onto the last wagon, his mane of gray hair whipping in the wind.

Searching around the pot, she found a makeshift weapon: a turning bar that was used to adjust the gears beneath the mechanical. Swinging would be difficult with her broken ribs, but at least she had a weapon.

Heron positioned herself at the bottleneck near the steam mechanical. The narrow path that connected the steerage to the wagons would provide her best line of defense, though she wasn't sure how long she'd hold out against soldiers much larger than her. One parry of weapons would leave her kneeling in agony.

The first one climbed over the last barrier between the wagon and the platform that held the mechanical. Flames reflected in his eyes and she could see him easily. In a passing thought, she hoped the destruction in the city hadn't damaged the Iron Road, or they'd all die when it crashed into whatever obstacles had landed in its path.

Glancing ahead to the streets, she saw men and women in bucket lines throwing water onto burning buildings. Their feeble efforts were swallowed by the flames that even Heron could feel from this distance. They passed the line quickly and Heron saw the fear and fright in their faces as their lives were consumed by the fire.

The first soldier leapt onto her platform and moved around the steam mechanical. He was twice her size and held his gladius confidently. Heron crouched behind the pipes and waited. When the soldier stepped onto the section of platform next to the steam pot, she stuck the turning rod through the maze of pipes to actuate a lever. Steam burst from a hidden port right into the soldier's face, he dropped his weapon as his face was melted by the hot water. Heron stepped forward and pushed him over the side, ignoring the sickening crunch as he hit a building right on the other side of the Iron Road.

The second soldier was not far behind, but he'd seen her trickery and ducked beneath the steam port that she'd released. Heron backed up and held the turning rod in her hand.

The soldier swung at the rod, knocking it from her slick fingers. The weapon spun into the street as the buildings flew by. The soldier raised his weapon, preparing to strike when they shot through a gap between two buildings and entered a wide square. The Iron Road ran along the side and thousands of people huddled together at the center point between the buildings. Even the soldier paused, seeing the row of buildings crumble.

Then he regained his purpose and his jaw grew resolute. Heron was preparing for the worst when an explosion shook the earth and they were showered in rocks and dust. Heron threw herself behind the shielding and clamped her eyes shut as heat and flame swirled around them. The explosion had come from nearby.

When she was finally able to open her eyes, the soldier was gone, knocked from the speeding craft by flying debris. The third soldier was lying on his face on nearest wagon, his head crushed in by a stone block. The steam mechanical was damaged, the pot dented and a few pipes bent, but miraculously, it was still working.

Then she saw him, Senator Silius. He'd thrown himself behind the shielding on the back wagon and survived. As they sped past flame and destruction, screams and shouts, bucket lines and clumps of survivors, Heron and Silius glared at one another. Heron knew what she needed to do and moved first, headed towards the connection between the steam barge and the first wagon. Silius, sensing her escape, moved to climb over the barriers between them.

She reached the back of the barge and knelt down, ignoring the sharp pain in her side. The pin that held the barge to the wagon was stuck in the hole. It was the width of two fingers and had a round loop on the end to pull on. Heron climbed onto her rear, set her legs on the wagon behind, and reached between her legs to tug the pin. Hooking her good leg around the edging of the wagon, Heron tried to pull it forward so she could get the pin out, but the weight of the wagons were much too great for her to budge it.

Silius climbed over the last barrier and moved towards her location after picking up the gladius from the fallen soldier. Heron looked away, and considered jumping from the speeding craft, but she didn't think she'd survive the landing. With the burning city reflected on his face, Silius moved toward her.

With all her strength, Heron pulled at the pin, but it wouldn't budge, nor did she expect it to, given the speed they were moving. Heron was about to move to her feet and flee to the front of the barge when the whole craft banked hard on a turn and she felt looseness in the pin. She yanked it free with a cry and was about to pull her feet back when Silius dove forward and grabbed her mechanical foot.

The two sections separated and Heron felt herself being tugged into the gap. Heron hooked the arm with the missing hand around the nearest pipe but she knew she wouldn't be able to hold on long. Silius tugged gleefully on her leg, yanking as she tried to kick him in the chest, but he turned to avoid the worst of the blows.

As the force of the wagons slowly dragged her towards death, Heron knew she only had one way out. Fingers tired from clawing at levers, caked with blood, and slick with sweat, worked at the buckles around her leg. Silius didn't quite understand what she was doing until she was on the last buckle, and then he started pulling frantically on her leg.

As the last buckle unclasped, the mechanical leg fell away and the sudden change in momentum toppled Senator Silius over. His body careened off the iron rod and then the wagon jumped as it bounced over his body.

Without the steam barge pulling them, the wagons slowly fell behind and Heron sat on the edge of the platform, numb from the fighting and fleeing, the last visage of Silius, wide-eyed with surprise as he tumbled into the gap, imprinted on her vision.

Heron noticed the clay roofs of the western workshops passing in great haste and realized she was coming to the end of the Iron Road. She scrambled onto her belly and crawled to the front, slamming the stopping lever backwards, but nothing happened. The steam barge flew at a rapid pace toward end of the Iron Road.

A quick glance at the piping told her the problem. The earlier damage had pinched closed the control of the lever. There was no way to stop it now. Heron struggled to one leg and took a terrifying look at the ground hastening by and decided to stay on the barge.

Not far away, the orange lights of the raging fire played against the sea. Legless and armless, Heron leaned against the shielding and watched the end approach, cursing the pinched line that kept her at top speeds. Growling, she hopped to the other side and lay down on the platform and used her foot to kick the pipe that ran from the steam pot to the mechanical. It was as big as her fist. If she could cut off the steam the pistons would lose power and grind to a stop. The pipe was thick and each kick barely dented it, but even the slight reduction in diameter was slowing the pace. She knew she didn't have much time. She kicked again and again and again, and the pipe was only half closed.

When the steam barge whined against the last turn, she knew there was only a straight shot and then a stone wall that she would smash against. Another kick pinched it three-fourths closed and the pistons wheezed to a slow churn, but the barge had too much momentum.

Steel cried out as the barge whipped through its final turn. It was never meant to round the bend with this much speed. Sensing little time left, Heron wrapped herself in the hot pipes, ignoring the sting against her flesh so she might brace herself for the impact. Wrapped in the steam mechanical, she could only look up through the ticking pipes to witness the crimson burial flames of Rome dancing against the sky. As the barge whisked past its unloading station, Heron chuckled grimly and her last thought was to wonder if this served as revenge for the fire that destroyed the Great Library.

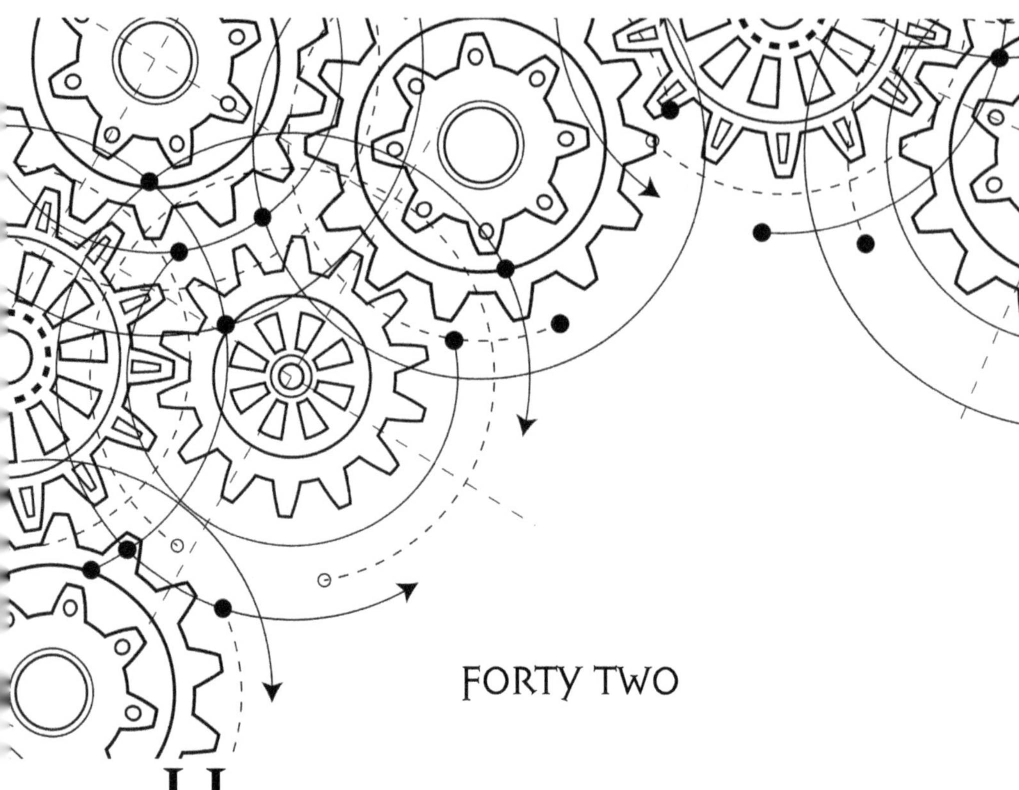

FORTY TWO

Hands carried her. Gentle palms and fingers on the underside of her knee, the small of her back, her neck, her shoulders. She could have opened her eyes but it was more peaceful to keep them closed. She felt like a corpse being carried to its burial. Maybe she was a Queen of Egypt, dried and husked for embalming, being readied for entombment in the Khufu pyramid, or better yet, the one she'd constructed in the desert south of Alexandria.

With her eyes closed, the pain was distant, as if it were somebody else's pain. But the hands were gentle. They kept her knee from bending, since the top layer had been seared off when it landed in the embers. There were other burns, two on the wrist from wrapping herself in the piping, another on the neck in the shape of a half-moon from the explosion at the villa, not to mention her legs. The hair had been crisped off and every pore was raw from being glazed with flame. Two or more ribs had been broken; it was hard to tell truly how many since it was just a patch of grinding beneath her armpit on the right side. Even her mouth had taken injury, biting her tongue when the steam barge slammed into the stone wall, but she didn't taste coppery blood as she thought she might. She didn't feel much of anything at all.

When Heron decided she'd had enough of the darkness, she tried to open her eyes, but they wouldn't budge. Like stubborn doorways nailed shut, they stayed closed. She wanted to lift her arm to tell them to stop, but it wouldn't move either, no matter how she tried.

She was aware people were talking above her, but she couldn't hear them. They were like tiny pinpricks of light, far, far away. Like stars, just as distant and unreachable.

Panic bloomed in her chest and then rage. Maybe rage could overcome this tomb of nothingness that held her in its grasp, but rage was swallowed whole. And this feeling, this awful feeling, was too familiar. She felt like an antelope trapped in the mud along the Nile, struggling, struggling, but only digging herself deeper.

The fear slid away as light penetrated her eyelids as if she were staring close-eyed at the sun. Except the light came as geometric shapes and dark purple hues rotating, as beautiful prized jewels. Heron was trying to decide if she was dead, when something in her right ear popped and sound rushed in.

"...there'll be nothing left by morning..."

Dry as the sands, her tongue was stuck to the roof of her mouth and trying to speak, she only managed to cluck it. She was about to try again when a distant roar silenced her thoughts.

"Freya's frigid tits, I think that was the warehouse where they kept the spark powder," said the voice after a time. "What a weapon Archimedes constructed. I felt the heat from here."

"What shall we do, Captain?" asked a second voice.

"Take the *Jörmungandr* away from the docks until the fires finish their raging. We can wait and hope the others get out," said the first voice.

Even locked in her motionless body, Heron could hear the hopelessness in his tone. She even knew his name, but it was hard to form the shape of it, but she strained...H...Hoth...Hoth the Black, that was it. She was on the *Jörmungandr*, Hoth the Black had found her. She became aware that she was lying on her back, but she still couldn't move, or even open her eyes.

"What do we do with her?" said the second voice, the one she didn't recognize. "I've never seen such a sorry piece of meat. If you wouldn't have been there to stop me, I'd have just thrown it back into the ocean."

The rage filled voice of Hoth answered back, "If you ever suggest such a thing to me, I'll cut your balls off and feed them to you, do you understand?"

"Apologies, Captain, I was just remarking on how bad she looked, no harm done," said the second voice, but she heard something less than apology.

"Now that she's stopped convulsing, let's move her to my quarters," said Hoth. "I want nothing but the best care for her."

Heron clucked her tongue again as she tried to form words.

"Did you see that? She moved her tongue," said the second voice.

"I did, I saw that," said Hoth.

Before she could try again, they both reacted as another explosion ripped through the city, shaking the boat as the heat wind passed.

"That was too close."

Hoth knelt beside Heron, placing a hand on her shoulder. "Fetch me some water. I want to make sure she can drink before we move her again. Whatever demons the fire burned into her, we need to cool them off first."

The thud of footfalls moved away. A gentle hand smoothed away the hair on her face. Heron tried opening her eyes again, but realized they were open. She wasn't blind, they'd placed a bandage against her face.

She shook her head and mumbled, "Eythhh...eythhh."

Hoth hooked a finger under the edge and pulled the cloth bandage over the crown of her head. Fire in the city reflected in Hoth's eyes as he gazed upon her.

"I'm glad you're alive," he said. "We saw the steam barge hit the wall. I didn't think there'd be anyone on it."

"Sethh...sethh..."

"Sepharia?" She nodded and his face grew grim. "We haven't seen her."

"Go...saaa...maaan."

The pain reflected in his eyes told her what his answer would be. "The city, you don't understand. Rome is burning, all of it. I couldn't send men if I wanted to. They'd mutiny before going into that inferno."

His man appeared with a pouch of water. "Thank you, Quadi. Hold her head up so I can give this water to her."

Her head was lifted and Hoth dribbled water into her mouth. Most of it ended up on her chest and the areas that had been burned awakened with pain as the cool water touched it.

"Seph. Must. Send. Men."

"I can't," said Hoth regretfully. "I won't." He frowned and looked away from her resolute gaze. "We'll wait out on the sea until the burning is done. Then we can send in a rescue party. It's the best I can do."

"Anyone?"

He shook his head again. "No Punt or Plutarch either. I can only assume they got caught in the fire. You were with Agog and Vestalis, right?"

She was able to nod her head, slightly. "Agog. Dead."

He straightened in reaction as if she'd said something he couldn't quite believe. Hoth glanced to the burning city with a question on his lips, but whatever he was going to say, he left it unsaid, shaking his head.

"Vestalis?" he asked.

She tried to shrug, but it only aggravated the broken ribs and she was left in the throes of agony. When it finally subsided, she caught her breath.

Hoth looked up as the deck vibrated with heavy footfalls, each one sending little spikes of pain through her side.

"Captain," said the newcomer, though she couldn't see him.

"What is it, Grimm?"

"The *Freyja* brings a message," said Grimm, his deep and gravelly voice weary with bad news.

"Out with it."

"Ships, Captain Hoth," said Grimm.

Hoth glanced over his shoulder. "From Alexandria?"

"Nay," said Grimm. "From the northern coast. Roman ships."

"And why do I care about a few ships?" asked Hoth derisively. "The steam catapults will take care of those."

"A few maybe, but they must have been hiding the rest of their fleet up north in the rivers. Biding their time until the revolt," said Grimm.

"How many ships?" asked Hoth, suddenly worried.

"Fifty, maybe a hundred," said Grimm. "The *Freyja* barely got away. Headed straight here to warn you."

"Curse these Romans," spat Hoth, he glanced up to Grimm, his jaw thick with anger. "Prepare the *Jörmungandr* to move. We'll head into the Mediterranean until they've passed."

Footsteps faded away.

"Sepharia," whispered Heron. "Must find."

"Apologies, *Michanikos*," said Hoth. "We'll have to wait until they're gone. The bulk of the Alexandrian fleet is scattered. Assembled, we'd thrash these fifty ships, but alone, I cannot do it."

"You...must."

"Don't worry," said Hoth. "We'll come back for her, and the others. It's not like the Romans can do anything either with the city on fire." He frowned down at her. "And you need to rest. You..." he searched for words, "don't look so good. Quadi, get the others. We'll move her to my quarters. You can care for her there."

Heron tried to protest, but it was like swimming against the tide. Soon, those gentle hands lifted her up and if she turned her head sideways, as painful as it was, she could see the city. The words, whatever they might have been, choked in her throat. She wasn't expecting to see what she saw. The upper deck of the *Jörmungandr* rode high above the water so she had a good view of the city. Not a single speck of the seven hills of Rome did not burn. A black cloud of smoke invaded the sky in an unending column, billowing northwest. Fields of embers as wide and long as the Circus Maximus glowed like a volcano with fallen buildings and tumbled stones lying in the ashes. It was as if she was gazing upon the surface of the sun.

Her brief viewing disappeared as she was carried into Hoth's quarters and set carefully onto a bed of silken sheets. Hoth stood at the end of the bed while Quadi mixed some gray substance in a glass jar, the brass spoon rattling at each turn.

"Rome..." was all she could say.

Hoth nodded. "Apologies."

Quadi tipped her head back and poured a nasty tasting liquid down her throat before she could protest, massaging her neck to make it go down. It tasted like sewer mud.

It didn't take long for the substance to take hold, given her injuries. A warm pit opened beneath her and she sunk into the silken sheets and as the tomb closed above her, one last word whispered across her lips.

"Sepharia."

FORTY THREE

The breath of winter gusted against the villa shaking the barren trees in a death rattle. Sepharia listened to its hollow moaning, wondering if the noise came from outside or inside her heart. Though what did she have to complain about, she decided. She was alive while so many had died in Rome. Even the poor souls who'd owned this farm had it worse. They'd welcomed the priest to their door, not knowing that his god Sobek demanded sacrifice. She refused to use his name, listing him only as *the priest* in her head.

Sepharia tugged on the coarse bonds around her wrists. For a one-handed priest, he knew his rope-lore well. Since he'd taken her out of Rome by way of a stolen steam chariot, she'd been bound. The gag he'd removed after they settled into the villa, but only if she promised not to speak unless given permission. Listening to the cries of the previous owners as he put the knife to them was enough to quench any thought of rebellious wit.

The smell of roasting chicken made her salivate as she sat alone in the candle-lit room. The villa was rustic compared to the opulence she'd grown used to in Rome, the walls and floor were made of wood, and tile was used sparingly, only as a backdrop in the little altar for the household gods. The owners had lived modestly, if well, as the priest found ample stores of grain, figs, olives, dried fish, and other foods in the cellar, enough to make a winter stay quite comfortable. Not that living with the priest who'd taken your father's foot and hand could be called comfortable, but so far he'd given no indication of what he was going to do with her. He was humming in the other room, a children's song by its cadence, though one she'd never heard before. And though she was quite frightened of the priest, she had the impression he wasn't going to hurt her, yet.

As if summoned, the priest appeared with a bowl of steaming white meat cradled in his arm and a loaf of hard bread balanced across the top. He set them on the little wooden table and dragged it next to her chair, humming the whole time.

"*Chomp!*" he tittered before giving her a smile that she thought no man who had killed so wickedly the day before should be able to give. If she hadn't known who he was, she would have smiled in return, but she did know, so she kept her lips clamped tight.

After pouring two cups of wine, he settled onto the chair across from her and placed his stump and hand in his lap as if he were waiting for something. His beady eyes drank her in and she tried to remain calm, focusing on the bundles of scrolls the priest had taken from the domus, for what reason, she could not guess.

"My Lord Sobek has many plans for you and I," said the priest, his beady eyes gleaming like onyx.

Quickened pulse throbbed against her neck like a great drum beating up from some unfathomable depths. The fear that she thought safely stashed away, burst through her walls as if they were damp papyrus. Sepharia swallowed the ball of ice in her throat.

"You may speak, daughter of Sobek's instrument," said the priest.

She let her gaze fall upon him, only briefly, for upon the pale sallow skin of his brow, lay a crown of sweat. Sepharia glared into her hands.

"What do you want of me?" she asked, more defiantly than she'd planned.

His smile twitched like the tail of a tiger. The priest lifted the pink, cracked flesh of his stump and held it before her eyes.

"It is not what I want. It is what He Who Dwelleth Amid Terrors wants," he said.

With her lower lip quivering, she said, "He wants death, that's what he wants."

The priest appeared wounded, lips pursed in disagreement. "Dear girl, death is a fact of life, it's what makes us shine so brightly. But death is the domain of Anubis, or Dis, or Hades, whatever you want to call him. That is not my Lord's realm. No, death for He Who Dwelleth Amid Terrors is an inspiration and without it, man would only be primitive beasts still banging stones together. For is it not the Nile crocodile that keeps men sharp and alert when they draw water at the river's edge? That is Sobek's gift."

Despite the fear raging in her heart, Sepharia leveled her gaze until it was matched with the priest. He seemed to take great joy in this development, and his eyes widened.

"See, girl," he said. "You burn brighter because you fear me, fear my god, maybe even one day your god, too."

"Never. And I'm not a girl," she growled.

A bit of laughter escaped from his lips, making her immediately regret her statement. "Well said. I suppose you're right. You're long past being a girl." He gave her a long knowing look. "But don't worry, my Lord Sobek has other plans for the both of us and those fruits are not mine to take."

"Then what are you doing with me?"

"With?" he mocked. "Together. Together, we are going to change the world as my Lord Sobek has revealed."

"Why me?" she asked, honestly.

An eyebrow raised. "Why you, rather than Heron?"

She nodded and he grew quiet and rubbed his chin in thought with the cracked stump, the fabric of his soot-stained robe falling around his elbow.

"I do not know," he said eventually. "My Lord has shown me many things. He revealed the fate of Rome to me even before I stepped into the city. He showed me the betrayals that awaited Heron. He's even given me glimpses of the future, of the world he would have us create with his permission." He looked up to her, his black eyes like portals to the Underworld. "But of Heron, your father and mother, he has hidden his purpose. Heron goes away from us on a journey of great importance, and I know not what it is, only shadows, only shadows."

She believed him. Believed every word of it. Whatever he believed his mad god had done to him, it'd also removed the part of him capable of lying. That much she could see. And he seemed despondent that he could not see. He had doubts and worries. Sepharia hoped she could use those doubts and worries to her advantage, to survive, and to eventually escape.

"What do you see in those shadows? About her journey?" asked Sepharia reverently.

The priest's gaze went inward and his body seemed to shrivel upon itself. "I see pain. Great pain. And the darkness of the unknown. I see a beast amid the jungles so great it would give even Sobek pause. And betrayal. There's always betrayal around the Broken One, a betrayal like no other."

"And then?"

The rictus of hard thought passed across his face and he looked to her, his face, the face of a man troubled by his own thoughts.

"I do not know."

She sat quietly, contemplating what he'd told her. She didn't believe in his prophecies, but knew her survival might depend on them.

"And what of me? What do you want me to do?"

He seemed to come out of his malaise. "You? O' admirer of Cleopatra." He laughed at her reaction. "Yes, of course, I know your thoughts. Sobek has shown them to me. He knows your secret desires, knows that this will bind you to him."

"Never," she said.

He laughed again, as if she were a child protesting her dinner. "You will. I have seen it."

"I wouldn't. Ever. Why would I help the person who took my father's limbs? Why would I help the man who was once the Alabarch and tortured so many good people in Alexandria? Why would I do such a thing?"

"For the same reason men and women still draw water from the Nile, despite the dangers, because sometimes to do nothing is worse," he responded.

She wanted to cross her arms, struggling momentarily against the bonds. "I won't," she said weakly.

He didn't respond and she tried to hide the shiver that passed through her. She glanced up defiantly. "So what will we do while we hide here?"

"Hide?" He laughed. "We leave tomorrow, once I've packed the steam chariot with supplies."

"Leave? We can't leave. It'll be winter soon," she said.

He patted her hand. "We cannot stay here. We're ahead of those fleeing the destruction of Rome, but not for long. Rome was a city of nearly five million and it held great stores of food, but now those supplies are gone and so are the artifices of the Empire. The Roman Empire is dead, burnt to the ground, turned to ash and given its burial. No, we cannot stay here. Once hunger turns to fear, any survivor of Rome will be an enemy of ours. We must keep moving, keep swimming against the current as those fateful jaws threaten to snap off our feet from behind."

The truth of his words was far too real. It was a sober pronouncement of their situation. She'd seen what hunger drove people to do in the Rhakotis district. She couldn't imagine what the survivors of the great city of Rome would do. Imagined the endless waves of hungry people, flowing towards them even now, expanding from the epicenter of Rome, like ripples from a rock into still waters. Except this was no rock. The destruction of Rome was like the world itself falling into the waters of creation, and the massive waves set like mountains against the sky, carving out darkness where once light had stood, a fearful mass threatening to break and topple onto the shore, carrying its destruction to the known ends of the earth.

"Where will we go?" she asked, though she knew the answer.

He smiled wistfully. "Back to the beginning. Back to where it all began."

She nodded and the words summoned themselves to her lips.

"Back to Alexandria."

§ § §

Continue Heron's adventure in Book Six of The Alexandrian Saga

VOYAGE
OF
ALEXANDRIA

OTHER BOOKS BY THOMAS K. CARPENTER

The Hundred Halls Universe

SEASON ONE
<u>THE HUNDRED HALLS</u>
Trials of Magic
Web of Lies
Alchemy of Souls
Gathering of Shadows
City of Sorcery

<u>THE RELUCTANT ASSASSIN</u>
The Reluctant Assassin
The Sorcerous Spy
The Veiled Diplomat
Agent Unraveled
The Webs That Bind

<u>GAMEMAKERS ONLINE</u>
The Warped Forest
Gladiators of Warsong
Citadel of Broken Dreams
Enter the Daemonpits
Plane of Twilight

<u>ANIMALIANS HALL</u>
Wild Magic
Bane of the Hunter
Mark of the Phoenix
Arcane Mutations
Untamed Destiny

<u>STONE SINGERS HALL</u>
Song of Siren and Blood
House of Snake and Tome
Storm of Dragon and Stone
Sonata of Shadow and Thorn
Well of Demon and Bone

<u>THE ORDER OF MERLIN</u>
The Order of Merlin
Infernal Alliances
Tower of Horn and Blood

ABOUT THE AUTHOR

Thomas K. Carpenter resides in Colorado with his wife Rachel. When he's not busy writing his next book, he's hiking, skiing, and getting beat by his wife at cards. He keeps a regular blog at www.thomaskcarpenter.com and you can follow him on twitter @thomaskcarpente. If you want to learn when his next novel will be hitting the shelves and get free stories and occasional other goodies, please sign up for his mailing list by going to: http://tinyurl.com/thomaskcarpenter. Your email address will never be shared and you can unsubscribe at any time.